THE TIDES OF RECKONING

BOOK 2 OF THE OUTLANDS SAGA

TYLER EDWARDS

The Tides of Reckoning

MESSAGE TO READERS:

Welcome back to the Outlands! One of the things I wanted to do in book 2 was expand on the world of the Outlands. At the back of the book, I have included a glossary of terms for words, objects, creatures, groups, and places. My hope is that this will be a helpful tool for you.

TABLE OF CONTENTS

CHAPTER ONE

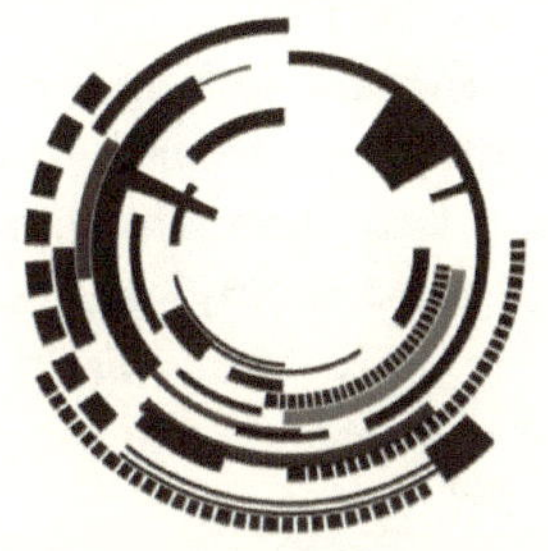

I wince as the dull blade gashes through the skin of my right arm. The wound feels hot, more like a burn than a cut as blood begins to seep from it. This is not going well. I slam my arm into my assailant's shoulder, knocking him back a few steps. He smirks as if amused by my attempt to fight him off. His hair is wild straw growing in all directions at once. His skin is like marbled leather covered in cracks, making him look more reptilian than human; his eyes roaming in their sockets as if incapable of stillness.

Recognition smashes into my chest like a fist. His clothes are unmistakable even in their worn and tattered state; it's the garb of an Outlands officer. He's from Dios. How long has he been here? How long has he been like this? My eyebrows climb my forehead as a deeper realization causes my eyes to stretch wider. This wild beast of a man was, at one time, a regular person. He could have had a wife and children. This could be anyone. Am I looking into a crystal ball? Is this my future? Is this what the Outlands is? A place where you die while you are still alive?

I cup my hand over my new wound and grit my teeth against the throbbing pain. It's not a serious cut, but the pulsing pain running up my arm is a distraction I can't afford. I'm going to need all my focus. My would-be murderer is fast—too fast; maybe he actually is part lizard. Becka is the fastest person I've ever seen, and she moves in slow motion compared to this guy.

One of the bubbles foaming from the corner of his mouth pops as his lips stretch into a terrifying smile. He cackles and my blood becomes ice. I'm glad someone is having fun. *Focus, Jett. Think.* I need something to catch him off guard or I'm dead. How? His movements are as unpredictable as they are quick. Hope drips away like the last droplets of water from a canteen. There's nothing I can do. Even though my energy knife is far more advanced than the dull, battered steel he is using, it does me no good if I can't hit him with it. I try to calm myself. What was it Victor always used to say? *It's not about speed, Jett, it's about timing. Don't try to go so fast you miss the perfect moment.* Ugh. Even when they are helpful, I don't want Victor's words in my head, reminding me of what he did.

It's hard to say how long I've been out here where time seems to be moving differently. This foaming lunatic is the first person I've seen since my exile. Now I'm wishing I'd kept my distance. I've come too far to stop now. Survived too much to let this guy end it all.

"We don't have to do this," I offer, holding up my hands up and out. He cocks his head to the side and more foam bubbles appear. His face seems perplexed, as if he doesn't understand my words. Great, no talking my way out of this one. He's too fast to run from. It's down to kill or be killed.

Sweat leaks from my hair as if each strand is a little faucet. The heat from the sun is like a bulky blanket pushing down on my body, making it harder and harder to stand. I exhale long and slow. He's just staring at me as he paces back and forth in a half-moon pattern. I'm happy for the reprieve, brief as it may be. My body aches. My breath feels labored and short. My eyes squint as I focus on him, looking for something I can use. He appears to be in his fifties, but he moves like he's still in the prime of his youth. Why give me the time? He has to know there isn't much I can do. Every attempt I've made has proven to be an impressive waste of energy. Why pull back? Why give me a chance? Maybe he's tired too? Since I can't outpace him, maybe I can outlast him.

Unlikely. My legs are too weak. The light blade in my hand feels like a heavy boulder. It's not like I've been able to sleep. Living in the place you've had nightmares about your whole life makes sleep hard to come by. It's so strange being here in the living nightmare that is the Outlands. It is somehow everything and nothing like I expected at the same time.

I blink and he's gone. In an instant, the space between us disappears. He's lunging for me, arms outstretched. I stumble back, surprised by his sudden motion. My vision blurs. Before I can lift my blade, I feel his tearing through my thigh. His dull knife feels more like it's ripping my skin than cutting it. My leg gives out, and I collapse to one knee, my free hand grasping the wound.

He dances back and forth in front of me as if he were listening to music that only he can hear. This isn't a fight. I'm not enough of a challenge to call it that. He's playing with me the way a child does with their favorite toy. I need to flip the script. *The key to winning any conflict is deception.* Victor's words invade my mind once again. *You must confuse your enemy. Seem weak where you are strong. Lure him where you want him to go by making him think it's the last place you want him to be.* I shook my head to wring his thoughts from my mind. Stupid Victor and his stupid voice.

That's it! I pull my hand from my leg. I can feel the blood coating my skin like a runny glue. I wipe it on my pants and grab for my pack. Outlands officers receive a small survival pack with about a month's rations and a few tools to give them a fighting chance. We're also given a crossbow, which would be really handy at a time like this, except I lost mine crossing the ocean of sand. At least I had my energy knife, though I don't know why they let me keep it.

I shield the survival pack with my body the way a mother would hold a child she wanted to protect. I keep an eye on my attacker. He stops dancing, stops moving, and glares at me with a sudden interest in my pack. *That's it; take the bait.* I make a show of trying to cover it even more. He creeps closer. Closer still. He lets out a sudden scream and lunges forward, trying to snatch at the bag.

I turn in a single motion, pushing the bag up and flinging it toward his face. He somehow manages to pull his body back and catch the bag before it hits him. Even caught off guard, his reflexes are incredible. That's what I was expecting. Protecting your face is basic instinct. As his hand swipes my pack out of the air, I spring toward him, pushing with every ounce of strength in my legs, my arm thrusting forward as fast as I can move it. My hand crashes into his chest, the blade of my knife disappearing inside his skin. He stumbles back, clutching his chest. His face is a mixture of surprise and confusion as he meets my gaze.

He looks at me as if I somehow betrayed him. He coughs and bloody foam spurts from his mouth as he collapses to the sand.

Air has never tasted so good. It takes me a moment to move. I tear a piece of fabric from my shirt and wrap it around the wound on my leg before hobbling over to confirm my attacker is, in fact, dead. I kneel over his body and pat him to search for anything I could use or that could tell me where he came from. He certainly wasn't a new resident of the Outlands. That means he's had to have food, water, and something resembling shelter. I don't really want to deal with more people like him, but I need to find a place to rest. No signs or trails to be seen. I search around for something, anything that might tell me where he came from.

The sky in Dios was a sapphire blue; here, it's a pale amber by day and an unsettling purple gray at night. The ground is a burnt-orange clay with deep cracks hiding all sorts of mysterious, creepy little horrors. Even the plants, which are few and far between, look twisted and corrupted. Everything here feels tough; I suppose anything surviving out here would have to be.

I wonder how the others are doing. Did they make it across the desert? Did they find a safe place? Concern makes my body tense. My imagination runs wild with possibilities. If something happened to any of them, I'll have to carry that weight with me forever. I need to find them: Lilly, Spike, Becka, Olivia, Kane, Telmen, and even Jensen. They are out here somewhere. Lilly was sent out alone. I can't imagine how difficult this must be for her. She wasn't like us. Growing up as an Artisan in Sector B gave her no experience in a hostile environment. They exiled her a month before anyone else. Why? Because Victor wanted power. Victor wanted to prove his worth, and he was willing to sell out his friends to set himself up.

Determination drives me forward. I will not die, not out here. Not before I bury my knife into Victor's beating heart. I will find my way back to Dios. I will do whatever I have to do to make him pay. Rage fills me with a heat that makes the scorching sun feel like ice on my skin by comparison. I'm going to find a way to—suddenly the back of my neck tingles. I tighten my grip around my knife. Someone or something is watching me. I scan my surroundings for any sign of movement.

The wound on my leg screams as I stand back up, spinning my body around to face whoever or whatever was creeping up on me. I hold my knife out and yell into the wind hoping to scare it away. There is nothing but the echoing of my voice followed by a sudden throbbing on the back of my head. My eyelids feel like boulders, my arms like wet noodles. For the briefest of moments, I am weightless. I hear more than feel my body crash against the dehydrated ground. The wind escapes my lungs. Suddenly I feel nothing, and I see nothing.

In the perfect dark, I see Lilly standing in front of me in her uniform with her yellow sash. We're not in the desert. I can't really tell where we are. Everything is black, except her. She's lit up like a spotlume. Her dark hair cascades down past her shoulders, glimmering in the light. I have so much I need to tell her, but I don't know where to begin. Her rosy lips form into a smile that makes me feel warmer than the sun beating down on me. She starts running toward me. She appears to move in slow motion. I race toward her, pushing with all my might. No matter how much we run, the gap between us doesn't shrink. As suddenly as Lilly appeared, she vanishes.

Victor is standing in front of me now. He smiles his warm, friendly smile; the same smile he uses to lure people into trusting him so he can stab them in the back. I dive at him, trying to tackle him to the ground. My body passes through his as he turns into black smoke and fades away. The smoke reforms into Victor's visage in front of me.

"What's the matter, Jett? You look upset. Don't tell me you didn't see it coming. I warned you so many times." He shakes his head, a smug smile growing wider across his face. "*Tsk, tsk.* I thought if I tried hard enough, I could teach you to think. But you're nothing more than a wild dog."

"Wild dog? You betrayed us! We were your friends! We were family! You sold us out for what? A title? A position? Power? I hope you enjoy it, you shinshew! I'm going to get back and when I do, you're heaped. I'm going to find you. When I put you down, I promise you it won't be quick."

He bursts out laughing. "You're only proving my point, Jett. It's all your fault. All of this. You couldn't be content with the life you had. You wanted a war. You wanted to bring down the Patriarch. I told you the cost would be too high. You wouldn't listen. Little Jett and all his rage wouldn't take no for an answer. You brought this on us all. Gibbs, Brelar, so many dead because of you. Everyone you care about is in the Outlands because of you. You're mad at me? For what? Being smart enough to get off the ship before it sank?" Victor shakes his head, and the rage inside me boils out of control.

I scream so loud it feels like daggers made of lava rush up my throat. I swing my arm wildly at Victor, cutting through him but never making contact. He shakes his head one last time as he turns back into a black fog and disappears. I press my hands against my knees as I pant heavily to catch my breath.

As if waking from a long slumber, feeling rushes back into my body. My limbs feel stiff like logs. I attempt to move to no avail. I can't even manage to pry my eyelids open. My joints throb with discomfort. I didn't think being dead would hurt this much. Everything around me is still black and formless, but I get the sense I'm moving.

"Why are we dragging this dry rot back with us?" a man's voice rumbles through my ears.

"Leave a body out here? This close to town?" The voice is feminine and firm. "You really do want to see the depraved, don't you?"

"Don't even joke about that. They don't come this close to the city."

"Just because they haven't, doesn't mean they don't. Doesn't seem worth the risk, does it?"

"I'm sure that's why Elder sent us out here to look for fresh domies."

"Yeah, that's weird. It's like he's obsessed with finding people and bringing them back. He's always so excited to meet them. Where do they go? Have you ever noticed they never stay in town?" the woman replies.

"He says they leave because they want to be in a bigger town where they will feel safer but, yeah, that no one ever chooses to stay—that seems unlikely."

My thoughts drown out their words. Well, I'm not dead. At least, I assume I'm not dead. I've never really died before, so I have no idea what it would be like. Something tells me the afterlife isn't a place where you hack in on random conversations. Slowly, the glue binding my eyes gives way. I groan as a wave of bright light crashes into me. I worked so hard to get my eyes open, and the first thing I do is close them again. The strange sense of motion I'd been feeling stops abruptly, and my head thuds to the ground.

"Domie's waking up," the man's voice bellows like a low, smooth roar.

A shadow blocks the brightness of the sun. My eyelids give way like a grinding gate lifting one chain link at a time until I am looking up at the stranger. Kneeling over me is a young woman, dirty brown hair pulled back into a practical ponytail. She's wearing something that looks like a light armor that covers her torso and shoulders underneath a weathered cloak of some kind. Her eyes are a rich green. In them is a softness that contrasts with the rest of her. Her exposed arms are lean and muscular. Her face is dirtied.

"Are you OK?" She sounds half annoyed.

I manage to turn my head a little before nodding. "What happened?"

"Great, another sand-brained domie. You passed out, obviously," the man blurted. I managed to turn my head enough to see him. He's considerably taller than the girl and similarly fit and lean. He's also wearing an outfit that looks like a combination of casual wear and armor. He has long, black hair pulled back in a ponytail, and his face is covered with spotty stubble.

"Did he just call me a domie?" I ask, looking back at the young woman.

"You'll have to forgive Cooper. He's—" she ponders how to fill in the verbal blank. "Direct. Though, in fairness, you were wandering the desert by yourself like a sand-brained domie."

"A domie?" I get the feeling it's not a compliment.

She grins down at me. "It's what we call people who are fresh out of the Dome."

"He's awake now. He can carry himself." Cooper releases the ankle he'd been dragging me by.

The young woman dusts off her pants. "Nearest city is Red Clay." She points toward a plateau.

"Wait," I protest. "You're just going to leave me here?"

Cooper laughs. "He does have a firm grasp on the obvious."

"I can hardly walk," I object again.

"You're in the Outlands now. Nobody is going to carry you out here. You figure it out or you die," the woman replies.

"Why'd you bother with me in the first place?"

"You were unconscious, so your survival was dependent on us. Now you are conscious, so your survival depends on you." Without so much as a glance back, the two of them head off in the same direction she pointed. I push myself up, wincing as I try to put weight on my injured leg. I don't have time for pain; I need to move. I force myself forward. I won't be able to keep up, but I can at least follow them. My right leg drags behind me as I hobble toward the steep rock walls of the mountain. I just hope I don't have to climb them.

A few minutes later, I notice the plateau is split by a gorge, almost as if a deep running river had carved through the stone and then dried up. The gorge seems to create a tunnel pass, winding through the mountain in the direction the young woman pointed. The stone walls are as tall as the cloud breakers in Dios, reaching so high they appear to have no end. Limping my way forward, I move toward the opening. By the time I reach the entrance, there is no trace of the two travelers. It's as if they vanished into the shadows of the rocky cliffs.

"Great, walk into the dark, scary gorge in the middle of the heaping Outlands all by your injured self. What could go wrong?" I say to myself. I let out a sigh and start my slow march into the canyon of doom. The pass is wide enough to drive a vehicle through, but there are so many jagged rocks jutting out that navigating it at a high speed would be almost impossible. Towering rock walls stretch as far as my eyes can see, shadowing the ground in an endless darkness. My imagination runs wild with all the hidden horrors its caverns could, and likely do, contain. That's my favorite part of the Outlands. It's a constant game of which is worse: my imagination or reality. Somehow, the answer often seems to be both.

The gorge winds like a slithering snake through the rocky wall. There's this feeling of dread and gloom just stepping into it. Midday feels like midnight. The deeper I move into the gorge, the darker it seems to get. A breeze brushes against my neck. My body surges with adrenaline as my goosebumps rage so hard it feels like something is brushing against me constantly. My whole body shivers, but the sensation won't go away. There are subtle noises all around me like something is trying to move without being heard. I wonder if this is how a deer feels when it senses the presence of a hunter. My instincts scream *run*. My mind urges caution. I scan the area, careful not to make any sudden movements. It feels as if a heavy gaze rests on my shoulders. Something is watching me. The path ahead is littered with caves while shadows dance behind me. I wrap my hand around the energy blade in my pocket.

I see something out of the corner of my eye—a shadow darting across a ledge on the rock wall above me. I turn my head, but there's nothing there. Flight mode kicks into overdrive. I should probably run, but in my condition, I doubt I'll be able to escape anything faster than an athletic turtle. I could hide. A cave would provide a good choke point, give me a small tactical advantage. The longer I'm here, the less likely I am to ever leave. Maybe I'm just being paranoid. It is so weird and dark. *Focus. Take a deep breath. Fear is in the mind.* I push on.

My gaze returns to the gorge path. Lining the gorge are a series of bright, glowing orbs spaced out irregularly but frequently all the way down the path. They remind me of street lumes in Dios. Did someone build these here? What made them turn on all of a sudden? Maybe they are triggered by motion? If so, why didn't my two new friends set them off when they passed through? As questions fill my mind, the tension starts draining from my body. The orbs make me feel like I'm at a festival back in Dios where they would string together all these little lumes everywhere. There was music and food and games of all sorts. It was also really easy for undesirables like me to slip in and feel like a regular person for an evening.

Maybe I'm just freaking out over nothing. I move deeper into the gorge, feeling suddenly more at ease than I have in days. The orbs are big, round, and beautiful. They emit this pleasant humming sound that makes me feel like everything is going to be OK. There are even some orbs on caves higher up the stone walls—enough to make this canyon feel less like a death tunnel and more like a happy stroll down the block at night. Fear fades from my mind. My worries fade with it. My body, which was on high alert, starts to relax. It's going to be OK. I'm safe here. My insides start feeling warm and toasty, the way they do after drinking a fresh cup of hot tea. My inner Victor screams at me: *The most dangerous enemy is the one who makes you feel safe.* Leave it to Victor, even Victor's voice in my head, to ruin everything.

Suspicion grows heavy in my mind. I look more closely. The orbs are perfectly placed at the top front of the cave entrances. Not a single orb as far as I can see is placed along the stone wall—only in front of caves. I crouch down and find a loose rock and scoop it into my hand. I take a step forward and toss the rock at the entrance to the nearest cave. It ricochets off the mouth of the cave and bounces off the dark clay ground below.

The lantern moves ever so slightly, and in an instant, I see three rows of razor-sharp teeth snap forward past the entrance of the cave and crash together where the rock bounced. I cover my mouth to keep from screaming. Closing around where the small stone had been was the mouth of an enormous creature. It looks like a giant fish with scaly skin and murky, glossy eyes. Its teeth come together with a loud crunch, and a cloud of dust swirls around it. The creature chomps a few more times, clearly disappointed at the lack of substance, before wiggling its mouth back into the cave and disappearing from sight.

It takes a minute for my heart to stop pounding. I reach down and select another rock, a slightly larger one. This time I hurl it at the stone wall across from the cave. It bounces loudly and rolls across the ground. Nothing. The lantern doesn't move, and no scary teeth come lunging from the dark abyss. I let out a sigh of relief. One last test before I dare to pass. I grab a small handful of pebbles and throw them into the air, so they land in the center of the path in front of the monster's cave. They bounce and roll about. No orb movement, no teeth. It seems that they only attack when they sense movement or noise near the entrance to their cave. Probably the point of the orb is to lure prey in, so they can strike.

Careful to stay as far from the cave entrance as possible, I move cautiously forward, repeating this process as I make my way through the gorge of death. Moving helps loosen up my injured leg, but every step sends a new spark of pain through my body. I hear something behind me. I spin to face it, finding only shadows and the tracks of my own feet. A few hundred paces later it happens again. Again, I see nothing when I turn around. I've made it this far. Despite consistent evidence to the contrary, I just can't shake the feeling that there is something watching me.

Relief washes over me like a breeze as I see the gorge open up and the light from the valley on the other side flooding in. I'm almost through. One more orb monster to pass, and I should be in the clear. Here's to hoping I was heading in the right direction. Just a little further.

A howl echoes through the gorge, sending a chill down my spine. I've heard howls before, but this sound is different—larger and more ravenous. My body tenses as I hear the scrambling and scraping of claws against clay rushing toward me. I back away, unable to pull my eyes from the direction of the sound. Fear makes fools of us all. Instead of rushing out of the gorge where I'd have some hope of evading my pursuer, I step back slowly, watching it move closer. Another howl, this one so loud I have to cover my ears with my hands.

I stumble, landing on my back. I push up and lean back in time to see as the creature stalking me bounds into view. Perched on a large boulder in the middle of the path, just a few feet behind me, is the largest wolf I've ever seen. It has black fur on its legs and back with a dark, tan-red underbelly and mouth. It has a long, thick tail with an almost spear-like point at the end. Its fur looks oily, as if covered in a clear coat of grease. This monstrous wolf is larger than a bear. Its mouth is stretched open and horrifying, filled with little dagger teeth. The back of its throat seems to glow like it's about to exhale flames. Sharp bones grow up from its ankles like spikes. It appears to have a second set of ribs growing on its back like a jagged bone saddle, complete with a bone collar that wraps around its neck. Like its throat, the creature's eyes glow with a red-orange blaze. Without question, the most terrifying feature of this monstrous creature is the bone horns growing out of the side of its head where its ears should be. They look like giant bone fishhooks.

I push against the ground with my palms, scooting back slowly, ineffectively. My head turns and my heart sinks. Moving around the rock and waiting next to the towering wolf monster are two more of his equally terrifying friends. I drive my heels into the ground, frantically trying to get traction but managing only to scoot myself back a few pitiful inches. The wolf creatures start slowly bridging the gap between us, forming a little half circle as they pace toward me. There's no escaping this. I couldn't outrun them on my best day, and I'm far from that. Maybe with my knife I might land a few lucky strikes, but there's no way I fend off all three.

Then, I see it: a little reflection of light on the black, greasy shoulder of the wolf monster. An idea forms in my mind. It's the kind of idea Victor would lose his mind over. He was never big on taking a wild shot and hoping for the best. Sometimes a wild shot is the only one you have. I scoot slowly back toward the source of the light, careful not to move fast enough to make the wolves pounce. I'd have to time this perfectly, and even then, it's a longshot. I glance over my shoulder to make sure I have the distance right. I slowly stand up, holding my hands out toward the wolf creatures as they growl. Thankfully, they still seem to be sizing me up before they commit to making me into their dinner. I step back, and they move with me, as if tethered to me. I exhale slowly and close my eyes. In a single motion, I turn and use my good leg to leap as far as I can away from the wolves. Throwing my body into a dive, I drop my shoulders and use the little momentum I have to roll forward before popping back up and running as fast as I can, which is not fast at all.

The largest of the wolf monsters, the one who had climbed on the rock, rushes forward with paws scraping against the ground. A surprised yelp rings out as the crashing of teeth clap just behind me. Bone-crunching, painful whimpering and angry growling fuse together to tell a compelling story. I glance over my shoulder to see the large mouth of the cave fish close around the wolf. It tilts its head back and clamps it teeth down again and again, chewing the massive wolf and swallowing it. The other two howl in rage and turn their attention to the cave creature charging at it. My heart beats so loud I'm nervous it will draw their attention back to me.

When I finally stop running, I've not only cleared the gorge, but I've made my way across an open plain. Panting, I dare to turn around. It seems I managed to escape my canine pursuers. My heart is a raging war drum. It takes me several minutes to catch my breath. I take in my surroundings. To the south, plains stretch as far as my eyes can see. To the east, there is a large forest of twisted, dark trees. Between them, a large area of rolling hills with what appears to be town. This must be the place the woman mentioned: Red Clay. I can't believe it; there is an actual town out here. We'd been taught our whole lives that nothing survives in the Outlands for long. Here I am, looking at a sprawling town. It's nothing compared to Dios but much larger than anything I expected to find.

The town is surrounded by a trench littered with spikes and other sharp-looking objects. On the other side of the trench is a palisade wall of interlocking wooden logs sharpened to a point. A sturdy bridge leads to an open gate with a large tower at either side. As I get closer, I see each tower is decorated with an alarm bell and adorned with a pair of guards. When I make my way across the bridge, I notice each of the guards is holding a bow. They haven't shot me, yet, but I don't want to push my luck. I stop and wait.

"Hello, I ummm . . . ," I start, not really sure what to say.

"He's with us," a familiar woman's voice belts out from behind me. I turn to see the young woman and the one she'd called Cooper walking up behind me. How did I get here before them? The guards nod and lower their bows. Cooper walks past me, lifting one arm over his head as he does.

"Congrats, domie. You made it to Red Clay." His words sound encouraging, but his tone sounds insulting and utterly unenthusiastic. "Always a pleasure, Kali. Good work out there," he says without turning around. A moment later he is out of sight. The young woman stops in front of me. "Come on, it's time for you to . . ." My vision blurs. Kali's words become distorted and unintelligible. Everything starts to spin and fade. Not this again . . .

CHAPTER TWO

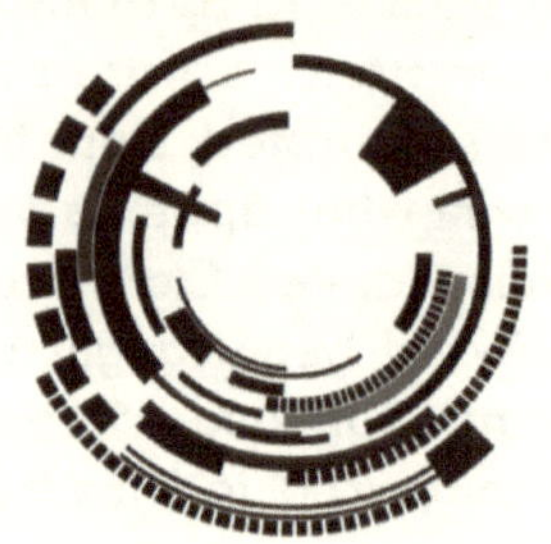

*B*eep. *Beep. Beep.*

Ugh, that's annoying. Nothing like slow incessant beeping to welcome you back to consciousness. I feel nothing. I see nothing. Am I dead? If the afterlife is just endless beeping, I'm going to be so nuked. I groan softly, and my eyelids slowly peel back. The bright light stings. I shake my head, forcing myself to focus. I glance around, careful not to move. I'm inside. The white walls are adorned with cabinets, screens, and other displays. The floor is white and looks strangely shiny and smooth. Lining the walls are counters holding all sorts of scattered equipment and devices. The room has one door and no windows. Am I in a hospital back in Dios? No, that doesn't make sense.

There are muffled voices in the background. I lay still, trying to focus in on them without drawing attention to myself. It's amazing what you can learn when no one thinks you're listening.

"He lost a lot of blood and was severely dehydrated. His oxygen levels were alarmingly low. I'm amazed he made it this far without passing out. We had to put him under. We treated his wounds, pumped him full of fluids and nutrients . . ."

I don't recognize the voice. He speaks calmly, confidently, and directly. Somehow that makes me feel like I can trust him. Weird.

"Did you give him the *Kathar Aera?*" I may not have known her long, but I already recognize Kali's voice.

"First thing we did. He should be able to breath normally now."

"His wounds?"

"He'll be sore for a few days, but the damage has been repaired."

"And when will he regain his nooma?"

My what?

"No way to know. It returns when it returns."

My body feels a surge of energy. I sit up and look for the source of the voices. Kali is standing next to a short, bald man with a subtle, thin, gray beard that lines his jaw. He is wearing a long, white coat and reading from a datapad.

"What is this place?" I blurt out.

The little bald man jumps back, clutching his chest and stumbling into the counter behind him. A silver tray holding lots of little, shiny, metal instruments slides back and ricochets off the wall, sending the tools it once contained flying in every direction. They clatter and clank against the floor.

"Great maroon sky, you scared the sun out of me!" he says.

Kali looks completely unphased by my sudden interjection.

"Did you really just ask what this is? You're in a clean room, lying on a bed after passing out, being treated by a guy in a long, white coat, crag." Kali just rolls her eyes.

I don't get the sense she likes me very much.

This was obviously some kind of medical facility, but in my defense, I just woke up, and finding a place like this where I didn't even think people could live is surprising. I rub my temples with my fingers to try to soothe a sudden surge of pain.

"How did I get here?"

The short man is still holding his chest, but his breathing is starting to return to normal. "Kali brought you in."

"What is all this?" I ask in disbelief.

"Remnants of the World that Was. Merchants brought most of these things here, salvaged from the forgotten cities. We've repurposed them."

"How do you keep all this running?" I ask, amazed at the amount of tech in the room.

He laughs. "Thank the Patriarch for that. To maintain their order, they exile anyone viewed as a threat. This includes doctors, engineers, and inventors. Many of the people who developed the technology in Dios were banished to ensure they couldn't use that technology to subvert the Patriarch's control."

"Wait, you are from Dios?"

He nods. "I am. I worked as a Physician in Sector A until an assessor caught me stealing medicine to treat an Undesirable who had escaped from the slums."

I wince. "What did they do to you?"

"Thirty-five lashes with a thrasher, two weeks in an isolated cell, then I was awarded the honorable title of Outlands Officer," he chuckles. "Good times."

"How long ago?" I ask.

"About nine years."

Suddenly I start to feel a little hopeful. "Wow, I didn't know people survived out here that long. The way they make it sound in Dios—"

"I wouldn't get too excited. Outside of the towns you're not likely to make it very long." He puts his hand on my forehead and then types a note into his datapad.

"That's encouraging."

"Feeling OK?"

I exhale. "Yeah, just a little zeroed."

"That's the medication; it should wear off soon."

"Have you seen anyone else come through here? I'm looking for my friends. They are about my age—"

"Is he good to go, Doc?" Kali asks.

He nods.

"OK, then, on your feet, domie; it's time to go."

"Go where?"

"To see the elder."

"The elder?"

"Are you going to repeat everything I say? That will get really annoying." She pauses for a moment. "Good. Now what do you say you close your crag mouth and follow me?"

I slowly slide off the bed. My legs feel shaky at first, like they've forgotten how to hold my body up.

"How long was I out?" I ask, turning back to the doctor.

"Four days."

No wonder I feel out of it. Not sure I've ever been still for that long before.

I nod. "Thank you," I say, extending my hand. "I'm Jett."

He shakes my hand with surprising enthusiasm.

"Tin Gray, but everyone calls me Doc. On account of my—"

"Being a doctor?" I interject before he can finish.

He chuckles and nods. My brain pulls a Telmen and starts racing with random questions.

"How is it possible to have all this out here? Where do you get your food? Your water? How do you generate energy in a wasteland?"

"Let's go, domie." Kali's voice is stern and impatient.

Doc waves off her objection with his hand. "Give him a minute; this is a lot to process. It's not going to hurt anyone to answer a few questions."

Kali glares at him. "Two minutes."

Doc just smiles back at her.

"We get water from a river that runs through the back of the town. We built a water mill and an underground purification source that pipes the water into our homes for drinking, bathing, and things of the like. The water is then cycled out and back through the filter to ensure none of it goes to waste."

I nod. "That's impressive."

"Most of our food comes from underground farms. We managed to find some old tech that replicates the effects of sunlight on plants, allowing us to grow crops beneath the surface. Additionally, most of the houses have little gardens. And we have teams of hunters. We also have some farmland outside of Red Clay, but it can get a bit dangerous at times as it attracts creatures."

"Wow, that's unexpected."

"We even have a projection screen in the Town Square where we can play vids for everyone. Don't do that often, though."

A ding sounds behind me as the elevator doors part, cutting off Doc's explanation.

"OK, time's up; we're leaving." Kali grabs my arms and tugs.

A part of me wants to resist on principle, but this doesn't seem like a good time to rock the boat. I follow her into an open elevator where we ride without exchanging a word. The silence is broken by another ding, and the doors slide open to reveal the inside of a log cabin. There is a wooden table, a few chairs, and some basic decorations. It is not at all what I expected to see. It's an odd juxtaposition from the high-tech medical facility below. This reminds me of stories I read about the World That Was. A group of people called Vikings made homes out of wood and covered them in animal furs. This feels like a

Viking home to me. A slew of questions rush to my mind. This must be how Telmen feels all the time. Maybe that's why he never shuts up.

Kali leads me down the main road through the center of town. We pass a blacksmith, a bakery, an apothecary, a general store—it almost reminds me of the Market Square. Between the wooden buildings I can see a row of houses, small but sturdy looking and in much better repair than the place where we lived in Dios. To our right the street slopes up, leading toward the top of a hill where a long, single building stood like a monument. It is surrounded by its own palisade wall and several guards armed with actual guns. This must be where the ruler of Red Clay lives.

The guards nod as Kali guides me into the long, wooden building at the top of the hill. We enter through a set of doors into a hallway. In front of us are another set of doors with another pair of guards. We walk in silence through the large double doors and into the main hall of the building. The floor is adorned with thick rugs. Long tables run the length of the main hall on either side of the center path. Furs and other fabrics drape decoratively from the high ceiling. At the back of the hall is a sort of elevated stage with a large chair built into the center of it. Sitting on the throne is an incredibly overweight man unlike anyone I'd ever seen. While Dios had people of various sizes, there was a general range. Anyone outside of that range on either end was at risk of getting stopped by an assessor. This guy looks like he eats even in his sleep. His hair looks like the bottom of a pan that was left on the stove too long. His face is covered in a thick, black goatee. For someone called Elder, he doesn't look that old.

I scan the room again, an instinct Victor trained into me. In each corner of the ceiling, I see the small lens of a mounted camera, each one with a tiny, blinking, red dot. Behind the throne there is a walkway decorated with a pair of armed guards. Four guards in a town this size seems like overkill. I can't be certain, but I suspect there is a separate door behind the throne area that would allow the Elder to come and go without coming through the main entrance.

Kali walks up to the front of the stage. She crosses her arms, holding each of her hands to the opposite shoulder and then kneels.

"Elder Schmitty." Her voice is soft and respectful.

"Ahh, if it isn't my little Kali. Tell me, what have you brought me today?"

"Brought you?" I blurt out in surprise. "Nobody brought me, I—"

A hand slams into the back of my shoulder and nearly knocks me over. I look back to see a tall man standing behind me. With short, dark hair cut tight on the side and back and left longer on the top. His skin is like midnight. His eyes are the calm before a storm. The way he holds himself seems simultaneously predator and prey. His muscles are coiled as if he is ready to pounce. There is something about him that makes me want to retreat into myself and not make another sound. He glares at me and shakes his head. Rubbing my shoulder softly, I turn back to face the fat man on the throne.

Schmitty nodded his head; it probably takes a lot of effort to keep that melon upright.

"Proceed," he commanded.

Kali lifts her head but keeps her gaze down as if not allowed to look at him. "Their information was accurate. He may have some use."

"Some use?" I shake my head. "Look, I don't know what's going on here."

This time I am ready as the man swings his fist at my shoulder. I step to the side, ducking down and driving my elbow back, catching him in the ribs. I hear the gust of wind escaping his lungs as I spin and knock him to the ground. Standing over him, I place my foot on his chest to pin him down as I glare into his eyes.

"Don't touch me." I try to sound tough, but it took all the energy I had to do so.

"I see what you mean, Kali; he has nooma. Tell me your name." The elder turns his attention to me.

"I'm Jett. Jett Lasting."

"Welcome to Red Clay, Mr. Lasting. I imagine it is rather shocking for you to find there is, in fact, life and civilization outside Dios."

"You could say that."

"That's what the Patriarch wants you to believe. They need the Outlands to be a slow and terrifying death, or they lose hold of their power over the people. The truth is a bit more complicated."

"How did you know I was from Dios?" I raise an eyebrow toward the king of chunk.

Something about this guy feels off. Maybe it's his size. Maybe it's that he sits on a throne while people are bowing down to him. Or maybe I'm just leery of this place because it's not what I expected to find.

"You are not the first visitor we have had from there. In fact, with the exception of Rowan, everyone here is an Outlands Officer or the child of one. We're all outcasts from the Dome city."

Kali backs up next to me and whispers, "Word of warning: you might want to get off Rowan before he kills you."

I move my foot and offer Rowan my hand to help him up. He shakes his head and gets up on his own. This seems to amuse the elder.

"Red Clay is the closest thing to Dios. Pretty much anyone who survives the Sand Sea ends up here. Where else would you be from?"

Elder Schmitty taps his nose as if that should mean something to me, or maybe his nose just itches. He keeps talking, but his words become undistinguishable sounds. My mind locks in so much on his previous statement that everything he says after becomes empty noise. *Those who survive the Sand Sea end up here.* Could it be?

My heart skips a whole sonnet as I look up at him. "My friends!" I blurt out, interrupting his monologue. Context, Jett. Give him context.

"Sorry, you were saying everyone who crosses the Sand Sea comes here. Has anyone else come through recently?" I can't keep the urgency out of my voice.

He looks at me, eyes narrowing and his face barely hiding his annoyance. I don't know why it takes so long to respond. It's a simple yes or no question.

"Yes, we have had recent visitors."

"Visitors? Recently? Where are they? Are they here? Are they OK? Can I see them?"

"Slow down, my boy—in due time. We will get to that. First—"

"I'm sorry; I'm not trying to be rude. I just need to find my friends. They were exiled because of me. It's my fault. I . . ." Why am I going into the whole story with this guy? I shake my head. "I need to find them. I need to make sure they are safe."

He held up his chubby hand and shook his head. "Yes, I believe your friends were here. But they are no longer in Red Clay. Take a breath. Relax. There is nothing that can be done tonight."

If they made it here, why would they leave? This would be the best place to wait until we all found each other. This is where we would wait. If they are not here, something is wrong. Elder Schmitty is hiding something.

"When did they leave?" Suspicion builds in my mind like the crescendo of a drum.

"Don't worry, we can help you find them. For now, let's get to know each other. Tonight, we can get you settled in. Tomorrow, we will discuss your friends." His voice is calm and methodical. His words move on a deliberate beat as if to encourage me to slow my pace to match his.

"If you could just—"

His demeanor shifts. His tone becomes assertive. "I said we'd talk about it *tomorrow*. Right now, you are a guest in my town. I will ask the questions. You will answer the questions. Understand?"

He's making it very clear. If I'm going to get his help, I have to play by his rules. I grit my teeth and take a deep breath. Fighting this wasn't going to get me anywhere. I nod in reluctant agreement. His smile is a bit too bright in response. He enjoys dominating others and asserting his power.

"That's better. Tell me about yourself, Jett Lasting." He idly strokes his black, oily goatee with his chubby fingers.

"What do you want to know?"

"What got you exiled, for starters?"

I sigh. "Well, I sort of helped lead a rebellion against the Patriarch."

That elicited so much interest he pushed his pudgy body forward and leaned his weight off the back of his chair.

"You led a rebellion?"

"Sort of. A group of beggar gangs and a guy named Grent started the rebellion. I ended up getting involved after I stole some important data. Victor devised the plan. We took over the Market Sector and tried to rally the people of Dios to rise up."

"And did they?" Schmitty sits on the edge of his seat.

"Would I be here if they had?" I counter.

He shakes his head before leaning back on his chair.

"I suppose not. Playing a lead role in a rebellion against the Patriarch, however—that says something."

"Yeah, it says I'm heapin' salvage."

"He also managed to kill a foamer. Took him awhile and he was injured in the process, but he didn't die," Kali added.

"Really?" Schmitty offers an approving nod. "Rebel leader, fighter, and recipient of a compliment from Kali. *That's* quite impressive."

That was a compliment?

"What's a *foamer*?" I ask. This seems to amuse the elder even more.

"You really are a crag. How many things did you kill while getting injured in the process?" Kali snaps.

"Where are your manners, Kali? A foamer is what we call . . . ," he pauses and waves his hand absently in front of his oversized face. "Are you familiar with doltine?" His voice sounds condescending as he prepares to lecture me on the meaning of a random word.

"The drug? Yeah, a lot of the Undesirables living in the slums were addicted to it." Maybe that will cut the lecture short.

"Yes, well here, the effects are little different. Doltine provides that great mental escape from the harsh reality that is life in the Outlands. The chemicals in the air and in the water the doltine is cooked with make the drug more unpredictable. You might get the greatest high of your life—or your skin may melt. This tainted doltine also causes mild mutations to a person's body. It makes them unnaturally fast, impervious to pain, and tends to rot their brain. They become like savage beasts. Most notably, it causes their mouths to foam constantly. Thus—foamers." He shrugs his enormous shoulders. "I've never heard of a domie encountering one and surviving. It's impressive. I could use someone like you."

"Look, I'm flattered, but I really just need to find my friends."

Schmitty nods and claps his hands together. "Yes, well we will get into that tomorrow. It seems we must cut this short. It is nearly time for the Dusk Descension. Rowan and Kali will help get you situated. Tomorrow we can talk about your friends and your future." He waves his hand in the air like he was holding an invisible flag, and several guards appear to help him up.

Before I can say another word, Kali leads me out of the throne room with Rowan trailing behind us. When we get outside, she gestures for me to follow her.

As we walk, I scan the town. Red Clay is about the size of the Market Square. Instead of housing thousands of shops, stalls, and stores, it contains mostly houses, each with little patches of crops behind them. There is a single row of various shops through the main street. I can see the small river Doc mentioned running under the palisade wall and through the back of the town, complete with a water mill and what appears to be a small energy factory. With the exception of a few buildings, everything is made of wood and covered in a layer of red dust.

My body jolts as I feel myself crash into something. I plant my foot to keep myself from stumbling. My hand catches hold of the arm of the person I crashed into—a woman wearing a heavy, bright-red cloak with a hood pulled up over her head—until the force of our collision causes it to slide off. It's so hot out here you could cook a potato by laying it on the ground. What sort of person in their right mind wears a thick robe with the hood pulled up?

"Excuse me, I—" Instinct kicks in; first thing you learn as a thief is how to size someone up. From her posture and the way she moves I can tell she is middle-aged, though she appears considerably older. She already has wrinkles like deep ravines. Her skin is weathered and cracked like overcooked clay. The dark pillows under her eyes indicate she's been missing sleep. Her unkempt hair would make a good home for baby birds. Jensen would say she has "street miles." She wears no jewelry or other accessories save for the gawdy gold necklace with the top half of a circle dangling from it. If she has any weapons, they are small and well concealed. If she had something worth stealing, I'd have snatched it. Habits are hard to kill. I chuckle and run my hand through my hair, a technique Victor taught us to disarm suspicion. It's amazing what you can get away with if people think you're dumber than they are.

The woman scowls at me with such ease, I imagine it's an expression she gives quite often. Before saying anything, she takes a breath. Her expression softens until she looks almost warm and friendly—almost.

"I don't believe I have seen you here before." She begins tugging on the sleeves of her cloak as if to fix wrinkles in it.

"I've only just arrived."

Her eyes light up. "Oh, how wonderful." She smiles even wider, but her face doesn't look happy. "I am Sister Janelle," she declares, placing her hand over her chest.

"I'm Jett." I'm getting a weird vibe as she stares at me like she's waiting for something.

"Praise to the merciful Bealz for delivering you here, my child." Her words are oddly enthusiastic.

"Your what now?" I raise an eyebrow.

"We are all children of the all-seeing Bealz. Tell me, are you a believer?"

"A believer in . . . what?"

She smacks her lips and reaches into her robe, producing a small, softbound book that she forces into my hand. "A believer in the promised Chosen One, of course. Long ago, Bealz made a pact with His servant to protect and bless the people through the servant's bloodline."

"I'm familiar." I really don't want to go down this rabbit hole.

"Good, good. The Sacred Text teaches that in the Last Days the holy bloodline will grow thin and appear to break. But in those darkest hours, when hope seems lost, the faithful Children of the Dome will find the Chosen One, who will bring about the restoration of this fallen world. Those who are found worthy, those who devote themselves to the teachings of Bealz and who live in service to Him, will be brought into the new paradise." Janelle grabs my hands in hers. "I see a light in you; the blessings of Bealz shine on you. I want to save you. You must join our order. For if you believe this book and follow these instructions, you may be saved."

I pull my hands back and lift the book up, inspecting it and hoping that will placate her.

"Thank you."

She reaches out and grabs my hands again, holding them in her own. This is uncomfortable. "You have come from the holy city. Tell me, what news do you have of the Great Prophet?"

"The prophet?" At this point I am actually starting to feel stupid.

"Yes, yes, the High Father." Her expression sours a little, her tone more agitated. "He is Bealz's chosen instrument. His bloodline is the link between Bealz and humanity."

Apparently, my expression of confusion is completely lost on this woman.

"I've never actually spoken to him."

"Of course, you've never spoken to him," she snaps before calming herself. "He doesn't speak directly to commoners. This would have been a public announcement."

"What announcement is that?"

"Has he found the Chosen One?"

"That's enough, you old crag. Leave him alone." Kali removes the woman's hands from mine and starts pulling me away.

I pretend to be disappointed as I look back at the woman.

"Do not let this Bealzless heathen lead you away! Read the words and believe! Praise the Eye, praise the Father, praise the Holy Dome!" she shouts as Kali completes my rescue.

"Best to avoid Janelle; she's a special kind of loopy."

"What is she talking about?"

Kali scoffs, "She believes she was called to the Outlands by Bealz himself and that it is her mission to serve as his ambassador here. Sand for brains thinks her exile was a divine mission. Ever since she got here, she's been trying to grow her following with anyone salvage enough to listen."

"And do they?"

"She'd be extremely dangerous if they did. She preys on the vulnerable to get them to join. She has a few followers; they call themselves Children of the Dome."

From Kali's tone, I gather this group is not particularly respected.

"It is their divine mission to find the Chosen One who will bring about their salvation."

"A *Chosen One*—like why are these things always so vague and cryptic?"

If I'm not mistaken, I think I see a smile form.

"There are no loopy religious fanatics in Dios?"

"I mean, there are, but they all work for the government."

Kali chuckles and releases my arm. "Come on, we don't have much time. There's a house at the edge of town that's vacant. You can settle in there until we figure out something more permanent."

"What is the rush?"

"The sun is almost down."

As she speaks, I realize the town is quiet. The few people I can see are all entering their homes and pulling their doors closed behind them. The entire town looks cleared out. Even the watchmen on the tower walls are descending from their posts and scurrying off like roaches. They didn't even bother to close the gates. I hear a click followed by a low humming sound. The perimeter just outside the palisade wall begins to glow with a light blue haze. It reminds me of the force shields in the Market Sector, just in a different color. If they have a protective barrier, why is everyone in such a rush? It's as if everyone knows something I don't. Considering the circumstances, they probably do.

"Do you have some kind of curfew or something?"

I try to make sense of the town's sudden shut down. What really crashes my system is the guards leaving the gate open and their posts unmanned. Those seem like two very important safety measures. There must be a reason for this seemingly clear neglect of basic security. Whatever the reason is can't be good.

"Something like that," Kali replies before looking at Rowan, who makes a quick series of strange signals with his hands. She shakes her head at him. Another series of hand signals, these ones looking more deliberate.

"I have a question. When I was traveling through the gorge, I saw these enormous wolf-like creatures with horns and——" I began.

"Nocstras," she interrupted. "Some call them night stalkers."

"Nocstras," I acknowledge with a nod. "Are they pretty common around here? I got attacked by three of them on my—"

"Seven," Kali responded.

"Seven?"

"There were seven of them."

My eyes narrow incredulously.

"Those things were huge; I wouldn't have missed four of them." My tone is a bit agitated. First, she leaves me to find my way alone. Then, she tells me what I saw?

"I wouldn't have thought anyone could miss something so obvious either, but like the sand-brained domie you are, you just stared stupidly at the alpha and didn't even notice the others."

Her tone makes me feel like I have done something to upset her, but we haven't interacted enough for her to have this much hostility. *Wait. How would she know about the nocstras?*

My eyes narrowed even more. "How would you—"

Realization slaps me across the face so hard I wonder if it will leave a handprint. Of course, the movement on the ledges. Someone was watching me, but they kept just out of sight. Kali taps the hilt to what appears to be a pair of energy swords at her waist as if to confirm my sudden epiphany.

"It was impressive how you used the terastrum to escape, I'll give you that."

"The *what?*"

Kali rolls her eyes. "The Traveler's Bane? The creature with the glowing orb. It killed one and distracted two more."

Her words sound almost like a compliment. Even her tone shifts. Maybe she doesn't totally hate me after all.

"It wasn't enough. The other four, that you apparently were too blind to see, gave chase. If we hadn't been there to cut them off, you'd be a bloated feeling in the belly of a nocstra."

There, it's back—that loathing tone to which I've grown so accustomed.

The sun began to hide itself behind the walls of the plateau, casting a dark shadow over the town. It would be night soon. An eerie siren rang out through a poor-quality speaker, making the sound supremely unsettling. Kali and Rowan looked at each other, a note of unease in their eyes.

"Shinshew," she groans. "OK, new plan. We don't have time to get you situated before dark. My house is closest; we can all stay there for the night."

Rowan nodded in agreement. It's strange, but I don't get the sense that these two frighten easily. I'm not sure I want to know what they are trying to avoid.

Kali's house is just a few buildings down. She closes the door behind us and moves to the middle of the room. I look around. Other than the wooden walls, it doesn't seem to offer any real protection, certainly not more than defending the wall and closing the gate to town would have. The house is a plain, open room. No bathrooms, bedrooms, kitchen or anything that would make this place livable. There's just a table and a couple of wooden chairs. Rowan and Kali pick the table up and hurriedly slide it against the wall.

Under where the table had been was a hatch built into the floor. Kali types a code into a pad on the side of the door and pulls it open. Under the door is another door, this one made of iron bars. Kali pushes in another code on a separate keypad, and there is an audible click. The door creaks loudly as she pulls it open. From where I am standing, I can see stairs descending into a barely lit space below.

"Inside, quickly." Her voice carries enough urgency that any desire to argue or question dissipates.

Here I am voluntarily entering a creepy basement dungeon—must be a Tuesday. I reach the edge of the stairs and turn, hesitating for a moment. Rowan is standing next to me.

"Jus—" I feel Rowan's hand grip my shoulder, thinking it's the subtle gesture reassuring me everything was going to be alright, until I hear more than feel his fist crash into my chest. The air feels hot as it abandons my lungs. My body keels over and I feel myself being hoisted up. Rowan slings me over his shoulder and starts carrying me down the steps. Kali closes the cell door behind us and types in another code. A faint sound like a motor turns, and the wooden door closes over top of the cage. Well, this is weird.

CHAPTER THREE

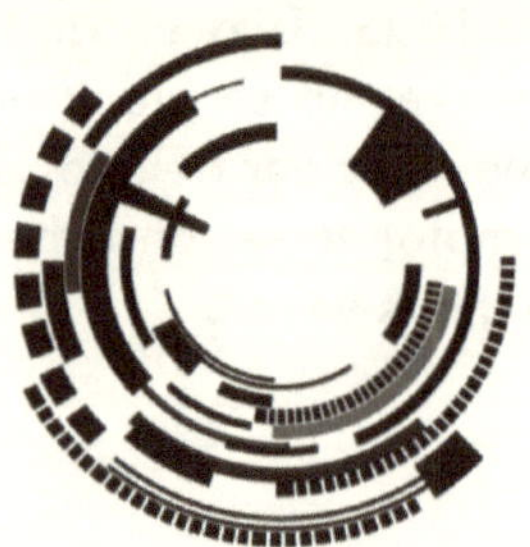

There's really nothing quite like finding yourself locked in a stranger's dungeon basement. When those strangers act like they are doing you a favor by putting you there, that's when things get confusing. Rowan flops me onto an oversized couch. I bounce ungracefully from the force.

"What? Do you think—" I start to protest, but I am dumbstruck by my surroundings.

The juxtaposition of the woodsman's retreat upstairs and the pristine luxury basement jars me. This is not a dungeon but luxury. It's how I picture the Primes living. The floors are sturdy like stone. They are smooth with an almost glossy coat. They look slippery but they are not. The walls are decorated with an odd mix of art and weapons. The weapons look like the original versions of energy weapons: swords, spears, axes, bows, shields—all made of metal. The basement feels part castle, part underground bunker, and part luxurious home.

Pain surges in my chest as I try to turn. My gut was still tender from the force of his blow. "You didn't have to hit me, I was—"

"Oh, he knows," Kali interrupts with a delighted smile. "He just really wanted to."

"Why?" I protest.

Kali chuckles, "He doesn't like having to let domies get the drop on him."

"What do you mean 'let'?"

Kali's chuckle turns into a full-blown laugh. "Wait, you thought your incredibly clumsy attack actually caught him by surprise?" Her laugh gets louder and makes me feel smaller.

She waves her hand in front of her face. "Elder Schmitty likes to see what new arrivals like yourself are capable of. He can't see that if Rowan defends himself because none of you would ever touch him. Part of the tribute we get to pay for being allowed to reside in his happy little town is that Rowan has to let crag domies get the drop on him. That and Schmitty is a racist shinshew who thinks it's funny to watch a Tribling get taken down."

"You want me to believe he let me take him down?"

"I really don't care if you believe it. People believe all sorts of things—doesn't make them true. The only reason you even made contact was because he let you."

"I find that hard to be—"

"To believe, I know, you've said. Every one of you thinks that because you didn't die in the sheep pen of your cushy little city that you're something special."

"I made it here, didn't I?" I protest childishly. Why am I trying to win her approval? It's stupid, but something about the way she talks gets under my skin.

"Wow, that's so amazing. You crossed the Sand Sea all by yourself," she says, shaking her head as if I was bragging about converting oxygen to carbon dioxide. "That's the least dangerous place here."

"Are you kidding? The heat, those endless waves of sand—I was by myself for four days. No food, no water, no shelter." *Why am I still arguing this? Shut up, Jett.*

"Right—there's nothing; that's what deserts are: nothing."

She pauses as if this information should somehow lead to an epiphany on my part. It does not.

"You want us to respect you because you managed to not die for a few days? I've been here since I was a child. Rowan was born here. Excuse us for being underwhelmed."

Well, when she says it like that.

"You don't know the half of what it takes to survive out here. Some places are dangerous because of what doesn't live there. Others are dangerous because of what does. Guess which one we are in?"

I exhale, holding my hands up in defeat.

"Look, I'm not trying to fight here. This is just a lot to take in. I don't have my bearings yet. I didn't even know people lived out here before last week. I thought it was a place to die a slow, horrible death."

Kali's expression softens slightly, and she shrugs. "It is for most. The rest of us get stronger and learn to survive."

We stare at each other. I force my teeth together to keep myself from talking as I try to calm myself down. I close my eyes and let out a slow breath.

"Can we start over?"

Kali shrugs in indifferent agreement. Rowan sits next to her, and they exchange a long look. His hands dance in a series of quick signals.

"He wants to know how you knew to avoid the orbs of the terastrum."

"What do you—" I stop before putting my foot in my mouth. "He doesn't speak?"

"He says plenty," she chuckles. "But no, I've never heard him speak."

"What he's doing with his hands—is that like another language?"

"In a sense. He uses signs and expressions to convey ideas."

"Interesting." I ineffectually try to mask my confusion.

"For example, right now he wants to know how you knew about the orbs."

I scratch my head, trying to figure out how to put words to it.

"How do you tell the difference between an easy mark and an undercover Red Cap trying to lure you out with a seemingly easy target?"

Kali and Rowan exchange a confused glance.

"You have to learn how to read your environment. When you're getting set up, there's always something out of place. Sometimes it's something small, like a guy walking back and forth in the same area too many times, or maybe a group of people sitting at a table not paying any attention to each other. Before you make a move, you learn to check for that thing that's out of place. The orbs were out of place. These beautiful lights set on a dangerous path—that made me feel weirdly safe. It felt off. Just because something makes you feel safe doesn't mean it is."

That response earns me an approving nod from Rowan.

Kali gets up and walks into the kitchen, making herself a cup of tea.

"Does everyone go underground like this every night?"

"Everyone who wants to see the sunrise."

"Is there a reason they don't lock the gates?"

"Most of the things that come out at night aren't deterred by gates. Skylari and aestroths just fly over them. Drukani and trematerras crash through them and then the gates can't be used when we need them during the day. Nocstras are about the only thing the gates could keep out."

"Those are all—?"

"Mutated creatures—and ones you should avoid if at all possible."

"What about the force shields?

Kali pours something into her mug and starts stirring it with a tiny spoon.

"They are effective as a deterrent but aren't strong enough to keep out anything that really wants to get in."

"If the gates don't keep the monsters at bay, why have them at all?"

"Wanderers, bandits, marauders. Mostly, gates will slow things down, give us time to get underground should the depraved come." Her voice almost trembles at the mention of the last one, which piques my curiosity.

"The depraved—you mean like the loopy monster-people parents tell their children about to get them to behave?"

"They are not loopy. They know exactly what they are doing. They understand. They don't kill because they've been driven mad. They kill because taking life is the only thing that makes them feel alive."

"Surely, you're joking. They're a tod tale."

There's a moment of silence before she responds.

"Of all the horrors that live here, they are the worst. The depraved don't just embrace death. They celebrate it. Delight in it. Worship it. They roam the Outlands like a swarm of locust devouring any life they find."

"You're making them sound like monsters, but they are just people, right?"

"Live long enough and you'll see; people are the worst monsters."

"But where did they come from?"

"No one knows. I think they just gave in."

"Gave in?"

She takes a sip from her mug.

"Fear is one of our basic instincts. It warns us of danger so that we can protect ourselves and get to safety. Prolonged fear is a dark void. What happens when the fear never goes away? When it becomes an overwhelming, unending, unrelenting force that you can't escape? The more fear surrounds us, the more it consumes us. The depraved didn't just look into the void, they became it."

"You've seen them?"

Kali shakes her head. "Not personally. Wouldn't be here if I had."

"Wait, you've never seen one, but you're convinced they are real?" My tone reflects my rising doubt.

"I've never seen the wind, but I've felt its presence." She lets that point sink in for a moment. "I've spent most of my life roaming the Outlands. I've seen villages wiped out with nothing but mangled parts and trails of blood left behind. I've seen video footage from datapads and security equipment. I've heard the stories. We've—"

"How do you know so much about them?"

"You'll see. Maybe one day you will too. There are many dangers in the Outlands, but the depraved are the main reason you don't want to be out at night. Some towns have force shields strong enough to keep them away. Others, like Red Clay, build underground bunkers."

"So how do you travel without getting caught outside?"

Kali sets her empty mug down. "There are way stations built to provide temporary underground shelter if you are lucky enough to find one. Or you find a nice cave or someplace out of view. It's still risky but it's manageable."

I slouch back into the chair. "I never thanked you for saving me from the Nocstras."

Kali seems suddenly uncomfortable and flustered. "It's not a big deal."

"It is to me. When I was exiled, I thought that was the end. I thought I was just going to wander through an endless desert until I died a slow, horrible death. Then, I met you, and ever since, I've had hope. Really for the first time since Victor."

"Victor?"

"Victor was my best friend; my brother really. In Dios, Victor and my other friends were all orphans in our own way. We found each other, and we became a family. We worked together, looked out for each other, and took care of each other. Life for people like us wasn't pleasant. I was tired of turning a blind eye to the injustice of the Patriarch. I wanted more. I wanted to fix the wrongs I saw in the world. I wanted to find my place in it. We started fighting back. We had a real chance to make a difference and then—Victor." I shake my head, trying to keep myself from getting worked up.

"Victor betrayed us; he sold out his friends to the Patriarch. I trusted him with my life. We all did. He got us sent here."

I spend the next hour or so telling them about my life in Dios—my friends, the rebellion, and the events that took place in the Market that led to our arrest and exile. At the end, Rowan leans forward, holding his right fist in his left hand and hiding his face behind them. Even this fails to cover the intense scowl on his face. Kali reaches out and touches his shoulder. Rowan sits back on the couch.

"You want revenge?"

For the first time, I sense a level of understanding or interest from her.

"Revenge, justice, redemption—you name it."

"Why not go back and kill him?"

"Even if I could find a way back into the city, my friends are out here somewhere. I need to find them and make sure they are safe."

Kali shakes her head. "They are probably dead."

"I refuse to believe that."

"You plan to leave, on your own, to go search the Outlands in hopes of finding your friends who may or may not be alive?"

I nod.

"What if there's nothing you can do for them?"

"I have to try."

"That's salvage. You'd be throwing your life away." Kali rubs her face in her hands.

"Maybe, but they are family."

"What good is family if it gets you killed?"

"Life has to be about more than just survival. Life is about having people who make it worth living. Don't you have anyone like that?"

"Your friends are that important to you? You'd die for them?"

"Yes," I say with conviction and without hesitation. "That's what family does. They risked their lives for me. They are in this situation because of me. I will do whatever it takes to find them and to make sure they are safe."

"What about your revenge? Who will bring Victor to justice if you throw your life away out here?"

"Victor will have to wait."

"The longer you wait, the harder it will be to kill him. If your friend is as smart as you claim, he will do very well in the Control. Might even make it to the Ruling Counsel."

How does she know about the Control? The Control is the Civil Branch of the Patriarch's leadership structure. If she were exiled as a child, how would she know about it?

"Why do you say that?"

"You're from Dios, and you don't understand how it's structured? The Patriarch is like a pyramid that's designed not to look like a pyramid. Everything is built to protect the High Father's image and make him look like a pious and humble man of the people."

"How do you know this?"

"My mother taught me."

"OK. Where did she learn it?"

Kali shrugs, "Life. If your friend led a successful rebellion, he has the Ruling Counsel's attention. They will make him an asset. The Patriarch knows how to protect its assets. While you're out here, he's there, climbing their ranks and getting further and further out of reach. You want revenge? You don't have time to waste."

I picture it in my mind, as I have so many times since his betrayal. I track Victor down and make him wish he'd died with his parents. Each time I picture it, I use a different method. It's amazing how creative the mind can be when motivated by malice. Imagining Victor beg for mercy, hearing him grovel and express how sorry he is, is like therapy. I relish the thought. Kali's suggestion that my window for gratification may be closing fills me with a sense of fear. What if she's right? What if I miss my chance? A consuming fire burns within me, driving me to find a way back and exact my justice on Victor. I take a breath. I picture Lilly's smile, hear Olivia's laugh, Becka's thoughtful words, Telmen's unending questions, and Jensen—well, not Jensen. Reason conquers impulse.

"I will not abandon my friends in pursuit of my revenge. That would make me no better than Victor." This earns me a dismissive shrug. That's my cue to change the subject.

"How did you guys end up in the Outlands?"

Kali chuckles, shaking her head. "Why on Bealz's dead earth would I share my story with you? I don't know you. I'd don't even like you."

Rowan gestures, and his hands flash between different signs.

"You can't be serious." Kali rolls her eyes in response.

The intensity of Rowan's nonverbal expression increases.

Kali exhales dramatically, "Fine, I'll tell him. Rowan wants to share *his story* with you: Rowan is a Tribling."

"I don't know what that is," I confess.

"A Tribling is a native to the Outlands."

"You mean he was born here?"

"I mean he's not from a city. Triblings are not descendants of exiles. They are natives to the Outlands; they've been here since the Great Collapse."

"I thought everyone outside the cities died in the Great Collapse."

"That is what the Patriarch wants everyone to believe. The best lies are half-truths. Most people did die. Whatever mutated and changed the animals killed most of the humans who weren't protected by the Domes. The few who survived were changed. His people are stronger, faster, more agile than most."

"That's why Elder Schmitty treats him the way he does?"

"Yes. Triblings are not popular. There's a lot of tension between them and most of the exiles who live in settlements. Some of that is a sordid history. Some is ignorance. Some is the fact that Triblings are polytheistic, which worshippers of Bealz find offensive."

"I see. Why doesn't he stay with his family—or other Triblings?"

Kali closes her eyes and lets out a long, slow breath. "There are many different tribes of what we call Triblings. They don't always get along with each other. Rowan doesn't have a tribe to go back to. His people were wiped out."

"And his family?" I ask.

"When Rowan was a boy, the depraved came to his village. He was sleeping at the time. His parents heard screams and managed to get him into a small cellar they had dug into the ground in their house. They were able to hide the cellar door just before the depraved broke in."

"What happened?"

"He watched through gaps in the wooden floor as his parents were killed and eaten. He hid there for three days in silence, watching them revel in the terror and death they caused."

"He has seen them."

"Maybe the only living person who has."

"They are as bad as the stories say?"

"Worse. The depraved are wretched creatures, a sort of death cult. What they don't tell you in Dios is that they file their teeth into fangs, graft spikes into their bodies using the broken bones of their victims, and sew their victims' flesh into their own like trophies. They cut out their own tongues. They paint their faces with blood. Do everything you can to avoid them. If they find you, they will torture you, kill you, skin you, and eat you. Only for the very lucky will it be in that order."

I feel a sudden knot in my gut, and my stomach turns. Of all the things

I'd imagined in my nightmares of this place, none of them came close to what Kali is describing. I take long, slow breaths as this reality washes over me.

"How do you fight something like that?"

"We don't fight the depraved. We run. We hide. We pray."

I turn to Rowan. "I watched my parents die. It was horrible, and it haunts me to this day. I'm so sorry. I can't even imagine what it must be like for you."

Rowan closes his eyes and nods. Maybe sharing our stories helps us bond a little.

We sit in silence for a few minutes.

"It's getting late. Get some rest. There's a spare bed in the room on the right. You and Rowan can fight over who gets that, and who sleeps on the couch." I've seen lightning take longer to disappear than she does as she bolts out of the room, closing the door to her bedroom behind her.

I look to the room with the bed and then to Rowan. He smirks, walking over to the room and closes the door behind him. Well, I guess it's the couch for me. The couch is surprisingly comfortable, especially after sleeping in the desert for the last week. My head hits the cushion, and the world around me disappears.

When I wake up, Rowan is sitting at the counter in the kitchen, sipping on a drink. I see no sign of Kali. Rowan silently slides a cup across the counter toward the empty seat next to him. Even from here I can see the steam peaking over the brim of the mug. It takes me longer than usual to get up. My body feels stiff, reluctant to move despite my repeated efforts. Once on my feet, I take a moment to stretch, hoping to loosen everything up and regain some mobility. It helps. Out of habit I tap my pocket to feel the hilt of my energy blade. Relieved, I sit down at the counter and take a sip from the warm mug. I choke, forcing myself to swallow what could only be some form of liquid tar. Rowan chuckles and glances up toward the stairs. Kali must have already left.

Sliding the cup away from myself, I grumble, "I can't drink that. It's safe to go up?"

Rowan nods and slides off his chair. I follow him up the stairs and outside. I was relieved to see it was still early in the morning. I thought I'd slept the day away. We walk in silence back to the main hall where I'd met Elder Schmitty the day before.

During my previous walk through Red Clay, I was distracted and didn't have the bandwidth to appreciate it. Today, I see the town is surprisingly large. Not like Dios with its cloud-breakers blocking the sky and creating giant wind tunnels. This town is almost serene. The constant roaring of hover engines, the steady hum of force shields and screen displays I was used to tuning out, are completely absent here, giving *quiet* a much richer meaning than I ever imagined. Ironically, this town, in the middle of the place I had been conditioned to dread my whole life, feels almost peaceful. Strange to think I could feel more at home in a place surrounded by dangers than I ever did in the haven that was supposed to be my home.

We walk in silence back to the main hall where I'd met Elder Schmitty the day before. As we approach, the two guards posted on either side of the door move together, blocking our path.

"Is he expecting you?" asks the one on the right. Rowan turns to face him. The guard, who a moment ago had been standing straight and confident, holding a rifle across his body, starts to cower. His head drops and without another word he steps away from the door. I recognize the posture, as the Patriarch conditioned it into us:

submission. Except the guard isn't cowering at the threat of armed soldiers or a seemingly all-powerful government but to a single man—and the guard is holding a gun. Maybe what Kali said about Rowan was true.

We walk inside. Sitting on his throne is the greasy-haired, impressively large elder, taking a bite of a giant leg of meat, its juices running down his face. The day is too young to be eating meat like that. He smacks his lips and wiggles up in his chair. A silent servant rushes over, holding an empty silver platter. Schmitty places the partially eaten meat leg on the plate and waves the servant off.

His smile looks incredibly inauthentic. "Oh, you have returned."

My heart races so much I don't even care that he's rubbing meat juices on his chubby face. "Yes! You said you'd help me find my friends. Please, do you know where they are?"

He holds up his hand to stop me. "You need to learn how things are done here. I don't appreciate you barging in here whenever you see fit," he says before leaning forward to make his presence seem more impressive. It might be intimidating if he wasn't comically large.

"Since you are new here, I will forgive this impudence." He looks so cheerful, like this is doing me some great favor. I don't care; if he can tell me where my friends are, it's worth it.

"Thank you. So—"

"Hold on, we are not there yet. I would like to know your intentions."

"My intentions?"

"Yes, if you are able to reunite with your friends, what do you intend to do next?"

I sigh. "I think we'd try to find our way back to Dios, but I don't know. I'm going one step at a time here."

Schmitty shakes his head. "Life is like a current. It flows in one direction. You can resist the current, or you can float with it. There's no going back. No one gets back into Dios. It is a fool's errand. You need to accept that. Everyone who has tried has died. Those of us who are still here are here because we gave up trying to go back."

"Look, my friends are out there. All I care about is finding them. Every minute I lose, they get farther away."

He nods. "I'm inclined to help you. But as I'm sure you can imagine, information is a valuable commodity. If I give you this valuable information, what do I get in return?"

"You want to barter?"

"Yes, in a manner of speaking."

My teeth grind together. My hand slides to my pocket, fingering the hilt to my energy blade. I'll give him some alternative motivation. Rowan's hand grabs my shoulder. Out of the corner of my eye I see him shaking his head. Why stop me? He can't seriously want to protect this scrap sink. I take a breath. It was my impulsiveness that got us into this mess in the first place. I don't have Victor to bail me out anymore. I need to think. I found a semi-safe place outside of Dios; a place that could be a home. If I attack the leader of this place, that's never going to happen.

The momentary silence is cut by the sudden sounding of a horn. This is not the eerie siren that marked the Dusk Descension. This is more of a bellowing bullhorn. Everyone in the room perks up. Schmitty points his finger toward the door and shouts something I'm too distracted to care about. Rowan is already out the door. I follow him.

Outside, armed men are rushing frantically toward the town gate. It's still weird not being able to identify who someone is or what they do based on what they are wearing. Everyone here seems to dress in whatever manner suits them.

Rowan is down the hill in a flash. I chase after him.

"Come on," Kali calls out, intercepting us as we approach the gate. She leads us to a ladder. We climb quickly. The ladder leads to a walkway along the inside of the wall. We race along it until we are next to the tower on the left side of the gate. The ramparts of the wall are covered with the citizens of Red Clay looking out at the scene below. Our spot gives us a clear view of the path leading into Red Clay.

Standing brazenly in the middle of the bridge leading to the now closed gates is a man. He's tall with broad shoulders. One of his eyes is covered by a patch, and he's wearing a long, brown coat that drapes from his shoulders all the way to his ankles. He stands like a soldier at attention, arms behind his back. Behind him, lined up in a menacing fashion on the far side of the bridge, is a large group of tough-looking thugs. *Well, this can't be good.*

CHAPTER FOUR

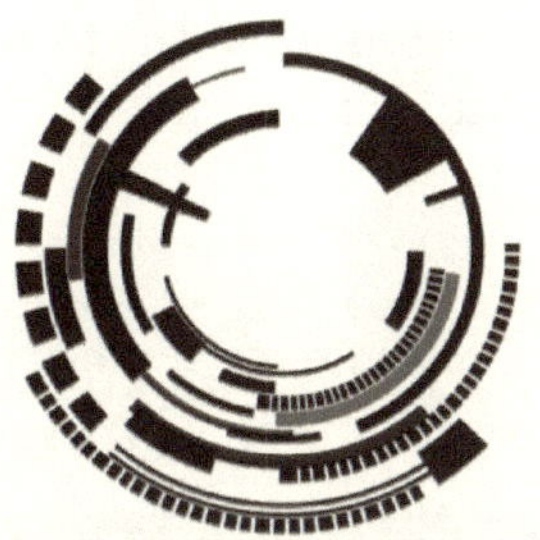

"**O**h, Schmitty," he bellows. "Come out and plaaaayyy." His voice sounds cheerful but also somehow angry at the same time.

"Who's that?" I whisper to Kali.

No response. She turns toward the gate. Rowan grabs her shoulders. She tries to push past him. He holds tighter, shaking his head. She keeps pushing, driving her feet into the wooden floor.

"Let me go, Rowan! Don't make me hurt you," she seethes.

He doesn't budge. She strains and twists, but she is no match for Rowan's strength. Her face is red, her teeth clench together as she pushes and fights to no avail. She is like a woman possessed.

"Gahhhh!" she grunts, kicking her feet back wildly. Rowan takes the shots without making a sound or letting go.

"What is going on?" I ask. Rowan looks over Kali's shoulders and just shakes his head. His eyes move to direct my gaze toward the one-eyed man at the gate. The gate slowly opens and an older, weak-looking man in an overly large suit slowly makes his way out onto the bridge. He is cowering, his body trembling as he approaches the one-eyed man.

"Greetings." His voice is soft and frail.

"Well, who in the Sheol is this?" the one-eyed man replies.

"Sir?" The man's voice shakes as much as body.

"You see, that's just bad manners. I ask for Elder Schmitty, and he sends this skeleton of a man. It's like he doesn't want to talk to me. After I came all this way for a special visit. It's just rude."

"I beg your pardon, sir."

"You can call me Morton. That's the name my mother gave me. Or King Ghood," the one-eyed man states.

"K . . . King Ghood, Elder Schmitty has instructed me to remind you that this is not how your arrangement works, and he requests that you return at the agreed-upon time."

Morton smiles brightly at the man, stepping closer and putting his hands on the tiny man's shoulders as if to comfort him. "Don't be afraid, friend. You are doing your master's bidding. It is honorable."

The older man seems to calm down some, shaking considerably less. "Thank you so much sir, I did not want to—"

Morton wags his finger in the man's face. "Shh, shh, shh. There is no need for that. I am here at your service. As the official ambassador to the Marauder nation and Marauder King of this territory, it is my solemn duty to ensure peace and prosperity between my people and your community. We are, after all, a family."

"Family, sir?"

"You should not cower or hide your face. You are a free man, speaking for the leader of this entire community." Morton puts a finger under the older man's chin, lifting his head to face him.

The gravitas with which he speaks makes him seem incredibly charming. He has a natural sort of magnetic energy. He seems so pleasant. That is such a relief. I expected things to go much differently.

"Tell me your name, friend."

"Lenard, sir." The old man leans back, assuming a more dignified posture.

"Lenard—I like that. Good strong name. You got kids, Lenard?"

"I do sir—two children and six grandchildren."

"Ain't that something? You're a lucky man, Lenard. Good for you."

"Thank you, sir. Would you like me to take a message back to our elder, King Ghood?"

Morton claps his hands together, flashing a bright smile. "Why, my good man, that is an excellent idea. If it's not too much trouble, please tell Elder Schmitty that—," Morton turns and grips something from under his long coat.

Before I can blink, a shining piece of steel sticks out of the old man's back. With a soft hiss, a blueish glow starts to pulse around the steel. I've never seen anything like this. It's a hybrid sword with an energy edge set around the blade that could be turned on or off. Morton pulls the blade free, swings it in an arc, and slices off Lenard's head. It hits the wooden bridge with a loud *thwuup*. Morton casually slides the blade back into its sheath on his hip. He kicks Lenard's head into the ditch and turns his gaze upward.

"Would someone please tell Lenard's grandkids they just lost their grandpa?" His voice is calm and sincere as if he's pleading. He even appears almost sad as he says it. "Let me make myself absolutely clear, so we can avoid situations like this in the future. When I ask for Elder Schmitty, I expect to speak to Elder Schmitty, not some feeble old sack of bones."

Shock freezes me in place. Disbelief clouds my mind. That didn't just happen. I must have missed something. Morton's actions are so contrary to his demeanor and speech that seeing them feels like a betrayal. I turn to Kali to try and make sense of what I just saw.

Kali looks down at the wooden walkway we're standing on. "Those are Marauders. They travel around demanding offerings in exchange for protection."

"Protection," I whisper back, "from what?"

"From them; pay and they leave. Don't pay and they murder us all. They create a problem, then they make people pay for the solution."

"People of Red Clay," Morton's charming tone rings out. "The Marauders work tirelessly and sacrifice a great deal to provide you with the protection you deserve. Your leader, Elder Schmitty, paid us with spoiled merchandise. Rotted to the core. We lost several men as a result of this act of willful aggression. Our code suggests that I purge all of you for this offense. But I am a reasonable and merciful man. I do not blame you for the ill-advised actions of your leader. Since he is too cowardly to own up to his nefarious deeds, the debt regretfully falls on you. We will return, at which point last month's offering, this month's offering, and additional reparations of four strong, able-bodied fighters will be delivered to us. If these conditions are not met, we will terminate our contract with Red Clay, and you will see firsthand what your offerings protected you from. You have three days."

Morton Ghood sighs before adjusting his coat. "I do hate all these unpleasantries. You made a mistake, but I am prepared to forgive you. Do not take advantage of my kindness."

"Offering?" I whisper.

Kali shakes her head.

Morton smiles gleefully, like a merchant trying to sell an overpriced item to an ignorant customer. "Just make sure your offering is ready when we come back, and we can be friends again. Okay?" He holds out his arms, inviting us to agree with him.

Even having just watched him murder an innocent old man, there is a part of me that wants to scream, "Yes!" It's like he has a hypnotic charm. I shake my head to break the spell his presentation has on me. Morton waves his arm in a little circle and pulls it in for a dramatic, low bow before he takes his leave.

Slowly the Marauders fade into the distance.

Marauders—a new threat to add to the pile of dangers the Outlands has to offer. How exciting. The scowl on Rowan's face matches the raw fury burning inside my mind. I didn't want to think about what I had just seen. There was no reason to kill that man. He was innocent and harmless.

Kali looks at me and then back to Rowan, who gives her a nod.

Her voice is assertive, but the notes of rage are unmistakable. "This is it; we need to go."

"Where?" I ask.

"It doesn't concern you, domie," she snaps.

"I could help."

"Getting in the way doesn't help." Kali shoves past me, nearly knocking me off the wall to the ground below. I stand for a moment, stunned and confused, before making my way down.

Passing the gate, I bump into Tin Grey.

"Jett, how are you feeling?"

"Confused, actually."

"I don't blame you. I can't believe he just killed Lenard."

"No, not that. It's Kali. She practically shoved me off the wall just now."

Doc exhales loudly. "She's going after him. I saw her storming up the hill toward the Main Hall."

"So . . ."

"She needs help."

"Are we talking about the same person? She doesn't seem to need or want help."

Doc sighs, "When she gets angry, Kali loses all sense. It's like her rage consumes her. If she's going to see Schmitty, that fire is going to grow. Crag girl is going to get herself killed."

"Why do you think I can help? She doesn't even like me."

"Doesn't she? You were unconscious for four days while I treated you. Did you notice that she was there when you woke up?"

"Yeah, so?"

"Did you think that was a coincidence? She checked on you every day."

"Really? Why? She doesn't even know me."

"You must have impressed her. Last time I saw her this invested in another person was when she brought Rowan to Red Clay. You have to stop her, Jett."

"Stop her from what?"

"The Marauder King—Morton. She's going to try to kill him."

"How is that my problem?"

"A life debt must be repaid."

"What?"

"She saved your life, Jett; you owe her."

"What do you want me to do? Knock her out and tie her up until she returns to her senses?"

Doc raises an eyebrow, "Hmmm . . . you wouldn't be able to if you tried."

"That girl doesn't need my protection."

Our conversation is cut short by the bellow of a nearby woman. At the end of the street stands Janelle. She's positioned herself on a makeshift platform and is shouting at a small crowd that seems to have gathered after witnessing Lenard's execution.

"Brothers and sisters, gather around. I see your suffering and your struggle. I have for you a message of hope! My children, it doesn't have to be this way."

Why are loopy people always so good at projecting their voices?

"We suffer because we have ignored the will of Bealz! His Chosen One remains lost. His tether to this world has become thin. Without it, we would be cast into eternal darkness. Hear me brothers; hear me sisters. We must bring the Chosen One back to the Holy City, and we will be saved! For it is written by the word of his prophet: those who serve the will of Bealz will receive life everlasting. I offer unto you the Mark of the Faithful."

Janelle lifts some kind of brand into the air, pointing the fancy fire poker at passersby. "This mark is the symbol of our devotion and our declaration of obedience. Admission into the paradise of Bealz is granted only to those who bear this mark."

She aims the poker in my direction, and I see the symbol on it. It's the top half of a dome with the image of an eye built into the dome.

Well, that's about enough of this. I start toward the Main Hall when Doc grabs my arm.

"I'll see what I can do for her but no promises." I look down at the short, bald man who nods in response before releasing my arm.

Despite being inside, Kali's voice blares all the way down the hill. The guards make no attempt to stop me as I approach. Inside the Main Hall, Kali is standing at the bottom of the steps, shouting up at Elder Schmitty, who is shoving spoonsful of rice into his mouth.

"How long are you going to just sit there, stuffing your face, while they take everything from us? We have people; we have weapons. We can go after them."

Elder Schmitty sets down his bowl of rice and leans back in his chair. He lifts one leg up onto a cushioned ottoman placed in front of him.

"Foolish girl, you know nothing. Marauders are warriors. They have greater numbers, more weapons, better training, and they survive in the wild. We wouldn't stand a chance. Do you think I enjoy giving away our hard-earned resources? Hmmm? We pay the Marauders because if we don't, they will kill us." His tone drips with condescension.

"You pay them because—"

"You are a guest here. Have you not enjoyed my charity? I have allowed you to stay, to come and to go as you please. I've even tolerated your little beast, disgusting as he is. Despite you parading that creature through my town, I instructed my men not to harass him. Now, after everything I've done for you, you challenge me. It's time you learned your place, girl."

I notice Schmitty's arm slide forward subtly on the arm rest of his chair. He reaches one finger under the bottom of the armrest and pushes up. Why would he have a button installed on his chair? My eyes move to the camera; the red flashing light stops blinking. That seems shady.

"My place? And what is my place?" If she's attempting to hide her anger, she is failing miserably. The two guards standing on either side of the elder step closer to him. Two more on either side of the room move their hands to their weapons.

"Don't play daft with me. It used to be women knew their place. They were seen but not heard. They did what Bealz intended without complaint. Now, you all seem to think you're entitled to more."

"More? Like having an opinion? Are you—"

"Opinions, ideas, a say—all of it disgusting. What is this world coming to? You want to make decisions, but you don't understand consequences."

"You need to shut your mout—" I take a step forward.

Kali grabs my arm and shakes her head. I force myself to swallow the piece of my mind I'd like to give Schmitty right now. Kali seems remarkably calm. Strange—she was practically foaming at the mouth at the sight of Morton Ghood. Schmitty insults her and her entire gender, and she doesn't bat an eye? His words make me want to climb the stairs and break his jaw so he can't vomit any more of this garbage out. Yet, Kali is as calm as a sunrise. I may never understand women.

"I don't blame you for being a woman. This is why the Sacred Texts forbid women from having authority, leading, and trying to teach men. It's not that you aren't important. It's that Bealz made you to serve us, so we could lead you better. You know this. Bealz made man first and made man better. Woman was formed second to serve, cook, clean, and give us children. We are not equals because we were not designed to be. There's no shame in being a woman. You just need to learn your limits. You are good at many things, but you weren't meant to make these kinds of decisions. You just weren't wired for it."

He did not just say that. My body is physically shaking. It's like disgust and rage are fighting for control of my reaction, and they are both winning. How can someone believe this nonsense? Why is she not more upset by it? I have a pit in my stomach. It takes everything in me not to rush the sad excuse for a man, throw him from his chair, and make him grovel for her forgiveness.

Kali's head turns down, but her piercing gaze never leaves Schmitty. Her brow furrows into a scornful glare. If looks could kill, there'd be nothing left of Elder Schmitty.

She takes a deep breath; her voice comes out measured and calm. "They demand more every time they come. Sooner or later, they will demand more than we can give. Then what will you do?"

"I'll not hear another word of this. I have endured your willful insubordination for long enough. You will listen to me now. You know what happens if we attack. Marauders have a code: "Strike one. Strike all." They do not tolerate resistance. Even if we won, which we would not, the other tribes wouldn't let it stand. It is not their way. If we fight, the full force of every Marauder tribe would crash down on us. They would grind us into the dirt to ensure no other town follows our example. Is that what you want? You want to turn Red Clay into an example of what happens when you cross the Marauders? Hmmm?"

As much as I hate how he's speaking and almost everything he's saying, he makes a valid point. *Only fools fight a war they cannot win.* Victor's words echo in my head. That's what he said to me after revealing himself as a traitorous shinshew. I'm tempted to say them here. I hate having to admit how right he was—again.

Kali's breathing is heavy as she attempts to control her anger. I recognize that anger, that slow rumbling frustration that boils over the pot of self-control.

"You can dress it up however you like, but your justifications are just excuses to hide your fear. We are not alone. We could form an alliance with the other towns."

"I already thought of that. The towns are too spread out. Even if we came to terms, no town would be able to help without leaving themselves undefended."

"We could join with the Outcasts or the Sandurans," Kali suggests.

Schmitty laughs, "Those zealots wouldn't lift a finger to help us. And the Sandurans? Ha, the brilliant mind of a woman."

"If the Marauders won't tolerate resistance, why haven't they wiped out the Moon Pack? They have been harassing and killing Marauders for weeks. No Marauders have come. No warnings given."

For the first time, Elder Schmitty doesn't respond. Kali presses her position.

"Why do you think Morton came early? They are scared. They can feel their grip loosening. This isn't the time to recoil. This is the time to strike."

This reminds me of so many conversations I had with Victor and Spike. Is this how I sounded to them? For the first time, I can see how unreasonable my impulsiveness must have looked. Funny how easy it is to see in someone else what I was so blind to in myself.

"The Moon Pack—that is an interesting idea. I hadn't considered aligning ourselves with an imaginary resistance force."

Now it was Kali's turn to stare in stunned silence.

"I've seen—"

"You've seen paintings on rocks. You wonder why I don't take you seriously? That proves nothing. You believe there's some mysterious group fighting against the Marauders because that's what you want to believe. Even if this imaginary group existed, you wouldn't even have the first clue where to find them. You are a fine fighter Kali, but you don't understand what it takes to lead. You don't know the pressures, the burdens. You would rush into conflict just to sate your bloodlust."

Kali breaks the momentary silence, "Better to die fighting than let them bleed us dry, then kill us anyway."

I want to shout, "preach," but it feels like the wrong time. Kali paces back and forth at the bottom of the stairs that lead up to the elder's throne.

Schmitty leans forward and slowly stands up. It took him a minute to secure his footing and to balance his weight, making what might have otherwise been an intimidating gesture lose its edge.

"I have made my judgment. You will accept it, or I will have you arrested. There will be no action taken against Morton Ghood or the Marauders."

"Coward," Kali mutters between gritted teeth.

I can feel the tension growing in the room.

Kali's arms tighten as her hand moves for the weapon on her belt.

"You know what he did. If you try to stop me from—"

Schmitty laughs heartily and slaps his own belly, making it jiggle. "I don't have to try, foolish girl. I snap my fingers, and you'll spend the next year in a prison cell. Speak to me like this again, and you and your pet friend will find yourselves banished." Rowan grits his teeth at the remark but manages to remain statuesque. "You forget that you are in *my town.* You will follow my instructions. Am I understood?" He glares down at her.

She glances over her shoulder at me as I put my hand on her arm.

"Not a good idea," I whisper.

Kali pushes my hand away and storms out of the room. She pushes past Rowan, who follows her out. I turn to do the same.

Schmitty's voice returns to its former facade of friendliness. "Mr. Lasting, we should continue our discussion about your friends, yes?"

Reluctantly, I turn to face him. He's already plopped back down onto his chair, his body still jiggling from the motion.

"I'm listening."

"I can help you find your friends."

"Really? You could have given me that information before but didn't. Why would you offer it now?"

"Well, I would like us to be friends. I can use someone with your skills."

"All I'd have to do in return is . . ."

Elder Schmitty smiles. "Nothing substantial. You keep an eye out for me. Let me know of anything that might need my attention."

"You mean spy?"

He sighs. "You make it sound like such a devious thing. Friends help each other. I help you find your lost compatriots, and in return, if say, someone was to share with you their intention to defy your friend and put this whole community in danger, you would tell your friend about it." He points to himself as if it wasn't abundantly clear.

"You know, a friend wouldn't use the safety of my friends to manipulate me."

"I'm not just offering you information. I'm offering to provide you and your friends with a home. You'd be safe here as a part of our community."

"Seems fair."

Schmitty nods, seeming pleased with himself. "Good, good."

"So about my friends?"

"*Tsk. Tsk. Tsk.* You'll need to prove you want to be friends before I give you that information."

Ah, the classic string-along scam. He doesn't really think I'm going to fall for that, does he?

"I better go; if I spend too long here talking with you, Kali may become suspicious. Then she won't tell me anything. How's this—you take the afternoon, and put together all the intel you have on my friends; I'll go see what she's planning. I'll sneak back here first thing tomorrow, and we can exchange information."

Schmitty smiles and claps his hands together like a happy child. "Ah, a wonderful plan. This will be the beginning of a beautiful friendship, I think."

I'm barely out the door when Doc grabs me and pulls me aside. "What happened?"

"What do you think happened? She yelled; he didn't listen. She wants to fight; he forbade it. She stormed out; here we are."

"Hmmm . . . Credits to creatures she's going anyway."

"Not sure what that means, but I'd take that bet."

"Hmmm . . . You need to go with her; try to talk some sense into her."

"Sorry, Doc. I have more pressing issues."

"You want to find your friends?"

"Elder Schmitty offered to share what he knows. At least that will give me a place to start."

"Jett, Kali is special. I don't want to see her hurt. She will come to her senses; she just needs someone to rein her in a bit."

"Why do you think that someone is me? I'm not exactly a calming influence."

"Schmitty won't help you but maybe I can. I'll see what I can find out to help you find your friends."

"So long as I do what you want?"

Doc shakes his head. "No. I'm going to do what I can to help you regardless. Because it's the right thing to do. Because it's what I would want someone to do for me. While I'm gathering that information, I am asking you—please help her."

For a moment, he reminds me of Spike. How could I ever say no to Spike? "Fine, I'll see what I can do. If she won't listen, I can't make her."

Doc hugs me tight, practically cracking a rib. "That's all I can ask. First, you're going to need a proper weapon. That glorified toothpick you carry isn't going to cut it."

"My knife?"

"That is not a knife. Go see Cooper—fourth house on the right. Tell him I sent you, and he will get you connected."

I follow Doc's directions to a small cabin just down the main dirt road. Leaning against the house with his ponytail pulled high on his head is Cooper; that makes finding the right house much easier.

"Well, if it isn't our new domie; what do you want?" he says with a casual smile.

He seems to think he's much more charming than he actually is.

"Doc sent me."

The disinterest on his face screams, "Why should I care?"

"He said I need a real weapon."

Cooper redoubles his expression.

Crash it, if he wants to be annoying, I'll play. I enunciate each word slowly and deliberately, "Doc sent me to get a new weapon from you."

"I'm just messing with you." He pushes the door to his home open and waves me inside. Cooper's house is almost identical to Kali's: four plain walls made of stacked wooden logs, a few pieces of sturdy furniture, and not much else. I guess they don't spend a lot of time indoors during the day.

His basement bunker is virtually identical in design to hers but very different in decor. Everything here is matching. The walls are white.

The dishes are white. The cups are white; it's like the color white threw up on everything. Every item is stacked perfectly. Every object is placed at a right angle. The walls are completely absent of decor or color.

Cooper walks over to the back wall of his weird, monochromatic life choices. I've never seen so much white. He pulls open a virtually invisible white panel—such a bold splash of noncolor to really accent the colorless room. He pulls a rectangular piece of metal from his pocket, then inserts it into a small hole on the panel. A glowing light scans him from the top down and then from left to right. The light flicks off with an audible click. The wall slides away, revealing another room—or rather, an oversized closet. The three walls are backlit with a blue-hued light and lined with shelves. Each shelf is covered in perfectly spaced hilts.

"Yeah, let me see your knife." Cooper extends his arm back without turning around.

Reluctantly, I pull the energy blade from my pocket and place it in his hand. He flips it over, inspecting it.

"Yeah, this is no good. They make these illegally with leftover parts."

"It's worked fine for me."

"It functions but not well. What does this give you, like a six-inch blade?"

I nod.

"Yeah, I see why Doc sent you to me. So what kind of weapon are we looking for?"

I shrug. "Maybe a gun?"

He shakes his head. "Yeah, that would not go over well with Elder Schmitty. He likes having all the guns to himself. It gives him a sense of power and importance. What are you using it for?"

"Not sure; he wants me to go keep an eye on Kali, and she's planning to take off after the Marauders."

"Gotcha. Well, a gun wouldn't do much good anyway. The energy beams fired from a gun are great against humans, but they don't have enough piercing power to handle the creatures you may encounter. Have you ever fought with any other kind of weapon?"

"Just guns and that knife. Apparently, my glorified toothpick isn't good enough."

"Yeah, unless you want to tickle them, this thing is useless. Tell me about your fighting style."

He turns his attention away from this obsessively organized rack of weapons and looks me up and down, assessing me awkwardly.

"I . . ." I really don't know how to answer that question.

He grins at me. Why is he—

His fist is so close to my face that I can feel the wind smack against my cheek. I pull my head back reflexively, barely dodging his swing. *You can't always avoid a fight.* Victor used to make us train multiple times a week just in case we got into a fight. Hearing Victor's voice in my head again makes me angry. *Make sure when you fight, you know how to win.* Instinct and muscle memory fuse together. I shift my feet and lift my fists, preparing myself.

Cooper slides forward and drives his fist toward my chest. I slap it away. His other hand comes flying up toward my face. I turn, barely avoiding a blow to the head for a second time. Combos are effective but also leave you exposed. I twist at the hips and drive my fist as hard as I can into his stomach. It connects with a loud *thwuump.* Cooper hunches over, a gust of air escaping his lungs. I hook my left fist into his jaw. The cracking sound echoes. The contact makes my knuckles throb.

Cooper's elbow swings toward my head. No time to dodge. Lifting my arm and moving in closer, I cut off the force of his strike, reducing the momentum of his attack and with it any impact it may have had. I drive my foot into the ground and push, causing him to stumble back off balance. Before I can press my advantage, his hands come up.

"OK, OK, OK," he chuckles and rubs his face where I'd hit him. "Good, I can work with that."

"Shinshew, what the heap is wrong with you?"

"Picking the right weapon is often the difference between life and death. The best weapon must be tailored to its wielder. Do you focus on speed, strength, or skill?"

"What does that have to do with trying to hit me?"

"Your reaction tells me everything. Watching you in the pass showed me your agility. That's not enough to pick the right weapon. I needed more. Now I see it; you rely on speed. You have strength but don't overexert it. You have training to both avoid and use effective combination attacks. You have good balance and an understanding of how to manipulate the momentum of your opponent. You react quickly and prefer fighting up close rather than keeping your opponent at a distance."

"You gathered all of that from a few seconds of fighting? How?"

He reaches into his weapon closet and hands me a black cylinder. It is slightly larger and thicker than the one for my energy knife. "Most people would attempt to avoid an elbow to the face by moving away from it. It's basic instinct. You moved closer. It was a smart move, as it set you up better for a counter, but not one most people would make. I think this will be the perfect weapon for you."

"How does it work?" I inspect the cylinder carefully.

"Squeeze the hilt once to turn it on."

I do so, and a beam of glowing, blue light projects out with a faint hiss. My eyes widen, as the beam is considerably larger than my knife.

"This is amazing."

"That's a twenty-four-inch beam. You'll notice it has a slight curve to it. It's more suited for your fighting style. Squeeze the hilt again to turn it off."

I give it another squeeze, and the blade disappears. I move the hilt around in my hand, getting a feel for it. At the bottom of the hilt, I feel a small mechanism.

"What's this do?"

Cooper smiles brightly. "Yeah, I knew I liked you. That adjusts the setting."

"What do you mean 'settings'?"

He seems very proud of himself.

"One thing your makeshift knife couldn't do is shift between different settings. On this, you can. Your default setting is the energy sword. Click it to the left and . . ."

I click the mechanism to the left and squeeze the handle. A smaller blade, much like my previous knife, appears.

"And if you click it to the right . . ."

I turn the blade off, click the mechanism two spots over, and reactivate it. A translucent blue shield, about two-and-a-half feet in diameter, protects my forearm.

"I've never seen anything like this."

"Yeah, you wouldn't have. It's my own design. It'll deflect most weapons and projectiles, but be careful. Using the shield for too long will drain the energy, and you'll have to recharge it." Cooper explains a few more things about the design, boasts about his creative ingenuity, and closes up his secret weapons closet.

"Did you make weapons in Dios?" I ask.

Cooper shakes his head. "No, I was a Merchant Liaison for the Market Sector. My job was to manage the goods coming in and out of the Market to ensure the Primes could find what they wanted and that nothing was too accessible for anyone else."

"How did you end up out here making weapons?"

"My father was a weapons designer in Dios. He'd come home after work, and we'd toy around with different designs. He wanted me to follow in his footsteps, but the Patriarch had other ideas. He designed some special weapon for them. A part broke because they tried to use it incorrectly. They labelled him a traitor, and our whole family got sent here."

"Heap, that's—"

"It's the Outlands; everyone here has a story like that. I'll play around with your knife and see if I can improve it some before you come back. Now you should get going, or Kali may be gone before you pick your jaw up off my floor."

I thank Cooper for the weapon and attach it to my belt.

Once outside, I can see the sun has already reached its zenith and has begun its descent. I take a moment to gather my thoughts. What was I doing here? Elder Schmitty has information about my friends, but I don't trust him. Am I really going to defy him by helping Kali? Something tells me he's not going to take that well. My mind wanders as I roam down the streets until I reach Kali's house.

Rowan is leaning against the doorframe to the front of her house, arms folded across his chest, leg up, resting one foot against the frame. He sees me and stands up straight. Something about his expression seems to say, "Took you long enough." For some reason, I find myself responding, "Cooper is really proud of his weapons—and a big fan of color."

That earns me a smile and nod.

"Is she downstairs?"

Rowan nods.

I find Kali on her couch, hands pressed together in front of her face, elbows resting on her knees as she rocks forward and back. Her eyes are fixed on some invisible thing in front of her. Rowan follows me down, and a moment later I hear the door sealing closed.

Kali stands, then paces back and forth, her face red, her eyes fixed on the floor as she tramples all over it. Suddenly she stops and stares at me as if sizing me up. The silence grows deafening.

"If you saw Victor again, what would you do to him?"

My hands curl into tight fists. My body tenses. Just thinking about it makes the cork containing my bubbling rage feel like it's going to burst.

I take a calming breath. "I would kill him. Slowly—after making him suffer for what he did."

Kali smiles in response. Normally, a smile is a warm affirmation. When one follows an expression of intent to commit murder, it's a little unnerving.

"I'm going after Morton. I'm going to find him. I'm going to kill him. If you get in my way, I will kill you, and Rowan will feed you to the Nocstras."

This anger is all too familiar. There will be no talking her down, no reasoning with her.

"I'm not trying to stop you. I came to warn you."

"About what?"

"Elder Schmitty wants me to spy on you and report back to him, in exchange for information about my friends."

"What did you say?"

"I told him I'd get some information and report back in the morning."

Kali's hand rests on her belt, her fingers brushing against her energy weapons. "Why? Tell me!"

"Because I trust Elder Schmitty about as far as I can throw him, and I doubt I could even pick him up, but I do have an idea."

Kali relaxes a little, her hands moving from her weapons. "What is it?"

"We could help each other."

"Oh, how's that?"

"We work together. I help you deal with Morton. You help me find my friends."

Kali scoffs, "What makes you think we need your help?"

"You're trying to kill the leader of an army. I have some experience with that. And you're going to need all the help you can get."

The feel of the room shifts suddenly.

"You've killed the leader of an army?"

"My friends and I, yes."

Kali smiles. "OK, domie, you got a deal. Just know that if you betray us—"

"You kill me; Rowan feeds me to the Nocstras."

"Look at that, you're not a complete crag after all."

Did we just have a moment? It felt like a moment. Just like that, I find myself rebelling against the governing authority of the first community I found after being exiled for rebelling against my previous governing authority. *I can't believe I'm doing this again. This better not turn into a habit.*

CHAPTER FIVE

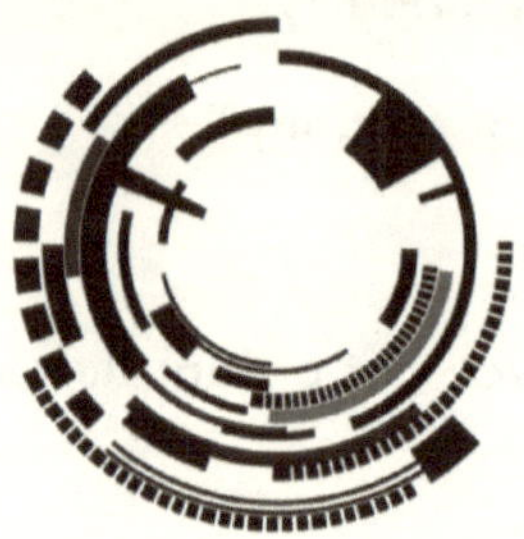

Rowan brandishes a small knife and walks over to us.

"Uh, Kali, what's he doing?"

"Making a pact," she says, like that should explain why he's walking toward me with a knife at the ready.

Rowan motions for me to give him my hand.

"Kali . . ."

"It's a Tribling custom. When two parties enter into an agreement to help one another, they form a blood pact. They are then honor bound to each other until both sides have fulfilled their commitment. The scar then serves as a reminder of their shared purpose, bonding them together."

Reluctantly, I extend my hand. "This like a little thumb prick or—"

I gasp as Rowan slides the sharp edge of the blade across the palm of my hand. As the blood starts to flow, he wraps my hand with a clean white cloth. He holds up one finger to his lips and then he repeats the process with Kali, who doesn't even wince.

Kali takes my hand and unwraps the bandage before pressing her palm against mine, so our fresh wounds touch.

This is not sanitary.

Rowan puts away his steel blade and retrieves a small energy knife. He activates the beam and then holds it between us. Kali takes her cut hand and holds it to the beam. This time she does wince as smoke rises, and the smell of charred meat fills the room. She grabs my hand and lifts it to the beam. It burns slowly as the heat cauterizes the cut.

"This blood pact is a sacred commitment. Refusal to honor it is punishable by death. If either of us try to back out, Rowan will be forced to kill us." Kali sits down at the island counter in her kitchen.

"Didn't think that was worth mentioning before we were bound to it?" I ask.

Kali shrugs, "No point in making a commitment if you don't intend to keep it. This way I know I can trust you to hold up your end."

I rub the tender skin around my newly forming scar. "Do you have anything that resembles a plan?"

Kali takes a digipad from her counter and starts drawing something on it before sliding it toward me. It bears the image of a yellow crescent moon with three lines, like bursts of light, coming from it. I've seen this symbol someplace before, but where?

"Marauders don't usually move in a large force like the one we saw earlier. Their main force stays at their base, and they send out scouts, or collection parties, to bring back offerings from the towns they protect. For the last month, we've been finding Marauder scouting parties wiped out."

"By some type of creature?"

"I don't think so. They weren't just killed; they were robbed. That and you know what creatures—Marauders, bandits, and the depraved—all have in common?"

I shake my head.

"None of them paint. We've found that image painted somewhere on the rocks nearby like a message or a warning at each location."

"You think there is a group deliberately taking out these Marauders?"

Kali nods and takes the digipad back.

"You think they will help us?"

"It's worth a shot. They spend a lot of time in the wilds; maybe they've seen your friends?"

I find myself suddenly invested in this plan. "Let's go find them, this Moon Pack."

"There is one other thing." Kali's tone changes.

"What is it?"

"There are three of us."

"Three," I repeat, suddenly second-guessing my commitment to this little escapade.

"We can make it four," she adds.

"Well, in that case, this will be easy."

"Jett." Kali suddenly looks stern. "I think I know where one of your friends is." She pauses for what feels like four-and-a-half lifetimes.

"Did you just lag? Are you pausing for effect? Who? Where?"

"The one with the scar; he's here."

I have considered that I wouldn't find all my friends at once. It would have been surprising if I had. What I failed to consider is that of all of them, the first one I would find would be Kane.

Emotions swirl together like a stew. When Grent told us Kane was a traitor, I never questioned it. I didn't trust him enough to give him the benefit of the doubt. Then, he shows up and shoots Grent, saving all of our lives. For the entire time we were in the cells waiting to be exiled, I didn't say a word to him. What could I say? *"Hey, so sorry I believed you were a traitor and wanted to kill you, then got you exiled to the Outlands."* Pretty sure they don't make techaposts for that. I guess I could send flowers.

"Where is he?"

"In a cell."

I roll my eyes while exhaling dramatically. "Of course he is. What did he do?"

"He killed three guards and then tried to kill Elder Schmitty," she says, almost matter-of-fact.

"Tried?"

"He probably would have succeeded if Rowan hadn't been there."

Now I know Rowan's not someone to mess with. Anyone who can stop Kane should not be taken lightly.

"Where are the cells?"

"On the far side of town. Across from the gate is a barracks where the soldiers and fighters train; underneath the barracks are the cells."

"So how do we get to him."

"Well, the good news is the cells are easy to access if you have a clearance chip, which Rowan does."

"How does he have that?" I ask.

"One of the conditions for our staying here is that Rowan serves as one of Schmitty's protectors—chip comes with the post."

"And the bad news?"

"There is no way to get to the cells during the day without guards seeing us."

"So the only way to get Kane out is to go at night when everyone else is belowground for the Dusk Descension?"

Kali nods in confirmation. "And we will have to get out of town before morning, or the guards will capture us anyway."

"That means traveling into the wilds at night when all the creatures are out, after everything you just told me."

"Nobody asked you to come."

"I know. I'm not going to find my friends if I stay here."

"You know that once we do this, we won't be able to come back."

This just keeps getting better and better. I'm starting to wonder if I'm signing up for the wrong service. Is this really the best way to find my friends? Would it be easier on my own? But there's just something about her.

"How long before we leave?"

"Few hours."

Rowan signs something to Kali, and she nods to him.

"He wants to know if your friend is going to cause trouble if we let him out."

I laugh. "Kane? Kane is chaos incarnate. I have no idea how he will react. I honestly don't even know how he feels about me at this point. If he'll join us, he's worth the risk."

"If he causes a problem, Rowan will—"

"I'll take responsibility for Kane."

Here's to hoping he doesn't kill me.

The world's creepiest warning siren blares, indicating the Dusk Descension has begun. Nervous energy pumps through my veins. Finding Kane is a start. One down, six to go. Rowan brings out four packs filled with food, water, and other rations and sets them on the counter. They were ready for this moment. I lean against the counter, trying to enjoy my last moments of peace. Could be a long time before we have a safe place like this to rest again. Out of the corner of my eye, I notice Kali staring at me. Is she sizing me up? Trying to figure out how useful I will be?

Nothing builds anxiety better than the calm before the coming storm. Loud beeping pierces the room as Rowan types on the keypad at the bottom of the stairs. The steel bars blocking the opening in the floor retract. It's time to go. I grab my bag to follow him. Kali grabs me, holding me back. Rowan disappears from view.

"Not yet. He's going to make sure everything is clear before we head up."

"Why is he—"

"That's what Rowan does," she explains.

Somehow her explanation doesn't really make anything clearer. Before I can press the issue, Rowan's head pops into view.

"Time to go." Kali pushes past me, bumping my shoulder unnecessarily as she does. I grab the extra pack and ascend to the surface.

The dark skies and glimmering stars of the night have always made me feel peaceful. Something about the quiet of night made the troubles of the day fade away. But here in the Outlands, dread wraps itself around me like a blanket. I know what dwells in the darkness. Fear ruins everything.

We make our way across town, darting cautiously between buildings. Even if all the residents and guards of Red Clay are underground, there is no sense in drawing needless attention from anything else that could be watching. It takes a few minutes to reach the barracks. Rowan hands the access card to Kali and then turns to keep watch as she unlocks the door before pushing it open. Directly in front of us is another wall, separating off a smaller section the guards use for training. A wide and undecorated hallway stretches in either direction.

"Which way?" Kali whispers.

Rowan points to the right. The hallway runs to the end of the building before making a sharp turn and heading straight back. Unlike the previous section, this hallway was lined with doors on the right, all closed. At the end of the hall is a solid steel door with another access reader. We reach the end of the hall, and Kali uses the access chip. The steel doors grind as they part, revealing an open, square room with a set of elevator doors on the back wall. This room has a single window covered in iron bars and decorated with a small, somewhat realistic looking, potted plant.

Once inside, Kali hits a button labeled with a "C," and our steady descent begins. The elevator reaches the bottom with a click and a subsequent ding before the doors part, giving us access to the cells below. Motion-sensor lights click on, filling the air with a soft hum. Rowan guides us past a series of secured doors, each with their own access pad and small square window.

He stops five doors down and punches a code into the pad next to the door. There is a grinding of gears, and the thick, white door clicks and pops out and away from the wall. Rowan pulls it open. Inside, sitting on the floor, is Kane. His head is tilted back, his knees bent in front of him, and his arms are draped casually at his side. He looks like he's meditating. For a man in prison, he doesn't seem too bothered. Typical Kane.

He looks at Rowan with a suspicious glare before noticing me. His disposition changes drastically. In a moment, he's on his feet and has crossed the room. Rowan steps out of the way, giving Kane direct access to me. Thanks, friend; you're the best. I tense up, tightening my hands into fists. I slide my leg back for balance. If he wants a fight, I'll give him one.

Kane's face holds an aggressive scowl. His eyes are blazing. His hands are clutched in tight fists save for the accusatory pointer finger, which he aims right at me.

"You!"

Nothing like a healthy dose of guilt to get the blood pumping. He's just out of arm's reach. I start to bring up my hands, trying not to look like I'm ready to fight while also being ready if he decides to start one. Why can't crazy people behave more predictably? He takes another step. I inhale, bracing myself for—

My arms suddenly press against my chest as a firm grip pulls at my back. Is he hugging me? What is going on?

"You," he repeats, squeezing me so tight I'm starting to wonder if this is an attack disguised as a hug.

"It's so good to see you, my friend!" I feel him lift my body off the ground.

"You're . . . not angry?"

Kane releases me and takes a step back; his face looks genuinely confused.

"Why would I be angry?"

"I mean, we thought you were a traitor," I start.

Kane shrugs, "Eh, I'm not sure I'd have thought any different if the tables were turned. I mean, I'd have killed you before you had the chance to prove your innocence."

Why is he smiling like that information is comforting?

"I got you exiled."

For some reason, I feel compelled to list all the possible grievances I may have caused him.

Kane stretches his arms out, spinning around. "That you did. I can't thank you enough. I'm in your debt."

I am truly at a loss.

"You . . . wait . . . What?"

"In my wildest dreams, I never would have imagined a place like this exists. I've never felt so alive, so at home, you know?" He walks over and slaps his hand down on Rowan's shoulder, pointing at him like a proud father bragging on his child.

Rowan glares at him before eyeing the unwanted hand on his shoulder. I have to resist chuckling. In Rowan's eyes I can see it all. He is not loving this.

"I really don't."

"My friend, I could have lived a dozen lives in Dios and never met a fighter who could best me. This one did it easily."

"I held my own against you," I protest.

"You survived me for a few seconds, when I wasn't actually trying to hurt you. There's a difference," Kane grins and slides his arm across Rowan's back to his other shoulder.

Rowan's expression sours even more. I know that look. I've seen it on the face of every woman Jensen ever talked to. It's a combination of anger, confusion, and repulsion.

"You're happy he beat you?"

"Defeat teaches us more than victory. He's given me something nothing in Dios ever could."

"Which is?" Why do I even ask; I'm not going to enjoy the answer.

"An opponent worth killing."

"Woah, woah, woah, you can't kill him. We came here to break you out," I object.

"Not today, then. Maybe tomorrow." Kane winks playfully.

Rowan seems completely unphased.

"You're happy you got exiled?" I hope to change the subject.

Kane tugs on Rowan's shoulder. Rowan shrugs his arm off and shoves him away. This only seems to amuse Kane more.

"I'm thrilled! Dios never felt like home to me. I didn't belong there. Fighting is life. Those people, meandering like lost sheep with their heads down in fear. They aren't living; they just don't know they are already dead. This place is full of life!"

"It's filled with death," I correct.

"Exactly! The threat of death and the daily avoidance of it is what makes life worth living."

Yup, he's an absolute looper.

Kane looks over my shoulder at the door. "Spike?"

"He's still in Dios, as far as I know. I wanted to wait for him, but I didn't have enough supplies. They could keep him for a month. There's no way to know."

"I wouldn't worry about Spike; he's a tough shinshew."

Kali clears her throat. "Care to explain yourself?"

Kane shakes his head. "What part of me do you want explained, sweetheart?"

"Why did you try to kill Elder Schmitty?"

"He deserves to die."

"No argument there, but why do *you* want him dead?"

Kane raises an eyebrow. "Your man here is the one who stopped me. You've come here to break me out. Now you're asking me why I wanted to kill the guy; you admit deserves to die?"

"I'm the one asking the questions here." Kali glares at him.

Kane turns to me, almost giggling. "I like her."

"Answer the question," Kali presses.

"I wanted to kill the elder because I found him distasteful. When I was set free from Dios, I made my way here. Figured I'd track down your girl—make sure she was safe."

Kali seems to tense up and her face sours.

"You saw Lilly?"

Kane shakes his head. "By the time I reached Red Clay, she was already gone. I was second to leave, so I figured the others would show up eventually. So I waited and watched."

Kali looks confused. "The guards didn't report your arrival until a few days ago."

"I'm a fighter, sweetheart, not a fool. I wasn't just going to walk into town by the front gate. I'd no idea what sort of place this was. They saw me when I wanted them to see me."

"Call me sweetheart again," Kali warns through gritted teeth.

"The speedy little girl with the dark hair; what's her name?"

"Becka?"

Kane snaps a finger. "Becka, that's it. She showed up three days after I did. Saw her go in to meet with the elder. Just before nightfall, I noticed one of the elder's guards following her. When everyone else made their way into their homes, the guard approached her. She was suspicious and made a run for it. He chased, but you know he wasn't going to catch her. Shinshew, that girl is fast. I thought that was odd, so I decided to have a little chat with the guard. He was a little shy at first but I explained things, and eventually he came to see it my way."

"What did you say to him?" Kali asked.

"He tortured him," I answer for Kane.

Kane smiles. "Turns out he was acting on orders from the elder to capture and detain anyone who came to Red Clay. Specifically, anyone who came by themselves or wouldn't be missed. I thanked him for his information, expressed my displeasure at his life choices, and went on my merry way."

"What do you mean, 'expressed your displeasure?'" Kali asks.

"You killed him and buried his body," I answer.

Kali's hand drops to the weapon at her side.

"Like kindred spirits we are! Quite right." Kane's eyes are glistening.

Kali sighs. "So that's what happened to Baker. You killed him for trying to do his job."

Kane shrugs. "I felt a little bad. He was just following orders. But trying to take a young girl against her will—*tsk*, that's just not something I can tolerate."

"You're a killer; what—"

Kane's eyes flash, and a smile forms on his face. "I am a killer. I am not a predator. I kill fighters. I kill people who enter into conflict knowingly and willingly. Those preying on the weak, the innocent, and the defenseless are vile, wretched people who do not deserve to live."

"Becka's not exactly defenseless," I correct.

"No way was she their first. If they targeted her, how many others did they take? How many people came here seeking refuge, believing they'd found a safe place, only to find themselves an easy target?"

Kali's hand slides from her weapon, and she turns her head. "You are . . . not what I expected."

Kane shrugs and returns to his story, unphased.

"Olivia showed up a week later. Guards grabbed her before she made it through the gate and before I could get to her, brought her here through a hidden entrance in the back. Jensen and Telmen showed up—same thing. I started casing the place to see how to break them out. A single elevator in and out doesn't make that easy."

"Unless everyone leaves as soon as it starts getting dark," I interrupt.

Kane chuckles, "I was finalizing my plan when early in the morning— just before sunrise—I noticed a small group of thugs near this secret back entrance. Their leader was missing an eye."

"Morton!" Kali exclaimed, suddenly invested in what Kane was saying.

Kane nods. "He met with Elder Schmitty. They shook hands, and a few minutes later, guards brought Olivia, Jensen, and Telmen out, bound together. The thugs took them away, and the Elder came back inside, acting like nothing had happened. I decided to deal with him before going to find them. That's when your man here took me down."

"Wait," I blurt out loudly.

Kali and Kane both turn to look at me. "What is it?" Kali asks.

"You know what this means?"

Kali shakes her head.

"The man you want to kill and the friends I want to rescue are in the same place."

"Well, isn't that convenient," Kane smiles. "Guess we are working together?"

Kali seems to be sizing Kane up. "We will need to see Doc first."

"Why?" I ask.

"He needs the Kathar Aera."

"The what?"

Kali sighs dramatically. "When you crossed the Sand Sea, did you notice your breathing becoming labored?"

"Now that you mention it—yeah, I did. I thought it was just fatigue."

"It's the Outlands. There's something in the air that gets into your body when you breathe it in. The Kathar Aera is an inoculation. Without it, the toxin slowly moves through your body, squeezing your lungs closed bit by bit until you suffocate."

"Light-blue liquid—stick it in your arm?" Kane asks.

Kali nods.

"Some bald man stuck me with that the day they locked me up."

Kali shrugs. "We're good to go."

"What about Becka, Lilly, my friends? Won't they need this too?"

"They probably got it when they first met with Elder Schmitty. He likes to use that to build trust. He certainly gave it to your friends before selling them. As for the others, it won't matter. If they didn't find a way to get it, they'll be dead by now."

"Great." That's hopeful.

"We really need to get going." Kali turns to the door; Rowan has already made his way out.

Kane rubs his hands together excitedly. "Oh, where are we going?"

"Kali wants to kill the leader of the Marauders. Then, you know, if we survive, we will go find our friends."

Kane smiles brightly. "You see, how could I ever be mad at you? You're so much fun. Let's go kill some people." His laugh is off-putting as he walks out of the room. *How do I keep ending up in these situations?*

Kane stops before the elevator, pushing a side door open and stepping inside.

"What are you doing? We have to move," I insist.

"Got to grab my tools—be right out." A minute later he steps out, adjusting his coat before giving me a nod.

"Can I ask you something?"

Kane looks at me and waits.

"You tried to kill the elder because he sold the others to the Marauders?" I ask.

Kane nods.

"Why? Why would you risk your life for them?"

"After we took the Market—before Victor sent me to find Gibbs—he pulled me aside and made me promise to keep an eye out for you guys if the time ever came where he couldn't."

"Why would he tell you that?" I snap.

"I assume he wanted to ensure your safety."

"Funny way of showing it—selling us out and getting us exiled."

My blood boils just hearing his name.

Kane smirks. "When the pieces of a puzzle don't fit, it usually means you're missing something."

"Missing?" My blood is lava in my veins. "What am I missing, Kane? My best friend, who was like a brother to me, betrayed us—sold us out. He sentenced us to die slowly in this place while he gains title, power, and comfort working for the same government that killed our parents. We had a chance. We could have changed the world. He let the Patriarch in. He got us captured. He got Gibbs killed. He got us exiled. Everything that has happened to us is because of him. Tell me, Kane, what I am missing?"

Kane shrugs. "Can't say. Life is cause and effect. We see the effects— the action a person takes—easily enough. How often do we see the cause of those actions? How often do we really know what motivates the actions we see? It's easy to judge someone based on their actions without ever really understanding their motivation."

I shake my head. "It doesn't matter now. Let's get going."

We make our way out of the underground prison and back through the barracks. Stepping outside, I rub my arms, as the cool night air whisks over me. We hurry our way through town, my heart pounding louder than our footsteps. I'm not sure why, but I feel on edge as if someone or something is watching us. It feels like that a lot out here. It's unnerving.

Rowan is in front, setting the pace. When we've all cleared the town gates, he slows from a stealthy sprint to a hurried walk. We follow a winding path between the hills headed back toward the gorge that leads to Dios. The path twists and turns, leading us around Red Clay and away from the Domed city. As we travel, the hills grow taller. I start feeling like I am wandering through the tunnels of Dios, only outside.

The canyons and hills serve as a sort of natural shield, hiding Red Clay from view. A multitude of paths through the hills split off, creating a web of alternate routes. I can't imagine how anyone would be able to track us through this. Still, I can't shake the feeling of being watched.

I scan the horizon frequently for any sign of movement. Victor taught us to be vigilant, to know our surroundings, and to be prepared for all possibilities. How can you prepare for possibilities when you have no idea what they are? We continue for hours until the dark's hold on the sky wavers, and light threatens to peek over the horizon. Kane is eerily quiet, which works to unnerve me even more.

"What exactly is the plan now? Just charge ahead and hope we find the Marauders?" I ask as I catch up to Kali.

"We know they came from this direction. For now, we need to get far enough away that we won't have to worry about being spotted by patrols from Red Clay. Then, Rowan will find their trail, and we will track them to wherever they set up camp."

"Just like that? Find their trail? How do you—"

"Rowan can track pretty much anything. Even if he couldn't, the tracks of a small army are hard to miss."

My mind wanders for a moment before I crash into Rowan with a thud. I stumble back, catching myself before freezing in place. His body is motionless; his eyes are fixed on the horizon. I don't need words to know what's happening. It's the same reaction we had whenever we stumbled across Levites in Dios. Danger is close.

CHAPTER SIX

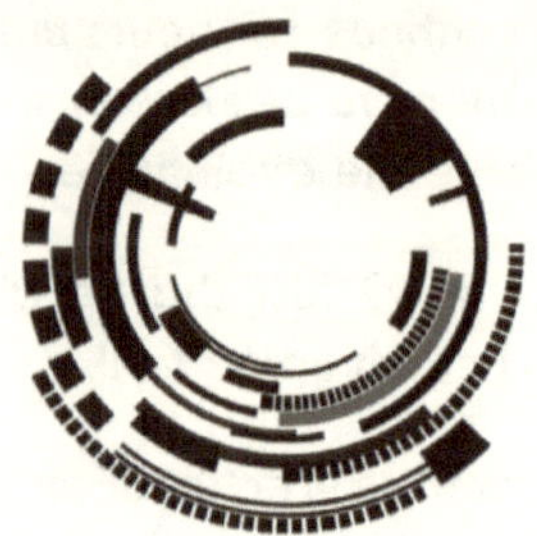

"Don't move," Kali whispers, hunching down.

Always nice when someone states the obvious. My eyes dart back and forth, looking for some sign of what Rowan was seeing. Out of the corner my eye, I see it. Two eyes appear from behind a boulder in front of us. Small and low to the ground, the eyes reflect even the faint night light. Whatever it is, it looks too small to be dangerous. Am I missing something? Relief washes over me as the creature moves into view. It's a raccoon; it's a little bigger than I've seen before, but that's it. I sigh, holding my hand to my chest—so much adrenaline for so small a thing.

Streaks of light move over our heads. More adrenaline surges as I look up. Floating above us is a surprisingly large butterfly. Its wings are the most beautiful things I've ever seen, trimmed with orange and blue iridescent lines in an intricate pattern and casting a bioluminescent glow that pierces the darkness. Its wings look like liquid light dancing whimsically upon the air. With each flap of its wings, sparkling powder floats around it like slow-motion fireworks. My jaw drops as I stare. My mind is consumed by the beauty of the glowing light. All my worries fade away. The stress, the fear, the rage that has burned within me since my parents were murdered—it all disappears. Nothing exists but this peaceful, wonderful light.

A sharp pain in my shoulder draws my eyes from the butterfly. Rowan is standing in front of me, pointing to a hole in the side of the hill, his expression stern and forceful.

"We got all worked up for a butterfly and a raccoon?" There's just something about it that feels so comical I can't stop myself from laughing.

"Not a butterfly," Kali says, grabbing my arm and tugging me away.

"Are you seriously worried about that—"

Kali shoves me into a burrow in the hillside. Kane grabs me and pulls me in until the butterfly is just out of view. Kali pushes in, crowding the hollowed-out spot in the hill. Rowan stands in the opening, looking out with his arms folded across his chest.

"Seriously, that thing is dangerous?"

"That thing is an aestroth," Kali growls, her voice dripping with annoyed frustration.

Rowan pulls out something shiny from his pocket. I can't make out what it is. He flicks his wrist. The raccoon jumps and hisses, baring its teeth. The mid-sized rodent tucks its head down and bites the metal pin sticking out of its shoulder. It jerks its head, pulling the object free and spitting it to the ground. The raccoon's saliva is a greenish color. It hits the ground with a hiss, and the clay begins to sizzle.

"Did it just spit acid?" I ask in surprise.

"Yes," Kali answers.

The aestroth's gentle, directionless dance turns into a swooping descent, its curled tongue straightening into a giant needle and piercing into the raccoon. The raccoon snaps its jaws at the large insect, barely missing it. Out of nowhere, another aestroth plummets down, landing on the raccoon. Another, then another—each with its glowing, flapping wings engulfing the creature. They swarm around it, covering it completely. The air is filled with a sucking, slurping sound. A moment later the aestroths flap away, lighting up the path until they disappear from view. I glance down at where the racoon had been. All that was left of it was a dehydrated hide. They'd sucked out its blood, organs, muscles—even its skeleton was gone.

"Shinshew." I stare in disbelief.

"Aestroths are drawn to blood. They use their tongues to pierce, then drain, their prey."

"How did they—"

"They excrete a toxin that liquifies organs and bones. Then, they suck all the liquid out, effectively mummifying you," Kali explains as if this was just some normal thing that happens.

I blink, trying to process that. "Even the butterflies here kill you." *This place is proper heaped.*

"I wouldn't stare at them either. The powder they emit is hypnotic."

This place just keeps getting better.

Kali looks at Rowan, who shakes his head. "OK, well, this is as good a place as any. We'll rest here for a bit."

"We're far enough out?"

"Should be."

My body feels simultaneously too amped up and too worn out to sleep. Laying on the hard ground of a burrow, packed tightly in with three other people, doesn't help either. I force myself to lay down and try. Surprisingly, I sleep.

When I wake up, I am alone in the burrow. I rub my eyes and stretch slowly, climbing to my feet. It's bright, nearly midday if I had to guess. Kane is crouching over his bag, picking through some of the sealed food options. Not sure what he's deliberating; the choices are dried meat or other dried meat. Kali is sitting on the mounded top of the hill across from our little burrow. Rowan is nowhere to be seen. I pace back and forth along the path. Sometimes moving helps me clear my mind.

Kane looks up from rummaging through his pack. "You're going to wear yourself out doing that."

"My friends are out here somewhere. I need to find them."

"How does treading about like a lunatic accomplish that goal?"

"I have to do something."

"What good is doing something when the something you do doesn't help?"

"I just need to—"

"Wait, you think all of this is your fault."

"I don't think that. It's a fact. If I hadn't insisted on getting involved, on doing something to fight the Patriarch, none of my friends would be in this situation."

"I see. So your friends, they are mindless sheep that do whatever you say?"

"What? No, what are you—"

"Oh, you forced them against their will?"

"No," I scowl, heat rising in my core.

"Let me get this straight; your friends can think for themselves and chose to follow you of their own volition without you forcing them in any way, and yet, somehow what happened to them is your fault?" Kane taps his head with his finger. My boiling frustration falters. *Did Kane just make sense? That's scary.*

"Maybe you're right. I just can't stop thinking: what if something happens to them? How am I supposed to—"?

"What if they die out here? What if they don't? What if they would have died in a freak accident in the city if none of this ever happened? What if they live longer out here than they would have in Dios? You can never know what if—only what is. *What if* is a waste of time."

"What?"

"You can carry the weight of the world on your shoulders if you wish. It doesn't change anything. You have no more control over life or death than you do when the sun rises or sets. Death comes when it comes. No one knows when or how. All we can do is live until it claims us. Anything else is arrogance." There is a surprising wisdom to his words. Strangely, the burden I've been carrying feels lighter.

Footsteps. I spin to face the sound, my hand grabbing for the hilt of my energy blade. Out of the corner of my eye, I see Kali slide down the hill toward us. The path ahead leads to a steep rock wall and a canyon path that forks, creating a passage to the left and another to the right. Dashing into view from the path to the right is Rowan. He's running toward us at full speed, waving his arm toward the hill Kali just slid down. I gather from my incredible powers of deduction that he expects us to follow this instruction quickly.

We rush up the hill, climbing over its summit and sliding down on the other side to lie across its gradual slope. Just as we peek our heads back over the hill to look at the path below, voices come from the canyon pass. A moment later, four people dressed in long, brown coats appeared at the crossway.

"Patrol from Red Clay," Kali whispers.

"I thought you said they wouldn't come out this far," I challenge. She shrugs.

To ensure I am safely out of view, I slide down the back slope of the hill a little farther. Our position allows us to see the path without being in view ourselves. As long as the patrol remains on the path, we're stocked. How would a search party have gathered and gotten ahead of us? This is just a coincidence. They aren't looking for us. They are just passing through. There's no reason for them to search too carefully.

"Shinshew," Kane mutters under his breath.

I start to ask but then I see it. My gut drops as if I'd just swallowed a giant boulder. Even if the patrol was just passing through, Kane's pack sitting out in the open a few yards from a mummified raccoon fur might give them a reason to inspect their surroundings. Maybe we can talk our way out of it. Better prepare for a fight just in case.

"What's that?" A woman's voice is followed by the rushing of boots.

They found Kane's pack. We are heaped.

"This pack is from Red Clay," a male voice replies.

"Someone is here. Fan out; search the area. Weapons ready."

"Freeze!"

My heart thuds in my chest. How did they find us so quickly? My mind digests the information, and my confusion grows. The command came from farther away. It also sounds different; the new voice is deeper and distorted as if through a helmet. The four people we'd seen weren't wearing helmets. I spin back onto my stomach and look over the hill.

Six soldiers covered head to toe in body armor come charging toward the path from the canyon entrance. Their faces are covered by black helmets with glowing-red visors. They look and move almost like they are robotic. Each one carries a large assault rifle. Even from here, I can see the red emblem of an eye inside a triangle inside a circle: the unmistakable symbol of the Patriarch.

Shouting and panic erupts below us. One of the four patrolmen starts firing at the soldiers in black. He misses, and the soldiers in black fan out, calling out commands and firing back.

"Nonlethal on the woman! Kill the others!"

That's weird. When did the Patriarch start worrying about killing women?

Kali slides farther down the back of the hill to completely remove herself from view. It's probably a good idea, but I just can't bring myself to look away. One of the patrolmen goes down immediately. The other two don't fare much better. The patrolwoman fires, desperately trying to track and hit any of the constantly moving soldiers in black. A blast of blue light hits the woman. She screams as it knocks her onto her back. Their fight is over as quickly as it started, leaving me with ample questions, like what are Patriarch soldiers doing out here?

The six soldiers swarm in on the woman, surrounding her in a half circle as she groans on her back.

"Lift her up," one barks in his distorted, robotic voice. Another lifts the woman to her feet. Another stands behind her and binds her arms.

"Scan," the group leader commands. One of the soldiers holds his datapad up in front of the woman's face. A faint blue light shines out as he scans her face, lifting his forearm up and down.

"It's not her," the soldier reports.

"Execute." The solider behind the woman wraps his arm around her neck, puts a hand on her head, and jerks suddenly. A loud snap echoes around us. I cover my mouth to keep from gasping as the woman's body slumps to the ground, lifeless.

"Move out!" The soldier who scanned the woman holds his arm out, and his unusual looking datapad starts projecting a wide beam of light. He rushes out ahead with the other soldiers falling into formation behind him. At least they are running in the opposite direction.

We wait in silence to ensure the soldiers are gone. After a few minutes I sit up and look around.

"What was that about?"

No one replies.

"What is the Patriarch doing out here?"

"We should get going." Kali's voice seems shaky. Maybe seeing the woman get her neck snapped upset her?

"Have you seen them before?"

Kali stands up and slings her pack over her back. "I've no idea, Jett, but I don't want to be here if they decide to come back."

We make our way down the hill and resume our journey. The rock cliffs here are different than the ones I passed through on my way to Red Clay. These are a brownish-orange color. I stare up in awe of the sheer size of them. I was too tired and too injured to appreciate the magnitude of the rock walls I passed through before. Even though these are much smaller, they are still a sight to behold.

The path splits, and Rowan turns to the right.

"Is that a good idea?" I ask. "Scouts and those Patriarch soldiers came from that direction."

Rowan gestures using two fingers to simulate legs walking across the flattened palm of his other hand. Then, he points to the right.

"That's the direction the Marauders went."

"Could we go around?"

Kali and Rowan exchange a glance. Rowan shrugs.

"If we can climb, we can follow this path to the left. There's an outcropping that we can cross, then make our way back. It's a bit more indirect, but it keeps us out of view of the pass and would let us see any approaching threats," Kali answers.

"Might be worth the risk," I posit.

"I'd certainly rather deal with a scouting party from Red Clay than Patriarch soldiers," Kane adds.

"Fine, come on. I hope you can climb." Kali tosses her cloak back away from her legs and starts climbing up the cliff wall. Rowan does the same. I've never tried rock climbing before, but the jutting ledges create plenty of holds, making the climb relatively easy. Once on top of the cliff, Rowan guides us along the plateau, following the path that leads left. The path suddenly opens into a large canyon. The canyon is filled with large creatures—the biggest I've ever seen. They look like bulls, but they are twice the size of elephants. Their heads are long and squared at the end. Coming off each side of their head is a pointed horn. From a plate on their neck grows two much larger curved horns with a razor-like edge. Unlike bulls or elephants, they have a long, thick tail with a bulbous tip. They look like giant dinosaurs.

"What are those?"

"The Triblings call them trematerra; it means shakers of the earth," Kali answers.

"Are they dangerous?" Even from our elevated position they look massive.

"They can be. Most of the time they keep to themselves. Just don't wander into their nesting grounds, don't try to steal their eggs, and don't shoot them with an energy rifle. Everybody good? Can we go now?"

"That last one seems oddly specific. You tried that, didn't you?"

"Shut up, Jett."

Rowan obliges by leading us to a place where the rock juts out from the plateau we are on to the plateau on the other side of the pass—like a naturally occurring bridge—albeit a thin, uneven, terrifying bridge. The rock bridge is at the edge of the pass before it opens into the trematerra canyon.

"Why would you try to shoot one? They are huge!" I try to distract myself as I make my way across the thin rock bridge.

As soon as I reach the other side, Kali spins around, grabbing my shirt, pulling me close to her face.

"Yes, they are huge. You know how many people you could feed off one of those things? Even at full power, all an energy blast does is make them mad. Turns out shooting it more just makes it angrier."

"What happened?"

"I practically caused a stampede."

I cover my mouth to keep myself from laughing.

"It's not funny. They will run down anything in their path. Once they are worked up, there is no stopping them."

I drop the subject, not wanting to agitate her further. We walk in silence for a bit. To our right, I see the crossroads where we started, now well below us. The plateau provides a sense of security. Up here, I feel out of reach. We follow the path for about an hour before Rowan stops and points down.

"Time to head back down," Kali instructs.

I look down the pass, which is clear for as far as I can see. That's comforting. Once back to the path below, we resume our journey. A few paces in, I notice something. Partially tucked behind a tall, dried-up bush, I see something yellow.

"Wait," I shout.

"You make one more joke, I'm just going to leave you out here." Kali looks back at me, her eyes narrowing.

Ignoring her threat, I walk over to get a closer look, pushing the branches of the bush aside. Painted on the rock wall is a yellow crescent moon with three lines—like beams of light—coming out of it. It's definitely the same thing Kali drew before, and I know I've seen this before; I just can't place it.

Kali pushes me out of the way. "That's it; that's the symbol for the Moon Pack!" She puts her hand on the yellow paint and takes a deep breath.

"The paint is fresh." I slide my fingers over it.

A rare smile covers Kali's face. "I knew they were real. Rowan, we need to find them. They could help us."

"Help us?" Kane scoffs. "How does some paint on a wall help us?"

"This symbol has been popping up all over the area. Every time we find the bodies of Marauder scouts, this symbol is nearby."

"Your point?"

Kali glares at Kane, and her voice becomes rough and forceful. "My point is the enemy of my enemy is my friend. This group is fighting against the Marauders. We share a goal."

"That's an assumption you can't afford to make, sweetheart. You might share an enemy. You might not. You have no idea what their motivation is or what this symbol means. Even if you're right, and you do share an enemy, what good is that to us?"

"Is this some sort of joke?"

"Not a very good one if it is. Unless this Moon Pack has enough soldiers to bring down the Marauder army—which they don't—they can't help us."

"How do you know they don't?"

"Think about it, sweetheart. If they could bring down the Marauders, why would they waste their energy taking out scouting parties one at a time? This is what you do when you can't face an opponent head on."

"It never hurts to have allies. Plus, there's strength in numb . . . ," Kali's words trail off as she watches Kane. Kane opens his pack and pulls out the mummified raccoon skin.

"Gross, why did you bring that?"

Kane holds up a finger before I finish my sentence. He hangs the dehydrated carcass from a ledge, holding it in place with a small rock and letting the fur dangle like a banner over the stone wall.

"This is Morton—disgusting piece of human filth—represented adequately by a rotting racoon corpse." Grunting loudly, Kane picks up a large boulder from the ground. He deposits it into my arms and slaps me on the back.

Shinshew, this thing is heavy.

Kane then grabs a smaller loose pebble from the ground.

Kali crosses her arms. "Is there a point to this little object lesson?"

"Which rock would you say is a greater threat: mine or Jett's?"

Kali sighs and points to me. "The boulder."

"You'd think so. It makes sense. The big rock is stronger and can do more damage. Here's the problem; Jett, throw your rock at the raccoon skin."

"Seriously?" I protest.

"Just do it."

I hoist the stone and hurl it as hard as I can in the direction of the skin. The rock is so big and heavy, it's more like I'm pushing it into the air and hoping it goes far enough. It does not. Despite my forceful shove, my rock hits the wall under the raccoon skin with a loud *clang*, then a *thump* as it sinks into the clay ground.

"Your method is inconsistent with your mission. You want to make your force bigger. Bigger is not always better. You are thinking like a warrior when you need to think like an assassin. This job is about precision, not power. You need a razor, not a broadsword." As if to illustrate his point, Kane draws his arm back and swings it, flinging the small pebble in his hand. It hits the center of the raccoon skin with enough force to leave a welt on it.

Rowan nods in approval, placing a hand on Kali's shoulder softly.

"Oh, shut up." Kali shakes her head at him. Rowan smiles and turns back to the canyon path. We follow him through the canyon, turning and weaving, as the path forks numerous times like a labyrinth. Kali was right; the path we are following looks heavily trafficked. Morton had to have come this way. There's that feeling again like a gentle current of electricity rushing over my neck, making my skin tingle.

Kane, who has been bringing up the flank, steps up behind me.

"I know what you are thinking," he whispers in my ear.

"What's that?" I keep my voice down as well—not entirely sure why— but he whispered, so now I'm doing it.

"You feel it too, don't you?"

Sure, double down on the cryptic. That's not weird.

"You're going to have to be more specific."

"Someone is following us," Kane whispers.

Well, that is definitely more specific.

"Yes!"

"Our little friend has been following us since Red Clay." Kane glances up without moving his head.

I follow his gaze. Above us, on the ledge of the rock wall to our right, a shadow moves, darting out of view into a recess in the rock.

"We need to tell—"

Kane grabs my arm and holds it firmly. "Don't. If you draw attention, they will run."

"We have to warn Kali and Rowan," I protest.

Kane chuckles, "Trust me my friend, they know. Our stalker is not particularly good."

"Well, then, we need a plan."

I see a rock jutting out from the ground ahead. I casually veer toward it. I make a show of bumping my foot against it and tumbling to the ground holding my leg.

"Ah . . . oh . . . ," I groan, gripping my ankle.

Kali and Rowan rush over. Kane looks down at me, confused.

"What happened?" Kali asks.

"Shhhh," I whisper.

Kali nods, kneels down over me, and bellows out, "Wow you really jammed it good, didn't you?"

"What are we doing?" Kane whispers.

"That fork in the path ahead—that's where we make our move. Rowan and Kali take the left path. Kane and I will take the right. When we get to it, run. It'll force our stalker to act without thinking. Whoever they follow becomes the lure. Their job is to draw them out. Do something to get them down from the ledge, or at least keep them in one place. The other group becomes the snare. Their job is to circle back and spring the trap."

Kane adjusts the pack on his back. "That's not bad."

Kali and Rowan nod in agreement.

"Victor calls it a pincer maneuver." If I'm stuck with Victor's schemes bouncing around in my head, I might as well get some use out of them.

Rowan helps me to my feet. I pretend to hobble for a few steps before smoothing out my stride. We take our time getting to the fork. When we reach it, Rowan and Kali sprint down the left path. Kane and I do the same to the right. I glance back over my shoulder but can't tell if the plan is working.

"Looks like we win," Kane says, sprinting beside me. He points. Sure enough, along the ledge I see the silhouette of our pursuer following behind us.

I shout, "Cave on your left—go!"

Kane veers to the opening in the rock wall. I rush in behind him. Now, here's hoping there's not something in the cave more dangerous than our pursuer. The cave isn't very deep. It has just enough room for us to get out of view. It's dark enough to hide us from someone standing at the entrance peering in. Now we wait and see. If our stalker is determined to track us, they will likely hold their position until we emerge from the cave. That should give Rowan and Kali time to corner them.

A dark, cloaked figure rushes past the mouth of the cave, then peeks in. Moving slowly, our pursuer steps into the entrance. I liberate the energy blade from my belt and hold it at the ready. The figure turns suddenly as Kali and Rowan rush into view, cutting off our stalker's escape. Kane and I charge from the back of the cave. The cloaked figure steps back. Kali swings her leg low, grabbing and slamming our cloaked pursuer to the ground with a loud *thud*. Kali's movement is swift and quick as she plants her knee on our pursuer, using the weight of her body to pin them to the ground.

CHAPTER SEVEN

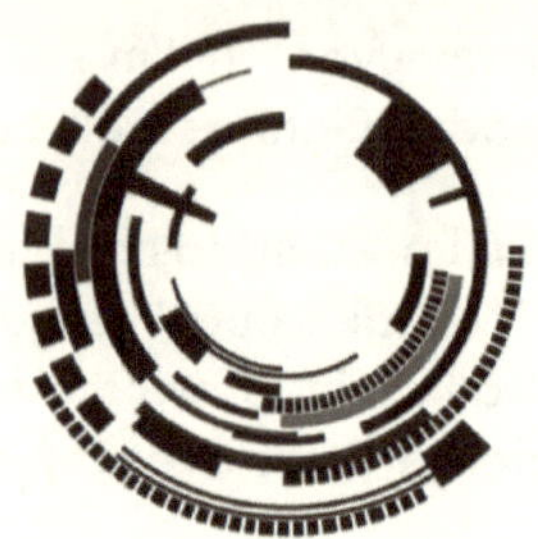

"**O**w, how did you—" the voice is female and familiar.

My eyes go wide, and I rush over, practically knocking Kali to the ground as I push her off.

"It's OK, it's OK! I know her!"

Elation, relief, hope, and joy form a happy medley in my soul. I lift the cloaked figure up, and the hood falls off her head. I wrap my arms around her and hold her tight, laughing hysterically while tears run down my face.

"Becka!"

"Jett!" She hugs back, squeezing much harder than I am. It's like she's trying to compact all my guts into a smaller vessel. Despite the physical discomfort, solace washes over me like a cool breeze. Just hearing her voice makes the cloud of my concerns fade away. She pushes me back, holding her arms straight out without letting go of my shoulders. She tugs on one shoulder, then the other, spinning me around and inspecting me. "Are you OK? You aren't hurt? How long have you been out here?"

I laugh. "Becka, you're starting to sound like Telmen."

She pulls me into another hug, this one much less painful. "Oh, shut up."

I glance down and see her shoes, worn and dirty but for the bright multi-colored shoelaces that have been methodically scrubbed clean. Becka burns through shoes at an alarming rate, so she doesn't bother taking care of them. Her shoelaces, on the other hand, she treats as if they were blessed by Bealz himself. Ever since I've known her, she has insisted on wearing these obnoxiously bright shoelaces.

"Still wearing your lucky laces, I see," I said, expecting my tease to bring her hug to an end, but she does not let go.

"You know I don't believe in luck." She squeezes me tighter.

We hug for another minute before I step back. "Kali, Rowan—this is Becka. She's—"

"I'm his big sister—by choice, not blood." Becka smiles and shakes both of their hands.

"Sorry about the—" Kali points to her head and shrugs.

Becka waves her hand dismissively. "Don't mention it."

"Becka, what are you doing out here by yourself?" I ask.

"I'm not by myself. There is a group of us working together and fighting against those horrible Marauders."

"You're with the Moon Pack?" Kali's eyes light up.

"Pack? Please tell me they are not calling us a pack. We are Moon's Raiders."

"Moon's Raiders definitely sounds better," I add.

"I don't care about the name; you're fighting the Marauders!" Kali's voice is loud and oddly forceful.

"Fighting may be generous. We are annoying them. We attack their scouts and smaller patrols—not enough to do any real damage."

"That's something. If we worked together, we could find a way to kill Morton," Kali says.

Becka turns her head, looking away. A moment of silence passes before Becka takes a deep breath and looks into Kali's eyes, her tone softer than before. "I'm sorry to say, we can't help you with that."

"What do you mean you can't help us? We could work together; I'm sure there's a way," Kali protests.

Becka shakes her head. "I wish there was. I really am sorry."

"Becka, do they have the others?"

Becka sighs.

"I suspected as much. Do you know how long?"

"About three weeks," Kane answers.

"That's not good. The Marauders take their pledges—that's what they call their hostages—and systematically break them down. It's not unlike what the Patriarch does with Levites. While they work to break the person down, they also train them to think like a Marauder, talk like a Marauder, and fight like a Marauder—until they are Marauders. If they have our friends, it's only a matter of time."

"All the more reason we should work together." Kali makes no effort to hide her agitation.

"The Raiders are not assassins. We are fighting to free the people he has enslaved. Killing Morton doesn't help with that," Becka explains.

Rowan puts his hand on Kali's shoulder to get her attention. She pulls her shoulder away from his grip.

"Not now, Rowan," she snaps, keeping her gaze focused on Becka. "Morton is the head of the snake. Cut off the head, and the snake dies. Killing Morton is good for everyone." Kali grinds her teeth together as she speaks.

Rowan grabs her shoulder again, and again Kali pulls away.

"Why don't we just—" Becka starts.

A soft hum pierces the air as Rowan's energy weapon sizzles to life. A blue lance projects from his extra-long energy hilt. In that moment, everything else stops.

"Well, well, well, what do we have here?" comes a voice from behind us.

The rock wall on the other side of the pass harbors two small caves, one on either side of the cave we are in. Emerging from the caves two by two are a motley group of men. The men fan out, creating a half circle around the cave, effectively cutting off any route of escape. Despite their well-placed trap, they seem disorganized and undisciplined. These are not Marauders. They are thugs. This unkempt and homely bunch is brandishing a mixture of steel and energy weapons that appear to be as diverse as they are. Their clothes are worn and tattered. They look like they've been living in these caves, or at least, spending a lot of time in them.

Rowan readies his energy lance, dropping into a fighting stance.

"Ah, ah, ah." The apparent ringleader, a short, thin man with a patchy goatee, wags his finger back and forth. Two green laser dots appear on Rowan's chest, moving slightly back and forth. He glances down at them and stops. "Let's everybody just remain calm, shall we?"

"What do you want?" Kali asks.

The short man smiles warmly. "Only what you owe us. You have wandered down our path. That means you need to pay the toll."

"A toll? Is that what you're calling it?" Kali asks, her hand on her weapon.

"You can call it whatever you like; it makes no difference to me. We will be taking your weapons and your valuables." The ringleader smiles as if he's doing us a favor by offering to rob us.

"Is that right?" There's a note of defiance in Kali's voice.

"We have you outnumbered and trapped. We also have two gunmen on the ledge behind me. If you try to resist, we will also be taking your lives."

This is not good. Even if we were able to thwart them on the ground, the two gunmen on the rock ledge above will make short work of us. We have no chance. If we resist, we die. If we surrender our weapons and supplies, we also probably die. It's perfect, almost poetic, really. I survived the Beggar Gangs of Dios for years, survived a rebellion, and survived in the Outlands only to meet my end at the hands of a group of bandits.

"You did this!" Kali whirls around and points a finger at Becka.

Becka glances over at me, then back to Kali. "I certainly did not!" she protests.

Kali steps closer, pushing her finger against Becka's shoulder, but her eyes move away from Becka as if she's focused on something else.

"Bandits just so happen to show up right after you?" Kali can't really think Becka had something to do with this, can she?

Becka pauses as if in shock and then takes a step back. "What? I don't have anything to do with—"

Kali steps forward, shoving her again. This time Becka takes a few steps back.

"Liar!" Kali shouts, her face red, her voice like fire as she speaks through gritted teeth. The bandits move in closer but make no attempt to intervene. Kali grabs Becka by the collar with both hands and drives her back into the wall of the cave just inside the entrance.

Becka shoves Kali's hands away. Kali reaches for her energy sword. She's no match for Becka's speed. Becka's clicks her energy knife, and the small blade sings to life. Becka jabs clumsily at Kali, who steps to the side with ease before her energy sword activates. This is getting out of hand.

I push between them. "Kali, what are you doing?"

"She brought them, Jett. She set us up!"

I shake my head. "Becka would never do that."

"Wouldn't she? The Outlands changes people."

"I'm not going to let you hurt her."

"Think about what you are doing, Jett," Kali warns, nodding slightly.

"I am."

"We have a blood pact; you want to violate our agreement to protect the girl that sold us out? You do this and . . ." She lets the last few words go unspoken. As if not saying Rowan is going to kill you makes it any less clear.

Rowan turns from the bandits and steps next to Kali, pushing Becka and I back further into the cave. There's something odd about his expression; he seems almost amused. This step back moves us into the shadow of the cave. We are still visible to the bandits on the ground, but Kali's sudden altercation with Becka has allowed our group to move out of sight from the ledge above. Kali just took the gunmen out of play. Not sure how that helps us, since they can just wait us out. I feel like I'm missing something. Whatever they are playing at, I might as well go along with it.

"Now!" Kali shouts.

I hear a click and then a hiss as a metal canister bounces and rattles across the hard ground, rolling toward the right side of the cave. Dark gray smoke erupts into the air.

"Fire!" the bandit leader shouts. Green bursts of energy crash harmlessly into the ground. The gunmen don't have a shot, but they fire anyway.

Kane rushes into the smoke, disappearing out of view. Green bursts of light pierce the gray cloud. The gunmen start firing wildly into the smoke. From the other side of the smoke, I hear two screams. They are undoubtedly Kane's handywork.

"Get them!" the bandit leader shouts, and his small posse of degenerates charge toward us.

Kali, Rowan, and Becka fan out in perfect unison. Becka charging at the right side, Kali at the left, and Rowan the middle. I stand perfectly still, doing my best opossum impersonation. I can hear the gunmen still firing, but their blasts aren't landing anywhere near where we are.

My brain snaps to attention as I see a large bandit with thin hair and ragged clothing, wielding a massive steel maul, moving in behind Becka. Becka's back is turned as she's struggling to fight off another bandit. I charge toward the larger man, sliding on the ground to cut him off before he can get to Becka, my energy sword roaring to life as I square off against the much larger man.

The bandit stops in front of me, pulling his maul over his head and slamming it down. I jump back, barely dodging it as his maul smashes into the ground where I had been standing, leaving a hole in the rock floor of the cave and sending little shards of rock spraying in every direction. I dash toward his side, swinging my sword at his stomach. He is too slow to counter or move, and my beam cuts him across his chest. He drops to his knees with a loud thud, looking down in surprise at the wound on his chest. He tries to stand up, but I drive my blade through his back before he can. His body crumples to the ground with a thud.

Becka's bandit opponent is lying on the ground, disarmed but alive. He's the only one still breathing. The smoke has finally started to clear, allowing me to see the aftermath of our encounter. Kali stands over four dead bandits; Rowan is surrounded by nine, including the ringleader, and there are two more just past where Kane's smoke cannister had gone off.

"Please, don't kill me," the bandit pleads from his back.

Becka looks down at him. "You tried to kill us. If I let you go, you'll just end up hurting someone else."

"N-n-no, I won't! I swear to Bealz! I'll never do this again," the man begs. "Please, I have a family. I-I-I was just trying to provide for them."

Becka shakes her head. "Find a better way. If I find you out here again, I won't be so generous," Becka warns before gesturing to the bandit to leave.

He nods again and sprints off, not even attempting to gather his weapon before he goes.

"Not sure that's a good idea," Kali says, walking over to Becka.

Becka shrugs. "Everyone deserves a second chance. Hopefully, he will do something good with it."

Kali shakes her head, but a smile forms on her face. "You played that well."

Becka grins proudly. "It took me a second. That was a clever plan."

The two exchange compliments back and forth as I stare, trying to figure out how they coordinated that so smoothly.

A few minutes later, Kane walks up with two new rifles over his shoulder and an oddly wide grin on his face.

"That was a blast," he says. "Can we do it again?"

Kali rolls her eyes in response.

"Come on, let's go see Lilly," Becka smiles.

"Lilly? You're with Lilly?" My excitement is an erupting volcano.

Becka rolls her eyes. "Jett, you are remarkably dense sometimes."

"What? Why?"

Becka pulled out a brush and a little jar of yellow paint. She slides the brush over the cave wall behind me, drawing a crescent moon with three lines coming out of it. She points to the moon. "What's this?"

"A moon."

"And what's this?" She points to the lines, interrupting my protest.

I sigh dramatically. "Lines." This painfully patronizing demonstration was preventing me from getting the information I wanted. I've known Becka long enough to know that if I try to rush her, she will slow down and make it take longer. She says it helps me learn patience. I think she just likes driving me loopy.

"They are rays of light, Jett," she corrects. This does not spark the revelation she seems to expect.

"Rays of light and a moon. How is that—"

"Moons . . . light . . . Lilly . . . Moonslight . . . Lilly is the leader of the Moon's Raiders."

Yup, I am completely salvage. Now that she says it, it's painfully obvious. Why didn't I realize? Why didn't I—My mind flashes to the Market Sector. That's where I've seen it before! Not long after Lilly and I had an encounter with a drunken Red Cap, I saw that very symbol painted on one of the buildings. That makes no sense; why would she have painted it there? Was she . . . ? My mind spirals into a winding staircase of questions. I shake the thoughts from my head.

Kali steps between us. "Not to interrupt this little show and tell, but can you take us to meet with this Lilly now?"

Becka catches my arm as I start to leave. "I know this isn't the best time to ask, but how are you holding up?"

"You mean from the bandits? I'm fine."

"No, Jett, not the bandits. How are you doing with what happened?"

Oh, she's asking that question. I sigh and look away. "I'm fine."

Becka puts her hand on my shoulder and forces me to look into her eyes. I hate when she does this. It's like some kind of sorcery that makes it almost impossible to argue with whatever she's about to say.

"I know what Victor did hurt you. It hurt all of us. I am still in shock. Every time I think about it, I want to scream and cry at the same time. Our friends are being held by a ruthless thug, going through Bealz knows what because Victor betrayed us. We trusted him. We put our faith in him. When we needed him the most, he—but I can't even imagine how much worse it is for you. Jett, what Victor did was terrible—maybe even unforgiveable."

Why does sharing in suffering feel so comforting? It's like hearing her express the same rage that burns inside me gives validity to how I feel. For some reason, the flames don't feel quite as hot.

"The worst part is, I keep remembering all these other things, these great moments that I used to treasure. Now, they are all ruined," I say.

"Betrayal has this way of tainting everything else a person does. It's important to remember, Jett; people are more than one thing. For a long time, Victor took care of us, looked out for us, sacrificed for us. He kept us alive. None of us would have made it as long as we did without him."

"That's what makes it worse!" My words rumble out through grinding teeth.

Becka nods, "I know. All I'm saying is, Victor was a big part of your life. Don't let one bad memory ruin all the others."

"Why are you defending him?" I counter.

"I'm not, Jett. I'm protecting you. You have so much heart. I don't want to see Victor's betrayal make you bitter."

"How could anyone be bitter with you around?" I ask.

"Jett Lasting, the Outlands are certainly making you smarter." Becka winks at me.

"We better get going," I suggest, hoping to end any further mention of Victor.

"Yes, I'm sure Lilly will be very excited to see you." Becka winks at me. Just the thought of seeing Lilly again fills my body with warmth and makes my heart pound like a conga. We step outside of the cave entrance; Kali is standing there, tapping her foot and looking annoyed.

Becka leads us back in the direction we came. We weave through the canyon for a while with no sign of anyone or anything. I'm starting to wonder how close this camp really is. Just as I'm about to ask her if we are getting close, Becka stops. She places two fingers in her mouth and whistles loudly. A moment later a rope ladder swings down, smacking against the rock wall and bouncing off it.

Becka smiles proudly with her hands on her hips. "Welcome to the Moon's Raiders. The guards at the top are going to take your weapons. It's nothing personal. Just protocol." No one is happy about it, but everyone agrees except Kane, who protests endlessly.

Climbing a rope ladder up the side of a cliff makes it feel much higher than it looks. At the top, two men in gray-hooded cloaks help me over the edge and onto the plateau above. The long, flat, elevated rocky plain stretches out over the horizon with sporadic rock walls climbing higher into the sky. The plateau provides an elevated position over the valley below. To the south, I see several tents set up, built in a little circle around the entrance to a cave. Men and women in a wide variety of garb are rushing and moving about. By my count, there are more than one hundred people.

"Weapon." One of the guards who helped me up extends his hand. I turn it over to him reluctantly. He drops it into a burlap sack.

"When do I get that back?" I ask.

"When I give it back to you," he grunts. That's helpful. Hard to argue with the accuracy of his tautology. Kane takes a little more persuasion before handing over his weapons. He also has an alarming number of them: one in each boot, one in his belt, two in his coat, one in his pack, and another tucked inside the bracer he wears on his right wrist. It's almost comical watching the guard's face as Kane pulls yet another weapon and adds it to the sack. By the time he's finished, Kane deposits more weapons than the rest of us combined. After that display, the guard decides to pat him down just to be certain.

One of the guards walks us to the camp, stopping just before we get there. He turns and puts his hand on Rowan's upper chest. "We will be watching you, so don't try anything, understood?"

Rowan grits his teeth and pushes forward. I look at Kali; she seems angrier than Rowan does. Why warn him specifically? Wouldn't they be watching all of us equally? I'd think, if anyone, they'd want to keep an eye on Kane.

The guard then leads us through the open tented area to the cave entrance. Two guards stand on either side of the entrance. I notice two large, almost circular rocks, one on each side of the entrance. As we pass, Becka walks up behind me.

"This is our base of operations. I've heard it was originally used by the Sandurans."

"Really?"

"Yeah, there is a kitchen, enough beds to house a small army—all sorts of stuff. They must have used it for something. The cave forks ahead. The path leading down goes to a large, open cavern with a natural spring. It provides clean water and a safe place to sleep at night. We are taking the path up to a room cut into the stone. It's our command post."

"These paths seem too big and neat to be naturally occurring," I comment.

"They aren't. These tunnels were carved out of the rock by Sand Wurms."

"Sand Wurms?"

"Giant rock-eating snakes."

"Delightful."

We reach the fork and take the path to the left that winds upward. The rock walls are adorned with regularly placed clear jars filled with a blue-green liquid that illuminates the tunnels. Becka notices me staring at them.

"We call them Aluma. They function like lumalight, but rather than using energy, it's an organic liquid that generates the light."

"Where do you find it?"

"You don't want to know." Becka makes it clear that I won't be getting any more information from her. She loves doing that. Brat.

The tunnel opens to a large room with a small hole that lets in natural light. Around the walls are barrels, boxes, and other containers. In the middle of the room is a large table with a single chair at its head. Apart from the guards, there is a single man in the room. He's standing at the head of the table. He looks up as we walk in. The man is wearing a thick vest with leather pauldrons extending over his shoulders and no sleeves. A short, gray cape hangs over his back, giving him the appearance of importance. His midnight-black hair is cut short and brushed forward.

"What is *he* doing here?" The man slams his hands on the table and darts toward us.

I half expect steam to shoot out of his ears as he approaches.

"Brock, where is Lilly?" Becka's voice is calm but firm. She speaks slowly, as if trying to calm him down with the pacing of her words.

"She's with the scouting crew, mapping a new set of tunnels. Now answer my question, Becka. Why is he here?"

Becka steps between me and the charging bull of a man called Brock. She extends her hands toward him to slow his approach sooner.

I'm not sure what to say here. For someone I've never met, he certainly seems very angry with me. He does look familiar. I'm certain I've never met him, but I can't shake the nagging sensation that I've seen him before.

"Brock, you need to calm down." Her voice somehow sounds like a warning without sounding threatening.

Brock reaches his arm over Becka's shoulder, pointing his finger at me. "You don't even know what you've done, do you?"

"I—"

"You wanted to be a hero, wanted to change the world; little Jett Lasting didn't get a fair deal so heap everyone else, right? Did you ever stop to think about whose lives you'd destroy in the process? Do you even care? My family was torn apart because of you."

I swallow what feels like a boulder of guilt. It sinks to my stomach and threatens to drop me to my knees. The worst part is I have no idea what he's talking about. So many people died; so many lives were changed in our failed rebellion. It seems I've destroyed this man's life, and I have no idea how. I close my eyes and lower my head in shame.

"Brock, I understand you're angry. This is not the way to deal with it. Why don't we step outside and talk privately?" The calm of Becka's voice has a stern note to it.

"You don't give orders here, Becka; get out of my way or I'll—"

I step in front of Becka, putting myself between Brock and her. "You don't want to finish that sentence. You got a problem with me, you can—" I feel his fist crash against my jaw and taste warm copper in my mouth. I expect another blow to come but it doesn't. Instead, I hear a grunt. A click echoes in the room, and a glowing blue blade appears at Brock's throat.

"That's my friend, boy. Get ahold of yourself before I do it for you." Kane's head appears over Brock's shoulder.

How did he get behind him so quickly?

I rub my jaw. "You didn't want to stop him before he hit me?"

Kane shrugs. "It sounds like you deserved that one."

Brock's eyes get wide as his head is pulled back. "What is this? Who are you?"

"I'm the guy who got a weapon past your guards. Probably a good idea to do as I say." Kane smiles like he's having the time of his life.

"Guards!" Brock shouts. There were six guards in the room. At his command they all step forward, weapons at the ready.

"I wouldn't do that," Kali says calmly.

Brock sneers, "You've got one weapon between you. He kills me, you all die."

"We don't need weapons. My friend here is a Tribling," Kali grins. The guards exchange glances and mutter to one another. Kali folds her arms as Rowan silently scans across the room.

"Is that supposed to mean something to me? You salvage—"

Kali smiles and turns to Rowan. "Can't say I didn't warn him."

Rowan moves so quickly he seems to vanish. One of the guards flies back, clutching his stomach, weapon clanging against the floor. The next turns his energy spear but too late. Rowan lifts it, drives the shaft into his face, pulls the weapon free, and discards it before knocking him to the ground. Guards three and four charge at him. Their weapons bounce harmlessly away before their bodies crash to the ground, followed by groans of pain. I've never seen someone move the way Rowan does. His body flows like water, adapting instantly to whatever his opponent tries. Guards five and six falter, their warnings shaky as Rowan circles around the table. He stops in front of them and glares. The two guards drop their weapons and hold their hands up in surrender.

"That's enough! This is not why we are here. Kane, let him go," I shout. Kane waits a moment before disengaging his energy blade and shoving Brock against the table.

Becka leans over next to Brock and whispers just loud enough that I can hear, "You hit my little brother again, Brock, and you'll wish Kane had used his knife on you. Understand?"

Brock coughs, rubbing his throat with his hand. "What do you want? Come to finish what you started in Dios?"

"Look, I don't know who you are. I know a lot of people were hurt in the rebellion, and we were a part of that. I'm sorry; I'm sorry for every person who suffered because of it. I truly am. We were trying to make things better. In the end, we only made them worse."

"The good intentions excuse? Really? You think that changes anything?"

"That rebellion was going to happen with or without us. People in Dios are suffering and dying every day at the hands of the leaders who are supposed to protect and care for them. Doing nothing in the face of tyranny and oppression gives permission to those in power to keep doing it."

"Save your speeches for someone who cares. What happened to my family wasn't because of some rebellion. It's because of you."

"Me? I don't even know who you are."

Becka walks over to the table. "Jett, meet Brock—Brock Moonslight."

My eyes widen, and suddenly I remember why he looks so familiar. He was on the broadcast with Lilly when they showed her and her family being arrested.

"You're Lilly's brother?"

"Yes, I'm Lilly's brother."

Meeting Lilly's family is off to a strong start.

"What about the rest of your family; where are they?"

"Still in Dios. My dad still has a lot of influence. After serving for twenty years, all he wanted was to enjoy a quiet life with his family. Thanks to you, the only way he could keep his family out of the Outlands was to rejoin the Defense Force. Of course, they were stripped of their class and sent to live in the Rim. Twenty years of his life undone because of you."

"If your dad made a deal, why are you and Lilly here?"

"Lilly was connected to you, the rebel leader. There is no world where the Patriarch would let that slide, even with my father's connections. The only way he could spare everyone else was to disown her publicly. I wasn't about to let my little sister get exiled alone, so here I am. Now do you see what your actions wrought? You didn't just separate my family. You broke it."

"Brock, I'm so sorry . . ."

"Oh, you're sorry. That makes it all better. Thank you. I had to watch my father, the strongest man I've ever known, weep as he disowned his precious baby girl. It broke his heart. The name he worked his whole life to build—ruined. But you're sorry, so all's good. We lost everything, but don't worry about it—you're sorry."

"That's quite enough, Brock," a familiar woman's voice comes from behind us. I freeze in place so completely I'm certain my heart forgets to beat. I turn slowly to see her standing at the entrance. Her dark hair is pulled back with a light-blue ribbon, worn almost like a headband.

The ribbon matches a light-blue cape that accents the faded-brown, padded, leather armor that covers her torso and shoulders. The blue looks much better on her than the yellow ever did.

CHAPTER EIGHT

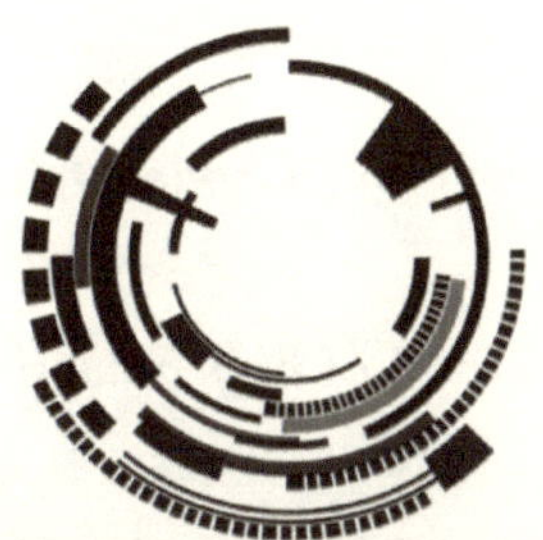

"**L**illy." I exhale more than say her name. I barely finish turning before her body crashes into mine, her arms wrapping tightly around my neck.

"Jett! You're here! You're alive! I was so worried." She pushes me back and starts inspecting me much in the same manner Becka had.

I laugh, "You're worried? I was trapped in a cell for almost a month after they exiled you. My worries had worries."

Lilly rolls her eyes, but I see a faint smile on her lips. Becka groans deliberately. Seeing her again brings back a rush of feelings that I have no idea what to do with. Do I hug her? Kiss her? Shake her hand? *No. Not that one.*

"How did you find us?" Lilly hops up on the table, kicking her feet slowly.

"We were traveling around and noticed Becka following us because Becka is the worst spy ever."

"Hey!" Becka slaps my arm.

"You might as well flash lumelights and play music."

Becka glares at me, folding her arms.

"Then why'd it take you a whole day to notice her?" Kane snickers.

Traitor.

"See." Becka points at me triumphantly.

"I'm so glad you're safe." Lilly's voice is sweet and sincere.

"You've no idea how much of a relief this is. This place—this is impressive."

Lilly blushes and tucks a strand of hair behind her ear as if she knows it drives me crazy. "Thank you."

"How did you end up leading a group of Raiders?"

Lilly sighs, "Someone had to stand up to Morton and that shinshew of a town Elder."

"That's not much of an answer," I challenge.

"When Brock and I got to Red Clay, we met with Elder Schmitty. I knew there was something off about him. I just couldn't place what. A mysterious man in a cloak approached us; he kept his hood up to keep us from seeing his face, but he warned us it wasn't safe to stay in Red Clay. He escorted us out of town, told me about the deal Schmitty had with the Marauders, and warned me not to come back. He pointed us to a town called Dragonvale. We didn't get far before coming across a group of bandits who were intent on robbing us yet seemed reluctant to do so. We started talking. They didn't really have a leader, but the man who spoke for them told me they all had loved ones taken by Morton's Marauders. They were robbing merchants and travelers to try and get enough to buy their loved ones back. They were desperate and terribly unorganized. I offered to help."

"You offered to help a group of bandits who were trying to rob you?" I ask.

"I offered to help a group of victims who had family members sold as slaves by a shinshew human trafficker," Lilly corrects. At this point, it shouldn't surprise me but it still does.

"So they just made you their leader?" I ask.

"It wasn't quite that simple. When I offered to help, the man who spoke for them, Nickola, recognized me. I taught both of his children back in Dios. He vouched for me and suggested to the others that they follow my lead. Who knew teaching would make me so popular? Ever since then, we've been organizing, planning, and working to liberate their friends and family."

"That's part of why we are here. Morton has our friends," I say.

Lilly slides off the table and turns around, looking away from me. "I feared as much. Becka said he tried to grab her. I'd hoped we could intercept the others before they got to Red Clay but no such luck."

"We can work together to rescue them."

"It's not just them, Jett. Morton has a lot of people. If our estimates are correct, he has over two hundred slaves."

"Two . . . hundred." I shake my head, trying to process that. "What does he do with them?"

"It depends. They have servants who cook, clean, and set up their camps. Others, he conditions." The tone of her voice is grim.

"Conditions?"

"Uses mental, physical, and emotional training to break their will and turn them into something else," Kali interjects.

"Can we rescue them?"

"Oh, rescue them?" Brock grunts derisively. "I got an idea; why don't you just go ask Morton to let them go? I'm sure if the great Jett Lasting said please, he'd be happy to do it."

Lilly walks over to the head of the table. "Brock, why don't you lay out the scouting report from the Marauder camp?"

"You can't seriously be considering helping him after—"

"Brock, the report please."

Brock begrudgingly unrolls a giant scroll and flattens it over the table. On it there is a crude drawing of a large camp showing an outer fence, towers, tents, and a series of buildings.

"Our scouts estimate they have around three thousand soldiers." Becka points to the tents on the map.

Lilly nods. "Which rules out direct confrontation. We don't have near the numbers to face them."

"What are their defenses like?" Kali leans in, inspecting the drawing more closely.

"The camp is surrounded on three sides by cliffs. The only way in or out is through the front gate. They have towers placed incrementally and patrolled by guards regularly." Lilly points to the towers on the drawing.

"Force shields?" Kali asks.

Lilly shakes her head. "Just the gate."

Kali and Rowan exchange a glance. Rowan makes a series of signs and Kali nods. "How do they avoid the depraved?"

"What? Are you superstitious? I don't think an army of trained warriors spends a lot of time worrying about tod tales." Apparently Brock's disdain for me pours over to anyone who associates with me, even Becka. I thought it was impossible not to like Becka.

"We could use darkness as a cover, sneak in at night, and—" I try to change the subject but don't even get the thought out before Lilly cuts me off.

"That's going to be tricky. The towers are guarded day and night. They are spaced out in a way that would make it almost impossible to take out one guard without the others noticing, so there's not even a way to create a blind spot to sneak in. Even if you could, our best guess is they are keeping the captives somewhere around here." Lilly points to a row of buildings along the backside of the camp.

"We don't know for sure; that's just our best guess," Becka adds.

"The one way to get to them without the tower guards seeing you would be to weave through the tents, which are arranged to be deliberately confusing. The tents are set up in sets of four, each opening to a small central courtyard. They are packed so closely together that you have to move into each courtyard to get through them, which creates a lot of exposure. The tents are tall and identical. On the ground, it'll likely be very disorienting. Imagine winding through a labyrinth without making a sound or getting spotted. Once you're through, you have to find the prisoners, free them, then navigate back. There's no way you'd be able to get hundreds of people out without being spotted."

"Hundreds? It's just three people." Kali looks up, confused.

"You want to rescue three people and just leave the others behind?" Lilly escalates from confusion to full on bewilderment.

"How are they your problem? Are you friends with all of them?" Kali asks.

"No, but they are innocent people who need our help."

"It's not like you owe them anything. Better to save a few than no one at all."

"What happens to the ones we leave behind when the Marauders find out some are missing?"

Kali shrugs.

"They get punished."

"So? That's not our fault."

"How is that mmm——" Lilly exhales and turns around for a moment to catch herself. "Jett, help me out here."

I look between Kali and Lilly. "They are our friends, Lilly. We have to rescue them. I don't care about anything else. I wish we could rescue everyone; I do. But I'm not going to leave our friends in the clutches of a madman simply because we can't rescue everyone at once."

Lilly's face looks like she's just eaten something very bitter.

"That's disappointing. I'm sorry; I can't help you. We are not equipped to fight the Marauders. We can't risk a team on an incursion that has almost no chance of success. We don't even know for sure that this is where they are being held. They could be anywhere. I'm sorry; there is nothing we can do."

My head understands what she's saying. It makes sense. It's reasonable. Yet, it feels like a rejection. I came here asking for her help to rescue *our* friends. She's saying no. Her reasons, logical as they may be, don't change the fact that she is refusing to help me when I need her. I was willing to storm the Temple Sector in the middle of a rebellion when the Patriarch captured her. That's what you do when you care about someone. Is this how little her friends mean to her? There's a time to fight for a cause, but when the people you care about are in trouble, that comes first right? Suddenly that sweet girl I've known since I was a child doesn't seem so sweet. The warmth I often felt just thinking about her has cooled several degrees.

"That's rubbish!" Kali's frustration makes me jump a little. "You claim they are your friends, and yet, you're just going to leave them in there?" My heart sings in agreement.

Lilly puts her hands on her hips. "How does getting a bunch of people killed help my friends? Hmm? I don't want to leave them in there. I don't want to leave any of the slaves there. But I need a plan that doesn't involve throwing away my soldiers' lives on a rescue attempt with next to no chance of success."

"That's nice; I like how you're hiding your cowardice behind a facade of caring for the many." Kali curls her lip as her weaponized words take flight.

Lilly blinks. "I like how you're hiding your callousness behind a facade of caring for the few."

"Tsk. Got it. Don't count on you to have my back if I'm ever in trouble."

"Don't confuse my sensibility with apathy. You don't think I care? You don't even know these people. They are my friends. I want to save them. I'd do anything I could. But the difference between us is that I am responsible for the lives of every person here. I can't put them at risk on a fool's errand."

My mind and heart wage war against each other. How can Lilly be so dismissive of our friends? Why is Kali fighting harder to rescue them? She doesn't even know them. Is this who Lilly is? She'll risk her life to save her students or to save strangers, but she won't lift a finger to help save our friends? I know she's being practical, and her position is reasonable, but it feels cold and uncaring.

"The difference between us is if my friends were in danger, there's nothing that could stop me from rescuing them. You can dress it up however you like; what it boils down to is that your friends need help, and you are too scared to do anything about it."

Becka and I exchange a glance. I open my mouth to try and put an end to this argument, but no words come out. The two women stare each other down—Kali breathing heavily and red faced, Lilly's arms folded in a calm disdain.

Lilly takes a breath, then continues in a slightly calmer vein, "Look around. The people here are not warriors. They are exiles like me who have spent most of their lives keeping their heads down and trying to blend in. This place is their nightmare. They are terrified of the Marauders. These people are trusting me to keep them safe, but they haven't followed me long enough to storm into certain death on my command. I told them I would help them get their loved ones back. I can't do that if I throw their lives away to serve my own interests."

Lilly and Kali glare at each other in some strange sort of test of wills. I half expect to see sparks appear between them.

Brock slams his fist down on the hard wood table to get attention. "I keep telling you we need allies."

"Like whom?" Becka challenges.

"Heap, we could talk to those crazy cultists, for Bealz sake; we can't be the only ones who have a problem with the Marauders," Brock suggests.

"We've tried that. Nobody likes the Marauders, but no one is willing to fight them either. That's why we can't risk sneaking into their base. They are too powerful," Lilly replies.

"What if we had a way that could work?" My brain finally rejoins the party.

Lilly and Kali continue to stare for a few moments before Lilly finally breaks eye contact. "What did you have in mind?"

"Well, if we can't get in, what if we can lure them out?" I ask.

"We're not putting our people at risk for you," Brock snaps.

"Brock," Becka warns.

"I get it; you don't like me," I cut her off. I don't want her getting caught in the middle of his issue with me. She doesn't deserve that. "I can't undo all the wrongs that have been done. At least, I can try to make some of them right. This isn't about me or how you feel about me. Right now, there are people, including our friends, being held by the Marauders. Some of them are there because of me. I need to fix it. I'm asking you to put aside your issues with me and help them. They don't deserve what happened to them any more than you did. Don't do it for me but for their sake."

Brock rubs his face with his hand. "Fine."

Lilly tries to hide the subtle grin on her face. "Tell me what you're thinking."

"You've been attacking their patrols, right?" I ask.

"Yeah," Brock answers reluctantly.

"How does their main force react? Do they send out search parties? Mobilize? What do they do when they realize one of their parties isn't coming back?" I try to think of all the questions Victor would ask in this situation. I have no idea what to do with the information, but maybe asking the right question will help formulate a better plan.

Brock scratches his head. "They send out three squads: one investigates the site; one watches, typically from an elevated position; one flanks around behind the investigating unit to flank anyone who might approach."

"That's smart," Kali nods approvingly.

"Maybe if we could take out the three squads, that would be enough to lure out the main force," I posit.

"That's a big risk. Even if we could do it, we'd need all the Raiders to pull it off. We might lure the Marauders out, but there wouldn't be time for a team to sneak in," Lilly explains.

She's right.

"We need a way to lure out their main force and draw them far away from their camp. Something big they can't ignore—like an army." Ideas form together in my mind as my plan starts to take shape.

"Oh, an army. Wow, what a great idea. You crag! If we had an army, we wouldn't need to lure them out. We could just fight them," Brock replies.

Apparently, being willing to work together does not include any measure of civility.

"That's why we've been attacking their scouts and smaller parties. We can chip away at their numbers, but we are nowhere near being ready to fight them," Lilly adds.

"You keep attacking their scouts, and all your men are going to die," Kali warns.

"What makes you say that?" Becka speaks quickly enough to ensure Brock can't comment.

"The Marauders have a code: Never back down. Never let a slight go unanswered. Never show weakness. Never allow resistance. Never tolerate defiance. You've been lucky so far. That just means they are biding their time," Kali explains.

Brock turns his ire to Kali. "We don't need tips from you. We've been doing this for a while now. It's working. We are careful."

Kali smiles sweetly at him. "That's exactly why you're going to lose. You won't see the trap coming." Kali gives Brock a disapproving glare. Everyone begins arguing back and forth, pointing out flaws in each other's plans. It's like they care more about winning the argument than they do about coming up with an effective idea.

"We don't need an army," I say loudly and then wait, letting the chaos of the room die down.

"You want to explain that?" Brock crosses his arms in front of his chest, pushing himself up to look bigger.

"Victor used to say the key to victory is in deception—to appear strong where you are weak, to look like you are moving when you're standing still, and to appear numerous where you are few. We don't need an army. We just need it to look like we have one."

"What sort of shinshew——" Brock starts to protest.

Lilly slams her hand down on the table. "That's good; if we set up a camp, make it look as big as possible from a distance, that might work."

"What happens if they send in scouts to check out the camp?" Kali asks.

"We need to set up in an area that's open enough that the scouts won't risk trying to approach." I point to a spot on their map. "Here."

"It's not far enough away. Even if they deployed their full force, you wouldn't have time to sneak in, rescue the prisoners, and get out before they returned." Lilly shakes her head in frustration.

I press my hands together. "Then we will have to slow them down. In order for their army to get to the camp, they will have to pass through this narrow area. It's perfect for an ambush."

Lilly sits down at the table, looking defeated. "That won't work. Even if we took the higher ground on the cliffs above, they'd make short work of us."

"What about explosives? Put some here," Kane gestures to the map, pointing to several different locations. "Also, here and here. That would slow them down and reduce their numbers; then you mount a quick attack to distract them—at least until the smoke clears. If we wait for them to pass and have enough explosives, we could blast this area and cut off their way back. Then, they'd have to go up and around. That would give you plenty of time."

"We don't have explosives. We can't get explosives. Otherwise, we'd have done so already," Brock grumbles.

Rowan signs something to Kali and she chuckles.

"Yeah, he is pretty slow."

Brock glares. "What did you say?"

"Explosives are easy if you know the right people. I know the right people," Kali smiles confidently.

"Step one: setting up the camp. We build it wide but not deep. It doesn't need to be functional, just to look good from a distance. Then, it's just a matter of making sure their scouts find it." This is the same tone Lilly used when we were kids, and she was about to start bossing me around.

"You don't think they will notice the lack of sound or movement coming from an army camp?"

Finally, Brock brings up an almost valid point. I wasn't sure he was capable of it.

"We'd need to leave a small team there to move around and make as much noise as possible. When the Marauders show up, they take off, hide, and meet back here once the mission is done," I explain.

"So three teams: one that sneaks in and rescues the hostages—all of the hostages." Lilly emphasizes the last phrase while staring at Kali. "One team to ambush the Marauders and one to make the camp look occupied. It's crazy enough; it may work."

"Seriously, sis, this is absolutely—"

"What's the point of all this if we aren't going to try to help people, Brock?"

Brock's jaw drops; he looks betrayed by her question.

"To stay alive."

"Cowardice runs in the family, I see," Kali snaps.

Lilly covers her face with her hands, breathing heavily into them. When she finally brings her hands down, she glares at Kali.

A soft knocking breaks the building tension.

"Sorry to interrupt ma'am." A young Raider stands at the entryway.

"What is it, Kyle?" Lilly pulls her angry gaze from Kali, but the frustration is still painted on her face.

"I think you're going to want to see this." He motions with his head for us to follow him.

Becka catches my arm again. "Hey, don't let Brock discourage you. He's just—"

"A scrap sink?" I finish for her as the others pile out of the room.

Becka grins. "Yeah, he is a bit. Reminds me of Jensen sometimes."

I laugh.

"Jett, you're smarter than you think. You never had to apply yourself when Victor was around, but listening to you, I could almost hear Victor's voice. You're starting to think like him."

"Thanks, Becka, but we should—"

"Already waiting on you," Becka smiles as she runs out of the room disappearing from view. I chase after her, struggling to keep up. We leave the command cave and make our way outside. At the far end of the plateau, the cliff provides a nice view of the path below. Raider Kyle motions for us to get down as we approach. We drop onto our stomachs and crawl to the edge of the cliff, looking down to the canyon below. Brock pulls out a pair of Zoomers and starts passing them down the line. Lilly, who waited for Becka and I to arrive, crawls up last and takes the Zoomers.

"What do we have?" she asks.

"Small Marauder scouting unit there," Kane points.

"Those are pretty common around here," Lilly replies, lowering the Zoomers.

"You see a lot of those?" Kane adjusts where he is pointing. I lie down next to Lilly and try to see for myself. It's too far to see clearly, but I can make out movement. Lilly hands me a second pair of Zoomers while looking through the others herself. Moving toward the scouting unit are six soldiers in black armor with red visors.

"Are those the same—" I ask.

"Yes," Kane replies.

Gunshots pierce the air as the Patriarch soldiers cross paths with the scouting unit.

"What are they doing?" I ask.

"We have seen them before. I think they are looking for someone," Lilly replies.

Within seconds the gunfight is over. The results are similar to the last time, except this time they left two people alive to scan. After the scans, they snap their necks and move on.

"That's not our problem. We just avoid them and—" Kali pushes off the ground, standing up.

"I think it's a woman," Lilly continues.

Kali freezes in place. There's a moment of silence. "Why do you think that?"

"Well, they take special care not to kill the women."

"They just killed everyone down there," Kali objects.

Lilly nods, "But they didn't kill the women until after they scanned them. It's the same every time. They kill the men immediately, scan the women, then kill them. My guess is they are searching for someone important—a woman. They want her alive. That's why they don't kill women until they've confirmed they are not the woman they are looking for."

"That doesn't make sense. The Patriarch teaches that women are inferior to men. Why would they go through so much trouble to find a single woman in the Outlands?" I ask.

"We don't know that's what they are doing." Kali's tone is strangely dismissive, like the discussion annoys her for some reason.

"Are you OK?" I ask.

"I'm fine. I just think we need to stay on task. You've got friends to rescue. I've got a king to kill. We can speculate about a half-dozen Patriarch soldiers later."

CHAPTER NINE

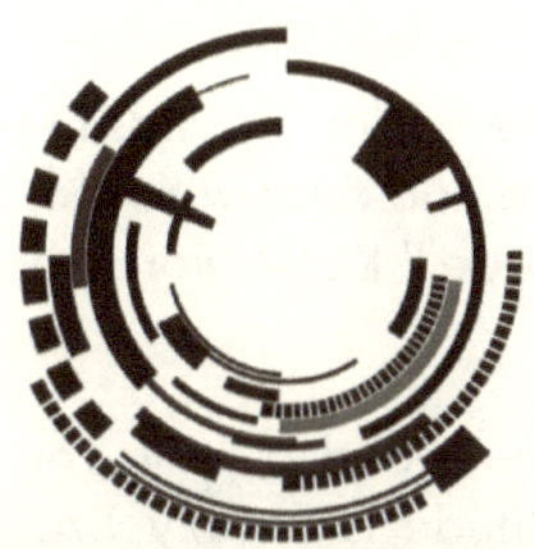

Back at the cave headquarters, we circle around the table. The tension in the air when we left seems to have been replaced with a frail calmness. We have a plan that helps everyone get what they want. Lilly stands at the head with Brock hovering next to her shoulder like a guard dog.

"Let's go over it again. Step one is set up: building out the camp, acquiring explosives, setting up the ambush site." Lilly waves her hand in little circles as she talks.

"We will also need a way to get the Marauder scouts to find the camp, or we may be sitting around waiting for a long time," Becka says.

"Leave that to me. None of this matters if we can't get those explosives. Kali, you know how to get them?" I ask.

Kali leans forward and points to a spot on the map. "This is Dragonsvale. It's the largest town in this territory and home to the Dark Market. You can find pretty much anything imaginable there if you know the right people and can pay the right price."

Kane lets out an excited grunt.

Lilly taps a finger over her lips. "OK, good, I can send—"

"Rowan and I can handle it," Kali interrupts.

"We'll deal with Morton first; I know how much that means to you," I say.

Kali seems shocked by this. She closes her eyes and takes a deep breath. "That can wait."

"Kali—"

"Morton isn't going anywhere. Your friends need help now. We rescue your friends first. Then, we can deal with Morton. It's . . . it's what my mother would want me to do." Kali's words ooze reluctantly from her lips.

Our eyes lock for a moment, and a smile forms on her face. "I don't know what to say." Gratitude is a cozy fire burning inside me. We smile at each other, and something about her expression keeps me from looking away. First, she argues *for* rescuing my friends, then she decides to put aside her own goals to help me. Is this appreciation I'm feeling? Or something else? There is a warmth in her eyes that pulls me in. I force myself to look down, ending our little gazing contest. Kali clears her throat.

"Besides, if things go right, this will draw Morton into the open, and that will make it easier for me to kill him." This practical expression makes her offer feel lesser. It felt like we were having a moment, that maybe what Doc was saying about her was true. Silly me, she's still just helping us to help herself.

Lilly points to the site for our decoy army camp. "Alright, I'll bring the Raiders here. We'll gather what we can from the area and start setting up the fake camp. Kali and Rowan will get explosives from Dragonvale and meet us at the campsite as soon as possible. If all goes well, we should be able to rescue the hostages, free our friends, and strike a crippling blow to the Marauders all at the same time." Lilly looks so natural, so comfortable giving orders, it's as if she were born to do it.

"Jett, are you with me or with her?" Kali asks. Why does she word it like that? This seemingly casual question feels layered and multifaceted. Suddenly all eyes are on me. Great, no pressure, Jett; just got to unravel the subtext of the question, figure out potential ramifications of each answer, and do so without delaying a response too long.

I freeze. My gaze moves instinctively between Kali and Lilly. Lilly's eyes seem larger than normal as she bites at her lip nervously. I need to say something here, but what? Why does it feel like I'm not just picking a side but picking a person? With each passing second, Kali's expression seems to grow warmer while Lilly's colder.

Kane puts his arm around my shoulder. "We'll both come. You'll need the extra hands to carry back the supplies."

Kane, you brilliant psychopath! That completely disarms the decision bomb thrust at me.

Lilly forces a smile before her expression shifts to a calm, blank expression that makes reading what she's feeling very difficult. She turns to Kali. "Do you need more?"

Kali scratches her head. "The explosives aren't particularly heavy, but there's only so much you can fit in a pack. I'd rather not encumber us too much in case we need to be able to move quickly. If you can spare six men, that would let us carry enough in our packs to get the job done."

Becka walks around the table and stands next to me. "I'll go with them as well. Someone has to keep Jett out of trouble."

"How long do you need?" Lilly's hand seems to be shaking as she shifts something on the table.

Kali starts counting on her fingers. "Dragonvale is about three days travel by foot. Might take a day or two to gather everything. Let's say ten days to be safe."

"OK. Gather the supplies you need, eat, and rest here for the night. I'll set you up with six of my Raiders and have them ready to travel in the morning." Lilly taps her knuckles on the table, and everyone starts to shuffle out.

"Jett," she says softly, lingering back as the others file out. I wait for everyone else to leave before turning to her. Brock was the last to file out, staring ominously at me before finally stepping out of view down the tunnel path.

Lilly walks around the table and stands just in front of me. The tension makes the air feel like a thick, heavy gelatin. I'm not sure what I expect here or even how to feel. Do they have a book for what to say in a newly blossoming romantic relationship when seeing each other for the first time since you destroyed her family and got her exiled with what will likely be a death sentence? I can't be the only one whose been in this situation.

"Sorry about Brock." Lilly looks down, shuffling her feet.

"He does seem to like me a little too much. You might ask him to ease up."

The tension lessens with her soft chuckle. "He just won't stop talking about you. Jett this, Jett that. I think he may have a crush. Should I be jealous?"

I reach out and put my hand on her arm. "Are you doing OK?"

Her smile brightens. "I am. Seeing you makes things better. It's been a challenging adjustment. Life is difficult here."

"I can't even imagine. What you've done here, well, it's pretty incredible. I'm just sorry you had to."

Lilly cocks her head. "What do you mean?"

Her question catches me off guard. "You didn't deserve this. You should be in Dios with your family where you'd be safe."

"Is that what you think I want?"

Confusion is like a mud pit. The more I wiggle around in it, the deeper I sink. "Do you not?"

She breaks eye contact and sighs deeply. "Jett, can I ask you something?"

"Of course." I get the sense I'm not going to like where this is going.

"Do you think I'm fragile?"

"What do you mean?"

"My dad was a soldier. He always calls me his little princess. He treats me like I am some frail piece of glass that might break at any moment. I know his heart is in the right place; he just wants me to be safe. I love him for it. I'm not some delicate flower that needs to be protected from every gust of wind. You're always apologizing and acting like everything bad that happens to me is your fault. It's a little insulting."

It's my turn to break eye contact. "Brock told me what happened to your family because of me."

"Brock blames you for what happened. I'm not Brock. What my brother fails to accept is that I'm a big girl. You didn't force me to do anything. You stood up for what you believed in. You fought, and I think you still fight, for the good of others. I like that about you. When everyone else just kept their heads down, you tried to do something to make the world better. I don't care that it didn't work out. I care that you tried. I respect the choice you made. I'm asking you to do the same for me. I made my own choices. I can live with the consequences of them. What I won't stand for is you acting like my choices don't matter because whatever happens to me is because of you."

Her words might as well be a stun blast. My mind and body seize up. "I—"

"Jett Lasting, if you even try to apologize to me again, I'm going to smack you in the back of your head."

"I'm definitely not sorry. I was going to suggest you apologize to me." Our eyes meet again. Despite her frustration, her words have lifted a burden from my shoulders. This whole time I've been blaming myself for what happened to everyone else. I hadn't considered that, even if I am somewhat responsible, blaming myself too much could actually invalidate their choices. Weirdly, this helps.

I look around the now empty room and then back to her. She smiles at me before looking down at her feet.

"I missed you."

I smile. "I missed you too."

The words themselves feel weird. I mean them; I just don't really feel them. I did miss her, but for some reason, things are different between us. A silent stillness lingers in the air as neither of us move or speak. I'm not even really sure what to say at this point. A flash of disappointment passes her face before being replaced with a shy smile.

"You know I hate this, right? Olivia, Jensen, and Telmen being inside a Marauder camp—it keeps me up at night. I don't want you to think I don't care. I do."

"I get it; you have other responsibilities to consider." I try to see where she's coming from, but something about her reluctance to help our friends doesn't set right with me. The more I try to rationalize her position to myself, the less warmth I feel toward her.

"There are a lot of people who are hurting out here. I don't have the luxury of playing favorites. I can't just leave hundreds of people to the Marauders because we don't personally know them, you know?"

I try to stop my mind from spiraling, but with every passing thought my view of her diminishes. She can't even tell me she cares about our friends without justifying why she wouldn't help them? Noble as she may be—impressive as she may be—what good is caring about someone who isn't going to have your back when you need them to? I don't want her to feel guilty. She's standing on her principles, regardless of how impersonal they may be. As much as I try not to be disappointed by her, I am.

"We've got a plan now, so we're stocked. I just want to know my friends are safe."

She sighs. "I want that too."

Her words feel hollow. She's made her position quite clear. While she might want them to be safe, she isn't willing to risk anything to make it happen. When she was in danger, even Jensen was ready to charge into the fight. When the shoe is on the other foot, she needs a noble cause to lift a finger? What does that say about her? As much as I admire her desire to save everyone, her refusal to consider a rescue mission for our friends is frustrating. She's known them since we were kids. Is it that crazy to care about them first?

I'm not sure it even would have struck me until I saw how passionate Kali was. She was offended at the thought that Lilly wouldn't do whatever it took to save our friends. Kali was right. I'm not sure the girl I've had a crush on is the person I thought she was. Saying you care is easy, but it's meaningless if you don't show it. The wedge between us becomes a chasm as we stand in silence, neither of us sure what to say.

"One more thing. How well do you know Kali?" She keeps her voice hushed, but the concern is blaring.

"Not well. She's the first person I met out here. She sort of saved my life. We made a blood pact, so that's something. I promised to help her, and in exchange, she helps me. We've been together ever since. Why?"

"There's something off about her." Lilly's warning feels strange. The girl I hardly know is more committed to helping me rescue my friends than the girl who has known us most our lives. I can't help but wonder if it's guilt that's driving Lilly's suspicion. Is her issue really Kali's agenda? Or is she just worried that Kali is acting like a better friend?

"Off? What do you mean?"

"When we saw the Patriarch soldiers, she was nervous. Did you see how quickly she tried to change the subject?"

"Lilly, I think you may be reading into it. Kali's right; it's really not the most pressing issue right now."

Lilly sighs. "I'm telling you; I've got a feeling about this. I know that look. Jett, she's hiding something."

"If you're so suspicious of her, then why were you so quick to offer extra men to help?"

Lilly doesn't respond for a minute. "I'm not saying she's a bad person or that she's not going to help us. I can just tell there's something she's not saying."

"What am I supposed to do with that, Lilly?"

"Look, maybe I'm still reeling from Victor. I never thought he would betray you. It may be nothing; I hope it's nothing, but please, just be careful."

"Thanks for the domes up."

There's an awkward tension between us as we make our way out of the room. Our paths split as she continues down into the lower part of the cave while I step outside. Kane drops a pack onto the table in front of me. It's already stocked with food and water for the journey. I start inspecting it to double-check.

With a loud *thwomp*, a sack slams down in front of us. I look up to see the guard in the gray cloak who had confiscated our weapons. He pulls the burlap sack open. Seeing his weapons again, Kane smiles bright enough to light a cavern.

"No hard feelings, eh?" Kane slaps the man's shoulder, gesturing to the knife he slipped past him. The guard grunts and walks off without a word.

"I don't think he likes you very much." I grab my energy blade from the sack and return it to my belt.

Kane shrugs.

He'll definitely lose sleep over it.

"Eat?" Kane suggests. Down the winding cave tunnel, we make our way to a large room that seems to function like a great hall. It's lined with tables, chairs, and other supplies. This was a far more established base of operations than I expected. Toward the back of the open cavern were three tunnels that open up to other large rooms used for sleeping and storing supplies. In the back corner, farther from the tunnels, they've set up a kitchen and dining area in the recesses of the rock.

A group of three women and two older men are setting food in large trays onto tables toward the back wall. One of the women standing behind the first table rings a bell. She's older than most of the Raiders—probably about sixty. She has thick, curly, black hair and a dark mark on her neck that looks like the remnant of a bad burn. The

Raiders start shuffling over and forming a line. Two of the women start distributing plates to each Raider in line.

"'Bout time, I'm starving," said an impressively large man who looks to be part boar. He stomps to the front of the line and reaches his hand toward a stack of rolls piled up in a basket.

Schhtckk. A wooden spoon slaps against the top of his hand, and the sound reverberates, silencing the chattering Raiders. The large man pulls his hand back, holding it against his chest and rubbing it with the fingers of his other hand.

"It's not time yet." Her glare is stern and, yet, somehow not angry. In a room filled with people, it's quiet enough to hear a squirrel sneeze. The large man stares at the much smaller woman. She doesn't blink; she just stares right back at him. I'm frozen in place as I expect to see him rip her in half.

The Raider breaks eye contact and looks down at the floor. He's not a burly brute anymore but a scolded puppy. "Sorry, Vesta, I forgot."

"Well, that's OK. I appreciate your enthusiasm. Why don't we let our guests eat first?" Vesta looks over at us and waves us forward. The large Raider grumbles and steps to the side, giving us space. Kane doesn't even hesitate. He walks right up in front of the man. Vesta hands him a plate and starts plopping food down on it.

"You remind me of my Grams. She wasn't afraid of nobody. I'm going to like you," Kane smiles, quite taken with the cook.

She waves him on. "Well, that's nice, isn't it? Please keep moving. There are lots of hungry people waiting to eat." The dismissal only seems to thrill him more. I smile politely and thank her as she fills my plate. The line moves smoothly, and soon we make our way to a nearby table. The clamor and commotion of a room full of people eating and talking fills the air like a long, steady rumbling of thunder. When Kali and Rowan come in, Vesta waves them to the front of the line.

"Our guests eat first, boys," Vesta warns, and the Raiders in line step to the side again, not hiding their displeasure. Several Raiders who just finished collecting their meal detour from their trek to a table and approach Kali and Rowan.

"We are taking in all kinds of strays now?" one says.

"I don't know about you, but I don't much feel like eating with some dirty Tribling," another snaps. Rowan turns to face them. This is not going to be good. Kali quietly sets her tray down and grips her energy weapons. Her killing these Raiders is not going to go over well. Sliding from the table, I rush over, hoping to disarm the situation before it gets out of hand. In a flash, Vesta crosses to the table and is standing between the group and Rowan.

The old cook pulls the plate from one of their hands and slides it back onto the serving table. "Well, I suppose you won't be eating at all, then—any of you." She proceeds to confiscate the plates of each of the Raiders involved.

"Come on, Vesta, you can't tell me you're OK with this filth," one of the Raiders protests.

"Well, the only filthy thing here is your manners, young man. You can go to bed without supper. Maybe a rumbling stomach will teach you to get a grip on your rumbling tongue." Missing a meal is a small price to pay. Vesta just saved all their lives, and they don't even know it.

Lilly walks over to the Raiders, staring at them angrily. "You crossed a line, Walter. I will not tolerate this sort of behavior. Everyone here will be treated with honor and respect. If you have a problem with that, you and your friends are welcome to leave. We will wish you luck in the wilds on your own. What's it going to be?"

She lets her words hang in the air, her eyes fixed on the men. Their rowdy behavior shifts to a submissive demeanor.

"We've no problem, boss," Walter replies.

Lilly turns to Vesta, the fire in her eyes fading as she exhales steam.

"Good, then, it's settled. Vesta, my men need to eat."

"Well, then, you should teach them how to behave. No one who talks to people that way eats my food."

Lilly starts to say something but decides against it. She turns to the culprits. "You heard her. No dinner for you."

The group protests loudly until the large boar-looking Raider walks over. They take one look at him and storm out, grumbling to each other.

Vesta takes one of the confiscated plates and offers it to Rowan. "Here, why don't you take a double helping for the trouble?" Rowan nods and walks toward our table holding two heaping plates of food.

"Nice take!" Kane cheers. Rowan's plate hits the table. Kane leans over, reaching his fork, trying to snag a piece of meat from Rowan's second plate. Rowan smacks Kane's hand away so smoothly I hardly saw him move.

Kane scowls for a moment before laughing it off. "Fine, keep it all for yourself."

"Listen up," Lilly raises her voice to address the room. "These are my friends. We are going to be working with them moving forward. One of them is a Tribling. Anyone has a problem with that, you have two options. Keep it to yourself, or find yourself alone in the wilds because you will not be welcome here. Am I clear?"

The room echoes with a chorus of, "yes, Ma'am!"

"Hmm, maybe she's not so bad after all." Kali takes a bit of her food.

"Yeah, she's something else," I agree.

After dinner, I make my way outside. The Raiders hustle about, moving their tents and supplies inside the cave entrance. The sun casts its fading amber light over the plateau. The picturesque setting is calm, almost serene. I stare out at the colorful sky, letting myself drift into pointless thought. It's almost time to head in. Almost.

Becka's hand rubs across my back. "It's going to be OK. They are going to be OK."

"I hope you're right. I'd feel a lot better if Spike were here."

"Wouldn't we all?" Becka chuckles. "Spike makes everything better."

"Do you think he's OK?"

"I am certain of it. Spike would never let himself die while his friends are in danger. He's too stubborn for that." Becka slides her arm across my back and pulls me into a side hug.

I sigh.

"Want to tell me what's bothering you, then?" Becka asks.

"You remember what Victor used to say? 'Even the greatest strategies unravel when they encounter reality.'" My imitation of his voice earns me a vigorous eyeroll. "I can't stop thinking; what if something goes wrong? What if I've missed something? What if my plan gets a bunch of people killed? How am I supposed to live with that?"

"It's a good plan, Jett; have a little faith. I don't know what will happen. What I do know is that whatever happens, you don't have to deal with it alone."

"I am so glad you're here—that you're safe. I don't know that I could do this without you."

"Of course, you couldn't. You're hopeless without your big sister."

"Can't argue with that."

"Have you thought at all about what's next?"

"You mean what we'll do after we rescue everyone, and we're all together again?"

That comment brings a smile to her face. "Yeah, what then?"

"We will have to figure that out together."

"What about Victor?" Her voice softens as if she's nervous to even pose the question.

I sigh, taking a few steps away from the cave entrance and looking up at the darkening sky. "I let my rage consume me in Dios. I acted on impulse and without thinking. I was a fool. As much as I want to make Victor pay, if I have to choose between keeping the people I care about safe and punishing the one who put us in danger, it's not a contest."

She rests her head on my shoulder. "I'm proud of you, Jett."

Hearing those words from Becka floods my entire body with joy; for a moment, I feel at peace. We stare at the sky in silence, enjoying this final moment before turning in for the night.

With the exception of a pair of guards standing in front of each stone, we are the only two still outside the cave entrance. A shadow passes over the ground in front of us and then is gone. That's strange; there weren't any clouds in the sky. Becka starts to walk toward the cave. Without thinking, I grab her arm and pull her as hard as I can. Her body jerks back, and she stumbles at the sudden, violent direction change.

"Ow, why did—"

Two large, green, clawed legs crash loudly into the stone in front of us where Becka would have been had I not grabbed her. She screams and stumbles back. In front of us is an enormous creature, easily six feet tall. Its green exoskeleton looks like plate armor. Its shoulders are spiked pauldrons. Spikes line its entire back, giving it a dragon-like appearance. The creature's head is shaped like an eagle with a long beak and red, shiny orbs for eyes. It has four transparent, shimmering wings extending out from its back. The top two are much larger than the bottom. The wings look delicate but are at least strong enough to allow the creature to fly. *What fresh Sheol is this?*

The blue stream of my energy sword sings to life as I shelter Becka behind me.

"I'm going to distract it. When I do, run."

"I'm not leaving you here," she protests.

"No arguing—just do it."

"Jett Lasting, don't you think for a sec—"

"You don't have to leave me to die, Becka. Call for help. Just get to the cave and stay there."

Becka nods. I fix my eyes on the creature's red orb eyes. The color and overall look of the creature reminds me of a praying mantis. I've always thought a praying mantis would be terrifying if they were larger. Turns out, I was spot on. It's a small comfort in a time like this. Its head bobs back and forth menacingly. A series of quick clicking sounds fill the air. At the end of each of the mantis-creature's arms are semi-translucent, crescent-shaped blades that look like a reaper's scythe. I can't tell if they are flexible like the wings or sharp like a razor. I'd rather not find out.

Behind the creature I can see the guards from the cave rushing toward us. I just need to keep its attention on me long enough for them to—*heap*. The guards thrust their energy spears forward into what would have been the creature's back. Their spears find nothing but open air as the creature effortlessly leaps into the air, landing behind us. It's fast—way too fast.

CHAPTER TEN

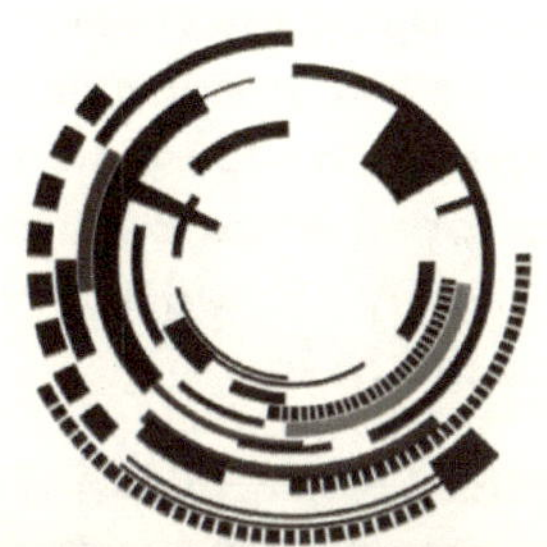

"**R**un! Now!" I point and push Becka toward the cave. She takes off and passes the two guards, who turn to run with her. I follow, looking over my shoulder. The creature was facing away when it landed but quickly spun around toward us. It leans forward and shrieks. The sound makes my blood churn. Digging my feet into the ground with each step, I shove my body forward as fast as I can go. Becka is practically to the entrance of the cave. The guard to my left is just a step or two ahead of me. The guard to my right is falling behind. Glancing over my shoulder, I see the creature surging toward us, gaining on us at an alarming rate. The monster-bug shrieks. We're still too far from the cave entrance; there's no way we will make it in time.

The creature swings its scythe out and slices through the guard behind me. Unhindered by the process, the creature leans forward, using its arms like legs and charging like a bull. Becka disappears into the cave. At least she's safe. Then, I realize the cave is open. If I don't do something, this thing can get in.

The loose dirt and pebbles rattle together as I slide to a stop. I spin to face the raging creature. *Here lies Jett Lasting, who tried to walk the thin line between courage and stupidity and ended up on the stupid side. Story of my life, it seems.* There's no way I can match this creature's speed. I don't like my odds in direct combat either.

Every good thief knows there is a difference between being fast and being quick. Maybe if I time this just right. Move too soon and the creature will have an open lane to the cave base. Move to late and I get splattered like a bug on a windshield—wouldn't that be ironic?

Legs tense, my hands squeeze the grip of my energy blade and then I draw my arms back. Just one more step. The creature lowers its head to crash through me. Leaping to the side, I swing my energy blade around. The blue beam slides along the creature's shoulder, slicing next to its spiked shoulder pauldron. It screams in pain and topples to the ground, sliding a few paces on the loose stone. I hit the ground and roll, using my momentum to spring back to my feet in a singular motion. Pros: that worked, and I slightly injured the creature. Cons: now the monster is between me and the cave.

The creature is already up and rushing toward me, scythe arms drawn back, ready to slice. The blade-like claws shriek as they slice through the air, getting closer and closer. Something hits me, knocking me to the ground. My eyes close reflexively. There's a heavy weight on my chest, followed by a blunt pressure as Rowan pushes off me and stands to face the creature.

The speedy swing of its scythe hurls at his head. Rowan ducks below it and steps closer to the creature. That's brave. *Stssstchk.* An energy knife sticks into the creature's shoulder. I see Kane grabbing for another blade. The creature shrieks and turns back and forth. *Stsstchk . . . Stsstchk . . . Stsstchk, Stsstchk, Stsstchk*—a series of glowing-blue energy arrows pierce into the creature's back like needles in a pin cushion. Kali slides across my vision. She's attached her two energy hilts together, turning them into an energy bow. She twists the handles and then pulls back, a blue arrow appearing and then releasing. This one whistles past the mantis monster, missing its target. The creature dashes quickly toward her. Kali pulls her handles apart, and where she had been holding a bow, she now holds an energy katana in each hand.

Kali rushes the attacking creature and throws her momentum forward, sliding on her back under the creature's attack. Her blades slice at the creature's legs, cutting them and making the mantis monster stumble to the ground. Kane leaps onto the creature's back, stabbing it repeatedly while Lilly runs in my direction. The monstrous creature flails and slashes wildly, roaring into the air. Kali and Rowan move in perfect synchronization, striking and dodging around the creature in an elegant dance. Kane slides into the mix as well, although lacking the refinement of the Kali-Rowan duo.

The mantis monster collapses under the constant barrage from the three fighters. The blue light of Rowan's energy lance zigzags back and forth, swirling and dancing through the air before being buried inside the mantis monster's chest. The creature shrieks, voice fading as it collapses to the ground with a thud.

"I love it here." Kane puts his foot on the monster's back and pulls his blade free before jumping down to the ground.

Lilly practically crashes into me. "Jett, are you OK?"

I nod, still catching my breath. Rowan gives me a subtle approving look as if to say, "Well done, now let's head inside before more of these things show up." That's probably what he means anyway.

Once inside, the guards on each side push the stones together to seal the cave entrance. The stones leave a small gap just wide enough for the guards to squeeze through. Then, smaller rocks are stacked up in the gap to seal the entry. It's crude, but it's better than nothing. The lights in the entrance are carried down into the main room below.

Before I can even make it down the path, Becka grabs me and hugs me tight enough to make my shoulders ache. "You had me so worried."

A hand slaps my shoulder as Kane passes by. "What a fantastic way to end a day."

Lilly shoves Kane, nearly causing him to topple over.

"One of my men was cut in half by that thing; maybe not a good time to laugh about it."

"What *was that*?" I ask.

"The Triblings call them skylari," Kali answers, walking up behind me. "It means death from above."

I shake my head, starting to process what just happened.

"Skylari are ambush hunters. Lucky it didn't get you when it first attacked. Luckier that this one was alone."

"Shinshew, are they not normally?"

"It depends. They tend to be solitary, but it's not uncommon for them to group together and travel as a swarm. Sometimes they even form hives, have a queen, and stay together. That's when you're really heaped."

"Swarms? Of those things? How do you survive that?"

"Find a good hiding spot. Or water—they hate water—and fire."

At what point does this place run out of horrors?

We descend into the large cavern below where a few groups of Raiders are standing around talking. Apparently, encountering a skylaris causes quite the stir. I recognize one of the groups as the squad that Vesta sent to bed without supper. Seeing us walk into view, the group approaches, blocking out the entrance into the main hall.

"You see what happens when you let the Bealzless fiends in?" The man makes sure to speak loud enough to attract an audience. His goons nudge him on with affirming support.

"Walk away, Walter," Lilly warns.

"Walk away? You can't be serious, boss! A Raider is dead!"

"I know. I was there. Where were you?"

Walter shifts, her question threatening his resolve. "This is a sign! We are being punished by Bealz."

"Are you seriously blaming Rowan? He's the one who killed the thing," I protest.

"The Sacred Texts teach us not to associate with the corrupted heathens, or the wrath of Bealz will fall on us. We need to get rid of him before more of us die."

"I know you're shaken up, Walter, but this is not—" Lilly's voice is calm but firm as she tries to de-escalate the man.

Instead, his voice rises. "How many Skylari attacks have there been before today?"

"None," one of his goons answers.

"And how many Raiders were killed by monsters before today?"

"None," the group now answers collectively as more Raiders gather around. This could get ugly.

Kali's weapons are in her hands as she steps forward.

Lilly extends her hand, cutting Kali off. "OK, let me make sure I understand you. A Raider was killed by a monster. You're suggesting that's not just tragic; it's also a punishment from Bealz for our allowing Rowan into our camp. Is that right?"

"Yes, boss." Walter nods excitedly as if having won a great debate.

"When your brother was killed by a bandit, was that Bealz's wrath as well? Rowan wasn't around then."

The smile fades from Walter's face as he considers Lilly's question. The crowd that had been cheering in support of Walter goes quiet. "No . . ."

"When your cousin got attacked by a drukani and died later from his wounds, was that Bealz's wrath? When you were exiled from Dios? When your friend was killed by the Patriarch? Was that all Bealz's wrath? Rowan wasn't there for any of that. I understand you're hurting. You're afraid. I am too. I don't want to see any one of you die. But we cannot let fear overwhelm our reason. We can't blame someone because something bad happened."

Walter's gaze drifts down; he almost whispers, "I'm sorry, boss."

"Not to me, to Rowan," Lilly corrects.

Walter turns to face Rowan. "I'm sorry."

"Get some sleep, Walter. That goes for the rest of you as well. One of our Raiders is dead; we should be focused on remembering him, not quarrelling with each other."

The sleeping room was quite large. The cavern walls were lined with beds stacked three high to save floor space. Additional beds were set in a series of columns in the middle of the room, leaving ample space for people to move about. One of Lilly's Raiders, a man with light brown hair and an asymmetrical smile, leads us to a couple of unclaimed beds. We thank him and climb onto the beds.

"It's exciting to meet you. Lilly told us all about you. Never thought I'd meet you face to face. I'm looking forward to spending more time with you." He flashes his uneven grin. His eagerness and enthusiasm almost remind me of Telmen. Funny how something like that can make you feel a bond to a total stranger.

"We are leaving tomorrow," I reply.

"I know you are; I'm coming with you. Lilly said you needed extra hands, so I volunteered. I'm very excited." That last bit was self-evident.

"Well, good to meet you." I try to politely wrap up our chat so I can rest.

"And you! Oh, I'm Kyle by the way." It takes a few minutes of small talk and several forced yawns before Kyle takes the hint and lets us go to sleep.

I close my eyes. My dreams are haunted by my final moments with Victor, playing on repeat. Each time, I try to make sense of his parting words: "I'm sorry," he whispered. What did he mean by that? Sorry for betraying us? Sorry for how things turned out? Sorry we were going to be exiled because of him? What exactly was he sorry for? I can't shake the feeling that I'm missing something. Victor has this way of making you think he's doing one thing when he's doing something else entirely. Is my anger at his betrayal blinding me, or am I just trying to wishfully convince myself that my friend isn't the monster he seems to be? I wake feeling like I'd run a marathon in my sleep.

Getting ready is pure chaos. Eating, gathering supplies, meeting with Lilly's Raiders, saying goodbye, and heading out. It's a storm of activity that leaves me feeling like I'm forgetting something important. As we set out, Kali and Rowan take the lead. The Raiders follow close behind.

Kyle falls back, walking next to me with a big dopey grin on his face. "I am so excited to be traveling with you: the leader of the Nightlings, the leader of the Market Rebellion, and . . . ," he says, looking at Becka, ". . . and one of the other people involved."

That was a painful attempt at inclusion.

"Kyle, you better watch—" I start.

"No, it's OK. I'm sure Kyle knows the only important people in a rebellion are the ones the Patriarch puts on the broadcasts. Couldn't be anyone else involved."

Kyle gulps. "I didn't mean any offense. I just . . . didn't know what to call you," Kyle fumbles.

"Can we help you, Kyle?" Becka's annoyance oozes from each word.

"No, I'm just excited and a little nervous. Are you nervous? You probably don't get nervous." Now he's really reminding me of Telmen.

"Why would we be nervous?" Kane growls.

"Well, we are going to be traveling at night. What if we come across," his voice gets low and he whispers, "the depraved?"

Kane chuckles and puts his hand on Kyle's shoulder, squeezing tightly. Kyle winces and tries to squirm out of the grip, but Kane doesn't let it go. "You know what they say; death rarely comes quickly with the depraved."

Kyle squirms more, still unable to get out of Kane's grip.

"Don't toy with him, Kane," I scold.

"Fine. I wouldn't worry about it, boy. It's hard to come across things that don't exist."

"You don't believe in them? I hear rumors all the time. There are packs that travel in this area," Kyle protests.

"Rumors? I'll believe it when I see it," Kane snipes back.

"You should hope we don't," Becka replies.

"Oh, don't tell me you buy that old tod tale too?" Kane scoffs before starting to sing:

> "Eyes black as night.
> Teeth filed sharp.
> Quiet boys and girls,
> Or they'll eat your heart.
> Mommy cries, daddy cries,
> Everybody screams.
> You'll still be alive,
> As they tear you from your seams.
> When you hear them coming,
> Hide inside your homes.
> Rattle, crack, rattle, crack,
> They even eat your bones."

I recognize the tune. We all do. Every kid in Dios sang that song. The grim lyrics sit in stark contrast to the cheery melody and tone. Unnerving by design. I wish Kali hadn't told me about them. I wish I could dismiss them as easily as Kane does. Just the possibility that what Kali told me is true adds a subtle terror to the journey. I've never, in the entire time I've known him, wanted Kane to be right so badly. I know deep in my core he isn't.

Kali shouts at us and picks up the pace. We are practically jogging.

"She's a bit impatient," Becka comments.

"She's a bat out of Sheol. Do you always travel like this?" Kyle marches up on my other side.

"She's on mission." Kane adjusts his pack as we walk. At this point Kali and Rowan are far enough ahead that we'd have to shout for them to hear us.

"We're all on a mission. Isn't that why we are going to Dragonvale?" Kyle asks.

"That's our mission," I explain. "Kali has another goal."

"What is it? Lilly has told us so much about you guys, I feel like I already know you, but what's her deal?"

"Hard to say, Kyle. She's not exactly forthcoming with personal information."

"That's weird. You think she's hiding something?"

"Why all the questions?" Kane interrupts.

Kyle laughs and rubs his hand through his hair, face painted with a dopey expression. "Ever since I was a kid, I dreamed of adventure. Hearing the stories of other people's adventures—it's like an escape from my ordinary, boring life. Craziest thing that ever happened to me was getting exiled."

"Why were you exiled?" I ask.

"You know, I don't really know. Last year, during the Middling Days, an Assessor tested me. I have no idea what I did wrong. He just said I failed. They took me away. Next thing I knew I was being called an Outlands Officer and sent out here." Kyle laughs as if it was nothing more than a hilarious misunderstanding.

What a strange man.

Our pace doesn't let up for most of the day. By evening, my muscles are cramping and burning. My body is so exhausted that the rock I sit on when we finally stop to rest feels like a silk pillow slowly engulfing me. We eat in relative silence, sitting around a small fire Rowan built in the middle of the canyon. A few feet up the rock wall is an opening that leads to a hollow large enough for us to sleep in while also keeping us out of view of the canyon below. It isn't totally secure, but it is the best we could hope for in these conditions. It doesn't look comfortable, but at least it's a break from our long march of doom. Our little band chats pleasantly, exchanging stories for a bit. The Raiders complain about the unnecessary pace we are traveling at.

"Why are we in such a hurry?" Kyle asks.

"The less time we can spend out here in the wild, the better." Kali's stares down the canyon pass intently.

"Are we going to travel so quickly tommor—" Kyle starts.

Rowan holds up his hand, and we all go quiet. Spinning around, Rowan waves us toward the rock wall, his face grim. I've never seen him look grim. Even while fighting the skylaris, he was stoic.

"Into the hollow—quickly. Quietly." Kali whispers through gritted teeth. Her quiet words carry the intensity of a scream. Rowan rushes to the fire, stomping at it. Three of the Raiders move to the wall and start climbing up into the hollow and out of sight.

"What? Why? W—" Kyle asks.

Kali grabs him by his shirt, lifts him up, and pushes him toward the wall. Becka and Kane climb in next. That's when I hear the voices on the air, faint but growing louder. *Someone is coming.* From the sound of it, a sizable group. Rowan's expression still strikes me as odd. It isn't earnestness I see in his eyes—it's fear. Like a canary on a ship, he senses something I don't see. Rowan is still kicking out the flames as the last of our crew climbs out of sight. Rowan and I are the last two. I grab his arm and pull him toward the wall as the voices get louder, echoing around us.

"Leave it," I whisper aggressively. Putting out the fire will do no good if they see us climbing into the hollow. At least in the hollow we have a chance of avoiding detection. The gap in the rocks was big enough to crawl through with a little maneuvering. I climb up and Rowan follows, sliding next to me as we pack into the tight space like sardines.

Lying on our stomachs in silence, we wait. Light peeks in through the opening below us, giving me a view of the ground below. I can't see much, just a thin strip near the base of the rock wall we are tucked in. It's like peering through the crack under a door. The dusk-induced darkness gives us just enough shadow to feel safely out of sight. I can hear one of the Raider's hearts pounding violently in his chest. The surge of adrenaline courses through me. It's as familiar as seeing an old friend. Almost getting caught comes with the territory as a thief.

"What do we have here?" comes a voice from below. I can see boots walk over to the embers of our fire, followed by shadows and movement. From the voices and overall volume of the discussion, I guess there are at least twenty people in this party.

"Someone was here not too long ago," a second man speaks.

"Fan out boys; we've got company. King Morton will want to meet them."

Great. Marauders.

The crunching and stomping of boots on the ground resounds. I can see flashes of movement. Our position is well hidden at first glance, but even in the low light, if they look in the right spot, we're heaped. I ready my energy blade; in the event they do find us, I'm going to be ready.

Two Marauders lean against the rock wall underneath us, making my heart race even faster.

"You got more doltine?" one asks.

"What happened to the last bottle I gave you?"

"I drank it," the man sniffs loudly.

"This stuff isn't cheap."

"Come on, man, you know how stressful things are back at the camp ever since they brought those new recruits. I'm not sleeping. I just need a little bit to take the edge off."

I hear the distinct sound of metal bottles clanging together.

"Fine, but this is the last time. You want more, you got to pay."

"Yeah, whatever you say; give it to me."

Well, at least they aren't taking the search seriously. I hear the Marauder twist off the top of his bottle and the loud gulping sound of him chugging something from it. I start to relax. The only thing these two are searching for is escape.

A crackling, rattling noise echoes through the canyon. It's a strange sort of off-putting sound. The Marauders stop moving to listen. I feel Rowan turn, sliding from his stomach to his back. His eyes are wide, legs pulled up to his chest, hugging himself in an upside down fetal position. The impact of seeing so fierce a warrior looking so fragile chills me to my bones. Horror grips my entire being, and I don't have the slightest idea why. Imagination is the scariest monster of all.

"What's his deal?" Kyle whispers.

Kali's eyes are raging flames as she turns and grabs his collar. "You say another word, we all die."

Kyle opens his mouth to protest but thinks better of it. Rowan charged a skylaris, was unphased by aestroths, and terrified armed guards. What could cause him to react like this? The rattling, crackling noises grew more pronounced; whatever it is, it is getting closer.

"What's that?" one of the Marauders asks.

"Get ready; something is coming," another shouts.

Dread in its purest form is something I've never experienced before. Not in our fight for the Market, not when being captured by Commander Stone, not even trying to fight an endless army of Patriarch soldiers. I've been afraid before, but this dread is new. My imagination kicks into overdrive. Thoughts flow through my head at the speed of light. Kali looks panicked as well. What could this be? A single skylaris didn't bother Rowan or Kali. They looked like they were having fun taking it down. Maybe this is a swarm? Or one of the other creatures Kali mentioned? The Outlands contains a seemingly unending list of terrors. This one feels different. My heart pounds. My breathing is labored. I glance around; everyone else seems to feel the same way.

I make eye contact with Kali and mouth, "What is it?" I'm not actually sure I want to know the answer. An idea flashes in my head that makes my blood run cold. *Please, don't let it be that.*

CHAPTER ELEVEN

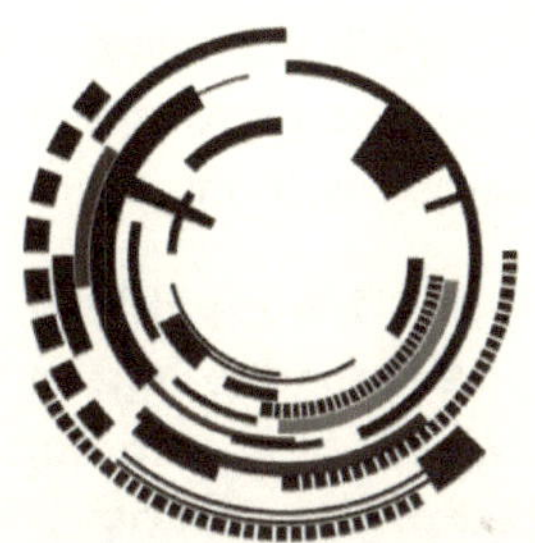

Kali doesn't respond. She doesn't need to. My skin crawls as if I were laying on an invisible anthill. Fear and imagination should never overlap. The results are unpleasant. *Torture you. Kill you. Skin you. Eat you.*

Creaaaacgnn. The strange noise echoes around us. Eleven people are crammed into a tight hollow, practically laying on top of each other, too nervous to even breathe.

"Oh, Bealz, no! It's—" the man's voice falters as fear overtakes him.

"Depraved!" shouts another. We inhale in unison, trying to keep from reacting to the word. Bursts of light fill the valley as they fire into the distance. The creaking keeps coming. The rattling growing faster and closer.

"Stay back! Stay back!"

"Euaaahhhhhh!" The first cry of pain erupts. I hear a thud. More screams. Begging. Groaning. The screams are so loud I cover my ears.

Rrraaaaack! The noises grow more and more unsettling. A strange scent like rotting cabbage with garlic wafts into the air. It's so strong it makes my eyes water. In a few passing moments, the gunfire goes from rapid to faint. The chatter between Marauders is gone. The screams fade, leaving behind a cacophony of other more disturbing noises.

Knnnnntttcccchhct. Biting. *Ssshllluuuchhh.* Tearing. *Hrarchh.* Chomping. *Obmmtch.* Chewing. *Tkcht.* Snapping. Gnawing. Grinding. Ripping.

Oozing. All of it loud enough to assault my ears even through my hand barriers. My stomach turns and threatens to expel all of its contents. My eyes close so tight it makes my head hurt. I try to think of something else, but the reality of what's happening a few feet from us is an immovable object in my mind. I can hear the Marauders, still groaning, pleading for an end. I wouldn't wish this on my worst enemy.

Craaaarrrrrrrr. The light fades. The audible horror continues. My body shivers so hard it hurts. Each sound brings a vivid visceral image to mind. I see them cutting away, eating, ripping like hungry scavengers tearing at a carcass—except the carcass is a person . . . and the carcass is alive. If this is what the Patriarch had in mind when they made us believe the Outlands was worse than death, they may have undersold it.

It feels like time is being stretched. Each moment seeping rather than flowing along. Rowan is not the only one shaking now.

Then, silence.

Why did they stop? Have they seen us? Heard us? Fear lassos my heart and drags me into a pit of despair. The group of Marauders fell in seconds. We are trapped in a tightly packed hollow. What hope do we have?

A rattling, grinding noise, like a chain made of bone being shaken, pierces the air. Carnal, guttural, wild groans echo, followed by dragging, scraping sounds. The onslaught of noise grows fainter, moving off into the distance. They are leaving.

For the first time in what feels like a day I take a full breath. I roll onto my back and look up at the rock ceiling above us. No one says a word for the rest of the night. No one sleeps. No one moves.

The sun rises the next morning, shining its bright light on the canyon pass. Rowan, who seems to have recovered his nerves, slides down to the ground to ensure the path is clear. A few minutes later, he waves us out. I expect to see mutilated bodies left partially eaten strewn across the pass. When I slide down to the ground below, all that remains are some discarded weapons, a few tattered pieces of fabric, and several long, thick trails of blood that disappear in the direction we came from. Somehow the lack of visible carnage seems worse. What possible reason could they have for taking the bodies? I love when my brain fixates on questions I really don't want answered.

"Bealz, protect us," Becka mutters under her breath.

Even having heard Kali's description, I had my doubts. After what we heard last night, I don't know that I'll ever be the same. A realization smacks me in the temple; Rowan didn't just hear those things. He saw them. Not just for a night; he saw them for days. He was alone as a child, and he had to face that. A sudden, strange desire to hug him washes over me. I resist the urge. We used to tell stories about the depraved to freak each other out. We laughed and joked about them. They weren't real. Or so we thought. With most things in life, imagination exceeds reality. Reality, in this isolated instance, was far worse.

Rowan leans his head against the rock wall of the mountain pass. Kali puts her hand on his shoulder and holds it there. The two stand in silence for a moment. Eventually Kali removes her hand and gives Rowan some space.

"I can't believe they are actually real. Those sounds came from people?" Kane almost seems scared.

"That is what happens to a person driven beyond madness. There is darkness inside all of us. For most it is small, hidden, easily contained, so it rarely—if ever—rears its head. There's only so much death you can witness before that darkness takes over, before it consumes any humanity you have left. For some, the only way to cope with the monster is to become the monster." Kali's words come slowly as if she's pushing them one at a time by force of will.

"Don't you go telling me that anyone can turn into that," Kane barks back.

"The only way to survive them is to become them," Kali counters.

"What does that mean?" I ask reluctantly.

"The depraved are relentless. If you run, they chase. If you fight, they break you apart piece by piece. Death is their religion. They don't rush it; they savor it. They don't just want to kill; they want to convert. They never kill everyone. They make some watch. Sometimes someone snaps and joins in. Either you die, or you become an agent of death. I'm not sure which is worse."

"Bealz above," Becka says, holding her stomach as if about to vomit.

"They seem like monsters. They are more like a cult—a cult that worships death. They are happy to recruit any who would join them. All you have to do is willfully sacrifice every ounce of humanity you have," Kali adds, staring blankly in the distance.

"How many of them are there?" Becka asks.

Kali shrugs. "No one knows for sure. There's a territory east of here no one enters; we call it the Depraved lands, as it belongs to them. As the stories go, the depraved have been around since the Great Collapse."

"Are they common in this area?" Kyle asks.

"Not typically. We can discuss it more, but it's best we don't linger."

We return to our rapid marching pace, heading in the same direction the depraved came from. Everyone is either too tired or too shaken up to speak. When we stop for lunch, Kali informs us that if we keep it up, we could make it to Dragonvale by nightfall. That's why she's been pushing so fast—to shave a day off our journey. Motivated by the vision of sleeping in a town, we keep pace with her. Sure enough, as the sun is setting, we exit the canyon and can see a large town on the horizon. We should be able to make it before dark. I'd much rather sleep safely in a bed than have to find another rock hole to hide in.

Ahead of us, I see the silhouettes of a group of people moving toward the town. I get the sense that they are coming from the same direction we are. Knowing the Patriarch has a strike force roaming around makes me suspicious. I put the thought out of my mind as we escalate from jogging to sprinting. To our right, and floating well overhead, I see the glowing luminesce of a small swarm of aestroths. Seeing the liquid light dancing so whimsically, I almost forget how dangerous they are. From a safe distance, they are beautiful. Watching them as we make our way toward the gates soothes some of the fear inside me. Good news is, we reached Dragonvale a day ahead of schedule.

The sun sets on the horizon just as we reach the town gates. Dragonvale is much larger than Red Clay. Surrounding the town is a large stone wall, fifty feet high. Walking the ramparts are guards with energy rifles. Towers are stationed regularly and evenly along the walls. On the tops of the towers are thick, black rods.

Sttiisssssts. The rods activate and the pale green light of a force shield connects between them and down in front of the stone walls. It's similar in design to the shield around Dios; it's just missing the arching canopy to fully enclose it. The perimeter is tall enough that it's hard to imagine much getting over it. We're not even through the gates, and I'm already impressed.

"Who goes there?" One of the guards on the wall shouts. I glance up to see a dozen rifles trained on us. Little, green lasers dance over my chest as they line up their shots. Hospitality at its finest. Rowan pulls his hood over his face and keeps his head down as if trying not to be noticed.

"We are a group of—" Kyle responds.

"I can see you're a group. State your business," the voice shouts impatiently.

"We are, uh, here to rest and, uh, gather supplies," Kyle's voice waivers.

"State your affiliations," returns the commanding voice.

"Af . . . affiliations?" Kyle repeats in the form of a question.

"Dragonvale Code 116: any person or persons entering the town must declare any affiliations or other known associations prior to entry. Dragonvale has a no-tolerance policy for hostility between Marauder tribes, bandits, or any other group without proper permits. We are under the protection of High King Lancer Ashuri, and any violation of the Peace Accords will result in termination of all parties involved with extreme and unwavering prejudice." He must have recited this speech a thousand times as it comes out almost mechanical.

"We are part of Lilly's—" Kyle starts.

Kali smacks him in the chest. "We are here from Red Clay as emissaries. We've come to trade and be on our way."

"Kali? Is that you?" comes another voice; this one female. The laser sights drift down and disappear.

Well, that's comforting.

"Gina?"

"You vomitous mass! You still owe me credits."

A grin forms on Kali's face. "Well, I can't pay you from down here, now, can I?"

There's a click followed by a *Sttiissssssts*. The green glow in front of the gate—and only in front of the gate—vanishes. A moment later, the gate lifts up into an unseen compartment, allowing us passage. Once inside, the gate and shield close.

Where Red Clay felt like a rural village made with wooden buildings and dirt streets, Dragonvale reminds me of a castle from The World That Was. The streets are paved with flat, gray brick lined with the faintest white seams between them. Elevated sidewalks connect to wide stone streets adorned with tall lumelamps. Shops, taverns, and various buildings frame either side of the streets. Dragonvale is a large circle. The stone walls curve and stretch out in either direction. Apparently, the shield walls provide enough safety that people here do not practice a Dusk Descension.

"This place is incredible!" I could see myself living here.

My attention is drawn from the sprawling town to the source of raucous chanting. Walking along the outer street just in front of where we are standing, I see twenty people in thick, bright red robes walking side by side in two neat columns. Their hoods are pulled up, cloaking their faces. Around their necks are gawdy gold necklaces with the top half of a circle. As they get closer, their words become clear: "Praise the Eye, praise the Father, praise the Holy Dome." They repeat this again and again. The group passes by us, continuing on their path unphased and uninterested in our presence.

"What's that about?" Becka asks.

Kali shivers. "The Children of the Dome have a compound here. Best to avoid them if at all possible."

"Why?" Becka questions.

"They are a fundamentalist cult with a fanatic devotion to their sacred purpose. They are as dangerous as it gets," Kali explains.

"Being passionate about what you believe doesn't make you dangerous," Becka snaps, her tone defensive.

"Oh, so you're OK with locking children in a closet for weeks at a time without food to try to make them have visions?"

Becka's mouth drops open.

"Or kidnapping people, forcing them to convert, and holding their families as hostage to ensure their unwavering devotion?"

"Bealz above, they do that?"

"And more," Kali answers.

"How can they justify that?" Becka's clearly struggling with the idea. Becka has a complicated history with belief. She grew up in the Temple Sector, learning all about the teachings of the Patriarch. While her connection to Bealz has never wavered, the things people do in His name often drive her crazy.

"In Dios, the High Father is obeyed and feared right?" Kali asks.

"Right."

"The Children of the Dome don't just fear him, they worship him. They see the High Father and the Dome itself not just as gifts from Bealz that should be honored but as if they were extensions of Bealz Himself. They believe if they can win converts and get them to follow their rules, they will save that person for eternity. It really doesn't matter what they have to do to a person because, compared to eternity, it's worth it."

"That is not what the Sacred Texts teach. The deliverance of Bealz isn't something to be earned. They are twisting the message," Becka protests.

"Maybe, but that's what the Children of the Dome believe. Their beliefs drive them to try and force everyone to convert before the 'Chosen One' is revealed."

"The 'Chosen One'?"

"Yeah, some mysterious person connected to the High Father who will change the world." The notes of disdain in Kali's voice are unmistakable.

"Avoid the loopers. Got it," I interrupt. I love Becka, but I'm too tired to listen to her spiral into this debate.

"Dragonvale can be a rough place, but it is the only place you can get the supplies we need."

"Can I suggest we find a place to sleep first?" I ask. "I think we're all pretty zeroed after last night."

Becka closes her mouth and nods. To her credit, no one takes a hint like Becka.

Kali nods and leads us through town, down one of the main streets to an inn. Kali leads us inside. The front doors open up to a wide lobby with a desk in the middle and a closed-off office space behind it. On either side of the desk are well-lit staircases leading down. I guess they still try to sleep underground. We get two rooms, each holding six beds.

"I've never been to Dragonvale before. This is quite the adventure," Kyle says.

"After last night, seeing a new city is what stands out to you?" I ask.

Kyle just shrugs. Now that I think about it, his excitement is a welcome distraction.

"Why did you want to come with us, Kyle?" Becka asks.

"I signed up with Lilly's Raiders because I wanted to be a hero. I wanted to make a difference. Lilly would tell us stories about you; I was so inspired. I wanted to be like Jett Lasting: leader of the Market Rebellion." Kyle strikes a pose.

"I guess Lilly didn't tell you the story of how bad we lost." I try not to sound annoyed, but acting like what happened was something to celebrate or honor doesn't sit right with me.

Kyle drops his pose and sulks like a scolded puppy. "I'm sorry, I didn't mean to offend. I just—I'm excited to be part of something. To do something that really matters, you know?"

"It's fine; you just reminded me of something a friend once told me."

"What's that?" Kyle voice jumps two octaves.

"War seems glorious from a distance but only to those who don't get too close to it." I recite one of the many Victor quotes that never leave my mind. Trying to get him out of my head, I look around. I see Rowan is already in his bed asleep.

"Kyle, if you wake me up with your incessant talking, I'm going to cut you with a dull, rusty blade, you understand?" Kane glares at him.

Kyle gulps and nods before climbing into his bed and staring straight up at the ceiling, stiff as a board.

The next morning, we gather for breakfast in a room at the back of the inn. An assortment of breads, fruits, and other items are placed on a counter in the back of the room. A long, thin table is set in the center of the room, surrounded by cushioned chairs.

Becka looks across the table at Kali. "What's the plan for today?"

"Don't have one for you. I will meet my suppliers. Until that's sorted out, there's not much you can do. Feel free to explore, rest, keep Rowan company—do whatever you like. Let's meet back here tonight and go over the next steps then."

"What do you mean keep Rowan company?" Becka's eyes narrow.

"It's not a good idea for him to leave the inn," Kali answers.

"Why?"

"The more he's out, the more likely someone notices him."

"Notices him? What do you mean?" Kyle asks.

"He's a Tribling," Kali says.

"Oh, right, he's a Tribling . . . but why does that matter?" Kyle counters.

"Kyle, some people form nasty prejudices against others based on nothing but their own ignorance. While we know Rowan is a wonderful, beautiful person, others see him as less than such simply because of where he comes from," Becka explains.

"Really? Why would people dislike Triblings?"

"Several reasons. For those who have faith in what the Order teaches, the existence of Triblings is considered an offense against the Sacred Text of Bealz. After all, the High Father himself declares that life in the Outlands is unsustainable. Therefore, anything that survives must be unnatural. Some consider Triblings abominations. Those who hold extreme views, like The Children of the Dome, believe killing Triblings is a service to the Holy Dome and is the will of Bealz—another good reason to avoid them." Kali makes no effort to hide the disgust in her voice as she talks.

"What's the other reason?" I ask.

"Many years ago, Outlands officers started moving east and building settlements beyond Kal Var. Before long, the settlements would go dark. Scouts would investigate to find the towns had been wiped out, and all the people were gone. They assumed it must have been the Triblings. When in doubt, blame the Bealzless savages who helped survive in the first place."

"They never bothered to get any proof?" I ask in disbelief.

"Who needs proof? The Triblings worship false gods; they must be up to all sorts of evils. Anytime something goes wrong in a settlement, the first thought is that the savage Triblings must be behind it."

"Based on what?" I press.

"Fear of the unknown mostly. Proximity builds harmony while distance breeds distrust. Even though the Triblings helped the first Outlands officers get established and build settlements, they were never invited to live among the exiles. When the exiles needed less help, they started getting focused on differences in Tribling customs. It's a cycle really. The Patriarch punishes people for being different. The exiles who were punished for being different turn around and punish the Triblings for being different. Funny how people so often become the very thing they hate."

Her words ring oddly true. "Did they ever find out what really happened to the settlements?" Becka asks.

"They did. Today, the lands to east are known as the Depraved lands. Yet, the Outlanders continue to blame the Triblings despite knowing they had nothing to do with it," Kali explains.

Becka seems shocked. I don't see why. It doesn't sound that different from how the Patriarch views Undesirables.

"It's easier to perpetuate the wrongs of the past than it is to admit they were wrongs in the first place," I add.

Becka puts her hand on Rowan's shoulder and rubs his arm softly. "I'm so sorry, Rowan. No one should have to feel that way."

Rowan smiles softly, offering her a subtle nod of appreciation. At least, I think it's appreciation.

We finish breakfast and leisurely make our way out of the Inn. The streets are a flurry of activity as people dash around in every direction. Even the way people walk outside of Dios is different. In Dios everyone marched as if they were soldiers, trying to avoid standing out in any way. Here, the variety of motion, the pace—everyone moves differently. Some people are swinging their arms, others practically skipping as they walk. It's unusual.

Kali and I are the first to head outside.

"I'm excited to look around—see what Dragonvale has to offer."

Kali hands me a thick plastic card. "Do not steal anything. The penalty for stealing in Dragonvale is immediate beheading, so go ahead, make your jokes."

I cough. "That's a bit extreme, isn't it?"

"It's effective. Harsher penalties tend to reduce crime. It'd be a shame to ruin that face of yours," Kali smirks and then looks away before rushing off without looking back.

That was odd.

Something bumps into my shoulder just enough to make me adjust my footing. I turn to see Becka walk up behind me.

"So that's why things with you and Lilly seem so weird." An accusing smile stretches across her face.

"What are you talking about?"

Becka pushes me. "Oh, just think! Not that long ago you couldn't even talk to the girl you liked. Now you've got two interested in you."

"Is your progress bar stalling? There's nothing between—"

"Who are you trying to fool, Jett? I see the way you look at her, those glances you exchange. That little smile you try to hide whenever she talks to you."

"You've crashed; Kali can hardly stand me," I protest.

"Is that so? She seemed pretty excited that you were coming."

For some reason, my face feels warm. "I don't know what you are talking about."

Becka gives me that confident smile she has whenever I play right into her hands. "Is that so? Then what are you doing here, Jett Lasting?"

"Getting explosives—that's why we are all here. Set a trap; rescue our friends. Any of this ringing a bell?"

"That's why Kali is here. You didn't have to come. When she asked if you were going with her or staying with Lilly, your eyes went to her first—then to Lilly."

I smush my face into the palms of my hands and lift my head up.

"Teasing aside, Jett, I don't want to get in the middle of whatever it is going on with you and Lilly. But if you start chasing after some other girl while Lilly's sitting around wondering where you stand, I'm going to throttle you, got it?"

I grumble, "Becka, that's not what's happening. I'm not sure how I feel about Lilly. Things have changed, but I don't want to overreact to that."

"Nothing wrong with being unsure, Jett. Just don't be one of those guys who plays games. Figure out what you want, then be decisive."

"Kali and I are not a thing. We're friends, sort of . . . I think."

Becka smiles. "Just remember, big sister's watching."

"Becka!"

"I've said my bit. Don't mess with my girl, and I won't have to bop you on your head. Let's have a look around. It'll be like the old days back in Dios. I want to hear everything that's happened since you were exiled."

We wander around, checking out various shops and exchanging stories of our Outlands adventures. While the shops here don't carry nearly as much tech as was readily available in Dios, the amount of contraband is extraordinary. In one of the shops, I find a bright pair of shoelaces, which I purchase while Becka is distracted and sneak into my pocket.

The shops are filled with all sorts of things we couldn't find in Dios. Most notably—books. There are so many books about The World That Was; the same books the Patriarch would arrest someone for owning. I wish I had time to scoop them up and read them all. Something about struggling to survive makes maintaining a reading habit feel impractical. Counters are adorned with snacks, portable aluma, Kathar Aera, and all sorts of other practical knickknacks.

"Wait here; I'll be right back," Becka instructs before stepping back into the shop we had just exited. I pace back and forth at the storefront, nodding to the occasional passerby. What's taking her so long? I turn at the corner of the building, only to crash into someone. I feel him catch my wrist as we bounce off each other.

"Sorry." Instinct kicks in, and I start scanning the man. His posture, his clothing, his hood pulled over his face—I've got nothing. That is very suspicious. It's like he's deliberately dressed to mask any identifying feature he may have.

"It was my fault—wasn't paying attention to where I was going," the man says. There's something about his voice. My suspicion goes up. Kali warned me about the dangers of thieving, but this is a classic move. Crashing into someone provides a perfectly innocent and excusable distraction that makes swiping their valuables rather easy. My hands move to my coat to inspect for missing items. Nothing is missing. I feel a weird lump in my pocket that wasn't there before. My brow furrows.

"Nice to see you again, friend. Be well."

Heap, I just got played. He must have known bumping into me like that would make me suspicious and used the distraction to slip past me without me noticing him. He's good. I spin around, trying to catch sight of him. Three people walking toward me block my view. He timed his move perfectly, using other people as a screen for escape. He's really good. I move between them as they pass, but the man has disappeared. *For the love of Bealz, what have I gotten into now?*

The bell over the shop door chimes and Becka emerges, holding a single book. She smiles brightly and stuffs it into the pack I have slung over my shoulder.

"Did you see a . . . ?" I start before realizing there's no way she could have.

Becka raises an eyebrow as my words drift off.

"Never mind; what's this?"

"A gift—I know how you love the history of The World That Was. The shopkeeper said this is the best work he's ever seen on it."

"Really? That's fantastic. Thank you!" I hug Becka tightly with my arms around her neck. The book is nice, but the moment she's created is far more meaningful. In the midst of this anxiety and tension, with the weight of our friends being imprisoned by murderous Marauders, this little gift creates a strange moment of levity and gives me a sense of peace. Typical Becka, always finding just the right thing to make me feel better.

"What's all this?" She pats my back and laughs.

"This world doesn't deserve you, Becka, but I'm glad you're in it."

She smiles, her cheeks reddening quickly. "OK, enough of that. We should go check on Kane—make sure he hasn't killed anyone."

We wander around the town, getting a feel for its layout. One of those lessons Victor ingrained in us: *The first thing you need to do in a new place is familiarize yourself with your environment. Know your surroundings.* Even if we aren't going to be here long, the proverbial shinshew can go cattywampus at any time. With our luck, it would be soon. It's always good to be prepared.

"This place is pretty nice. Maybe we should just stay here after we rescue everyone."

Becka looks around as if considering it. "That's an idea. Dragonvale does seem rather peaceful. We've only been here for a few days; we don't really know what this place is like yet."

"I found these." I reach in my pocket and pull out a brightly colored set of shoelaces.

Becka's eyes ignite as she grabs the shoelaces and inspects them, giggling happily. "OK, you're right. We should never leave this town."

"Maybe it's time to give those old laces a break. They did their time; let them rest in peace."

She shoulder-checks me. "Not on your life."

"I've always wondered what the deal is with those shoelaces anyway. It seems like you've had those laces on every pair of shoes you've owned for as long as I've known you. Becka, that's a long time for shoelaces."

Becka looks down at her shoes. Silence fills the air. Finally, she looks up at me. The smile on her face fails to mask the sadness in her eyes.

"My dad gave these to me. I saw them in a store when I was a kid and I begged him to let me have them. He said no. But then, a few weeks later, he surprised me with them. I had done really well on my Potter test, and he wanted to show me how proud he was."

"Wow, that's really cool; I don't know why I never thought to ask before."

"They are the last thing he gave me. Two weeks later I was expelled from Potter training, and my dad disowned me—said he wished he'd never had a daughter and that he never wanted to see me again."

"Heap me." I just stare blankly, not sure what else to say.

"The past is the past. No reason to let it dampen the present."

"Why do you keep them if they remind you of something sad?"

"They don't. They remind me of something happy. It's the last happy memory I have of my family; that just makes them extra meaningful."

"Nothing rains on your cheery nature, does it?"

She just shrugs and tucks the shoelaces into her bag.

"Seriously, though, this place seems great. There's no Patriarch, no Levites, no Red Caps, no Beggar Gangs, and no oppressive caste system telling us we are worthless human filth."

"But we don't know anything about the problems it does have," Becka replies.

"That's oddly pessimistic of you."

"Is it? I don't mean it to be. I guess I'm just a bit more cautious these days. I'm not sure I could just settle down here anyways. Dios feels unresolved to me. Does that make sense?"

"You can't just walk away. Despite how terrible it was, it was our home," I confirm as we round the corner.

I jump back, grabbing Becka's shirt and pulling her back with me. I press my back against the wall. She slides next to me. One of the benefits of spending so much time with someone is that you learn to communicate without words. Becka stays pressed against the wall while I peer around the corner. I motion for her to look, and she slides beside me.

Standing on the other side of the street is a group of men in all-black body armor, wearing helmets with glowing-red visors. Each has a large, high-tech rifle slung over his back. The majority of them are standing at attention, facing us while one paces back and forth in front of them issuing instructions.

"Are those the Patriarch soldiers we saw earlier?" Becka asks.

I shake my head. "There were only six before. This is a lot more."

"What are they doing here?"

"Let's get closer; maybe we can hear something."

"We really shouldn't," Becka protests.

"Come on, for the first time in our lives, Patriarch soldiers have no reason to be suspicious of us. We're just two random exiles wandering through a town of exiles. We will just walk by, act natural, and they'll never be the wiser."

I can feel Becka's resistance. I don't blame her. Everything we've ever done has been to avoid the Patriarch. This feels counterintuitive. One of the things that made Victor so good at planning is he was always well-informed. If we are going to survive out here, we need to know what we are up against and what our enemies are up to.

After a moment of hesitation and deliberation, Becka places her arm in mine and we cross the street, acting completely casual. There are plenty of other people moving around the soldiers; no reason for them to notice us. We turn and start walking toward the soldiers. This feels so weird. My brain is screaming at me to run the other way. Sheer force of will keeps us on course. As we approach, I can feel Becka's grip tightening against my arm.

"Remember, stun blasts only until you are sure. We cannot risk killing her," the pacing solider shouts at the others.

Lilly was right; they are looking for a woman.

"Squads two and three—you will be heading to Red Clay. We have an understanding with the village leader. All the women will be gathered in the Great Hall. You will enter, scan them, and if she is not among them, leave."

"Question, sir," one of the guards shouts out.

"Speak, soldier," the commander replies.

"How do we know all the women will be there? Couldn't he just be pretending to cooperate?"

"Excellent question. While Squad three is scanning the women in the Great Hall, Squad two will have the bio-tracker. If she is near Red Clay, the tracker will light up."

"If she's there, sir?"

"Well, then, you'll have to execute the entire village, won't you?"

The soldiers cheer.

Who cheers at the opportunity to kill a bunch of innocent people? As if I needed another reason to hate the Patriarch. Our slow pace won't allow us to hang around any longer. We could turn and make another pass, but that's risky. We reach the edge of the sidewalk and stop. This will buy us another moment or two.

A small rock slams against the wall of the building behind where the soldiers are standing, ricocheting off the stone. The soldiers erupt into action, rifles aimed and ready. Standing on the far side of the street, casually tossing a rock into the air and catching it as if he doesn't have fifty guns pointed at him, is a man wearing a long trench coat with a patch over his eye. I move back, trying to duck us into the alley. What is he doing here?

"Ah, ah, ah, gentlemen. Dragonvale's rules are quite clear about violence within the town walls. You shoot me, they kill all of you. Nobody finishes their mission." Morton Ghood smiles his warm smile and extends his arms out before rubbing a finger over his eyepatch.

CHAPTER TWELVE

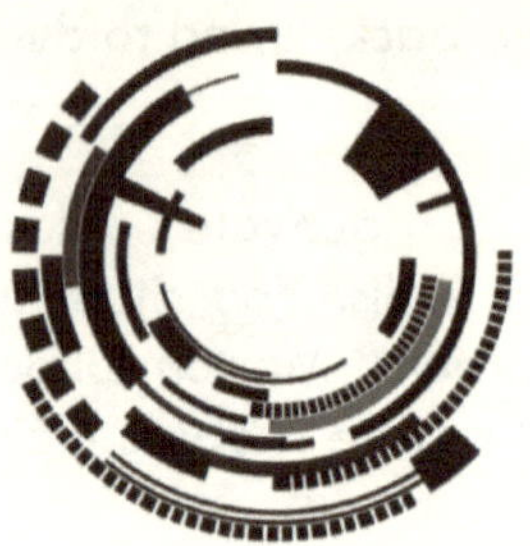

"What is the meaning of this?" the commander barks.

Morton smiles and holds a hand over his heart. "Thank you for asking. It means so much to me that you care. Here's the dilemma I'm facing; maybe you can help me with it. I couldn't help but overhear that your men were going to Red Clay and that you'd be tramping your filthy Patriarch boots in my town. Begging your pardon, but I can't be having that."

"Our business in Red Clay has nothing to do with you, Marauder scum!" The commander's voice drips with disdain.

"Now, now, that's just a hateful thing to say. You've gone and hurt my feelings." Morton puts one hand on his cheek and makes a pouty face. "But Sheol, I'll forgive you. That's just the kind of person I am. Let's get back to it. I know you're not really from around here, so you don't know how things work. Let me explain it to ya. Red Clay is mine. This whole territory is mine. I hate it when people mess with my stuff— makes me feel all kinds of angry. You know what I'm saying? You got business in Red Clay; you've got business with me. And I don't do business with a bunch of fascist scrap sinks."

Dragonvale's city guardsmen box in the street, surrounding Morton and the Patriarch soldiers, completing the powder keg.

The Vanguard commander walks over, standing in front of Morton. I hadn't realized how tall the commander was. "We are the Vanguard of Dios. We have a holy mission given to us by the High Father himself. You do not want to get in our way."

Morton grins. "Imma make you a deal right here. It goes against all my principles, but since I'm in such a good mood, here it is: you take your little men, you march back to your little city, and you never come back here again. And in return, I let you live."

"And when I say no?"

Morton reaches up and grabs the commander by the back of his head, pulling the taller man down against his own forehead. His words are quieter, and I can barely make them out. "I'll start by breaking your knees. Then, I'll take your hands—keep you from getting ideas about putting yourself out of your own misery. Then, I'll drive a hook through your shoulder and drag you into the depraved lands . . . and leave you there for them to play with."

The commander shouts, looking over his shoulder, "You've now threatened an officer of the Patriarch. Captain! Send a word to headquarters: the Marauders are now to be treated as hostile and shot on sight. Request additional forces to deal with his associates." He turns back to Morton. "I gave you a chance. Now your kind will be purged from the earth like the pox you are."

"I can't even believe my name will be in an official Patriarch memo. You've gone and made my day." Morton holds his hands over his heart and bats his eyes. "Ya'll know how to make a man feel special."

"Know this, scrap sink. Once your lifeless body is rotting in this Bealz-forsaken land, my men and I will take everything that's yours and burn it." The commander turns around to walk back to his men.

"Just one more thing." Morton grabs the commander by his head, jerking his own arm suddenly. A loud snap echoes, and the commander's limp body falls to the ground. "See, I'm really not supposed to do that," Morton shrugs.

The Vanguard soldiers raise their weapons. The city guardsmen do the same, shouting commences back and forth.

Morton holds up his hands. "I'll leave this to you, then. Have fun," he says to no one in particular and walks out of view.

"Why aren't the guards arresting him?" I whisper.

Becka doesn't respond. Morton just killed a Patriarch commander and walked away like it was nothing. He seems to hate them as much as we do. A civil war rages in my mind. My idealist self knows Morton needs to die. He's a monster. I made a deal with Kali. My pragmatic self can't help but wonder—if he's a monster who hates the Patriarch, could we not be fighting on the same side? His Marauders would be a great start in building an army. In our situation, we don't have the luxury of being picky with our allies.

Becka's tug on my arm snaps my mind back to attention. "Jett, we should get out of here." She's right. I'd rather not be around if the situation escalates. We head down the street, away from the soldiers. As we turn the corner Kane is casually leaning against the wall. That's suspicious. He has one foot kicked up on the wall and is using a small blade to clean dirt out from under his fingernails.

"You two come to watch the show?" Kane grins without looking up.

"How long have you been here?" I ask.

"Long enough. Should tell Kali that Morton is here. Probably the best chance she'll have at getting her revenge."

He's right. This is a great opportunity for Kali. Selfishly, I can't stop myself from thinking if she kills him now, it could interfere with our plan. I don't want to risk rescuing my friends, but can I really keep this from her? I'm too ashamed of my own thoughts to give them voice.

"You're right, we have to tell her." The reluctance in Becka's voice makes me think she's wrestling with the same thoughts as I am.

Kane pushes off the wall and stands up straight. "Come with me."

"Where are we going?" Becka challenges.

"I have someone you should meet."

"We've been here for less than a day," I protest.

Kane just smirks and starts walking. We follow him down the street, then turn into an alley and down a few jagged steps to an underground tavern. The door glows with a sign of a flask of frothy ale and the words: The Thirsty Traveler. Catchy. The tavern is dimly lit. Scattered booths and tables encircle a central bar. A thick haze wafts in the air. Kane leads us to the back where a man is seated in a corner booth surrounded by a half dozen empty pint glasses. Another glass is held firmly in his hand.

"These are your friends?" the man says, eyeing us slowly.

"They are," Kane answers.

"Kane, who is this, and why are we are talking to him?"

Kane slides into the booth and signals for a beer. "Jett, Becka; meet Raggy Brookton."

The man lifts his drink to us before downing the remaining amber liquid and lifting the empty glass above his head.

"And why are we talking to him?" I press.

Kane smiles and leans back on the booth as a server slides him a glass of ale. "Raggy here is a sort of expert on the Marauders."

"What does that mean?"

"He was the Marauder king in this territory before Morton ousted him."

Raggy turns his head and spits right onto the seat.

I guess we will remain standing.

"That shinshew stole everything from me. But my new friend says you're going after him."

"What if we are?" I shake my head at Kane disapprovingly. I don't particularly like that he's sharing that information with strangers.

Raggy smiles; his teeth are yellowed and rotting. "Well, then, I'd be happy to help."

"Exactly how would you help us?" Becka questions.

"Tell them what you told me," Kane instructs.

"You want to kill a king; you're going to have to deal with the Law of Retribution."

"The *what*?" I ask.

"The Law of Retribution." He leans toward Kane. "You said they was informed."

"Explain it to them," Kane nods.

"Fine, but I's wants another drink for the lesson."

Kane agrees.

"The Law of Retribution is part of our Code of Honor."

"Honor? I watched Morton murder a harmless old man, cut his head off, and kick him into a ditch like he was garbage. What honor?" I object.

"I didn't say the code was moral, did I? Now, if you're done interrupting me, first thing yous need to understand is the Outlands is divided into territories. Each territory is claimed by a tribe. The leader of each tribe is their king. Each tribe is self-sufficient and self-governed for the most part. We all answer to High King Ashuri. Nobody crosses him or defies his instructions. High King Ashuri is the one that sets our code, which is a set of principles all Marauders live by. It's our way of life. Do you know the code?"

"Vaguely; I've heard it referenced before," I answer.

"Never back down. Never let a slight go unanswered. Never show weakness. Never allow resistance. Never tolerate defiance. Take what you did not sow. Break what you did not build. Die with your weapon in your hand. This is our way."

"Anyone who follows this code can become a Marauder?" I ask.

"Nah, Marauders aren't just a creed. We are a breed. Being a Marauder—it's in the blood, it is. That's what Morton don't understand, see. He's a false king, taking people hostage and makin' cheap Marauder knockoffs. It ain't proper. It ain't right."

"Is there a point to this?" I make no effort to hide my annoyance.

"You want the point, here it is: the Law of Retribution states that if a Marauder king is killed, all Marauder tribes must unite in order to punish those responsible. So if yous go off and kill Morton, the Marauders will come like the plague and kill everyone."

Becka sits down and puts her head in her hands. "Everyone?"

"That right; women, children, it don't matter none. They will hunt down and kill anyone they find until they feel their honor is reclaimed."

"So if Morton dies?" I question.

"Hundreds, maybe thousands, of people die right along with him. Can't have people just killing Marauder kings, now, can we? What sort of message would that send?"

Message? What am I supposed to tell Kali? *I know we have a blood pact and all, but as it turns out, you can't kill the guy you're obsessed with killing. Sorry.*

"You is lucky. See, I know the ways around it. I know how you can kill Morton without getting everyone in the area dead as a result."

Hello, hope, my old friend.

"Well, then, please continue."

"The best way around the Law of Retribution is to send Morton to Roth Shalar."

"Roth Shalar?"

Raggy seems confused by my repetition but then nods and clarifies, "The field of fallen warriors."

I shake my head.

"If yous want to hear more about our beliefs, I needs more ale."

Kane whistles for another round.

"Lovely. Now, how a Marauder dies is important because it determines where he spends the afterlife."

"That's not right," Becka challenges.

"Wasn't asking ya, was I? You want to hear this or not?"

I put my hand on Becka's forearm to stop her from arguing further.

"There are three places of the dead: Roth Shalar, Roth Thrune, and Roth Despor. Roth Shalar is the warriors' paradise and where every Marauder longs to go. Only warriors who die in battle with their weapon in their hands can enter Roth Shalar. Marauders who maintain their honor in life but fail to die in glorious battle go to Roth Thrune. It's like an empty field." He shrugs, "It's nice enough, but boring. Lastly, there is Roth Despor. That is the place of shame. It is for cowards, traitors, and Marauders who have lost their honor."

Becka looks like she's about to burst, but she manages to keep her mouth shut.

"Being killed outside of battle—by an assassin, say—is a shameful death that would result in the person ending up in Roth Despor. Shaming a tribal king in such a way is considered a blight on Marauders everywhere. It is a shame that cannot go unpunished. So if a king is killed outside of combat, all the tribes gather to reclaim their lost honor. Only way to do that is to find and execute those responsible. Most of the time, the other kings come in, wipe out a town or two, and declare they found the culprits. Course, they don't really care about the dead king. They do it because whoever succeeds in restoring honor to the Marauders gets to take the territory of the dead king as their own—his land, army, resources, all of it. That's the Law of Retribution."

"Basically, if Morton is killed outside of battle, other Marauder tribes will come in and just start murdering everyone they find?" Becka asks.

"You've got it," Raggy confirms.

"You said 'there are ways' before; I assume that means there is more than one?" I suggest.

Raggy snaps his fingers and points at me. "Exactly. There are two ways a king can be killed without the Law of Retribution taking effect. First, if he dies in battle. Second, if he challenges someone to a duel and loses."

"When a king dies in those ways, what happens?" Becka asks.

Raggy empties an entire glass of ale in a single drink before slamming the mug down on the table and wiping the foam from his lip. "It depends."

"On?"

"How he dies. If the king is killed in battle, his second-in-command becomes the new king. Mixed bag where things go from there."

"What's the other way?" I press.

"If the king challenges someone to one-on-one combat and he's defeated, the person who defeated him becomes the new Marauder king. If someone defeats the Marauder king, that means they have the blessing of Gar Oath."

"Who is Gar Oath?" I ask.

"He is the Almighty Warrior, the king of the gods, and the Lord of Roth Shalar."

"There is only one God, Raggy. Bealz is His name," Becka says.

Raggy shrugs and reaches for a fresh pint of ale. How he's still sitting upright at this point, I don't know.

"I'm not interested in converting, girl, but thanks."

"If someone defeats a Marauder king in one-on-one combat, they become the new king? No Law of Retribution?" I try to keep things on track.

"Ya, the dead king is honored because he died in battle. No shame brought on the Marauder name, therefore, no Retribution required. Trouble with that option is, you can't just challenge the king. He has to challenge you," Raggy explains.

"All Kali has to do is get him to challenge her, and she can get her revenge," Kane smiles, taking a large draw from his glass.

"Her?" Raggy looks over. "You never said nothing about no 'her.'"

"Why does that matter?" Becka asks.

Raggy shakes his head. "There's no honor in challenging a woman. No self-respecting Marauder would do it. Women are too weak."

"You've not met Kali," I counter.

"Doesn't matter. No king would ever challenge a woman; it would bring shame upon him. Even if he did, being defeated by a woman would bring greater shame to the Marauders than him being assassinated. If a woman kills him, the Law of Retribution still applies."

Kane's head sinks as he leans forward in his seat.

"Raggy, I need you to be very clear and very specific here. The only two ways of getting rid of Morton without enacting the Law of Retribution are if he is killed in combat or if he is defeated in a duel against a man that he challenges, correct?"

"Didn't I just finish saying that?"

"I have a question." Becka smiles sweetly with her lips, while glaring at Raggy with her eyes.

Raggy glances at her. "Well?"

"How are you still alive?"

"What?" he grumbles in annoyance.

"You were a Marauder king, right?" she asks.

Becka, you clever girl.

Raggy nods his head and sits back like a peacock strutting. "Yes, I was."

"So how, then, are you still alive?"

"Why yous keep asking me that?"

Sharp as a marble, this one.

"You told us there were two ways to get rid of a Marauder king; both involved killing him. We can trust the accuracy of your information because you yourself were a Marauder king. Yet, you are very much alive; well, you're still breathing anyway."

Raggy scowls, "You've got some nooma talking to me like that."

"I'm not challenging you. I'm trying to understand. If we can't kill Morton without bringing on the Law of Retribution, maybe we can get him removed as a king?"

Raggy slinks back into his seat. "That won't help yous. A king can, if he so desires, give up reign and become a King Emeritus. He remains untouchable and, in the eyes of the Marauders, is still to be respected as a king, just one without any power."

This is going famously.

"Can I ask why you surrendered your rule?" Becka's tone is like honey.

"Law of Retribution doesn't apply to a king's family. Nothing in the Marauder code protects them. I have a daughter that I kept secret. Morton found out about her. Came to me demanding I turn my rule over to him, or he would torture her and then kill her. He couldn't kill me—even now as a former king, he can't do nothing. But he keeps my daughter in his camp, so if ever I try anything, he will punish me through her."

"That's despicable," Becka says.

Raggy nods, "It is—why yous think I'm giving you this information? Only person on this earth Morton cares about is Morton."

Morton is self-absorbed; I wonder how we can use that against him? We continue talking with Raggy for a while longer to see if he has anything else useful to share. While some of his information is interesting, none of it is particularly practical in our situation.

"Thank you for the information," I say, extending my hand to his.

"Put an end to Morton Ghood, and you can consider us even," Raggy growls.

We exit the tavern. Fresh air never smelled so sweet.

"That was surprisingly helpful, Kane. I'm sorry I doubted you," Becka concedes. "We're going to tell Kali," I say.

"Think that's a good idea? If she knows he's here, I doubt she'll be able to stop herself," Kane says.

"He's got a point. She doesn't seem to have much handle on her anger."

Did Becka just agree with Kane?

"She has the right to know."

"Jett, if she—" Becka starts.

"I know the risk. She chose to put her revenge aside to help us rescue our friends. She's proven she can handle this. Even if she hadn't, this is not our decision."

"And if she goes after him?"

"She won't. Kali is angry, but she's not going to condemn hundreds of people."

"You're willing to bet their lives on that?" Becka presses.

"If we don't tell her, we might as well call ourselves the Patriarch. Justification is a slippery slope. Even if you have a great reason the first time, it gets easier and easier."

"That hardly makes us the Patriarch, Jett; we're just trying to—"

"Protect her from herself? Isn't that exactly what they do? Suppress, conform, mold people for a greater good. Protect them from themselves. The greater good is just a pleasant excuse to do wrong without having to feel guilty about it. If we decide for her, we are taking away her choice and with it her right to become who she wants to be."

Becka sighs, "I hope this doesn't come back to bite us."

"Me too."

We head back to the inn. Outside, one of the Children of the Dome is shouting at passersby like a merchant trying to entice customers. Why'd he have to set up right by the front door?

"Come brothers, come sisters, hear my warning! The chosen one is coming. The chosen one will soon be found. He will rise to the highest throne and all his faithful will be taken with him to paradise. Fear not! The chosen one will accept all who come to him. Come, or you will burn in the fires of his wrath. When he rises, these cursed lands and those who are not with him will be consumed! He shall purge this world with the fires of his faithful!"

No wonder everyone was giving him a wide berth. It doesn't seem to bother him, though; he just repeats his message all the louder.

Kyle is waiting in the lobby when we step inside. "Hey guys, welcome back. Kali asked me to give you a message. She's waiting in the back room of Yuri's Tavern. She'd like you to come as soon as possible. Just a few blocks down this way," Kyle points, smiling brightly. "On your right."

We nod and head back outside, once again passing Mr. Turn or Burn on the corner.

We find Yuri's and descend into another belowground tavern—this one larger, and considerably nicer than the Thirsty Traveler. It also lacks the charming smoke-filled haze the other tavern afforded us. At the back of the tavern, an open door reveals a second stairway descending into a small room. Rowan steps past us and stations himself at the top of the stairs as we descend. I wonder how he got in without being noticed.

Two taverns in the same night; at what point do I join a support group?

The second basement is quiet. Gray stone walls decorated with colorful tapestries drape from ceiling to floor. The room hosts a seating area with a couch and three cushioned chairs forming a nice little circle on a fuzzy, red rug. Kali is sitting on the couch with a woman I don't recognize.

"Well, your friends finally made it," the woman says. She is a petite woman with blue eyes and leathered skin. Her auburn hair is cut short, barely covering her ears. Her face rests in a squinting expression, making her look perpetually suspicious. She wears the uniform of a city guard, a smooth, gray jacket tucked into matching gray pants with a green stripe running from the collar across the shoulders and down the sleeve. Over the heart is an embroidered green patch with black trim in the shape of an arrow. Inside the patch is a black dragon with outstretched wings. I've seen the same symbol on flags and guards all around town.

"Jett, Becka, Kane." Kali stands up and motions to the guardswoman, "This is Gina. She's a friend of mine."

"Is that what we are?" Gina seems amused by the suggestion. Kali rolls her eyes dramatically in response. The smile on her face suggests playfulness.

"What's going on, Kali?" Becka asks.

"We hit a bit of a snag with the supplies." Kali sits back down and motions for us to join her.

"I don't like the sound of that. What kind of snag?" I sit across from her.

"Nothing serious; I anticipated it. The kind of explosives we need aren't just stocked on shelves. Sometimes the dealers who acquire them want more than just currency in exchange."

"Let me talk to him; I'm certain we'd come to an understanding." Kane sounds a little too enthusiastic about his offer.

"Sure, then I lose one of the best contacts I have."

Kane waves his hand dismissively. "You're no fun."

Kali ignores his protest. "Jett, I'll need you to come with me to meet him in the morning."

"Why me?"

"He needs the skills of a thief. Said he wants to meet you before going into detail."

"Why's your friend here, then?" Kane asks.

"I wanted you to meet her. She's going to run interference with the city guard tomorrow," Kali explains.

"I'll come too. Two thieves are better than one," Becka smiles.

Kali raises an eyebrow. "From what Jett tells me, I'm not sure you qualify."

Becka gasps before turning and punching me in the shoulder. "What did you say? I'm a great thief. I've never been caught."

"Hahaha, Becka you are absolute rubbish as a thief. A blind man would see you robbing him." That earns me a much harder punch.

"It's a finesse job. Sorry, Becka." Kali's consolation seems strangely sincere.

"What are we stealing?" I ask.

"He wouldn't say. Just that it's valuable and quite rare."

"Which means it will be difficult to steal."

I don't like where this is going at all.

"Yes, and you'll have a tight window in which to do it."

"You want me to steal something rare and valuable a day after you warned me not to steal anything because if I get caught, the guards would lob my head off?"

"That a problem?"

"Not at all; just making sure we were on the same page."

"Better—we may even be reading the same book." I find my eyes fixed on hers for a moment before I am able to shake them free.

"I don't like this," Becka protests.

"If you can think of another way to get a bunch of lightweight, high-impact explosives, I'm all ears." Kali leans back on the couch, waiting for a response. Becka finally shakes her head. Kali claps her hands together and stands. "Alright, then."

"Actually, there is one more thing we need to discuss." I glance over at Gina and then back to Kali. "Privately."

Gina nods and excuses herself. "I'll guard the door till you're finished."

"Thanks, girl." Kali and Gina kiss each other on the cheek before the guardswoman heads out.

"Could you ask Rowan to come over here?" I shout to her as she walks away. A moment later, Rowan sits down where Gina had been.

"What's this about?" Kali looks between us suspiciously.

"It's about Morton," I respond.

"What about Morton?" Her tone gains an agitated edge.

"He's here, in Dragonvale."

Kali practically leaps up from her seat. "He's here? Where is he? Take me to him!"

"Kali, you can't go after him," I say firmly, hoping my tone will calm her down.

She ignores me and starts toward the door. Kane moves to intercept her. She turns back, now frantically pacing in the middle of the room. "No, you're not backing out on me. We have a blood pact. I swear—" Kali threatens.

I hold my hands up and try to calm her down. That accomplishes nothing.

"Jett, he's here. We won't get another chance like this."

"Kali." I keep my voice calm as I gesture to the seat. "Please sit down. We need to talk."

"What's there to talk about? This is perfect! He's away from his army. We can handle a few of his lackeys. Why are you stalling? This is my chance! I'm going to kill him!"

"If you do, then hundreds—maybe thousands—of innocent people will die with him," Becka states plainly and without emotion.

Kali stops pacing and looks to Becka, then to me. "What is she talking about?"

We explain to her what we learned from Raggy Brookton about the Marauder code and the consequences of killing a king. Tears well up in the corners of her eyes as she slumps down onto the couch.

"How do we even know we can trust this guy? Some random drunk Kane met in a bar? Come on!" She's reaching, grasping for something. I've been there, felt that. It's like she's drowning in the sea of how unfair life is, reaching against all reason for anything to grab hold of. All she's really doing is splashing water around.

"He's not a random drunk." Kane sounds offended. "If there's one thing I know how to do, besides killing of course, it's gathering intel. That's as reliable as credits in the market, sweetheart."

"What is it with you and this guy, anyway? Ever since you saw him in Red Clay you've been sheol-bent on killing him. Why? Because of what he did to the old man?" I ask.

"Because of what he did to my mother."

A hush falls on the room. All eyes are on Kali. Suddenly she's not a fierce warrior woman with an impenetrable armor for skin; she's a scared little girl shrinking in on herself in search of a safe place.

I reach out and put my hand on her knee. "I'm sorry. I understand if you don't want to talk about it. If you'd like to tell us, we'll listen."

"Why do you care? You don't know me." Her tone sounds harsh but insincere, like she's trying to push me away all while hoping I won't let her.

"You did save my life. That's usually a good way to start a friendship."

My words seem to knock her off balance. She breaks eye contact and covers her mouth with her hand as if trying to hide a reaction. "You think we are friends now?"

I smile. "Well, I would like to be. Friends get to know each other. I've told you plenty about me."

Kali remains in a silent stare for a moment. I sigh, realizing she's not going to share. Even after all of this, she's not going to open up.

"My father was . . . is," she corrects herself, "an important man in Dios. He had a thing for young, attractive women. Women like my mother."

I'm so shocked I refuse to even blink out of fear that it will somehow shut her down.

Kali takes a breath before continuing. "When she got pregnant with me, she hid it from him—managed to keep me a secret for almost eight years. Eventually, he found out. To avoid a scandal, he had her branded an enemy of the state and exiled us. My mother carried me across the Sand Sea and brought me to Red Clay. It became our home. Elder Schmitty had just become the elder at the time. He promised we would be safe there. For a time, we were. Then, Morton came along, wanted to make her his bride. She wasn't interested in that, so she turned him down. Turns out he didn't like being told no. He murdered her in the Town Square in front of the entire village. And he laughed about it. I watched him drag her by her ankle all the way through town. Then, he stood her body up, leaned her against the wall, and drove a spike through her chest to pin her in place. No one told him no again after that."

I can see her fighting back emotions. Her strong demeanor can't hide the sadness in her eyes. I move to the couch next to her and put my hand on her shoulder softly. "I am so sorry."

I wish there were words that could make that better. Sometimes all we can do is be there for each other. I take a breath, letting the moment settle.

"Can I ask her name?"

Kali seems confused by the question. "Her name?"

"I think we all live twice. Once in our bodies, once in the minds of those who love us. The more we talk about those we've lost, the more they live on in us. One of the greatest pains of losing someone is feeling like they are forgotten—that you are the only one keeping them alive in your memory. There's nothing I can say to make that pain better. Maybe you don't have to carry the weight of her memory alone. It sounds like your mother was an amazing woman."

Kali nods and sniffles softly. I feel my body pulled in as she wraps her arms around me and hugs me tight. It's strange the way shared tragedy can bond people together. Kali feels warm and comfortable as she holds me. Becka's words replay in my brain—*don't be one of those guys who plays games. Figure out what you want, then be decisive.* Becka is right; I need to be careful.

"Her name was Valami," she almost whispers to me. She holds me in this embrace for another moment. I feel her shoulders suddenly tighten as if she suddenly realized what she was doing. She sniffs again and pushes off me, standing up quickly. Her cheeks are pink, her eyes flooded with unreleased tears.

A quiet understanding settles over the room. I want to say something, to offer some words of comfort. No good comes from singing songs to a heavy heart. In moments like these, the best support is a silent presence.

"It's just not fair," Kali protests. Her voice is soft, almost defeated. "I've waited my whole life for a chance to kill that man. Now, I finally have one, and you're telling me that if I do, I'm going to be responsible for the deaths of countless others?"

Becka puts her hand on Kali's shoulder. She nudges me out of the way and sits down next to her. "Don't worry, we'll find a way to deal with Morton."

"You don't get it, sweetheart; that's not going to help," Kane says.

Becka puts her hands on her hips. "What don't I understand? Raggy told us how we could get rid of Morton without causing collateral damage."

"Be glad you don't understand," Kane replies.

"What's that mean?" Becka snaps.

"It means you didn't watch your parents get murdered right in front of your eyes. You've never felt that kind of hatred, that need. It's not enough for them to be dealt with," I explain.

Kane nods. "If she can't be the one to do it, it won't solve anything. Shinshew, it might even make things worse."

"I don't believe that." Becka shakes her head. "Revenge doesn't bring satisfaction. This has to be about more. It has to be about justice. Otherwise, we are just fueling the cycle."

"Spoken like someone who has never experienced it," Kane grunts.

"Brelar and Gibbs don't count, then? It has to be parents? Otherwise, it's impossible to know pain, trauma, hate? Come off it; right and wrong are not that fluid. There is an emotional impact to revenge. It may make you feel better in the moment, but it leaves a scar just as damaging as losing the person you loved. Revenge never leads to healing."

"They teach you that in Potter school?" Kane glares.

Becka steps closer to him. "You know wh—"

"There's no chance he was lying?" Kali's words silence the argument. Her tone is not questioning so much as pleading. I understand the feeling—wanting something so bad and there not being any good way to accomplish it. You end up grasping for straws.

Rowan signs something to Kali. Whatever he was saying seems to confuse her. She sniffs and rubs the backs of her hands under her eyes to wipe away the accumulated moisture.

Kali shakes her head. "How do you know he wasn't lying; you weren't even there."

Kane, Becka, and I watch his signs but can't make sense of them. We are at the mercy of Kali's response to glean what he's saying.

Kali shakes her head again. "When were you a Marauder?"

That draws all of our attention. She looks at him for a minute, eyes narrowing further.

"Why didn't you say anything before?" Kali questions.

Rowan gestures something quickly and then points at Kali, who gasps.

"I never asked? How would I even know to ask something like that?"

"Ummm . . . ," I hold the note to remind them of our presence and our inability to track what was going on.

Kali lays her head back on the couch and starts talking to the ceiling. "Turns out, before I met him, Rowan was a Marauder. They found him after he escaped the depraved and started training him to fight. He was with them for about four years, then we met, he left, and the rest is history."

"They just let him go?" Becka asks.

Rowan signs and a minute later Kali says, "Marauders are granted freedom from service if they complete what is believed to be an impossible task on behalf of the tribe."

"What did he do?" Becka asks.

Rowan shakes his head and folds his arms in front of his chest. I guess we aren't getting the details. This new revelation actually seems to calm Kali down.

"Are you OK?" Becka rubs her hand across Kali's back.

Kali nods slowly.

"We will figure out something. One way or another, we will find a way. We have a blood pact after all." I attempt to add a little hope.

Kali stands up. "Thank you. I just, I need to get some sleep. Jett, let's meet at the inn lobby in the morning?"

I confirm with a nod. I can't tell if she has accepted the news or if she's just going along with it to avoid the argument.

We get back to our room to find Kyle and the other Raiders are already asleep. I pull off my jacket and start to set it down. I feel it, something strange in my pocket. That's right! With everything going on, I'd forgotten. After bumping into that guy, I thought I felt something. I reach into the pocket and pull it out. My jaw drops, and I practically drop it. I flip it over in my hands, inspecting its scratch marks and familiar thin scrapes. I'd recognize this anywhere. This isn't just a datapad; this is *my* datapad. The same datapad the Patriarch had taken from me when I was arrested and imprisoned by Commander Stone. It is, but it can't be. For this to be here, not only would someone have to have stolen it but they'd also have to have left Dios with it, tracked me down and then slipped it into my jacket.

Who *could* do such a thing? Who *would* do such a thing? The question that plagues me the most is: *why?*

CHAPTER THIRTEEN

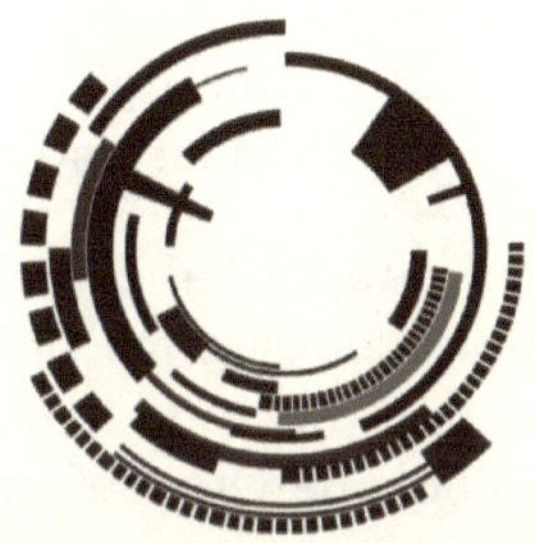

The next morning, I find Kali waiting in the lobby. She smiles when she sees me. She looks remarkably sweet and gentle when she smiles. After last night's revelation, I feel like I'm seeing her for the first time. I understand her—her anger, her pain, her driving need. I felt this in Dios. I had something she didn't. I had friends. I had people who cared enough about me to challenge me, calm me, and temper my rage. Kali has been living with this volcanic wrath her whole life. She's been dealing with it alone. I shake my thoughts about her from my mind. I need to focus. It's time to go steal something in a city that beheads thieves.

"Sleep well?" Kali asks, walking to the door.

"Not really; anytime I close my eyes I hear the sounds of—"

"Yeah, me too," she cuts me off.

We step outside into the noisy stir and chatter of Dragonvale's main street.

"Thank you." Her voice is so soft I almost don't hear it.

"For what?"

"I've never really talked about my mother before." She looks at me, her eyes almost pleading. This is new. Her voice sounds almost fragile.

"It must have been very hard to share that, but I'm glad you did. I find that having people you can share your struggles with helps make them more bearable."

She nudges me, catching me at just the right time. I stumble sideways, almost tripping over myself. She chuckles and raises an eyebrow.

"Don't laugh! I was off balance," I lie. Even playing around, she is remarkably strong. Kali starts leading me around the town, pointing out various places she likes and places to avoid. We follow the street around a turn, taking in a whole new row of shops.

"Can I ask you something?" I say.

"What is it?"

"When you were talking with Elder Schmitty, you mentioned allying with a couple of different groups."

"The Outcasts and the Sandurans?"

"I've heard of the Sandurans, read about them in Dios. I didn't know they still existed. The way the Patriarch talks about them—"

"Well, they still exist," Kali confirms.

"Can you tell me anything about them?" I ask, trying to suppress my zeal.

"I don't know much. They are mysterious and very powerful. They are well connected and well informed. Much as you might expect from the people who created the domes in the first place."

"Wait—what? The Sandurans built the dome around Dios?"

"Sand-brained domie." Unlike previous times she's called me this, her tone has a warm playfulness to it. "They built all the domes. The Sandurans were the ones who saw the Great Collapse coming."

"Of course, the Patriarch would change the histories to suit their purposes."

"Not just the histories. The Sacred Texts, too," Kali chuckles. "The High Father is the world's greatest narcissist from a line of great narcissists. When they took power, they wrote themselves into everything—made themselves the center of everything—so that they would be remembered throughout history as the saviors of the world."

"They changed the Sacred Texts?" I don't know why that surprises me; it's perfectly on brand.

"They took some holy books from The World That Was, copied down the teachings, and twisted them to suit their purposes. The Patriarch was able to defeat the Sandurans because they weaponized the faith of the people."

"Oh, Becka is not going to like this."

"It doesn't mean Bealz isn't real. It just means the version of the Sacred Texts used by the Patriarch have been twisted."

"What does the Patriarch touch that isn't?"

We turn up the next street, and my mind is racing with thoughts about this new revelation. I've always figured the Patriarch just used the Sacred Texts that fit their purposes. It didn't occur to me that they might have changed them too.

"Can I ask you something?" Kali stops walking and turns to face me.

I nod.

"Why did you tell me about Morton?"

"Should I not have?"

"No, I'm glad you did. It just seems like a salvage risk."

"How so?"

"You know how bad I want Morton dead, even if you didn't know why. I could've just said 'heap it' and killed him anyway."

I shrug. "You wouldn't do that."

"How'd you know?"

"I just do."

She nudges against me and smiles sweetly, looking more like a delicate, gentle woman than I'm used to seeing. Women are truly strange creatures. Once again, I have to force my thoughts away from her. This is not the time or place.

"Come on." Her grin evolves into a full-out smile, eyes sparkling as she looks into mine. I can feel any resistance I have to giving her the information she wants crumbling to ash.

"When we were in the cave, and you said you'd put aside your vendetta because it's what your mother would have wanted you to do. That says it all, really."

Kali avoids making eye contact, but I can see a subtle smile on her lips. She opens her mouth to say something, then shakes her head subtly. She clears her throat.

"It's about time for our meeting; you ready?"

I motion for her to lead the way. As we walk, she explains how these dark market deals work while giving me some specific instructions: Don't offer information that isn't asked for. Don't commit to anything until a final offer is presented. Don't ask questions unless you absolutely need to do so. Sounds a lot like haggling with merchants back in Dios.

"Most importantly, be prepared. He may try to test you. If he does, you need to impress him. Gregor is the only one who can get us what we need. He shuts us down, we're heaped."

Nothing like pressure before breakfast to really start a day off right.

The shop is a narrow stone building sandwiched tightly between two considerably larger stone buildings. It has a brown, wooden door with a gold handle. On either side of the door are long, green and white, chevron-patterned banners. Above the door is a sign that shows what looks like a lamp with the words "Heart's Desires" written on it. Makes it sounds like the kind of place I didn't care to enter. Kali doesn't seem bothered. She pushes the door open and walks inside.

The place is, to my relief, a sort of jewelry shop. Glass display cases form a barrier between the customer and the owner. Rather than jewelry, the cases are filled with holographic images of various weapons. The walls are lined ceiling to floorboards with mounted weapons as well as various other dangerous looking items.

"Does everyone you know have a giant room of weapons?" I ask.

Kali looks at me as if deciding whether to answer. "After my mother was killed, I knew I needed to get stronger. I learned to shoot, to use blades, to fight—I've been training my whole life so I could kill the man who murdered her. Getting the best training usually requires networking. Yeah, I know a lot of people who specialize in weapons."

That was a much deeper answer than I was expecting. It occurs to me that Kali would have fit in perfectly back in Dios. She's struggled and experienced loss. Where we learned to steal to survive, she learned to fight.

"Kali, you have returned. Is this your thief?" A tall, thin man with almost skeletal features steps into the room. Without lowering his upturned nose, he looks me up and down like he's scanning me.

The pompous scrap sink.

"Yes, Gregor, this is Jett Lasting. Jett, Gregor."

My hand extends toward his. I step toward him, tripping over an uneven patch of floor, my body crashing into his. He pushes me back to my feet with a scowl. "Not off to a great start," he sighs dramatically.

Even his sigh has an air of superiority.

Kali glares at me.

I wince and mouth, "Sorry."

The skin-wrapped skeleton taps his fingertips together. "Very well; come with me." He sounds reluctant. Gregor leads us into a back room and closes the door. He steps behind his desk before pointing to the two chairs on the other side of it.

"You were able to get what I asked for?" Kali asks.

"That was never in doubt. I have the items you requested. The question is, why should I give them to you? My reputation is on the line here. This job is sensitive. I require professionalism, skill, and finesse. You bring me a boy who stumbles over his own feet? I must say, I am not impressed. I very much was hoping to be impressed."

Kali grits her teeth. If looks could kill, the glance she gives me would result in a slow and painful death. "Gregor, can we just start over?"

"Crash that," I stand and interrupt. "You told me he was serious. I don't do business with self-important amateurs."

The look of horror on Kali's face as her eyes widen like a deer in lumelights is priceless.

"A what?" Gregor protests, seeming quite offended by the suggestion.

"He didn't mean that, he's just—"

"Oh no, I did. Only an amateur merchant would fall for such an obvious trick."

"Trick! You insolent—"

"You still don't even know it's missing, do you?" I fake a laugh for effect.

Gregor's eyes narrow, and he starts patting himself down.

"Wait, where is my necklace?"

"That's the first thing you noticed?" I reach into my pocket and pull out a gawdy silver necklace and toss it onto his desk. He scoops it up quickly and puts it over his head.

"I imagine datapads are hard to come by in the Outlands; the Patriarch typically confiscates them whenever they exile someone."

Gregor nods, "Yes, they are rare. I myself have one of course but—"

"Had one," I correct, pulling out the datapad I swiped from his wrist when I fell into him. Gregor's eyes practically pop out of his skull. I place the pad down on his desk and slide it toward him. "Alright Kali, let's go."

"What?" The anger on Kali's face has been replaced with confusion and disbelief. She stares at me, jaw hanging open. I offer her my hand, which only seems to add to her confusion.

"He obviously doesn't want to work with us, so let's go find someone who does."

"Wait, wait, wait." Gregor extends his hands as if trying to pull us back. "Please, forgive my rudeness. You have to understand that in my line of work, certain precautions are necessary."

I remain standing and pretend to be considering it. The longer he wonders, the more the negotiations swing in our favor. After a moment, I sit back down. "I suppose we can overlook it this once. Now, tell me why I'm here."

Gregor exhales in relief. "I find myself in a rather precarious position. I have a reputation for being able to acquire what others cannot. A group has contacted me to acquire for them—something quite valuable and rare."

"Unfortunately, this rare item is in the possession of another client," I say nonchalantly.

Gregor's mouth curls into a half grin. "How did you figure that?"

"Simple. You were upset that I appeared clumsy, which means you need finesse. Normally it wouldn't matter if I got caught as they'd behead me, and you would go on your merry way. Which got me thinking—why would finesse be as important to you as success? Has to be that you need something stolen without the person it's being stolen from knowing it's been stolen."

Gregor nods. "Yes, but how do you know it's another client? It could just be someone powerful who I don't want to make an enemy of."

"I considered that. The first thing you said was that your reputation is on the line. You don't become the guy who can get what no one else can without crossing some powerful people. What could put you in such a precarious position? If you have a client who wants something that you can't get, that's bad for you. Stands to reason the only thing that would give you pause is if taking that item could also damage your reputation."

Gregor looks pleasantly surprised. "Kali, it seems you have overdelivered. I am quite impressed. Mr. Lasting, if you can steal this for me, I'll will provide you with everything Kali has requested."

"Information or object?" I ask.

"Information."

I nod. "OK, what am I stealing, and who am I stealing it from?"

"At the far end of town, the Children of the Dome have a compound," Gregor begins.

"You want us to steal from those cultist loopers?" Kali protests.

"Yes."

"That's a bigger deal than you let on," Kali challenges.

"You think explosives grow on trees? They are not easy to come by."

"What do they have that you could possibly want?"

"Don't write them off so easily. The Children of the Dome believe the High Father of Dios is Bealz's link to this world. They believe Dios is the promised land. Anything related to Dios, they consider a religious relic. Somehow, they got their hands on a datapad. Not just any datapad, but a datapad that has access codes to the gates leading into the city."

"They have a datapad that can get them into Dios?" I ask.

That can't be a thing. Hope loves to rush off and leave reason behind. Could it be that there's a way back? If I could get my hands on that, I could get us back into Dios. We could return home!

Gregor nods. "Yes, on their own the codes are worthless, of course. The gates are hidden from the outside. In order to use the codes, you'd need to find an activation point, which would be almost impossible unless you had the design blueprints showing exactly where they were."

"How did a datapad with codes that important end up in the Outlands? How do you know the codes still work?"

"Dios was not always ruled by the Patriarch. The Patriarch lead a rebellion against the true rulers of Dios," Gregor explains.

"The Sandurans." My reply earns an approving nod.

"Quite right. When the Patriarch was seizing control, they banished all the Sandurans and their supporters to the Outlands. They didn't think to remove their datapads as, at the time, the Patriarch had no idea the gates could be opened from the outside. Even if they found out, the codes in the datapad are master codes that cannot be overwritten."

I try to keep myself from looking too interested.

"I see. You need me to sneak into a heavily guarded cultist compound, find where they have this datapad hidden, copy the information on it, and sneak out without being detected or raising suspicion?"

Gregor nods. "Essentially, yes, but I can tell you where the datapad is being kept within their compound if you can tell me how you'd manage to copy the information. As impressive as you may be, I don't see how you could pull it off. You'd need a datapad that could hack through the security of their datapad to copy it."

I hold up my right hand and pull back my sleeve, revealing the datapad I'd discovered in my jacket last night. I'd spent most the night checking to confirm it really was mine. Not only did it have all of my information, but it also had something special. I ran my fingers across the surface. A semitranslucent projection hums to life. "Gregory Seymor Fannie—oh, that's an unfortunate name. Age 51, male, born on—"

"That's from my datapad! How did you . . . ?"

"Cloned it when I swiped it; thought I might need to impress you a little more."

"On the contrary, Mr. Lasting, I'm not sure how much more I could be impressed. Now, please delete that," he smiles politely.

I leave my screen up while I do, so he can watch. When I am finished, he pulls up a scan of the compound. Spinning it, he taps on a room in the back, making it glow green on the map. "This is their vault. It's on the top floor, behind a sealed door that is under constant guard by a rotating pair of cultists. Once you're in the room, you'll likely find the datapad in a glass display case."

"Why do your clients want these codes?"

"I cannot share client information. Surely you understand."

"I do. But if I'm going to do a job, I need to know I can live with the consequences."

Gregor strokes his wire-thin mustache. "What I can tell you is that my clients hate the Patriarch and that doing this job will help them in their fight against the Patriarch."

That I can live with.

"Your clients are the Outcasts?" Kali asks surprisingly loud.

Gregor pauses for a moment. "You are familiar with them?"

"No one hates the Patriarch more than the Outcasts," Kali replies.

"Quite right. Their cause is to bring down the Patriarch and then lead all the exiles home," Gregor adds.

"It takes a lot more than getting into Dios to bring down the Patriarch," I say.

"Sounds like you have experience." Her tone is light and playful as a warm grin dons her face.

"Not the good kind; they don't exile you for winning."

"The Outcasts are well organized, well supplied, and well trained. If they had the means to get into Dios, they'd have a chance."

"Well, then, I suppose we have a deal." I extend my hand to Gregor.

He looks at it and then up at me before smiling and shaking it. "Excellent."

"I'll be in touch when the job is done. Make sure you have our supplies ready."

"Of course, Mr. Lasting. I look forward to seeing you soon."

Once outside, we waste no time putting distance between ourselves and the shop.

"Well, I must say, Jett, I'm quite impressed." Kali nudges me. "Who knew you were such a strong negotiator?"

"We dealt with things like that a lot in Dios. I watched Victor work out deals enough times; I guess some of it stuck."

"Well, you did amazing. How did you do it?"

"Grabbing the stuff is the easy part. The clumsier you look, the easier it is to make contact with someone without raising their suspicion. Necklaces are easy, provided you can find the clasp. One hand goes up, the other grabs the wrist for support." I demonstrate stepping toward her, putting my hand around the back of her neck and grabbing her wrist with the other. "The other hand grabs here. The other person is caught off guard, trying to make sure you don't knock them over—they don't notice what you're really doing." Our eyes meet as I finish my explanation. I grabbed her neck and wrist to illustrate what I did, but here I am, still holding them, just looking into her eyes.

"And how did you copy his information?" Her words are soft, her eyes fixed on mine. She makes no attempt to break away. All of a sudden, I feel nervous.

"Oh, I have . . . uhh . . . an application on my . . . uh . . . datapad." What is happening to my brain? What am I doing? I let go of her and step back, clearing my throat and averting my eyes. "The only impressive thing about that is the guy who designed it. The application allows my datapad to copy bits of information off other devices. All I have to do is push a button and keep them close to each other. I did that while he was walking us into the room." I shrug, trying to take my mind off what just happened.

Kali's cheeks are flushed pink as she fights off a persistent smile.

"What's next, Mr. Thief? How do we get this datapad?"

"Normally, I'd case the place for a few days—learn their patterns, test their responses, then make a plan from there. We don't really have time for that. But what if we used the same plan we have for rescuing the others here?"

"I don't follow."

"We create a big distraction to draw out the Children of the Dome. Then, while they are out, we sneak in, grab what we need, and get out. It'll be like a practice run."

"We may not need a distraction. If you can be ready in like an hour, the Children of the Dome are hosting a special service in the Town Square in honor of the High Father's birthday. They use the big celebration to try to recruit new members."

"We'll need to move fast. Can you have Becka and Kane meet me near the compound, and get Gina ready?"

Kali nods. "I'll find them and meet you at the compound as soon as possible."

"Wait, one more thing." I pull out a piece of paper and write a quick message on it. "Give that to Kane."

Kali raises an eyebrow. "Passing notes?"

I chuckle. "It's something I need him to pick up; he'll know what to do with it."

The compound, appropriately named, looks like a small castle within a castle. The compound's walls are only a few meters shorter than the walls around Dragonvale. At each end of the compound, they have built their own private watchtowers. The front door is an iron gate with a reinforced wooden door behind it. In Dios, we wouldn't have even considered robbing a place like this. It's too risky. Who needs reason when you can have desperation? I have Gregor's blueprints but no way of knowing how many cultists are inside.

While I wait for the others, I watch the outer walls. Thankfully, the city guard does not patrol this area very often. Two cultists wearing their bright cloaks stand on either side of the gate, looking menacing. They don't appear to be carrying weapons, but who knows what those bulky cloaks hide.

Time to process the plan. Step one: Get inside. Step two: Make it to the vault room. Step three: Find a distraction to draw the guards from their post. Footsteps behind me disrupt my list making. I glance back to see Kali and Becka.

"Where's Kane?" I ask.

"He'll be here—said he had to get something first," Becka answers.

I nod, turning my attention to Kali. "Any idea when they leave for their recruitment party?"

"Should be soon; we passed a group of them heading to the Town Square on our way here."

"Guard count?" Becka asks.

"Minimal. My guess is they will leave two at the gate and two inside to guard the vault."

"That would be fortunate," Becka smiles.

"You didn't start without me, did you?" I jump at Kane's voice coming from behind me. I'm not used to people being able to sneak up on me.

"Kali, you think Gina could get us up on that wall?" I ask.

"I don't see why not. Why?"

"People guard doors, not walls. We come in from above, sneak in from a place they aren't trying to watch. From there, we can use a rope ladder to drop down into the compound undetected. The two cultists who were in their watchtowers have already gone inside. With any luck, they will be going to the celebration as well. Kali, I'll need you to coordinate with Gina to keep the city guards from wandering this way. Kane, you'll be the lookout. When I'm in, you'll pull the rope ladder up, and stay out of sight until I signal. While I'm inside, you're my eyes. You see any cultists headed back, let me know."

"Lookout? Me?" Kane sounds offended.

"You have the most experience in gathering intel. If anyone is going to sense something is off, it's going to be you. I need your vision for this."

Kane smiles. "Well, how could I say no to that? How am I supposed to signal you?"

"Sing loud and act drunk."

"Why?"

"There's a celebration going on; everyone else will dismiss you."

"You better not be sidelining me, Jett Lasting," Becka warns.

"I wouldn't dream of it. You're coming in with me. We are going to disguise ourselves as cultists. We approach the vault guards, give them a drink, wait for them to pass out—you know the rest."

"Pass out? It'll take a long time to get them that drunk," Kali objects.

"Kane," I say.

Kane smiles and holds up a green, cylindrical pill. "Not with these."

"You are *not* poisoning anyone." Becka crosses her arms and glares.

"Easy, sweetheart. They'll wake up in a few hours feeling hung over and not remembering a thing." Kane hands me several pills, and I secure them in my pocket.

"Kali, one more thing. If anyone approaches that front gate before we are clear, you have to slow them down. I don't care what you do. You're our safety net."

Kali nods. After confirming everyone knows their part, Kali leads us to an alley. Gina is there, looking nervous. Weird. Her part is pretty innocuous. Even if we got caught, she's a city guard. She could just pretend to be arresting us. Why is she frantically searching the horizon? Maybe life as a thief has desensitized me to how nerve-wracking something like this can be. Still, it seems odd. She hurries us through the door.

"You got thirty minutes; after that, no promises. I'll meet you here on your way out," Gina says before grasping forearms with Kali, who immediately heads back out toward the front of the compound. Becka and I climb down the rope ladder onto the compound wall without incident. We make our way down into the structure. Gregor's blueprints show a laundry room on the top floor near where came in. In it we find dozens of freshly washed robes hanging on wall hooks to dry. We slide them on, pulling up the hoods.

"Yours still damp?" Becka asks, rubbing the sleeve of her cloak.

I nod.

The dampness made the already heavy fabric feel more like a suit of armor. Why would anyone choose to wear something like this regularly? It's restrictive and unpleasant.

The compound looks deserted. Even so, we move quietly and keep our heads down; no reason for unnecessary risks. In the kitchen, we retrieve several glasses and fill them with wine. I drop a pill into each glass. This was going almost too well.

We take the glasses with us and make our way toward the vault. Turning the corner, we see them— the two guards standing outside the vault. As they see us approaching, they straighten up and look alert. Unlike the guards by the front gate, these two very clearly have weapons.

"Praise the holy dome, brothers!" Becka's voice is gleeful and warm as she lifts the glass in one of her hands. The two guards exchange a glance, appearing confused.

"What are you doing here?" one asks.

"We felt bad you got stuck with guard duty for the celebration. So we thought we should bring the celebration to you!"

Smiles appear on their faces as we close the gap. Becka and I offer each of them a glass. They take the glasses but hesitate. Apparently our cover story wasn't quite convincing enough for them to just down whatever libations we brought them. *Think*. Victor isn't here to bail you out anymore. I feel my pulse quickening. We're in it now. I hadn't accounted for what to do if they didn't trust the drink offering. What sort of guard left behind during a celebration doesn't jump at a chance for a drink? Cults are weird. If they don't drink, we are royally heaped. With every passing second, the likelihood of them doing so lessens.

Becka rolls her eyes dramatically. "Oh Bealz, here." Without hesitation Becka reaches out and reclaims one of the glasses, lifting up and chugging it down. "You don't want it; I'll drink it myself. Sorry for trying to share the fun."

Becka, what have you done?

The guard who still had his glass starts drinking it. The other takes Becka's second glass and gulps it down. Good thing I put a pill in all of the glasses.

"Why aren't you drinking?" the first guard says, pointing to the remaining glass in my hand.

It'll be hard to rob you and escape if I'm passed out too.

"I may have started early. Shhhh, don't tell." I hold my finger to my lips and try to slur my words as much as possible before offering him my cup.

He smiles and drinks it. Now we wait.

"Why aren't you at the recruitment celebration?" one of the guards asks.

"We were; they sent us back early to get . . ." Becka's voice trails off. She's wobbling like her legs are made of overcooked noodles. That was fast.

"To get what?" the guard asks before slumping to the ground.

The other starts to say something before toppling over himself. Thankfully, Becka managed to stay upright longer. I catch her as she collapses. I lean her up against the wall and tap her shoulder. Sweet Becka saves the day.

The vault door requires a uniquely shaped key. One of the guards must have it. I root around in the pockets of their bulky cloaks before finding it in the final pocket of guard number two's cloak. The key clicks into the lock, and the vault door slides open.

The inside of the vault looks like a pirate's treasure trove. It's lined with shelves and displays, all containing random, mismatched items—some of which I recognize, many I don't. I wish I could look around and inspect all the strange wonders, but time is of the essence. I move quickly but carefully, scanning the room until I find the datapad. In Dios, Spike had designed and installed a hacking process on all our datapads. It allows me to unlock the information on the older datapad and copy it to mine without requiring any hacking skills on my part. It takes a couple of minutes to complete the process. I open a hidden storage section on my datapad, another boon from Spike's tech-spertice,

He'd partitioned off space on all of our datapads that was hidden from external scanning. It was a way for us to keep information secret from annoying Patriarch invasions into our privacy. With my secret digital compartment open, I copy the datapad again. The second copy takes a little longer. I'm growing impatient waiting. I keep hearing this weird sound.

> "May the road be soft unto your feet
> May the wind be swift and fair
> May the sun be warm
> And your heart be light
> And good fortunes find you day and night"

What a strange song to hear . . . *Shinshew.* That's Kane's voice! He's singing a warning. The moment the copy is complete, I set the datapad down. I need to get out of here and quick. Something catches my eye, and I stop. It pulls me like a gravitational force. Sitting on the counter are a stack of books. Toward the top is a large, green, leather-bound book with golden filigree letters. It's not so much the book that captures my attention but the glossy, golden letters spelling out the name of its author: Dr. Jacob Olander. I slide the other books off and pick it up to examine it. I've only heard the name one time in my life, but I'll never forget it. According to Victor, Dr. Jacob Olander was the proper name for our friend, Gibbs. He published a book? What was it doing out here in the Outlands? Why did the Children of the Dome have it?

The front cover reads: Bloodlines and Beliefs. Curiosity overpowers caution. I stack the other books back but deposit Gibb's book into my cloak. Time to go. I dash from the vault. The door slams closed with a loud thud. I should put the key back; that's the smart move. A missing key may raise suspicion. Something just isn't sitting right with me. I slip the key into my pocket before repositioning the guards. I pick up the glasses and set them upright near the guards. Anyone who sees the scene will hopefully assume they just got drunk and fell asleep. My mind keeps telling me to move faster, but my body feels sluggish and slow to respond. The door to the courtyard below closes, and loud angry voices resound in the compound.

"Those infernal Outcasts defile this holy day with their blasphemy. Get the clubs, boys; we'll put the fear of Bealz into them."

I slide Becka's arm over my shoulder and lift her up. Her unconscious body is dead weight and nearly pulls me to the ground. I strain against the force, managing to keep my feet under me. Slowly I half drag, half hobble down the hallway.

Boots are crashing against stone and getting closer. The compound has become a hornet's nest of activity. I make it around the corner. One hallway down; one hallway, a flight of stairs, two doors, a walkway, and a rope ladder to go.

Adrenaline surges, giving me a much-needed boost as I manage to clear the next hall without being detected. Pulling Becka up the stairs is a special kind of challenging. More than once I almost slip and send us both crashing. Finally reaching the top, I step out from the staircase and freeze as three cultists rush by. My heart skips like a rock thrown across a pond. They don't stop. Either they didn't see us or didn't register us as being out of the ordinary. I peer down the hall. I need to cross it and get through the next room, but to do so will leave us terribly exposed. I hear sounds coming from behind me. Heap. Someone is moving toward the stairs.

I grind my feet against the ground, pushing myself forward and dragging Becka with me. I make it across the hall. The sound of boots rushing up the stairs is getting close. I twist the door handle and shove my shoulder into it. The door swings open and I stumble through it just as I see a red cloak coming into view. I freeze, not knowing if he saw us or was too preoccupied to notice. When no one comes through the door, I carefully close it and make my way back onto the ramparts of the wall.

Kane peeks his head into view and waves us toward him. The rope ladder drops into place. Becka groans, apparently all the movement has started to return her to consciousness. Not enough for her to climb the ladder; that would be too convenient. Kane climbs down and helps me with Becka.

"What happened to her?" he whispers.

"She had to drink the spiked wine," I explain.

The two of us work together to carry Becka up the ladder, splitting her weight between us. Each step up is agonizing. My muscles burn from holding the tension of her weight for so long. When we finally get to the top, we lay her down and collapse next to her, gasping for air.

"Can you find another way back?"

Kane nods.

I quickly hand him my datapad. "Take this and Becka. Wait for me at the tavern where we met Raggy."

"What's this about?"

"Hopefully nothing; I just have bad a feeling."

"Don't like leaving you in a pinch, friend," Kane protests.

"Take it and go; that's how you get me out of the pinch."

Kane reluctantly agrees. He picks Becka up and carries her in the opposite direction.

Time to see if I am being paranoid. I follow the stairs from the exterior wall down to the room Gina had led us into. Gina is waiting there with Kali.

"What happened? Where are Kane and Becka?" Kali asks.

"We split up. Becka had to drink the spiked wine. Couldn't risk her slowing down our escape."

"I'll go help them; which way did they go?" Gina offers. Her voice eager.

"They will be fine. Besides, I got the prize. Let's get out of here."

"You got the inf—" Kali starts.

"I got it," I interrupt her forcefully, hoping she'd catch my hint and drop it. She gives me a puzzled look but doesn't ask any further questions.

"Fine. Good. Let's go." Gina pushes the door open.

We step outside and the door closes behind us.

"Well, well, well, who do we have here? Is that you, Kali girl? You've grown into a woman. A mighty fine woman at that. You're the spitting image of your mother."

I see Kali's body tense. I can feel the anger radiating off her—that pure hatred that drives away all reason. She knows that voice—as do I. It's the perplexingly charming voice of Morton Ghood.

CHAPTER FOURTEEN

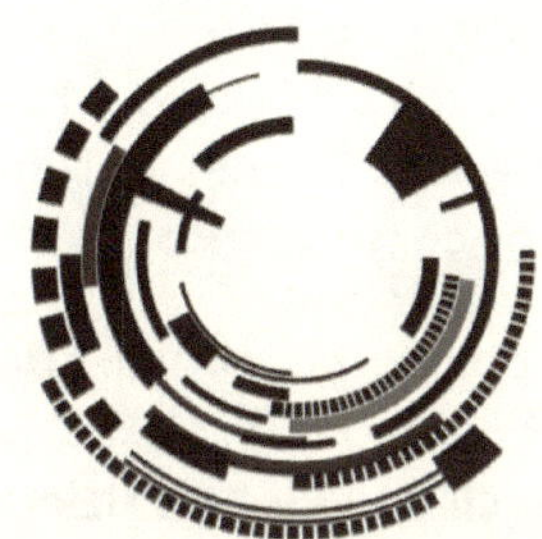

Morton stands closest to us with a dozen of his Marauder lackeys creating a human barrier to our escape. A scowl is painted across Kali's face. Her hand clutches her blade, but she doesn't draw it. It's almost as if she is frozen by fury. Silence fills the air. Gina is leaning against the door we just exited, hanging her head. Kali whirls around to face her.

"I trusted you!" she screams, lunging for the guardswoman. Gina doesn't move, doesn't make any effort to defend herself. The whistle of metal cutting through air and the shining glimmer of Morton's sword stops Kali in her tracks. The blade becomes a barrier separating Kali from Gina.

"Now, now, I don't mean to interrupt, but we have some business to take care of. Y'all can have your little lover's quarrel when we are finished."

Gina catches Kali's glare and somehow manages to hang her head lower. She looks like a disciplined puppy holding an invisible tail between her legs.

Kali turns her attention to Morton. "What do you want?"

He holds ups his free hand. "Easy, killer. No need to get nuked. I'm just here to take the stuff you just stole because I want it. You're going to give it to me because I want it. And if you don't, I'm going to murder you all kinds of nasty. Which would be a shame. I just got these boots, and I really don't want get blood on them. So why don't you make this easy on me, and give me *my* stuff."

"How did you even know we'd be here?" I ask, hoping to divert some attention from Kali. Even though she knows what's at stake, I'm not sure she'll be able to control herself. Flames of vengeance are rarely put out by streams of reason or consequence.

Morton turns to face me, pulling his sword back and tapping the flat part of the blade against his shoulder. "And just who might you be?" He walks around in a little circle like he's sizing me up.

"I'm Je—" I cough as Morton slams the flat edge of his sword into my chest. Sputtering as my lungs expel the air held within them, I feel a stinging pain in my chest. Clutching my stomach, I cough a few more times before standing back up. "I'm Jett."

"Well, Jett, didn't your mother ever teach you it's rude to interrupt when someone is talking?"

"My mother is dead," I blurt out. I'm not sure what I hope to accomplish with that.

Morton stops pacing, and he looks at me. "That's terrible. How did she die?" My brain knows he doesn't care, but his face and tone are so convincingly genuine, a part of me believes that he actually does.

"She was murdered," I answer, still catching my breath.

Morton sniffs. How does he manage to look sad? The look on his face— it's like I just told him his own mother had passed away. Morton puts his hand on my shoulder and rubs it softly, almost compassionately. A moment later he releases it and turns around. He paces back and forth before leaning back and shouting.

"Shinshew! This world is heaped. I know how hard it is to grow up without a mother. It's horrible. No one should have to endure that."

Kali and I exchange a glance. It feels like every muscle in my body tightens, refusing to relax just from being around him. Do I say something? Let him just continue rambling like an oddly sensitive madman?

He turns back to me. "Jett, is it?"

I nod, completely caught off guard by his sympathetic tone. "Yeah . . ."

"I understand your pain. I've felt it too. People say they understand but they don't. You and I, we are brothers born from the tragic loss of the most important person in our life." He pats me on the back and looks into my eyes. He speaks with such sincerity and conviction. Somehow his words are as comforting as if he were an old friend. Everything in me wants to like him. Nothing about what he's saying fits with what I know about him. He's sympathetic to the loss of my mother but he brutally murdered Kali's. How can someone who does that even pretend to care? Or is this all just an act? Is this some game he's playing at? I focus not on what he's saying but on what I know he has done. It's the only thing that helps me ward off his enchantment.

"You know what else you and I have in common?" I glare back into his strangely empathetic gaze.

"What?" he asks.

"Absolutely nothing." I shove his arm off my shoulder.

Morton laughs and points at me. "Oh, I like you. You remind me of me." What he intends as a compliment makes me sick to my stomach.

"We going to stand here all day pinging the firewall, or are you going tell me how you knew we'd be here?" I snap.

"Your friend Gina came to me, told me about this rare and expensive item you were planning to steal." Kane puts his hand on Gina's shoulder, which only seems to deepen her shame.

That's a relief. Gina's the one person who didn't know what we were actually stealing.

"Gina, how could you?" Kali's words pierce through gritted teeth. If Gina stared any harder at the ground, it might give way.

"Gina here is just repaying a debt—her fiancé, Jordy or Jimmy or some stupid name like that."

"Larry," Gina inserts.

Larry? Morton was way off. Morton's hand tightens on the back of her neck, squeezing as he grins.

"Did I tell you to speak?" He glares down at her.

Gina shakes her head as much as she can with his hand grasping the back of her neck.

"Her fiancé made some bets. Bets he couldn't pay. In order to keep all his appendages where Bealz put 'em, Gina here made a deal with me. It's nothing personal; she's just doing what any good woman would do—fixing the mistakes of her man."

Kali's glare remains unaffected by this news. Gina looks as if she's going to collapse in on herself like a dying star.

"Why don't you show me this rare and valuable item you confiscated from those loopers?" Morton smiles his effortless smile, finally releasing Gina's neck and walking over toward me.

"There's nothing to show. Just this." I lift the vault key we took from the guards.

Morton's entire demeanor shifts. His warm, jovial smile fades as his face sours into an agitated glare. Morton grinds his teeth as he turns to Gina. "Sounds like we've got a problem."

"He's lying!" Gina lunges forward and points at me accusingly. "He told Kali they got it! He said—" Her words are cut short as Kali drives her fist into Gina's face, knocking the guardswoman to the ground. Gina crumbles to the ground, holding herself up with one hand, rubbing her jaw with the other.

"Keep your mouth shut, you salvage scrap sink!" Kali points a threatening finger at her.

Morton chuckles and grabs Kali's arm, pushing her away from Gina. "You wouldn't be lying to me, would you, Jett? Not after we had that powerful bonding moment. You wouldn't do that, would you?" Morton smiles unnaturally wide. I can see an anger in his eyes. "I really, really hate liars." Morton paces in front of me.

"He is lying," Gina repeats, still rubbing her jaw. "The others must have taken it with them." Shinshew, now she's really done it. Kali lunges for her again. This time Morton catches her and pushes her back. Two of his Marauders restrain her but despite their considerable size advantage, they struggle to do so.

"Others, you say? Where are these others?" Morton turns to face me.

I need to stop him. Even if Kane found another exit, he couldn't have gotten too far dragging Becka's unconscious body with him.

I laugh as loud as I can, throwing my head back, trying to make my reaction seem as big as possible.

Morton's eyes narrow. Good, he's taking the bait. "What's so funny?"

"She's a city guard. City guards are complete rubbish. They all think alike."

Morton does not seem amused, but at least for the moment, I have his attention. Every minute I keep him talking is another minute for Kane and Becka to get away. Morton turns to his men; that's not good.

"You always have a shade!" I blurt out. Morton turns his attention back to me. I play it off like I'm bragging. "There's always a risk of getting caught, but if the guards can't prove you took anything, they can't do much, can they? All you have to do is make sure the one who got the goods is the one who doesn't get caught."

Hopefully that tod tale is a convincing enough distraction.

"You said you didn't get anything," Morton glares.

"No, I said the only thing of value I got was this." I extend the key toward him.

Morton growls, "I'm getting real tired of this."

I toss him the vault key.

Morton inspects it. "You must think me a proper fool. You want me to believe you went through all this to steal a key?"

"Believe what you want."

"Nobody goes through all that for a key."

"You're right. Our plan wasn't to steal a key. That key is a treasure in its own right. That key gets you into the vault, which is filled with treasures. More than we could have hoped to carry."

"Sure, and you didn't think to grab a single one?"

"That's right. The cultists were supposed to be out for the day. I'm sure you noticed them charging back into their compound. We had to alter our plans. It happens."

"Pat him down; find what he took," Morton commands. Two more Marauders step on either side of me, patting up and down my legs, my sides, and my arms. One pulls my energy blade and offers it to Morton. He waves his hand dismissively. "I don't care about his weapon." The other thug finds the book in my cloak. He taps it before reaching in and pulling it free. He offers it to Morton. Morton inspects it, looking displeased.

"What in the actual Sheol is this? A book?" He tosses Gibb's book to the ground.

"I think you're missing the point," I suggest.

"Check her." They pat Kali down as well but find nothing. Morton puts his face directly in front of mine, leaning in and glaring at me.

"Tell me, then, what point am I missing?"

I've never had a question feel so threatening.

"If I had stolen something, they would notice it was missing. Something goes missing you change the locks, you increase security, you make sure nothing else goes missing. That would ruin the opportunity. But a little key—that's easy to misplace, probably happens all the time."

If Morton has any experience with actual security, he'll see right through this bluff. Losing a key to such an important place almost guarantees locks getting changed.

"Since you didn't take anything . . . ," Morton starts as if reasoning it out himself.

"Exactly, the hardest part of stealing valuables is getting access to them. In giving you that key, I'm giving you the greatest opportunity you could ask for. That key is worth far more than whatever Gina promised you."

"Yet, here I am; I got all dressed up for you, and you didn't really bring me anything. That makes me sad." Morton shakes his head but appears slightly amused.

"Well, why settle for one treasure when you can have all of their treasures? Now that you have the key, all the hard work is done. Just sneak a dozen men in after nightfall, and you can rob them while they sleep."

"If I wanted to do it myself, I wouldn't have waited for you to do it, would I?"

"If I'd done it for you, it'd be meaningless. If I stole it and then you took it, you'd be Morton Ghood, man who took something from the skillful thief who stole it. Now, with that key, you can steal it all. Everyone loves a good heist story. Can you imagine? Morton Ghood, the master thief who pulled of the greatest heist in Dragonvale history. You'd be a legend."

Morton laughs, slapping his leg and turning to his goonies. "You see that, boys? That is how it's done. You weave a tale so the only option the other person has is to agree with you. The best way to do that is to appeal to their ego. Well done, you." Morton starts a slow dramatic clap. His Marauder goons awkwardly join in. It's really painful to watch. I have no idea if this is a good thing or not. At least he seems to have forgotten about the others.

I stare at him, forcing a smile. "We good, then?"

"You're an odd little parasite, aren't you? But I like you. I'm going to give you an extraspecial reward. I'm going to let you leave here with all your little bits in the same place they were when you got out of bed this morning. My generous pay for a job well done. Till next time." Morton whistles. He winks his single eye at us, and his thugs follow him down the street and out of view.

They've only just disappeared when Kali falls to her knees and begins hyperventilating. I rush to her.

"He was right there," her voices cracks. I pull her against me, holding her head against my chest while she sobs.

"I know," I whisper soothingly.

"I couldn't do it, Jett," she manages between gasps, tears running down her cheeks like two slow-moving streams.

"I know," I try to comfort her.

She sniffs, "I wanted to . . . I wanted to kill him . . . I didn't care what would happen. I didn't care . . . about the consequences. I was going to kill him . . . anyway. Seeing him so close . . . hearing him say my name. My whole body . . . just froze. I felt like that little girl again . . . Powerless . . . Weak . . . I failed her, Jett . . . I failed my mother . . ."

I let her words linger for a moment, so my response doesn't sound argumentative. I rub her back with my hand, trying to ease her mind. "You did not fail her. You did what she would have wanted; you survived."

A shadow moves over us. Gina looks down, her face wrought with guilt. "I didn't have a choice. He has Larry; he said he would kill him if I didn't."

Suddenly Kali stops shaking. She's no longer sobbing. With a loud sniff she drags her forearm across her face. A moment later she is on her feet. "You sold us out to *him!*" Her voice and volume raise like a battle cry. I can't tell if Gina knows about Kali's past with Morton. For her sake, I hope she doesn't.

Gina steps back. "I didn't have a choice."

"Only cowards pretend they don't have a choice. Everything is a choice. You just don't want to face the consequences of it." Kali pulls her blade from her belt.

I jump up, grabbing her arm to pin it to her side. I don't see her move. I feel her wrist twist away from my grip and then my feet sliding away from the ground. I land on my back with a painful thud.

"Kali, no!" I groan, reaching my arm up toward her.

"You can't be OK with what she did, Jett. She brought *him*." Kali glares at me.

"Look at her. Does she look like she feels good about it?"

Kali pauses.

"Listen, I understand why she did it. If I were in her place, if it were my friends, I don't know what I'd do."

I see her muscles relax a little. "You'd never sell someone out like that," she says.

"Maybe not, but it's an impossible situation. He has someone she loves, Kali. Can you really blame her for trying to save him? What if it was someone you loved? Would you really do any different?" I avoid bringing up her mother directly; that's a card I don't want to play— not unless absolutely necessary.

The blade in Kali's hand begins to shake with her fading resolve. Her arm falls to her side, and her eyes close. "Get out of here. Next time I see you, I will kill you."

Gina looks both relieved and somehow disappointed before scurrying off.

Standing up and dusting myself off, I cautiously put my hand on her shoulder. Kali turns and presses herself into me, holding her head against my chest. I put my hand on the back of her head and hug her against me.

"I don't understand why I fall apart whenever I think of her," Kali says so quietly I almost don't hear her.

"It's hard. There are so many things that can trigger those memories. I remember for years after my parents died, whenever I'd hear the slow dripping of water like from a leaky faucet, it would set me off. I'd see my mother holding her neck as the blood slowly dripped through her fingers. Once it started, it was like I was living it all over again."

Kali sniffs and looks up at me. "It never goes away, does it?"

I shake my head. "No, but it does get better. The more you let others in, the easier it becomes to live with the hole they left behind."

"Thank you, for being here."

"Always."

"I think I need to rest," Kali says.

I collect Gibb's book and tuck it into my cloak before taking Kali back to the inn where I change out of the cultist robes. Being back in normal clothing is such a relief. I place Gibb's book on my mattress before making my way to the tavern to meet Kane and Becka. When I arrive, Becka is conscious but is sprawled out at the booth and having a hard time keeping her head up.

"Jett . . . we dids its?" she slurs.

I can't help but smile. Becka doesn't drink, so seeing her inebriated is a special moment. "Yeah, we did it. Now we just have to make the exchange, and we are stocked."

"What happened to you?" Kane tosses me my datapad. I catch it and reattach it to my wrist.

"What do you mean?"

"Don't play salvage with me. We had a plan. You changed it. Somehow, I got here before you, despite toting this one the whole way. I'll ask you again—what happened?" Kane's eyes are piercing, like a hawk eyeing his prey. No sense in hiding it.

"We ran into Morton," I answer.

"You what?" Kane starts to stand up, but I gesture for him to stay.

"Turns out he has Gina's fiancé. Morton is forcing her to pay off his debt by giving him information he can use."

"Shinshew! And Kali?"

"She's OK—shaken up but OK. I took her back to the inn to rest. I should be able to handle Gregor without her. I'll make the deal this evening."

Kane nods. "That's a relief. What about Gina?"

"What about her?"

"Don't toy with me, friend; tell me you didn't let her walk away."

"What? She's a victim; what else would I have done?"

Kane shakes his head grimly. "Jett, she was in the room."

"So?"

"When we talked about killing Morton, she was in the room."

"She was guarding the door. She didn't hear anything."

"You sure about that? No chance she overheard us plotting to kill him? If she did and she tells him, all of this is for nothing. Your little plan only works if he takes the bait. He's not going to bring his Marauders out if he's suspicious someone is plotting to kill him. We can't take the risk."

"No, we are not discussing this. That is a line we don't cross."

Kane's expression sharpens. "What is wrong with you? I know you don't have a problem with killing."

"What you're talking about isn't killing; it's murder."

"Don't give me that; now you're splitting pixels. Dead is dead."

"There is a difference between killing someone who is trying to kill you and killing someone because they might have heard you say something that you didn't want them to hear. Gina is not a bad person. She just got caught up with one."

"I appreciate the sentiment, friend, but we can't afford not to. You want to get your friends back? Gina has to die."

"No, it's not right."

"I'm not saying it's right. I'm saying it is what's required. I hate it as much as you do; being stuck in that position is horrible. Heap Morton for putting her in it. But in it she is."

"Even if she did hear us, which we don't know, that doesn't mean she will tell him."

"The best predictor of future behavior is past behavior, my friend. She's already played her hand. If she has to choose between us and her fiancé, she'll sell us down river faster than you can say goat's milk. She's got to go."

"Victor once asked me, 'what's the point of changing the world if you can't live with yourself afterwards?'"

I can't believe I'm quoting Victor again.

"I understand what you're saying. You're right; it's a risk. I want to be able to look my friends in the eyes when this is done."

Kane stands up and pushes away from the table. With his face close to mine, he speaks through gritted teeth. "You can't look them in the eyes at all if they are dead. You want to risk that? Your friends dying because you didn't have the nooma to do what was required? Spending the rest of your life knowing they might have lived if you'd done something differently?" With that, he storms out of the tavern. No point in chasing after him; Kane's a shadow. He'd disappear the moment I gave chase. Besides, I can't leave Becka in a place like this. Not in her current condition. I slide into the bar and try to help her up.

"Jett, you're here."

Becka's voice always has a calming effect on me, even when she's completely zeroed.

I can't help but smile. "I have been, in fact. How you feeling?"

"I'm good, thanks. I'm hearing colors. They are loud."

I slide my arm under her shoulder and lift her up. "I've heard that about them. Come on, let's get you to bed."

Thankfully, Becka is conscious enough to carry some of her own weight. She can't walk or balance, but she manages to keep her feet under herself. Always the helpful one.

"Don't turn around." The voice behind me is stern and commanding.

I reach for my weapon.

"Don't. I'm not here to hurt you."

"Says the stranger in the shadows."

The man chuckles. "Still a lumegrin, I see. Nice to know the Outlands haven't changed you too much."

Wait, who do I know here? The voice does sound familiar, but I can't quite place it. "Get on with it, then. What do you want?"

"Firstly, let me express my condolences. We did not expect your friend to turn on you. A rather unfortunate turn of fate, I'd say."

"How do you know Victor?" My voice heats; I can't stop myself from starting to turn.

"Don't turn around," he warns firmly.

"Fine," I grunt and return my gaze forward. Becka hangs loosely on my shoulder, her words slurring incoherently; that drug had some kick.

"We have been watching you for some time now."

"Creepy. You coming up on a point?" I jeer.

"I see patience is still not a virtue that you possess. You have something we want. We can provide something you need. Perhaps we can come to an arrangement?"

"Hard pass. Been down this road before; don't care to do it again."

The man laughs. "We are not some beggar gang with delusions of grandeur. It seems unwise, in your position, to turn down potential allies. Especially without hearing what we have to offer."

"Fine, let's hear the sales pitch. If it has the words 'change the world' in it, I'm walking." Sometimes it's fun to push people's buttons. I find it can be quite illuminating. Everyone can pretend to be civil when they want something. How people respond when provoked is a bit more telling as to what they are really like.

"We share a common enemy, Jett Lasting, son of Matteo and Falli Lasting."

My eyes widen. My heart jumps inside my chest. My hands squeeze into fists. This stranger knew my parents? Is this some kind of trick? If he's as connected as he claims, getting that information would not be difficult. If he thinks casually dropping their names will earn favor with me, he's sorely mistaken.

"Mentioning my parents? Now you've crossed a line. I'm done with your games. You're going to explain, or I'm going to walk, and you'll never get the codes. That's what you're after right? It's the only thing that makes sense. I'm going to count to three. Then, I'm going to turn around. Anything else you have to say, you can say to my face. 1 . . . 2 . . . 3."

I turn, lugging Becka's body with me. Even though she is able to partially hold herself up, twisting her around is tricky. I stare at the man, or rather, not at the man but where the man should have been. In his place, stuck to the wall, is a note:

"Talk soon—

Signed – A friend."

Why do mysterious people have to be so cryptic? I examine the note closely to make sure I'm not missing anything. The handwriting, like the man's voice, is vaguely familiar. Still, I cannot quite place it. I pocket the note and head to the inn.

I'm not sure I like being this popular.

Though still groaning like a kid after too much cake, Becka is practically able to walk on her own. I keep my arm around her just to be safe. When we reach the inn, I deposit her in her bed, pull the sheets over her, and return to my room. Rowan is wearing a hole in the floor, pacing. Being shut up in a room all day doesn't seem to sit well with him. The other Raiders are all laughing and joking, playing a card game, and having a grand old time. Must be like a little vacation for them.

"Jett, you're back! Were you able to get it?" Kyle stands up.

"Yes, we're all set. I have to meet the merchant. I'll need your help bringing back the supplies. Can you get the others ready?"

Kyle nods. "Kali left a bit ago, and Kane isn't back yet."

"We will have to make do. Becka's . . . not in a position to help either."

"Can we carry it all with four less people?" Kyle asks.

"Shouldn't be a problem to drag across town. Just empty your packs of all our traveling supplies, and we're set." I pour out the contents of my pack onto my bed and sling the bag over my shoulder. "I'm going to go on ahead. Meet me at Gregor's shop as soon as you are able."

We part ways and I find myself walking the streets of Dragonvale alone. The sun is starting to set. Despite all that's happened, this is the safest I felt since leaving Dios. Maybe I should just forget about Dios; Dragonvale seems like a fine place to live.

I reach Gregor's shop and head inside. He's standing in the showroom when I enter. He extends his arms out wide, smiling like he expects me to rush in for a hug.

"You've returned! And with good news by the look of it. Come, come." He waves me back to his office. He's practically squealing as he sits down.

"Our supplies?" I keep my tone firm and direct.

Gregor extends his hand to the back of the room. Lining the wall are twenty chrome canisters, each about two feet tall. Next to the canisters, four stacks of ten chrome pucks.

"I trust that is to your satisfaction." Gregor slides two remotes across his desk toward me.

I deposit them in my jacket. "How do they work?"

"Each device has an activation switch. You can set them on a timer or detonate them with a remote. I included the second remote as a fail-safe or in case you wanted multiple people to have access. You can program the remote to each canister in a sequence where it automatically moves to the next one each time you click the detonator. You can program them to all go at once. Whatever your heart desires. The possibilities are endless. You've enough explosives there to bring down a mountain."

"Good." I open the code file on my datapad and transfer it to Gregor's. A soft *ding* indicates the process is complete.

"One last thing. I must insist that you delete the file from your datapad as well. My client insists that their copy be the only copy."

Just as expected. I let him watch as I purge the file from my datapad. It's a feature all datapads have when you want to remove something so completely that it can never be accessed again. When data is purged, it's like it was never there.

"Would you like to scan for copies?" I extend my forearm over his desk, knowing he could scan it all day but would never find the hidden copy. Predictably Gregor scans my datapad and nods happily, convinced there's nothing on it.

"May I make a suggestion?" Gregor asks.

"What's that?"

"Is it fair to assume you are not leaving Dragonvale tonight?"

"Not sure why that matters."

"It matters in that your accommodations do not provide the same security as I can offer. Perhaps I may, as a gesture of my appreciation, hold onto these for you. I can arrange for them to be delivered to you on the morning of your departure. That way you are unincumbered by them while you are here."

"That's a kind offer, or rather, that's the kind of offer that comes with a catch; so what is it?"

Gregor waves his skeletal hand in front of his sunken face. "The catch is simple; I want us to be friends. It benefits me to have connections with people of exceptional abilities. You have proven yourself to be quite effective. Allow me to do this favor for you so that perhaps in the future, should we have the opportunity to work together again, you might favorably consider it."

I raise an eyebrow. "You'll hold onto them, just to be nice?"

"Mr. Lasting, I did not get to where I am today by making enemies. I find that when you go just above expectations, it goes a long way to fostering what we can call fruitful partnerships. Consider this an investment in a potential future enterprise."

"Alright, Gregor. But if this is some kind of ploy—"

Gregor puts a hand over his heart and lifts it up. "Hand to Bealz, I have never failed to pay for services rendered. You tell me when you are leaving, and your payment will be waiting for you. Just consider, with your skills and my connections, we could achieve great things together." Gregor extends his hand. I shake it firmly.

"If you're playing me, my friend Kane will come to visit you. That is not something you will enjoy," I warn. Gregor nods in understanding. I make my way out of the showroom only to see Kyle just arriving with the other Raiders.

He looks at me with a confused expression.

"Are we not—"

"Not tonight—turns out our new friend offers a free delivery service. One less thing to worry about."

"We came all this way to get those explosives, and now you're leaving them here?" Kyle asks.

"I don't think he intends to back out. Plus, I put a tracker on his datapad when I nicked it before. He tries anything, we will know right where to find him."

The other Raiders head back, grumbling about their precious time being wasted. It's weird when grown men act like children.

Kyle lingers. "Jett, I was wondering if I might ask you something." His voice expresses a nervous excitement.

"What is it, Kyle?" I try to hide the annoyance in my voice.

I don't know what it is about him; he's nice enough. There's just something that doesn't click. It's like our bandwidths are incompatible. I have no reason to be bothered by him, but I am.

"Well, I was wondering if you could tell me a little more about Kali."

"Kali." I raise an eyebrow.

Kyle looks down at the ground and rubs the back of his head. "Well, the thing is, she's not like most of the girls I know. You two seem close. I was thinking maybe you could tell me about her?"

"If you want to know about Kali, why don't you just go talk to her?"

Kyle laughs. "Talk to her? Just like that? Are you serious? Have you seen her? She's so beautiful and so brave—and a little intimidating. You saw the way she fought that Skylari. I've never seen anything like that in my life. I wouldn't know where to begin."

"So why are you talking to me?"

"I was hoping you could help me figure out where to start."

"Oh no, I'm not getting in the middle of—"

I start to walk past him, but he catches my arm.

"Please, just a little bit so I have a starting point. Maybe just answer a few questions. Like was she born in the Outlands, like Rowan?"

The pleading puppy dog expression on his face is too much.

"Fine. No, she was born in Dios."

"Oh, I see. What is she, like twenty?"

"I don't know Kyle, probably. We're all pretty close in age I think."

"How long has she been out here?"

"She was exiled with her mother when she was around eight."

Kyle seems oddly excited about that. "What about her father? Was he exiled with them? The Patriarch usually exiles the whole family, don't they?"

I shake my head. "She doesn't know who her father is, just that he was someone important within the Patriarch. How does this help you exactly?"

"What? Oh, um . . . well, I don't know. I'm just asking questions. Got to start somewhere, right?"

"That's all I got. You want more? Go talk to Kali."

Kyle smiles. "An important mystery father. I wonder who that could be? Any ideas?"

"Goodbye, Kyle." I walk past him, this time with no resistance. What a strange man. Who am I to talk? I was so nervous around Lilly for months that I could hardly form a sentence.

The heart makes fools of us all.

CHAPTER FIFTEEN

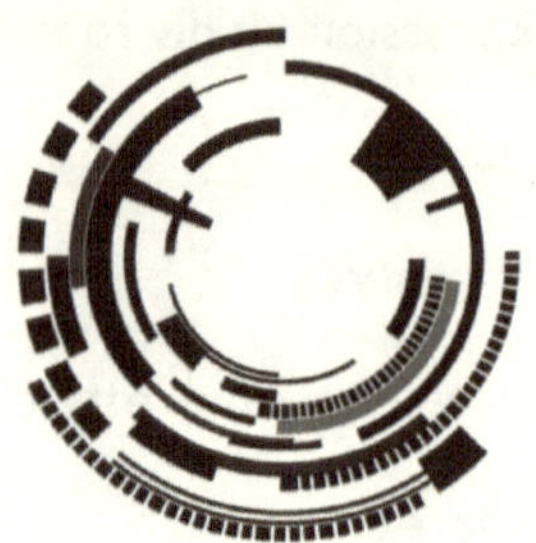

I hear the faint howls of what I assume to be a nighstalker in the distance. Something about knowing the danger outside the walls can't get me gives me a rare feeling of comfort as I walk the streets of Dragonvale.

Turning the corner toward the inn, I see Rowan leaving, heading toward the town gate. Probably on his way to get some fresh air. I remember going nutty on days Victor made me stay at the house—and even then, I could go outside. Rowan's been cooped up in a room by himself for days. I can't fault him for getting out. Even as I think this, a group of men group up, following behind him. This can't be good. I speed up, getting within earshot.

The gate is already closed, so Rowan turns to walk alongside the wall. The crowd follows until the guard towers are out of sight. Rowan turns to face the crowd.

Interesting tactic; I would have just run.

The crowd fans out in a half circle around him. There's almost a dozen of them.

"What do we have here? I'll be—looks like you were right, Bollinger." The man speaking stands in the center of the half circle, clearly the ringleader of this ragtag group of crags.

"Told you I saw him check in!" one, presumably Bollinger, jeers.

"Well, boys, it's time for community service. Let's take out the trash." The ringleader drives his fist into his open palm.

"We should turn him in. I bet he's the reason that poor lady guard went missing," another adds.

"Yeah! Maybe they'll even offer a reward," Bollinger notes. The little mob of fools start circling Rowan like sharks circling their prey. This must be what Kali was concerned about—a variety pack of scrap sinks flaunting their ignorance like a badge of honor. The men brandish a variety of weapons: a chain, a bat, steel knuckles, and a few makeshift blades.

My energy blade hisses to life, drawing the attention of the pack.

"One chance: Let's all just head home before things get out of hand." I try to sound as intimidating as possible, but I'm not sure it's enough to ward off twelve thugs.

"What's this, boys? Looks like our little Tribling brought a friend." The ringleader glares at me. "You know the only thing worse than a Tribling? A Tribling lover. There's nothing lower than someone who betrays their own kind." He spits on the ground in my direction.

"Walk away now, and we can forget this ever happened," I warn.

"What are you going to do? Murder us with your fancy sword? Use that, and the guards will come for you, for sure."

I twist the setting on the handle, and my blade turns into a shield. "I'm not going to use it on you. I just knew a bunch of crags like you wouldn't be able to stop yourselves from staring at the glowing light. Thanks for proving me right."

"What are you talking about?" the ringleader bellows, stepping closer to me with his chest puffed out.

I point. Behind him, four of the thugs who had circled around Rowan are lying on the ground groaning or completely incapacitated.

"Twelve on two is rough; eight is much more manageable."

"Get them," the ringleader growls, throwing his arm forward. I bring up my shield, deflecting his blow, moving inside it, and driving my fist into his chest. Pushing through the initial contact, I shove my fist up under his rib cage to knock the wind out of him. He keels over, gasping for air. Another thug charges toward me while yelling as if that will improve his fighting. I dodge his attack and catch his jaw with a left hook. One of the thugs wraps his arms around me. Pinning my arms to my sides, he lifts me up while thug number four rushes toward me holding out his knife. I tighten my core, pushing back against the man holding me, which allows me to drive my legs into thug four, sending him stumbling back and the knife bouncing down the street.

Before the one holding me can adjust, I wiggle and try to free myself, but he's too strong. I can hear Rowan fighting with the other group but can't see how he's doing. The ringleader recovers and walks toward me with a menacing look. He punches me in the face, hooking his right hand into my temple. I taste copper, and my head rings for a second. I see him winding up for a left hook. I wait until the last second, squeezing my core again to duck my head down and pull the man holding me closer.

The fist aimed at my face hits the man holding me instead. His grip weakens as he stumbles to the side. I tug my arms free. Using my momentum, I uppercut the overextended ringleader, knocking him back. Being outnumbered was proving quite the challenge. I quickly dash between each of my attackers, striking them once or twice before moving on to the next and trying to keep each off-balance while dealing as much damage as I can. Deflecting their punches with my shield works well and usually allows me to counter. I glance over to see Rowan knocking the last of his four to the ground. It looks like a massacre behind him as eight thugs lay unconscious or groaning in pain. Their weapons lay littered across the ground. My four attackers, on the other hand, while showing signs of exhaustion, are still very much capacitated.

Rowan turns and walks toward us without even seeming out of breath, though I would appreciate a bit more earnestness to his approach.

"Heap this," Bollinger shouts, dropping the bat he failed to even swing effectively and rushing back toward the gate. His exit starts a domino effect with the others. The ringleader takes the longest before realizing he didn't have a chance.

"You'll regret this; you'll see," he threatens and then chases after his friends, tail between his legs.

I keep myself from falling over by pushing my hands off my knees. Rowan pats me on the back. He holds his hand open to his lips and extends it forward.

"Don't mention it," I reply, assuming he was thanking me. I follow Rowan as he heads back toward the inn.

The next day, Kali seems to be in a much better place, whereas Rowan seems far worse. Being cooped up in an underground room all day and night is taking its toll. I don't think our encounter with the crag townsfolk helped matters. Thankfully, Becka appears to have recovered fully. The back room of the inn provides some privacy and a nice gathering place for our group to meet. We assemble there to plan our next steps. Most of the Raiders are eager to leave.

"We have what we came for. We can't just stay here; Lilly is waiting on us," said a short, balding Raider named Benji.

"We can't leave while Morton is still here," Kali counters.

"Why not? This mission is over; what are we waiting for?" Benji folds his arms defiantly. Kyle puts his hand on Benji's shoulder as if trying to pull him out of the argument. Benji sniffs.

"Because, Benji, the Marauders are not going to face an enemy army without their king. So as long as Morton is here, we can't do anything anyway," Kane sneers.

"We could still get the supplies back and get set up." Benji's really doubling down on this. The other Raiders stand behind him as if to communicate he speaks for all of them. Of the Raiders, only Kyle seems to be in disagreement.

"We could do that, but we have no idea how long he'll stay here. If we stay, we can keep an eye on him; make sure we know when to spring our trap," Kali insists.

"I get that, but we need time to set the explosives as well—make sure everything is in place. I'm just saying, it's worth considering."

"What if we did both?" Kyle asks. This silences the debate. "The explosives are light enough, right? Probably only take seven people or so to carry them."

"I'm not sure we should split up," Becka objects.

"After last night, it might be safer to get Rowan out of town. Maybe he could lead the Raiders back? Gets him out of this room, and he can keep them safe," I suggest.

"We don't need some Tribling to keep us safe, boy," Benji scoffs.

"Talk about him like that again, and you'll need him to save you from me," Kali snaps.

Benji's demeanor shifts. His pupils appear to be dilated, and he seems a little twitchy. "I didn't mean any offense, just that we can take care of ourselves."

"An extra hand isn't going to hurt," I insist.

"Actually, if it's all the same, I'd like to stay here," Kyle inserts. Little lovesick puppy doesn't want to leave Kali behind. It would be cute if it wasn't so glaringly desperate.

"Sorry, Kyle, it's going to take seven packs," I explain.

"I'll take one; after all we did to get the salvage things, I'd like to keep my eyes on them," Kane offers. It's a bit surprising, but it does make me feel a little more at ease knowing Kane would be with them. Everyone seems to find this acceptable.

"Alright, then; Kali, Becka, Kyle, and I will remain here. The rest will head back with the supplies to meet with Lilly and get prepared. Once we are sure Morton is returning to his headquarters, we will let you know. Just make sure you're ready when we get back. I'll reach out to

Gregor; make sure the supplies are here first thing tomorrow morning. You'll want to leave at first light."

The group splits. I close my eyes and take a deep breath, trying to calm my impulses.

Kali moves next to me. "You OK?"

"Yeah, I just hope we aren't stuck here too long. Every day we delay is another day my friends are stuck with those Marauders, having Bealz knows what done to them. Who knows if he'll make his move on that vault anytime soon?"

"I wouldn't worry about that. Morton is not a patient man. That key is a temptation he won't be able to resist for long."

"Let's hope so."

Kali puts her hand on my shoulder. "I know this must be hard. It's not long now. The finish line is in sight."

I place my hand on hers; it feels warm and nice. "Thank you." I give her a nod, and we step away from each other.

"Well, now that we've come this far, what's next? Are you still thinking you want to return to Dios after all this is done?"

I nod. "I'm not sure really. Part of me wants to, but I'm not sure there's a way to do it."

Kali smiles. "Are you familiar at all with the Outcasts?"

"Not really—heard them mentioned a few times. Doesn't seem like the Children of the Dome care for them much."

"No, no, they wouldn't. The Outcasts hate the Patriarch. They are determined to return to Dios and kill the High Father and then, of course, take control of the city for themselves."

"Naturally. Why is it everyone who claims to fight for justice also wants to claim power?"

"From what I understand, the Outcasts want a revolution. They want to tear down the caste system, remove the Patriarch, and bring all the exiles home. I've heard they have a base of operations here but I'm not sure where. They are pretty secretive with outsiders."

"That sounds promising. Why haven't you mentioned them before?"

"I honestly wasn't sure you'd live long enough for it to matter." She smiles warmly at me as if that should soften the insult. I suppose it does.

"How do we get in touch with them?" I ask as the Raiders file past us.

"I'll talk to my contacts, see if they can get me in touch with someone. I'll let you know if I hear anything."

"Great, when do we leave?"

"Actually, Jett, I really need to speak with you." Becka walks up beside me with Kyle in tow.

"Kali, I don't want you going alone. With Morton running around, it's not worth the risk," I say.

Kali raises an eyebrow, "Aw, are you worried about my safety?"

"Not even a little; I'm worried about what you'd do to Morton and the consequences from that."

This seems to please her.

"Kyle, will you accompany her?" Kyle's eyes light up, and he nods a bit too eagerly. Kali, on the other hand, seems far less pleased. That's what she gets for that safety comment.

"My source is shy. I can't just go bringing some eager domie along," Kali protests.

"Make him wait outside; tell your contact he's hired muscle." This time Kali is pleased while Kyle—less so. He gets over it quickly and starts talking almost immediately, trying to impress her. She looks over her shoulder, glaring at me as they walk ahead.

I mouth, "Sorry."

Kali just rolls her eyes.

Becka and I head outside and wander around town. She walks with a directionless purpose as she looks around, seeming almost paranoid before she pulls me into an alley and out of view.

"What has gotten into you?"

"We need to talk about yesterday," Becka insists, still looking around nervously.

"What about it?"

"The man, the one who spoke to you when we were leaving the tavern," she whispers despite there being no one within shouting distance.

"You remember that?"

She smiles. "I wasn't quite as out of it as I let on."

"Are you serious? I had to haul your heavy—"

"Watch it." She aims her finger at my face.

I choose not to finish the thought.

"Jett, I saw his face."

"What do you mean you saw his face?"

"Not a lot of ambiguity to, 'I saw his face.'" She enunciates each of the words dramatically.

I deserve that; it was a daft question.

"Jett, I recognized him. He's that guy you were talking to in Dios. The one who wrote you the note. You ran off by yourself like a crag to meet with him."

That's where I'd heard that voice before. It was Kegan. Realization is a cruel beast. It promises clarity and understanding but typically brings with it a slew of confusion and additional questions. What is Kegan doing here? How did he find me? Why does he keep showing up? As questions drum on my mind, Becka keeps talking. "Sorry, what?"

She sighs. "I was saying if he's here, maybe he has a way of getting in and out of Dios."

Realization flashes like lightning in my mind. I grab Becka's shoulders and kiss her on the forehead. "You're a genius! If he's here, there has to be a way to get back into Dios without the Patriarch knowing. Becka, we could go home."

Becka smiles at the thought. "I do miss that ratty old house; I wonder if they rebuilt it after the fire."

Sentiment—what a joyously irrational thing it is. We picture going home and returning to a season of life that has now passed. Even if we could get into Dios and make our way back to our old house, it would not be a safe place. Thank you, Victor.

We exit the alley and spend the rest of the day checking out shops, reminiscing, and dreaming about what we could do when we got everyone back together. In the final throngs of evening, we make our way back. This would be our last night before the Raiders leave, and our mission moves into its next phase. After tonight, we are one step closer to rescuing our friends. Boots clatter against the stone streets as a group of city guardsmen rush past us, rifles in hand. An alarm sounds, reverberating down the streets.

"What do you suppose that's about?" Becka inquires.

"Who can say? I'll go check it out."

"I'll come with you."

"No, you head back. Don't want you to push it too hard after yesterday; go rest."

Becka is less than pleased but finally agrees. We split up. I rush after the city guards to see what's going on. I follow them to the far side of town where the road meets the outer wall. In an open area, a crowd has gathered, cutting off the view of the other side. The guards push through the crowd. In their wake, I catch a glimpse: a body lying in a puddle of blood. Curiosity pushes me forward through the crowd. When the human wall closes too tightly for me to press through, I turn to the person next to me.

"What is it?"

"There's been a murder," the man whispers back as if scared to say the word.

"A murder? Who?"

"Couldn't say. Someone said it was some woman from the city guard."

This can't be a coincidence. My mind flashes to one conclusion after another, barraging me with an endless series of scenarios. I need to be sure. I need to see for myself. I shove my way through the crowd and see her. The only city guard who's name I know: Gina. Her body is sprawled out on the ground, a single precise cut across her neck. It wasn't an energy blade. That would have cauterized the wound or at least charred the skin. Gina's blood pools under her body the way a puddle would after a good rain. Suspicion and assumption breed conclusion after conclusion. It seems an odd coincidence that Gina is dead a day after Kane wanted to kill her. Would he do this? She was connected to Morton. He's loopy enough. Could be someone else entirely. She sold *us* out; perhaps we weren't the first. She could have enemies because she's a city guard. I take a long, slow breath, trying to slow my mind. *Never assume you have all the information, Jett. I hear Victor's voice in my mind. It's easy to solidify an assumption and confuse it with truth. It is not until you see all sides that you truly see.* Standing off to the side of the crowd, I see Rowan and Kali. Another possible twist on the suspects list. Or the alarm drew their attention as well. I make my way over to them.

Rowan gives me a subtle nod. Kali can't take her eyes off Gina's body. I put my hand on her shoulder. "Are you OK?"

"It's strange; yesterday I wanted to kill her for what she did. Now, seeing her like this, I'm sad." She finally pulls her eyes off Gina and looks at me.

Could be an act, but it doesn't feel like one. Plus, I don't see any reason for her to lie to me.

"The heart is a strange thing."

"I don't want to look at this anymore. Can we go?" she asks.

The streets are mostly empty as we walk back to the inn. The only people out beyond the crime scene are a group of doltine addicts passing a bottle back and forth in an alley. I find myself once again wishing Spike was here. I wonder how he is doing. Is he still in Dios? Was he exiled? Did he make it across the Sand Sea? A pot of anxiety occupies a burner in the back of my mind, slowly simmering my worries into full blown fears. A dark realization rolls into my mind like a storm cloud; I may never actually see him again.

We reach the inn, and I head to my room. So much has been happening, I almost forgot about Gibb's book. I retrieve it from the pack sitting next to my bed and inspect it. On the inside of the back cover is an "About the Author" section with a picture of Gibbs dressed in a nice suit and smiling warmly. He looks much younger in the picture than the Gibbs I knew. "Dr. Jacob Olander" is printed in big bold letters under the image. Seeing him like this is weird. My brain surges to memories I have of my friend. But this isn't Gibbs. Questions form faster than I can process them. What was Gibbs researching? Why was he staying with us? Were we part of his research? Were the things he said true or part of some concocted backstory? Were we just test subjects he was studying, or did he start to think of us as friends? Did the Patriarch know of his study? Did they sanction it? Was he working for them? With them? I shake my head, trying to free my mind from curiosity's merciless onslaught. I start reading about the man I knew as Gibbs:

Doctor Jacob Olander is a renowned researcher with degrees in Diosology, casteology, and history. He is widely respected as one of the leading minds in the history of Dios and is presently pursuing research into the impact of the caste system and its role in the High Father's goal of creating a peaceful and unified city. This work, Bloodlines and Beliefs, *is the shining jewel in his impressive and prolific writing career. Heralded by long-time friend and colleague Lorth Drant as "an insightful study in why our faith and the sacred bloodline are essential to the order and harmony of our great city." The High Father himself stated in a Prime Weekly interview that* Bloodlines and Beliefs *is one of his favorite books outside of the Sacred Texts.*

The book drops from my hands onto the bed. Just when I thought I'd put the questions away, this made it so much worse. Gibbs—our friend, the man who always outdid Telmen for Thief of the Day—didn't just work for the Patriarch—he was friends with them. I struggle to reconcile the person I knew with the person described in this book. We couldn't have just been research. He sacrificed himself to save Spike. Something must have changed. Did he just get attached to us? Was he seeing things differently after his time with us? Questions swirl through my mind like a cyclone, destroying any hope of sleep. Normally, I'd distract myself by thinking about Lilly. Doing so doesn't bring me comfort the way it once did. Ever since her reluctance to help rescue our friends, I don't think less of her—I just think of her less.

The next morning, a group of men drop off our explosives with a message from Gregor wishing us success in our endeavors. We say goodbye to Rowan, Kane, and the Raiders. We see them to the city gates, and they begin their journey back to our rendezvous location. We return to find the Town Square of Dragonvale abuzz with people chattering and rushing about nervously. Kyle approaches a fabric vender with his gift of questions. He returns a few moments later to report.

"It sounds like a group called the Outcasts are planning some gathering to recruit new members in preparation for some big event. Rumor has it that the Children of the Dome are planning to attack the Outcasts."

"They've got their permits?" Kali asks.

"Permits for what?" Becka asks.

"Dragonvale is a bit of a melting pot, housing people from different beliefs and backgrounds. Thing about melting pots is they often create powder kegs. To avoid things getting out of hand, Dragonvale allows groups to fight openly provided they obtain proper permits. It's how they control the chaos."

"They give people permits to kill each other?" I can't keep the notes of disgust out of my voice.

Kali nods. "Basically. There are rules that must be followed, but provided everyone abides by those, the guards just look the other way."

"Rules?" Becka's voice contains the same disgust as mine.

"No significant damage to property, no firearms, no hostages, no attacking groups or people who are not covered by the terms of the permit. Anyone caught violating these rules will be executed."

"How can they just allow that?" Disbelief drips from my words.

"That's the trouble with Dragonvale. There's constant civil tension between differing factions. Most of the factions here have additional charters in other areas. The mayor doesn't want to intervene and risk losing trade partners. When tensions rise, one or both parties can petition the mayor for a mediation, which is a nice way of saying the two groups battle until one side surrenders or is wiped out. The winning side is expected to clean up the mess after. These are the accepted terms and conditions for any conflict resolution between groups. That's why they ask about affiliations upon entry."

I rub my fingers, running through my hair. The whole thing sounds absurd.

"You can't be serious," Becka scoffs.

"As the grave, sadly. The mayor requires that the mediation be scheduled and a week's notice be given to the merchants and citizens to ensure any noncombatant has ample opportunity to make arrangements and avoid the mediation zone." Kali doesn't seem troubled by this system in the slightest.

I suppose orderly barbarism is better than normal barbarism.

"I can't believe this. It's the job of the community leaders to mediate and prevent conflict, not to offer permits for it. That's absurd," Becka grumbles.

"It's effective. Dragonvale has an incredibly low crime rate with less conflict than any other town in the region despite having the largest number of groups with conflicting ideologies."

"Bealz above, did they say when this mediation was supposed to occur?" Becka chimes in.

"Apparently it was announced this morning and is set for one week from today," Kyle answers.

Kali sighs. "That complicates things. Whether Morton leaves or not, by next week we need to be gone."

"Can't we just stay in the inn?" Becka asks.

Kali shakes her head. "Inns, taverns, any place we could access as guests are not safe havens."

I love it when a plan falls to pieces. Nothing to do about it, I suppose. We just have to hope Morton isn't loopy enough to stick around for it.

Over the next four days, we take shifts, keeping an eye on the city gates. We stay in pairs. Kyle remains insistent on pairing with Kali, who seems more and more annoyed each time they are together. His overeager puppy dog charm appears to be having a negative impact.

On my watch, I use the time to read through Gibb's book when Becka isn't stealing it from me.

"No, that's not what I'm saying." Becka flips to the middle of the book and points to a section. Look here:"

"In order to create a culture of true harmony and unity there must exist a shared belief amongst the population. Studies show that for this shared belief to be effective it requires devotion, practice, and sacrifice on behalf of the people. The sacrifice appeals to their nobler natures and motivates them to overcome themselves by shedding their individuality for the sake of the corporate good. The benefit of belief is that it allows the molding of a culture through the establishing of internal values and behaviors. For what the heart desires, the hands reach for. Uniting the people with common purpose and shared beliefs aligns their hearts toward unity."

I set the book down. "How does this not disgust you? It's like a guide for how to control and manipulate people."

"It's a study. He's not advocating for the Patriarch. He's simply expressing how to create a culture of unity."

"Is that right? What about this?" I flip further into the book and spin it toward her, tapping on the page that reads:

"The great burden of belief is that teachings may be interpreted many ways. However, if the system of belief promotes a singular focused medium for interpretation, like a prophet, this allows the teachings to be disseminated without division. The brilliance of the Patriarch's establishment of the High Father's bloodline as a holy bond between Bealz and Dios is that it creates a subconscious bond between the people and the Pontiff. For not only is the High Father the voice of Bealz but he's also the one who translates for Bealz, interprets Bealz, and is the people's connection to Bealz. Thus, to defy the High Father is to defy Bealz. To defy Bealz is to be condemned to eternity in Sheol. Thus, every action must be measured against a weight of not just temporary punishment but the eternal as well. Thus, the man who speaks for Bealz becomes Bealz."

"He doesn't say he agrees with it. He just notes that it's brilliant. In fairness, he's right. How many people never think to question the High Father because they just assume everything that comes out of his mouth is from Bealz?"

I hold up my hand. There's movement by the gate. Becka perks up and closes the book. Is this finally it? The small group stops at the gate and then turns back into town, just a passing merchant crew.

Four days and no Morton. With each passing day, the looming conflict grows closer. It's starting to look like we will need to leave before Morton does. I find myself taking long strolls at night, enjoying the peace and quiet. In all the years we lived in the ratty, old house in Dios, I rarely took the time to just think. I don't know why; everyone else did. Spike would meditate, Becka had a time for prayers, Olivia was always gardening in the backyard with every free second she had. Jensen went on walks, Victor was always thinking, even Telmen's endless waves of questions were how he processed the world around him. All I did was daydream about my parents.

The stars glisten overhead. The cloudless sky and cool evening breeze create a tranquility I haven't felt in a long time. It's too nice a night for such a dangerous place. This may be the only place in the Outlands where I can enjoy being out at night without having to fear endless horrors. It's amazing what the illusion of safety can do. I turn down a side street, wandering nowhere in particular. I'm so lost in thought I almost don't notice the three men step into the street, blocking my exit. That looks like a situation I'd rather avoid. I turn around, but before I can take a step, I crash into a large man in a tan coat. He's so large I bounce back a step after smashing into him. They must have been following me, waiting for this opportunity. But why? Who are they?

"You're coming with us," one says.

"No, thank you. I'm good, but I appreciate the offer," I reply.

"Lumegrin, it wasn't an offer. It was an instruction. You'll be coming with us. Only question is, will you be walking on your own feet or carried over Big Tim's shoulder?"

I wonder which of them is Big Tim. The one I'd crashed into would have made Grent look petit by comparison. The bigger they are, the more strain they put on their knees. Surprise is my biggest ally here. Without hesitation I drive my foot into the big man's knee. Pain surges through my foot so intensely that I see little dancing lights for a moment. Big Tim stands completely unaffected. He doesn't even wince.

That's insulting. I need a new plan. My vision goes dark and a thick, coarse fabric sucks into my mouth. I feel the sack pulled tight under my neck before my head jolts to the side, pain surging through my face and around my eyes. I feel my feet being lifted off the ground. I buck my hips, trying to free my legs, but I can find no purchase. My arms are pinned behind my back, and I'm being carried like a human stretcher. Wiggling is fruitless, but I do it anyway. If they are going to take me against my will, at least I'll make them work for it. It's a petty but gratifying rebellion.

CHAPTER SIXTEEN

The ground is smooth and cold as I crash into it. I groan and push myself up. Big Tim relieves me of my energy blade. Despite my rough transport, they make no effort to restrain me. Only two reasons for that: They are incompetent, or they do not see me as a threat. That's insulting. I pull the burlap sack from my head and toss it away. I'm in a strange room. It looks almost like a factory. Noisy machines clank in the distance, muffled by brick walls. Exposed pipes run along the walls and floor. Sitting in an out-of-place simple wooden chair is another man dressed in a long, tan coat with a gray undershirt and thick, black boots. I love it when a group of thugs coordinate their outfits. There's nothing really distinguishing on his clothing, nor anything particularly memorable about his appearance. The man looks at me and scowls before looking up at the henchmen behind me.

"Explain," the man scolds.

"Sorry, boss; he was resistant—didn't want the city guard to catch us trying to tie him up, so we just brought him here," the giant ogre called Big Tim responds.

"Resistant? You cornered me in an alley and demanded I come with you without so much as an introduction! I prefer to think of it as principled. I have a strict 'don't go anywhere with strangers you meet in a dark alley' policy," I object.

The man in the chair grits his teeth. "We will talk about your application of my instructions after we have finished with our little friend." He turns his attention to me. "You'll have to forgive our aggressive invitation. I don't particularly care for meeting with your kind."

"My kind?" What does that mean? Is he a different kind than me?

"You can change your outfit, but you're not fooling us. We saw you coming out of the compound, walking around town in your robes. No point in trying to hide it. Didn't know you were allowed to take your robes off outside the compound. Makes me think you're up to no good. What are playing at? Explain." He pulls a knife from his belt and dances it between his hands menacingly, or rather it might be menacing if he didn't almost drop the knife every few seconds.

I laugh, "Oh, you think I'm with the Children of the Dome?"

The blade freezes in his hand. He looks at me more seriously. "Explain."

It occurs to me that this could be a setup—a clever ploy to get me to confess to robbery. Since the penalty for that is beheading, I choose silence. These could be cultists in disguise, city guard, or someone else using this as a bluff, though there's something about disgust that is impossible to fake. I get the sense this is not a trap, but I need to be sure.

"Why would I explain myself to you?"

He brandishes his knife. "Because if you don't, I may decide to show you how much I loathe your kind."

"Sure, or you could be a city guard pretending to threaten me to get a confession."

"A confession to what?"

"Ah." I wag my finger playfully toward him. "Not that easy."

"I'm not a city guard."

"Oh, is there some kind of magic enchantment here that makes it impossible for city guards to say they are not city guards?" I make my tone as patronizing as possible.

He grumbles, "You're pushing your luck."

"Can you blame me? I like the way my head connects to my shoulders through my neck. The symmetry is quite lovely."

The man tugs at his gray undershirt and leans forward, revealing a small brand on his chest. The brand is of an eye—almost the exact design of eye used by the Patriarch—except this eye has been gouged out. Rather than being inside a triangle inside a circle, the gouged eye is inside a skull. Oh, the lost art of subtly. I stare at it for a minute before he sits back in his chair and grins.

"Outcasts don't take roles in Outland cities. We are not meant for this place. Now, explain."

Well, that's compelling enough. Plus, I find it's usually best to endear yourself to someone who is holding a knife.

"While I'm certain your men did see me in red robes, I am equally certain they didn't understand why I was in them. I'm not a member of the Children of the Dome. I was robbing them."

His gaze grows stronger as he considers my words. His stare goes on and on. This may be worse than the knife. OK, stab me, cut me, whatever you've got to do; just stop staring at me like a gargoyle. Eternity comes to an end before, finally, the man sheathes his knife and smiles warmly.

"So it was the Children of the Dome that had it all along. Gregor was smart to keep that a secret."

I shrug.

"Well, then, it appears we may have gotten off on the wrong foot. My name is Shane Lier. I am in charge here."

"And where exactly is here?"

"You are in the Dragonvale headquarters of the Outcasts."

This is their headquarters? I glance around, trying not to let my face reveal my skepticism. I've been curious about the Outcasts for a while but if this base is any indication of how organized they are, I'm not impressed.

"Word on the street is, you want to get back to Dios," I say before the silence gets too uncomfortable.

Shane smiles. "And why, pray tell, does that interest you?"

"Dios is my home—or at least it was. My friends and I were exiled for our part in a failed rebellion."

That catches his interest.

"Your friends—are they here?"

"Why?" I ask suspiciously.

"We've all been wronged by the Patriarch. An enemy of theirs is a friend of ours."

"No, they are being held by Marauders, presently."

Shane's smile widens. "Tell me your name."

"Jett Lasting."

The mood in the room seems to shift. Shane and his goons exchange meaningful glances. What the exchanges mean is beyond me. My name does not usually have this kind of effect. I look over my shoulder. The two guards who remain in the room look down sheepishly, avoiding eye contact as Shane glowers over my shoulder at them before finally returning his eyes to me.

"You're Jett Lasting?" Shane repeats.

"Last I checked."

"You led the rebels who took the Market Sector!"

"Well, that was more Victor than me, but I guess so. How do you know about that?"

"Know about it? We watched it. We keep tabs on the Patriarch. When you all took the Market, you changed things. For years our plans have been hollow words and plans on paper. After what you did, word spread. Now we are ready to fight. I feel like I'm meeting a celebrity! It's an honor!"

Shane extends his hand. I shake, not entirely sure what else to do. I pull his arm in and pat him on the back a few times. The moment lets me check him for other weapons; I don't feel any. That's good. One of the things I learned living as an Undesirable in Dios is you can never be too careful meeting new people. The ones you want to trust the most are often the ones you should trust the least.

"What happens now?" I ask.

Shane rubs his hands together, trying to start a fire with an invisible stick. "What a treat this is. We were very impressed with what you managed to accomplish. First time I've ever seen a rebellion in Dios that actually stood a chance."

He takes a breath and recomposes himself.

"Snowball's chance in Sheol, but sure."

"As you may know, the Outcasts exist to fight against the tyranny of the Patriarch and to free Dios and all its true citizens from their oppressive control. Most of us are Outlands officers who are here because we resisted and were banished for it. We plan to show the Patriarch the foolishness of putting all their enemies in one place."

"You'll have to forgive my skepticism, but I was there. I saw the black sea of endless soldiers crashing upon the Market like waves pounding the shore. For every soldier we killed, two more took his place. What could you do against that unstoppable force?"

"Well, since you ask. We have an army. Weapons? We've got them. Support from true citizens within the city? Got it. Promise of support from another city to aid us? We've got that too. A plan, a way into the city, access codes to move about the city—check, check, check. Anything I'm missing?"

"Yeah, follow-through."

Shane raises an eyebrow. "Explain."

"If you have all of that, what are you waiting for?"

"We've only recently acquired the codes; apparently, we have you to thank for that. We were starting to organize and mobilize our forces, but now that you're here, it changes things."

"Me? Why would things change because of me?"

"You have a reputation out here, Jett Lasting: The man who bloodied the nose of the Patriarch. Until you took the Market Sector, everyone believed the Patriarch was unstoppable—protected by Bealz himself they were. You made them bleed. For the first time in our lifetime, people saw Patriarch soldiers retreating. That inspires hope. If word spread that you joined us, our numbers would surge. Our support would grow. We'd have everything we need. We could launch the invasion, bring the Patriarch to its knees, and return Dios to its true people."

"How do they even know about me?"

"There are people in Dios who provide us with information. They send us reports, even vids. One of them sent us your speech rallying the beggar gangs. It stirred our ranks as well."

"They sent a vid of my speech?"

"Not just of your speech—of the battle. You'd be surprised how many people are working against the Patriarch out here. Those vids of you were played in every Outcast outpost I know of. Probably other places as well. We've never been so close to leading the true people of Dios home. This is a very exciting time!"

Hope flies like a kite in my heart, soaring above the trees, light and free. The only thing tethering my glee is a thin, nagging string tied to a handle I can't let go of.

"True? You keep saying true; what do you mean?"

"The true citizens of Dios are the men and women like you—who stand up, who fight, who resist the Patriarch's tyranny."

"So what happens to all the fake citizens of Dios?"

"Jett, the Patriarch is not just a small group of leaders. It's a system, a structure, a culture that must be destroyed. You can't build something new without tearing down the old. We must purge every vestige of the Patriarch's support. It's the only way to ensure its poison is eradicated from this world."

My kite of hope turns to an anvil crashing from the sky, threatening to squash me under it. "You want to just wipe out everyone who doesn't fight against the Patriarch?"

"I don't want to, Jett; I'm not a monster. I have to. It's the only way."

"Innocent people?"

"Innocent? You can't believe that. They have allowed this tyranny to continue for generations. They permit it with their silence, accept it with their inaction, and support it with their compliance. They are as guilty as the High Father himself." Shane's face has gone red and a vein throbs near his temple.

"What you are saying makes sense. I've been there. The Patriarch's power is predicated on the submission of the masses. If the people would stand united, they could topple the Patriarch in a day. I despise their indifference. I hate their inaction. However, I can't blame them. They don't know the power they have; all they can see is the power that presses down on them. They are afraid. They are lost. They are not guilty. They didn't do anything wrong."

"They didn't do anything at all. That's the problem. When you do nothing in the face of such injustice, you might as well carry out that injustice yourself."

I shake my head. "They are just trying to survive. You can't blame someone for not risking their lives in what seems like a hopeless battle."

"You did. You started something. You had a real chance at victory. These people that you are so quick to defend, did they defend you? Did they come to your aid? No. They watched. They let it happen as they always do. They are not blind. They know what the Patriarch is and what they do. How many lives has the Patriarch destroyed while they sat back and watched, doing nothing? They let the Patriarch continue because in their hearts, they want it to continue. Dios is meant to be a haven. Whoever controls it controls paradise. Only those who are worthy deserve it. When we take the city, we will remove anyone who was complicit, silent, or supportive of the Patriarch."

"Guards who are just doing their jobs, mothers who remain silent to keep their children safe, fathers who do nothing out of fear they might be responsible for getting their families sent out here to the Outlands— all these horrible people deserve to die?"

Shane sneers, "This is not what I expected from the hero of the Market Rebellion."

"I expected nothing of you, and somehow I am still disappointed." I stand up and start to walk away.

Shane calls out, and the two guards block my path. "I'm afraid I can't let you go."

"I'm not sure you have a choice."

"Explain," he growls through grinding teeth.

"Your fight is against the Patriarch. If you imprison me, someone famous for fighting against the Patriarch, it sends a mixed message, doesn't it? How do you think it'll look to all those people who believe in your cause when they see you holding the leader of the Market Rebellion hostage?

Shane's eyes narrow. "I could just kill you."

"That you could. It'll probably be great for recruiting. Join the Outcasts! We are just. We are honorable. We fight for the good of the people. We will kill you if you disagree."

Shane snarls, "That doesn't matter if they never find your body."

"We don't have to be enemies. Your 'let's murder everyone who doesn't risk their lives standing up to tyranny' policy doesn't work for me. So I won't be joining your little club. Why don't we just go our separate ways?"

Shane smirks confidently. "Doesn't work that way. You're either with us, or you're against us."

"I'd agree with you, but then we'd both be wrong."

"Explain."

"We both hate the Patriarch. We may not agree on the how, but we are allies on the what. We both want to see them brought down. You try it your way; I'll do it mine. We've no reason to fight each other."

"Sorry, I can't risk letting you go now that you know what you know."

"I thought you might say that." I pull one of the remotes Gregor gave me from my pocket. "While your goons were dragging me here, I planted a small explosive on each of them. I click a button, and their insides become outsides. Oh, right, and I put one in your pocket as well."

Shane looks down and moves his hands toward his pockets.

"Ah, ah, ah." I shake my head and lift the remote. "Don't try to get it out. You reach for it—I'll blow you all up right now," I warn. Last thing I need is him checking his pockets to realize there's nothing in them. My patting him on the back to check for weapons will give some validity to my bluff. He's probably thinking that's when I slipped it on him right now.

Shane glares at me, but his confident gaze seems shaken. "I let you go, what assurance do I have that you won't press that button the second you're out of the room?"

"None. You'll just have to trust me."

"That's a jagged little pill."

"Since I'm the only one in the room who's not into killing everyone who disagrees with them or seeking the genocide of an entire city, it's my word we'll be taking."

I step back and hold out my free hand. Big Tim reluctantly returns my energy blade.

"You're going to regret this," Shane warns.

What an amazing threat.

"I want you to wait here until I've left the building. You come after me—I click this button. You leave this room within the next five minutes—I click this button. You try to find the explosives within the next five minutes—I click this button. Got it?"

Their unified grumbles indicate they do. As I make my way past the guards. It occurs to me that I have no idea how to get out of this place since my head was covered on the way in. I step back into the room, looking at Shane. Well, this is awkward.

"Can one of your goons show me the way out?" I put on my friendliest smile. It's already weird—might as well have fun with it.

The smaller of the two grumbles and pushes past me. "Come with me."

I follow him through a series of corridors and past a couple of large rooms before he pushes open a creaky, metal door opening to the street. He remains at the door as I descend a series of steps onto the street below. No way this was their headquarters; there was no one else around, no guards, nothing. Can't even trust people who kidnap you and drag you to secret meetings anymore. What is the world coming to?

"Thank you. Now head back inside and wait."

I hurry down the street to get as much distance between me and them as possible. It's only a matter of time before they discover that there are no explosives. Hopefully, by then, they will realize this fight isn't worth it. Regular glances over my shoulder provide no evidence of a tail, but I can't seem to calm down.

Thick clouds roll, blanketing the sky and hiding the celestial lights. The clouds look strange, like they are sparkling with a green glow. It looks subtle at first, almost imperceptible. The faint, green light starts to pulse. An unsettling feeling comes over me. The streets are empty. Quiet at night is normal but not deserted. My senses heighten. Every window and door is closed. Red, flashing lights pulse from numerous places along the wall. I don't suppose it's a warning for something good. I take off in a full sprint toward the inn. It's still blocks away. I don't even know what I'm running from, but every instinct tells me I'm not running fast enough.

I see the glowing sign and the light from the inn lobby shining faintly through the clear door. I hear the rumble of thunder like a cosmic belly growling. Then, a gentle, familiar pitter-patter of a gentle drizzle but with an added *tssssss* at the end. I glance over to see a raindrop sizzling against the stone street like butter dropped on a heated iron pan. This is not normal rain. The sound is sporadic but growing. I slide to the door and pull—locked. I slam my hand against it again and again. Please, someone hear me. I shout at the door. The soft rap-tapping grows faster and louder. A droplet hits my shirt, and the fabric erodes away. My skin underneath burns. I rub the area, which only spreads out the pain. After all I've survived, death by rain is not how I expected to go.

A shadow emerges from the stairs and rushes across the lobby. The rain grows louder as its acid drops sizzle and splash against the stone. Kali twists at the door and pulls it open. I practically dive on top of her before she pushes it closed and reengages the lock.

"Sand-brained domie! What were you still doing out? Didn't you see the storm lights?"

"Actually, I was chatting with the leader of the Outcasts."

"Before the acid rain—are you mental?"

"I didn't choose the timing; they grabbed me off the street."

"That's not a good sign."

"No, it was not." I look out as the downpour begins. The droplets dance and sizzle heavily on the street. It's strange—it doesn't seem to be damaging the stone, but it burned through the fabric of my shirt and left a mark on my skin.

"You've never seen the acid rains before."

I shake my head. "It doesn't erode the stone?"

"No, it cleans it. Seems like the acid only really burns organic materials like cloth and skin."

"Is this common?"

Kali shrugs, "Common enough that most towns have a warning system for them."

"Glad we weren't traveling for this," I jest.

"Come on, I want to hear all about your encounter with the Outcasts."

The next morning, the rains have gone, and the streets look polished clean from them. Two more days pass; still no sign of Morton. Just knowing where my friends are, knowing the kind of situation they are in, means I have to talk myself off the ledge of impulsive rescue attempts multiple times a day. At least the Raiders should have had ample time to get set up. It's early in the morning. Becka and I are walking through the Town Square when Kyle comes rushing over. He slides to a stop in front of us, panting for breath.

"Morton! Morton's leaving. Saw him at the gates just now!"

"Where's Kali?" I ask, looking around.

"Headed back to the inn to get our stuff."

"We should go too," Becka suggests.

I take a deep breath and utter words that cause me physical pain. "We need to wait."

Both Kyle and Becka's jaws drop as they stare at me, apparently too stunned to speak. They look as shocked by the statement as I am in anguish for making it.

"We need to give him a head start," I explain. "Doesn't do us any good if we go bumping into him—or worse, if he spots us following him. We should gather our supplies and get ready; let them have a full day's lead. Tomorrow morning we go."

Packing up goes quickly. There's a part of me that's reluctant to leave. This is the safest I've felt since the beginning of the Market Rebellion.

When the four of us do start out, I realize how weird it is not having Rowan along. Despite his perpetual silence, his presence is noteworthy. Rowan's keen perception and awareness kept us out of trouble on multiple occasions. Not having him with us makes me feel even more on edge. Kyle continues his idle chatter, employing persistence as a romance strategy. It doesn't seem to be effective, but hey, maybe he just needs more of it.

"We're close, Jett; it won't be long until we have our friends back!" Becka's voice purrs with an excited energy.

"Then we just need to find Spike."

Becka puts her hand on my shoulder and shakes my whole body. "Bealz above, I miss Spike. I can't wait to see him."

"We're one step closer," I grin.

"Maybe one day we can go find a beach. There has to be one somewhere, right? Wouldn't it be amazing to go find one? Build a little life for ourselves; a nice, peaceful getaway where we could just forget all the troubles of this life. Doesn't that sound nice?" she chuckles.

"It sounds like a dream," I agree.

Becka has always been interested in the ocean. There were projections of it and images in stories of The World That Was. Every time it came up, her eyes would light up. She always said it looked majestic. She wasn't wrong. Nice to see that even after all this, her hope in a fantasy future hasn't waned. A beach—I'm not even sure it is real. Could just be another tod tale.

We return to the quick pace we used when traveling here. Kali must be part machine to move so quickly for so long without even appearing out of breath. Her pace makes conversing difficult. It's barely evening when she spots a cave in the rock wall about ten meters up. After our recent encounter with the depraved, we aren't taking any chances. A safe place to rest is more important than how far we travel. We climb up the wall and move to the back of the cave, which runs deep enough that even a lit fire wouldn't be visible from the outside. Can't light a fire in a cave, though; smoke doesn't have anywhere to go. We set up an aluma for light and sit around it.

Our time in Dragonvale allowed us to restock our supplies, giving us plenty to eat and drink. After demonstrating once again she wasn't going to let us stop for meals, we all make sure to fill up. We laugh and joke for a while, then grow quieter as the sun starts to set. Kyle is oddly quiet now. His leg bounces rapidly as he sits across the aluma from Kali. I do that when I'm impatient, but he seems more nervous than impatient as he constantly glances toward the cave entrance. Can't say I blame him; the last time we were here was traumatic. Even if that was the only time the depraved ever came through this way, the fact that they did makes the whole place feel uneasy.

"So, Kali, what's next for you when this is done?" Becka asks in a hushed tone. We might be out of sight, but Becka's smart enough not to draw attention by being too loud.

"Hard to say. Killing Morton has been this all-consuming pursuit for so long, I've never really considered what comes after that. Maybe I can finally settle down and feel at peace," Kali whispers back.

"That sounds nice. I hope you are able to find it, whatever that looks like." Becka's words bring a warm smile to Kali's face. She starts to reply but then freezes, eyes moving to the entrance of the cave. Kyle stands up, hand on his weapon. Do I hear voices on the wind? The noise makes me tense, but Kyle seems to relax a little. Maybe just knowing it's not the depraved is a comfort to him? More sounds, almost like boots marching. No—not boots—buzzing. It's a faint but growing buzzing.

Kali mouths, "Skylari."

I stand up and step toward Kyle, putting my hand on his shoulder and whispering, "It's OK, they'd have a hard time fitting through the cave entrance." I'm not entirely sure if my goal is to reassure him or myself. Fighting one of those things was difficult when we could move in the open. A swarm of them cornering us inside this cave would render us pretty helpless.

Kyle closes his eyes and lets out a heavy breath before sitting back down on the cave floor. The harmonic hum of wings as the large mantis creatures fly by drowns out everything else. Kali starts packing up.

"What are you doing?" Becka asks, keeping her voice low.

"We should go," Kali responds.

"Are you kidding? We can't go out there with that swarm of monsters." Kyle's objection sounds more angry than fearful.

"Best time to travel. That swarm will clear the canyon for a long time. Soon as it's gone, we go. We can push through and make it to Lilly's camp by late morning," Kali answers.

Something is off. While her explanation makes sense, forgoing rest seems like a desperate move. We have a relatively safe and secluded place to sleep, so why does she want to leave that to travel through the night? While her face projects a fierce confidence, her eyes are beaming with suppressed fear. I want to ask what's really going on. Something tells me not to.

Kyle shakes his head. "No, we need to stay here. We need to wait until—"

"You really think it's safer?" I ask. If Kali is this rattled by something, I trust her instincts. There's always time for explanations later.

Kali nods. "Without a doubt."

Becka starts packing her stuff. I do the same. Kyle's jaw is agape. He looks to the entrance and then back to us.

"No, we need to rest. We just ran all day. Now you want to go all night, too? That's madness," he protests. His shift in tactics weakens his overall position. I'd be more inclined to support him if he'd just stuck with being too scared to travel at night. It wouldn't win him points with Kali, but I could at least sympathize.

"Come on, Kyle, you wanted an adventure; this is what adventure looks like." I slap him on the shoulder. The melodious murmur starts to fade as the main group of Skylari is moving away from our position. Kyle sighs before kneeling down in defeated acceptance, packing his bag.

The buzzing grows faint as the swarm flies off into the distance and disappears from view. We wait a few minutes to make sure there are no stragglers before climbing down from our rest cave and continue our marathon jog to our rendezvous point. At least with the Raider camp we can sleep with a sense of security.

Kali was right. We travel through the entire night and don't hear or see another living thing. The sun begins to rise and on we go. We push through the fatigue, the soreness, the weariness of mind and body. Becka periodically goes to each of us, chatting and cheering us up with her relentless encouragement. Kali is driven by some unseen force, or maybe her time in the Outlands has made her so tough she doesn't get tired. Kyle has been silent since we left, pouting like a child who didn't get his way. As the sun rises, so does the temperature. Just as I'm ready to insist we take a break so we can rest our legs, the canyon opens and, in the distance, I see the camp.

Tents, flags, and supplies stretch as far as I can see. It's perfect. From here it looks like an army encampment. Even knowing that it's a mirage, I have to remind myself that it's not actually the base of a large army. Then, it hits me: This plan may actually work. Invigorated, we race toward the camp.

Rowan, Kane, Brock, Lilly, and a few others I don't recognize greet us as we arrive. Brock is wearing his superior scowl. Rowan tries his best to appear disinterested, but I can tell he's happy to see us. Lilly appears reserved. Things were confusing when I left, but her hesitancy now makes her feel even more distant.

Kane breaks the silence. "Welcome back; we were starting to wonder if you'd gotten lost. Any trouble?"

"Leave them alone, Kane." Lilly finally breaks her statuesque posture and smiles softly. Her eyes continue to move between Kali and me. "Why don't you get some rest? You look like you've traveled all night. When you're ready, we can discuss the next phase of the plan."

"Should we—"

"You should rest. We'll talk after," Lilly interrupts me.

I'm too exhausted to protest or object. I grunt and stumble my way to the tent set up for me. My body is so worn out I barely make it. I don't even remember lying down. When I wake, the sun is rising again. Everything hurts. It's like all of my joints are filled with flaming cement. Getting up takes way too long.

Vesta, the ever-thoughtful Raider cook, sets aside a large plate for me: strange meat—well-seasoned, some odd-looking but tasty vegetables, rice, and a piece of bread. Apparently, traveling a full day and night works up the appetite.

After finishing my meal, I meet Lilly and the others in the largest tent, presently serving as the command center.

"Becka was filling us in on your time in Dragonvale. Care to walk us through your experience?" Lilly asks. I tell her what we learned of Marauder culture—specifically the complications of killing a Marauder king—and about the Outcasts, Kegan, the Children of the Dome, and the Vanguard. Saying it all out loud really makes it feel like a lot has happened. Once the debrief is finished, Brock comes stomping over.

Brock bumps his shoulder into mine as he hands something to Lilly. It's good to know his charm has lost none of its edge while we were gone. Lilly looks at the note and groans, rubbing her temples.

"Why didn't you tell me this before they left? We could have had them bring doses back?" She glares at Brock so hard it gives me chills.

"What is it?" Becka asks.

"Our supply of Kathar Aera is getting low."

"Hasn't everyone already had it?" I ask.

"As I've been told, it doesn't last forever." Lilly sounds exasperated.

"She's right. You need to re-up every eight months, at least for the first few doses. If you survive long enough, your body will adapt, and you won't need it as often. Most don't make it that far," Kali explains.

"It's just frustrating because this inconvenience could have been so easily avoided; that's not your problem. Let's get back to the plan." Lilly motions to the table.

"Is everything in place?" I ask looking over the designs on the table.

"Yes, the plan is to leave a small force here to create enough movement to make the camp look convincing from a distance; when the Marauders arrive, they will take off. Our main force will split in two, taking the high ground on either side of the pass. When the Marauders come through, we will wait for them to inspect the camp. When they start back, we will use the explosives. Once the explosives are set, my Raiders will engage. We'll hit them hard and fast, then return to headquarters via two different routes. This should give you as much time as possible to rescue your friends while also hopefully dealing a mortal blow to the Marauders," Lilly explains.

"I've added some traps here and here and here," Brock says, pointing to places in the camp, "to take out a few more of them while we are at it."

"Bad idea," I respond.

"Oh, is it?"

"The space is too open; it won't do enough," I explain.

"It'll do something. Every bit helps," Brock retorts.

"It will give them a dome's up—make the real ambush harder to pull off. It's not worth it to take out a few scouts. We don't want to do anything that might make them suspicious," I counter.

"Who do you think you are? Some upstart Undesirable with delusions of grandeur? Unlike you, I was educated in Dios. I studied history and tactics," Brock boasts.

"Maybe you should have studied knitting—might play more to your strengths." Kali flashes a wicked grin. "Jett's right, any trap you set for their scouts jeopardizes the whole plan."

"Disarm your traps, Brock; it's not worth the risk," Lilly commands.

Brock scowls and storms out of the room, his cape flapping dramatically behind him.

"Kali, you're going to stay here with Lilly's Raiders." I turn to face her.

"The sheol, I am!" Kali looks at me as if I've just betrayed her.

Becka puts her hand on Kali's shoulder softly. "This is your chance Kali."

Kali pulls her shoulder free. "What are you talking about?"

"When Lilly's Raiders attack, this becomes a battle. This is your chance to kill Morton without repercussions. It's a long shot, and even with everything else, there still may not be a way to do it. But if ever there was one, this is it. This is your chance to avenge Valami. I'm not going to take that away from you. I'm sorry I won't be able to—"

Kali blinks and looks at me. "You remember her name?"

"Why is that surprising?"

"Most people hear without ever really listening. You didn't just ask her name to be nice. You actually care?"

"Of course, I do."

Kali stares for a moment as if unable to process that. She blinks several times before her eyes narrow, making her look determined.

"You'll need our help to rescue your friends," Kali protests.

"We'll figure it out. I'm not getting in the way of your—"

"No. I mean, thank you. It means a lot that you say that." Kali rubs her hand down her face.

"We have a Blood Pact; I'm not going to—" I say.

"We'll just have to figure something out later. Rowan and I are going to help you rescue your friends."

"Kali, I can't ask you to—"

"We're coming. Might as well accept it," she cuts me off again. Rowan turns and nods firmly. Victor's voice in my head tells me: *Don't fight a battle you can't win.*

"Thank you," I manage to get out despite my shock.

I will feel much better having them with us. I catch her eyes, green and glimmering with that same softness I saw when I first met her. Now, as she looks at me, I feel a strange warmth as well. The world around us seems to fade. For one moment, there is nothing but those green eyes.

Lilly clears her throat, replacing the warmth I was feeling with a sudden, overwhelming awkwardness. "I'll be here making sure we're ready on this end. Who's going with you?"

"You know I'm going." Becka walks over next to me, joined by Kali and Rowan.

Kane joins us, smacking me on the back and laughing. "No way I'm letting you have all the fun."

"I'll go, too," Kyle smiles, making a point to stand next to Kali. Why am I suddenly annoyed he is standing next to her? He's been fawning over her for days.

"Jett, your rescue team will leave once we lure the Marauder scouts in. You'll wait outside their base here." She points to a spot on the map out of view from the path leading from Morton's camp. "Once the main force leaves, get in and get out quick. We'll buy you as much time as we can. Get our friends to safety. We will meet you back at headquarters. From there, we can decide what to do next. Any questions?"

"One." Kane leans over the table. "What happens when something goes wrong?"

"What do you mean—when?" Brock balks.

"It's a solid plan," Lilly counters.

"Plans are always neat and tidy. Reality is messy," Kane retorts.

"Just don't screw up and we won't have any problems, will we?" Lilly snaps.

Kane steps back from the table. "Yes ma'am."

A few days pass like frozen molasses sliding downhill. Then, it begins: Marauder scouts are spotted. We wait another agonizing day to give the scouts the opportunity to return and report back. Then, finally, we are off. This time Kali struggles to keep up with my pace as we blaze ahead, making our way to the Marauder base.

We make our way through the pass. We come around a turn and I collide into something—someone. I stumble back and nearly fall over. Standing in front of me in the traditional garb of an Outlands Officer is a woman. She looks skeletal and thin. Her hair is dried out like a wire brush. Around her lips are a patch of bubbles. Shinshew. She lets out a cackle and swings the knife in her hand at me. I lean back, narrowly avoiding the steel edge as the others catch up. I reach for my blade when someone crashes into me from the side, knocking me down and almost into the rock wall. Another foamer joins the fray. Rolling to my feet as quickly as I can, I realize it's not just two but a whole pack of them.

CHAPTER SEVENTEEN

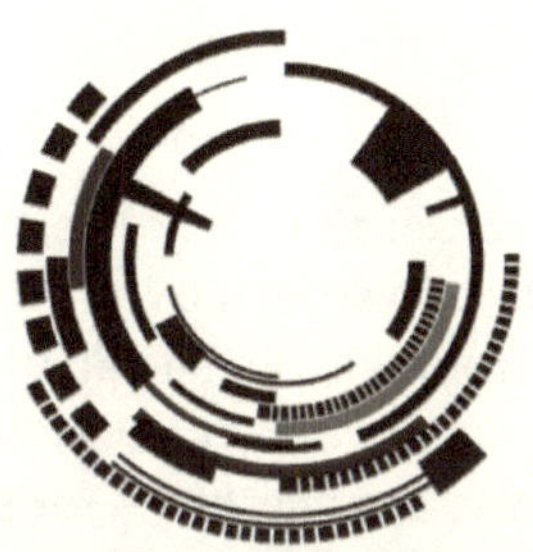

Becka rushes to me. "You OK?"

"Yeah, where did they come from?" I ask, readying my blade.

Kali activates her energy bow and fires a shot at one of the approaching packs. The energy arrow catches one of the foamers in the shoulder, but the foamer keeps coming.

"They roam around in packs sometimes," Kali answers.

Rowan dashes like a streak of color and cloth, cutting down the one that crashed into me before it could turn around. I scan the foamer herd, counting six more besides the one I bumped into. Kane laughs and gleefully charges at the foamer pack. Rowan charges with him while Kali fires arrows over their shoulders. Kyle seems too stunned to move, leaving Becka and I to deal with the last one.

The foamer roars and dashes toward Kyle. Becka dashes to cut the mad addict off. The female foamer grabs Becka and headbutts her. She stumbles and falters. I charge forward, swinging my blade at the foamer but miss completely as she rapidly changes directions.

This is going well.

"Kyle, snap out of it!" I shout. He turns to look at me but still doesn't move. The she-foamer rushes at me. Her arm lifts above her head as she starts to lunge. Suddenly her shoulder jerks back and her body twists as a blue bolt of energy hits her just below her chest. I shove my blade forward, taking advantage of the sudden shock. I see her try to adjust on the fly, but it's too late. Kali's arrow slowed her down just enough for my blade to find its mark. Her body slumps forward and collapses to the ground.

I turn to Becka. "Are you OK?"

She nods, still holding her head. To my surprise the pack of foamers is almost entirely wiped out. Rowan stands over one he's just killed. Only one other remains. The final foamer, a slender and sickly-looking male with patches of hair missing, looks around and cackles before turning to run away. Not much point in chasing him—he's way too fast.

A shadow passes overhead. Dropping out of the sky is the great green-armored Skylari. Falling like a rock, it dives at the retreating foamer. Its clawed feet grab the man by his shoulders and topple him to the ground as the Skylari lands on him. Roaring with delight it's wings flutter so fast they become an invisible blur as the massive mantis-creature soars up and out of view, carrying the foamer in its clawed clutches.

Out of instinct, I scan for more. The sky is as clear as a freshly cleaned pane of glass. We stare for a moment, too shocked to do much else.

"That was fun." Kane rubs his hands together, smiling far too genuinely for my liking. No sane person enjoys near death experiences like this. Kane's insanity breaks enough of the tension for us to resume our journey to the Marauder base.

The path leading in is wide. In the middle of it is a single boulder with a relatively flat top. The rock protrudes about four feet off the ground, splitting the path in two for the briefest of moment before returning to a single lane leading to the gate.

Along the base of the rocky cliff is a cave. It's close enough to the gate where we can watch traffic coming in and out but far enough to keep us safely out of view. A day passes. Then another. How long does it take to mobilize an army? Maybe they didn't take the bait. Maybe the camp wasn't as convincing as I thought. Maybe it was, but they just don't care about the presence of another army. Was all of this for nothing?

On the third day, there's movement at the gate. Finally. Marauders stacked in neat, even rows—armed and ready. At the front of the pack is the tall psychotic cyclops, Morton. Relief washes over me like a spring breeze as Morton begins marching his Marauders toward a fake camp but a very real ambush. It's not long now. It's almost time to rescue my friends. Everything I've been focused on since my exile comes down to this.

The Marauder army disappears from view. No more waiting. This is it. We sneak through the gate without any trouble. The few guards left behind are scattered and inattentive.

"Kyle, Becka, Rowan, you take the left side; make your way to the back of the camp. Kane, Kali, and I will take the right. We will search each building until we find the hostages, meet in the middle, and head back out." I look at them. Each nods in agreement.

Crouching low, we make our way along the outside edge of the camp just inside the perimeter, careful to ensure we remain out of sight from the towers above. Lilly's reports were right. If they had a full guard crew on patrol, this place would be impossible to sneak into. Thankfully, the Marauders only left a skeleton crew behind to serve as guards, which creates lots of gaps in their lines of sight. Weaving in and out of tents for cover, we dash through as quickly as we can. The further in we get, the lighter the guard details become. Nerves make my body shake. It's not the first time I've snuck into a guarded area, but the stakes feel higher than usual. The prize isn't just something to help us get by; it's my family. Failure has never been less of an option. Some twisted part of me would feel much better if this were Victor's plan. At least then, I'd be confident it would work. But this is no time to worry. We have a small window to work with and won't get a second chance at this.

The middle of the camp is completely abandoned, allowing us to run freely toward the back. No alarms, no shouting, no sound at all. Things are going well. Kali holds up her hand, and we stop suddenly. She motions with her head. I peek around the corner at a large wooden building. Standing in front of the door are two guards.

"Creatures to credits that's where they are keeping them," she whispers.

"I got it," Kane says before disappearing into the tent next to us. He dashes to the far wall of the Marauder base. He moves quickly, reverse-hugging the wall as he follows it to its end. Kane pauses, draws two blades and then turns the corner. He moves like a shadow, darting to the door and moving past the first guard. From our position we can see him move, but it's hard to make out what he's doing. A second later he is returning his blades to his belt, and the two guards are dead on the ground. This is it.

I shove the door open. Inside the wooden building is a long, open room lined with bunk beds. Each of the beds has a thick iron chain with a glowing red light attached to its metal frame. The chain connects each prisoner to the bed at their ankle. Excitement, nervousness, fear, and hope collide inside me all at once. I rush into the room, looking for my friends. There are no signs of guards inside the building. Just a group of prisoners in shabby, tan tunics covered in dirt and scrapes sliding out of their beds and walking as far as the chains would allow them. Murmurs of hope, whispers for help, and cries of desperation fill the air.

"Telmen, Jensen, Olivia," I call out.

A slow groan answers back.

"Jett? Is that you? What are you doing here? How did you find us? Where have you been? What's going on? Where did all the Marauders go?" Telmen's automatic question dispensing fills me with joy. I rush to him and wrap my arms around his shoulders, hugging him tight.

"You're OK." Unbridled relief floods through me.

Telmen taps my back gently and winces. "OK, but—ow! I'm a little sore; could you loosen up?"

I let go and look at him, smiling from ear to ear. "We're getting you out of here."

"Jett Lasting, I told them you'd come. I knew you'd find us." Olivia's voice comes from behind me. A second wave of relief hits me. I chuckle and fight back tears as I rush across the room to her. We practically collide as we hug each other, laughing as we are now both fighting back tears and losing.

"Olivia!"

"I never gave up hope. No matter what the Marauders did, I knew it was just a matter of time before you found us."

"I'm sorry it took me so long. I was doing everything I could to—"

"Stop with that. I know. We all do. We are family after all, and you don't leave family behind.

"Are you OK? Where's Jensen?" I ask.

Olivia looks down and sighs. "There's a switch on the wall that unlocks all the chains at once. Let us out; I'll take you to him." Something about how she says it makes me nervous. Kane finds a control on the front wall and clicks the release button. Kali starts gathering the other prisoners and giving them instructions for our escape. Olivia leads me across the large main room to a small set of backrooms. Telmen follows us in silence.

The door is unlocked. Telmen and Olivia exchange knowing glances as I push it open. The room is empty save a bed bolted to the floor in the middle and a few counters lining the wall on either side of the entrance. The metal bedframe has no mattress, just a metal slab. Underneath the bed are a pair of cables running to a large, rectangular box that looks like some kind of power generator. Curled up in the fetal position is a young man with freckled skin and sandy-brown hair all disheveled. He's almost unrecognizable. The bed has a post on each corner and around each post are chains binding Jensen to the bed.

"Olivia, we need a key; search the drawers!"

Olivia darts over and starts frantically rummaging through the counter drawers. Jensen doesn't move or make a sound.

"I don't see anything," Olivia replies.

Jensen is wearing a tattered, tan tunic and slightly darker, brown pants. I put my hand on his shoulder. No response. I look back and see the fear in Olivia's eyes. We've come this far. There's no way we are just leaving him here.

"Jensen, Jensen?" I shake him again. He moves enough to indicate he's alive but not enough to demonstrate any real consciousness. I shift my energy blade to the smaller knife setting and active it. I hold it to the chain, careful to keep it as far from Jensen's skin as possible. We can deal with the shackles later; we just need to get him free. My blade burns through one chain. I move to his other wrist. Pulling his sleeve up to get access to the chain on the other side, I see his chin. The scars of severe burns stretch beyond the shackle itself. I see what they were doing. The metal bed, the metal chains, the power generator—they've been electrocuting him.

"Taking too long; we need to leave!" Kane is at the door, shouting sternly.

"We'll leave when our friend is free. Why don't you go be useful and help tend to the other prisoners?" Olivia cuts him off, staring him down. Even having just watched Kane stealthly kill two guards, I'm worried for his safety.

The second chain falls away, and I move my blade to the chains on his ankles. As much as I didn't like it, Kane was right; this was taking too long.

"I don't think he's able to walk. We're going to need to carry him out," I say.

Olivia walks over to the bed. "They were rough on all of us, trying to mold us into their little soldiers. Jensen worst of all. He refused to give in; no matter what they did, he wouldn't comply," she explains.

"That sounds like Jensen—always has to be difficult." I try to lighten the mood, more for myself than anyone else. One chain to go. Gently, I roll Jensen onto his back. I step back, covering my mouth with my hands, my eyes watering at what I see. Jensen's face and neck are covered in bruises. The variety of color suggesting they have been inflicted over an extended period of time. His cheeks are puffy. A scar similar to Kane's but much larger and fresher runs across his face. He's been beaten. Repeatedly. Savagely. His lips and eyes are swollen; one so much so, I doubt he could open it if he tried.

"Jensen, if you can hear me, I'm getting you out of here." I start sliding him toward the edge of the bed.

"We'll get him; you get us out of here." Olivia steps in front of me. She and Telmen lift Jensen up, holding his weight between them. Olivia nods for me to lead the way.

Kali and Kane have been joined by Rowan and Kyle. They are all standing at the front door with the other prisoners at the ready. We make our way over to them just as Becka steps into the room.

"What's going on? What are we waiting for—" Becka's words cut short as she sees Telmen and Olivia carrying Jensen. A smile flashes for a moment before she sees Jensen's condition. A sob catches in her chest, and she looks away to gather herself. Becka walks straight up to them, extends her arms, and makes a big hug circle, careful not to press into Jensen's battered body.

"Are you—" she starts.

"We're OK. Let's just get out of here," Olivia answers.

"Rowan, lead the way. Get everyone out. We'll hang back and help with the wounded," Kali instructs before gesturing to Jensen. Rowan nods and starts the trek back to the Marauder gate. I count around two hundred prisoners, each silently following Rowan's escape route. How are we going to sneak all these people out without being noticed? Even with their reduced numbers, they aren't going to miss a parade of prisoners prancing away.

A scream pierces the air and with it, my heart. Gunfire seems to be coming from near the entrance. The prisoners start clamoring and gasping. Becka holds up her hands, trying to reassure them and calm them down. Just as things were going so well. Shouting and more gunfire. What is going on? It's not Morton coming back; they wouldn't be firing on each other. Is someone attacking? Are the creatures approaching? Please, whatever it is, don't let it be the depraved. Waiting isn't an option. The longer we are here the more likely the main force returns and traps us. We head toward the sound. With no other means of escape our best hope is that it is a small skirmish, and we can overpower whoever is left.

The line of escaping prisoners moves closer and closer to the gate. The sound of battle slows and seems to be moving deeper into the base. With any luck, we can slip past them without being noticed. A fool's hope is sometimes the only thing available. Rowan stops near the front gate. It seems the conflict has moved far enough inside that we have a clear escape route. It's almost too fortunate. We don't have time to question or even options to consider. Our best hope is to keep moving.

Kali gives Rowan a nod, and he takes the lead. Kane offers to take over for Olivia. She says something unladylike and shoves him away. Telmen and Olivia drag Jensen out next. They'll need the biggest head start. The other prisoners start filing out, keeping their backs to the wall and moving as quickly and quietly as they can. No one has noticed us yet. The longer it stays that way, the better.

"Movement at the gate, on me!" a voice shouts from somewhere in the sea of tents.

Now, we are heaped. At least it's not the depraved. Speed becomes more important than stealth.

"Run!" I shout. The prisoners race out of the base, following Rowan. A flash of black rushing between tents. *The Vanguard? What are they—*

"We need to buy them time," Kali shouts.

"Kane," I start.

Kane grins, already holding a pair of blades. "Thought you'd never ask." He disappears into the pile of tents.

"I'll draw their attention," Becka offers before rushing to one of the walls and climbing up. How did they find us here? Why now? They had no way of knowing the Marauders would be gone. *Be present. Focus.*

"The tents! Burn the tents!" I shout, rushing over to one and activating my energy blade. Keeping the blade just far enough from the fabric of the tent, I hold it in place, hoping the heat will be enough to set it ablaze. It is. With a rush, the fabric catches; orange flames dance up the walls of the tent. Kali follows suit. The flames generate a considerable amount of smoke, which should reduce visibility enough to slow them down. A short burst of gunfire erupts, followed by a quick scream.

Kali attaches her energy hilts to create her bow before drawing back an arrow. Out of the corner of my eye, I see Becka running along the ramparts of the outer wall. She's holding a gun from one of the fallen Marauders and is firing wildly into the tent area. I can't see the soldiers through the jungle of tents, but having seen her shoot before, I have to assume she's missing all of them. My attention diverts as I hear them firing, seeing the bursts of light crashing behind and around Becka while she runs. They are too close for comfort. Kali steps to the side and fires her arrow. The beam of light whistles through the tents. Another scream.

I scan quickly—the prisoners are all clear. Kyle is standing near the gate and he's the only other one in sight. Why is he just standing there? Did he really freeze up again?

"Kali, let's go." I move toward the gate.

"What about Becka and Kane?" she protests.

"They will catch up; we need to get clear."

Kali nods. We turn and run to the gate. Suddenly our path is cut off.

"I'm really sorry about this, but I can't let you go," Kyle smiles warmly.

"Kyle, what are you doing?" I ask.

"My job."

"Kyle! We don't have time for this." I try to push past him. He shoves me back before drawing and pointing a small energy pistol at my head.

"Jett, I admire you. Your persistence. Your determination. I'll admit it, I might even like you. I'm so grateful for all the information you gave me about sweet Kali here." He smiles and turns his attention to Kali. "We've been looking for you for a long time. I was starting to think we'd never find you."

"What did you tell him?" She looks at me accusingly.

"I didn't tell him anything."

"Oh, Jett, don't sell yourself short. Exiled at eight with her mother. Mysterious but important father. You told me everything."

"You, you asked for help talking to her, not . . ."

What have I done? Somehow, I've given away something important. I have no idea what. How is any of that important?

Kyle laughs. "You must think I'm pathetic to need help talking to a girl. What a joke. I was gathering information. You see, we've been looking for the *Filia Lucem* for some time. She's always managed to stay one step ahead of us. Even with a tracker on her, heaping old tech. We had this faint signal, but it would fade in and out, give us a general location but nothing specific. It's been incredibly frustrating. Thanks to you, all that is over."

"What are you—"

"I'm Vanguard, you crag. Tracking wasn't working out, so we used spies. Sent them all over to gather intel and see if we could find a lead on sweet little Kali here. No one ever did until me."

"You work for the Patriarch?" My hand grasps my energy blade.

Kyle clicks a button on his gun and shakes his head. "Course I do. Now that I've found the *Filia Lucem*, I'll be set for life. Thanks, Jett, I really couldn't have done it without you."

"Why did you wait until now to make your move?" I ask.

"On the way to Dragonvale, I wasn't certain. I didn't want to blow my cover over a guess. I mean, she's the right age, but the whole warrior woman thing gave me some serious doubts. Guess she doesn't take after her father. Who knew? I planned to take her on the way back. My team was approaching the cave, but they got pinned down by the Skylari swarm." Kyle grits his teeth. "Why do you think I was so resistant to travel through the night? But all's well that ends well."

"Sir." One of the Vanguard soldiers comes rushing into view. A moment later two more drag Kane between the tents. "He killed five of our men before we were able to subdue him. Kane groans and rolls onto his side. The soldier deposits his body in front of us. The remaining Vanguard soldiers, a group of twelve, circle around us.

"We will deal with them in a minute; first, scan her." Kyle points to Kali.

Kali raises her arms, ready to fight.

Kyle turns his gun back to me. "Ah, ah, ah. Any more of that, and they will pay for it."

Kali scowls and drops her arms.

One of the soldiers taps on his datapad. The blue beam of a scanner rushes over Kali's body and face. There's a quick, happy-sounding beep. The soldier looks up.

"Confirmed, sir; she's the one."

The one? What does that mean?

Kyle claps his hands together. "Finally, boys, we can leave this wretched sheol-hole and return home."

The soldiers cheer.

"Drag everyone outside. Our men as well. Leave no trace we were here."

The soldiers grab us and shove us out through the gates, leading us to the large boulder that splits the path. Kane is still lying on the ground groaning. They force me onto my knees across from Kyle. Kali is behind me with two soldiers struggling to hold her still. This is not going to end well. I just hope Becka's smart enough to stay away. We wait for a few minutes while the soldiers who aren't keeping us restrained head into the Marauder base and return, dragging the bodies of their fallen comrades.

"Nice of you to clean up. I'm sure Morton will appreciate it," I scowl.

"We need to make sure this looks like it was a Raider attack. Can't have Morton chasing us down before we get back to Dios with our prize. Don't worry, I'll leave your body here for him to find."

"You're not taking her," I protest, climbing to my feet.

Kyle puts his hand on my shoulder and looks into my eyes. A gunshot rings out. Instinctively, I clutch my chest, expecting to feel heat or cool or wet. There's nothing. One of the soldiers behind me drops to the ground.

"Contact!"

The Vanguard soldiers move into their combat formation, firing wildly at a group of Marauders charging toward us. I didn't even notice them approach. In the chaos that ensues, I duck down and grab Kane's shirt, dragging him away from the action. Kali grabs the arm of the guard holding her down and flips him over, slamming his back against the ground. Before he can react, she buries one of her energy blades into his chest. She rushes toward us. We slide behind the boulder, ducking down to stay out of the line of fire as much as possible.

"I can move; just help me up," Kane groans, starting to push himself up.

Kyle whirls around. "No! Don't lose Kali!"

He turns toward us, aims his gun, and fires. His shot flies wide as Becka crashes her shoulder into him just as he pulls the trigger. Now she'll have to circle around to avoid him. At least she's fast enough to catch up. She smiles and nods to me before taking off in the other direction while Kyle works to regain his bearings.

The Vanguard is falling back, firing and retreating toward the Marauder camp gate. They are outnumbered badly. Kyle curses and rushes to join them.

"I really hate when my friends have a party and no one invites me," Morton's unmistakable voice rings out. He's standing farther down from where we are but looking at the Vanguard. A small group of Marauders charge past him, chasing after the Vanguard.

I glance over and see the full force of his Marauder army marching into view.

"This isn't over!" Kyle shouts, retreating father into the Marauder base. The Vanguard is pinned down inside their base—not much hope for them. We are far enough away that if we ran, we'd have a good chance. Kali pulls on my jacket. I start to turn.

"Jett, we meet again." Morton and a few of his henchmen approach. "What am I going to do with you? On the one hand, we got all kinds of stuff from that vault, thanks to the key you gave me. On the other, my scouts tell me you and your friends stole all my trainees. After we had that bonding moment about our mothers? I can't believe you'd do something like this."

I picture Jensen's beaten face. My blood seers through my veins. He's baiting me. I just want this to be over. If I could just—

Kane grabs me—more leaning against me than pushing off me—but the result is the same. "No. This is not the time or the place."

A group of Marauders comes stomping up, dragging someone behind them. I can't make out who—just kicking feet at first. Kicking feet and a flash of bright, colorful shoelaces. My heart falls out of my body and bounces off the ground. Morton kneels down and lifts the woman up, spinning her around to face me while holding his arm around her neck. There's no way I can bridge the gap between us in time to do anything.

"A friend of yours, I see," Morton smiles. "Not as pretty as the other one. But she'll do. With some training—some torture—she'll make a great slave."

"Becka, don't worry, I'm not going to let—"

"It's OK, Jett; our friends are safe. That's all that matters. Just go. It's enough for me to know you're safe."

"Shut up, Becka, I'm not leaving you here. We are all going back. We are going to be together again." I take a step closer, trying to get within striking distance without him realizing what I'm doing.

"Will you listen to these two?" Morton puts his hand on his heart. "This may be the sweetest thing I've ever heard."

I'm almost surprised flames don't burst from my eyes. "Touch her, and I'll kill you!"

Morton laughs. "You've got nooma kid; I admire that. Hearing you two talk makes me feel all warm and cozy inside. Tell you what, I'm in a generous mood. Here's what I'm going to do. I'm going to go kill those Patriarch scrap sinks in my base. I'm going to let you go with a warning and a debt. You took my stuff. You're going to bring it back."

"Those are my friends," I snap.

He waves his hand. "I don't care about your friends. So long as you bring me replacements."

No way I'm doing that, but I'll tell him whatever he wants to hear to let Becka go. Kane's grip on my shoulder tightens. "Easy, take a breath. I've got an idea."

"Oh, before you go, one more thing," Morton says, smiling his charmingly creepy smile. Becka coughs. Blood spurts from her mouth. My mind tries to reject what I'm seeing. Protruding from her chest is the tip of Morton's steel blade. The metal is covered in Becka's blood.

CHAPTER EIGHTEEN

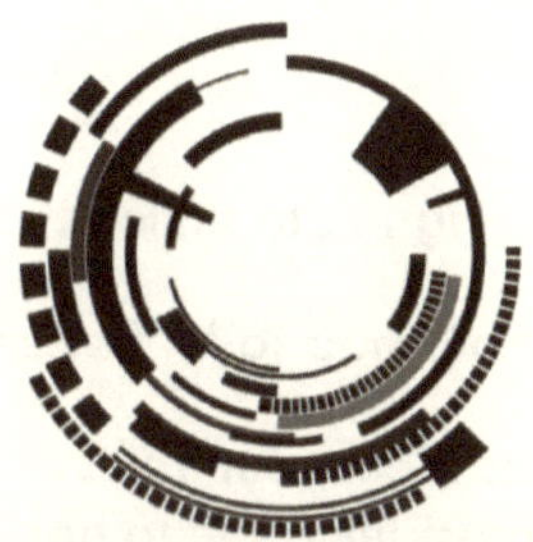

Kane plants his feet, but it's no use. I shove past him and run toward Becka. Morton pulls his sword free and pushes her with his foot in my direction. He turns and walks off like he's just thrown away a piece of garbage. I slide across the rough terrain, tearing up my knees, to catch Becka as she falls. I cradle her in my lap, my hand pressing against her wound, willfully deceiving myself into thinking she has a chance. Tears stream down my face, raining on the ground below.

"No, no, no, no, no, no . . . ," I repeat as if my denial could change the situation.

"That's your warning. See you next time, kid." Morton waves his hand without turning back.

My will splits into two. One part—my unbridled wrath—tries to drive me to chase him down and kill him here and now. The other part— overwhelming sorrow—makes my legs too heavy to move. Sorrow wins. My focus returns to Becka.

Her soft hand caresses my face as she wipes a tear away. "It's OK, Jett . . . I'm ready." Her words come out slow and are broken up by her short, heavy breathing.

I shake my head. "Shut up, Becka, you're not going anywhere."

She smiles softly and coughs. "Promise me . . . you'll keep them safe."

"Becka, I'm so sorry." I can barely look at her.

This was my plan, my idea; this is my fault.

"Shh, Jett, . . . do me a favor?"

"Anything."

"I want you . . . to keep living . . . to smile . . . to be happy . . ."

"Becka," I start to protest but stop to let her speak.

"When I met you . . . I was alone. But you . . . you became my family. You all . . . were the greatest thing . . . to happen to me . . . I wouldn't change a thing . . . not a thing . . . you hear me?"

"Then don't go anywhere and I won't," I plead as if there were some deal to be brokered.

Becka smiles, "I guess . . . this is . . . where . . . I leave you . . . The rest . . . is up to you . . . Don't you dare die, Jett . . . You have to live . . . for both of us now. Find a beach somewhere . . . and think of me, OK?" Her words are getting softer as my heart grows heavier.

"I love you, Becka," I say through sobs and tears. "You're the best sister anyone could ever have."

Becka coughs up blood as she tries to laugh. "I know." I feel her press her hand into mine. "Jett?"

"Yes?" I barely manage to speak through my tears.

"The shoelaces . . . would you . . . hold onto them . . . for me . . . to remember me?" Her voice is so faint, I can barely hear it.

I look down to see her brightly colored shoestrings. "I could never forget you, Becka. Not in a hundred lifetimes."

Her hand falls from my face and slaps limply against the ground. I hold her tighter to my chest, tilting my head back and screaming into the sky.

The main force of the Marauder army is getting close. I can't bring myself to move. Kali's hands slide under my arms as she lifts me up to my feet. Kane lift's Becka's body over his shoulder and starts moving away from the base. Kali tugs me along after them.

Somehow, we end up at the Raider base. Lilly and most of the Raiders are still gone. They probably have no idea how spectacularly my plan failed. Olivia and Telmen rush to us. Kane lays Becka's body down gently and steps back.

Kali stands next to me without a word.

Olivia covers her mouth and tries to stifle a scream as tears start cascading down her cheeks.

"This is your fault!" Telmen whirls and points his finger in my face. "You got her killed. Like you got Gibbs killed. Like you got all of us banished out here!"

"Telmen, that's not fair. You know he didn't—" Olivia objects.

"Oh, I know. The noble Jett Lasting never means for anyone to get hurt. But we did. We got captured. They tortured us, made us do things. None of this would have happened if you'd just listened. Spike warned you. Victor warned you. I told you this was crazy. No, you make choices, everyone else pays for them."

"Telmen . . . " I don't even know where to begin. His words are not news. They are the audible expression of what has been playing in my head since Dios.

"Do we all have to die before you're satisfied? What's it going to take before you—"

"You've said enough, boy," Kane scowls, stepping between Telmen and me.

"Oh, is that so? That's my thing, isn't it? Telmen is always talking. Maybe if you'd actually listen, I wouldn't need to talk so much. All of this could have been avoided."

"Telmen, you need to calm down. You're being—" Olivia tries to step in.

"No, it's OK. He's right. All of this is on me," I say.

"See?" Telmen taunts. "Even he knows it. It doesn't stop the destruction he leaves in his wake, but he knows it."

"Oh, shut up," Kali interjects.

Everyone turns to look at her. She steps between me and Telmen, her face red.

"Most people live their whole life without finding someone who would do for them what Jett has done for you. I thought he was crazy risking everything for his friends. From the moment I met him, he's thought of nothing, done nothing, except try to figure out a way to rescue you. He put his life on the line, faced horrors you haven't even dreamed of yet, to rescue you. You don't think he'd have traded places with Becka in a heartbeat? I do. I think he'd have laid down his life to save any one of you. He'd have been happy to do so. Bealz help me, I can't figure out why. Does he get a thank you? No, he gets this." She gestures to Telmen with a scowl. "I'd count myself lucky to have a friend half as caring as him. Shame on you. Why don't you just—"

"Kali, it's OK," I protest. Her words provide a slight relief as if chasing away some of the clouds of misery in my mind.

"No, Jett, it's not," she grunts out through gritted teeth.

"Whatever." Telmen stomps his foot. "I'm going to check on Jensen. Try not get anyone else killed." Telmen storms off.

"Jett, he doesn't mean it." Olivia tries to comfort me.

I don't want to be comforted. Everything is falling apart around me: Victor betrayed us; Gibbs and Becka are dead; Spike is alone somewhere; Jensen is hurt; Telmen hates me—leaving me with Olivia as the last remnant of my former family. When Becka left this world, she took the light with her. I sink into a black hole of despair.

Lilly and her Raiders return a day later. Kane and Kali handle the explanations. Kali heads off, but Kane lingers back and says something to Lilly in private. Meanwhile, I sulk in the darkest corner of the cave I can find. Becka's death seems to have dampened everyone's spirits. Even in her short time with the Raiders, she seems to have really made an impact on them. It's nice to know Becka never stopped being Becka.

Lilly insists on a service to honor her and say goodbye. I put forth my best effort, but my mind is in a daze of despair. They dig a hole in the ground and put Becka's body into it. Kali explains this is the way dead bodies are dealt with in the Outlands to keep them from attracting the depraved. I've never seen a burial before. It's strange to think you could walk over a person's remains without ever knowing it. In Dios, there wasn't enough space to bury bodies, so bodies were burned to ash.

At the departure ceremony, lots of people talk, but it sounds like they are underwater. Words become hollow sounds devoid of meaning. Faces are a blur of blank stares. Everyone tries to offer their sympathies. I remember this dance. I learned it after my parents were killed. I know they mean well, but if one more person tells me this is the will of Bealz, or she's in a better place, I'm likely to punch them in the face. Do they really think that helps? Are they actually trying to cheer me up? It's been a few days. It seems like they are trying to assuage their discomfort more than they are trying to comfort me in my grief. Heap this; I walk away. I need some time by myself.

I find a chair in the corner of one of the caverns just outside the retrofitted kitchen area and sit down. My fingers run over the colorful surface of Becka's old shoestrings as I clutch them like precious gems.

This is not what Becka would want—me sulking about, but I don't know what to do. It's as if a thick fog surrounds me and weighs everything down—my mind, my movements, even the beat of my heart feels irregularly slow. How do I shake this feeling? How do I let go and move on?

"Hey." Kali rubs my shoulder with one hand. She doesn't say anything. She just sits there next to me. A minute passes. Two more. Still not a word. No cheap condolence? No petty attempt at comfort? Maybe she understands how annoying those things are.

"I don't know what to do, Kali," I confess.

She nods. "You don't have to do anything."

"I know I can't just sulk about forever; I know I need to—"

Rowan walks up, standing on the other side of me. He places his hand on my other shoulder. Even without squeezing, his grip is strong. He nods to Kali.

"Triblings are forbidden from trying to comfort someone in mourning until ten days after the loss. They believe the pain of loss is necessary to heal and that comforting too soon cheapens the memory of the deceased. For ten days, they comfort their friends and loved ones by sitting in silence with them while they mourn. It's how they honor the dead."

I rub my eyes. "Really? It's a shame not everyone does that," I try to jest, but it only makes the pain feel worse.

"Jett." Her voice is firm but soft. "May we sit with you?"

Her words break me, and I collapse into a heap of tears and sobs. Kali sits down next to me, and I curl up against her. Kali pulls my head into her lap and runs her hand gently through my hair. Both of them sit in silent support, letting me weep like a child without any hint of judgment or disinterest. An embarrassingly long time passes before I've cried myself out. I sit up slowly and dry my eyes. Rowan hands me a soft piece of cloth for my nose.

"Thank you. This means a lot. If you don't mind, though, I'd like a little time alone." I whisper weakly. Two nods, no words in response. Kali gives me a one-armed hug before getting up and walking with Rowan out of the room. As they leave, I notice Lilly standing at the entrance. She looks as if she was about to walk in. Seeing them leaving, she walks away as well.

Sitting here in a little hole in a cave all by myself, I'm not sure why I wanted to be alone. I guess I'm not used to being so vulnerable with others around. Last time I wept like this, I was a child. Victor was the only one there to comfort me.

"Mind if I sit?" I look up to see Vesta standing over me with a sad smile on her face. I shrug and down she sits. "Well, I heard what happened to your friend, Becka; I'm sorry. I didn't know her for long. But she seemed quite special."

"She was." *Was. Ugh.* I'm not ready to be talking about Becka in the past tense.

"Well, I do remember this one time when she first arrived. A couple of young boys— not boys, but you're all boys to me. Anyway, the two were arguing about something, as boys do. Everyone was just watching them go at it. Becka just smiled sweetly and stood next to them. She asked one of them a question; I couldn't hear what it was. My ears aren't what they used to be. Then, she turned and said something to the other. She wasn't loud. She wasn't aggressive. She just spoke to them and with one sentence each, they shook hands, sat down, and ate a meal together. I've seen a lot of people do a lot of things in my time. That sweet, gentle, disarming of conflict—well, that's something I'll never forget."

Hearing her story made me smile; Becka was the queen of disarming conflict. Picturing it made the fog surrounding me feel a little lighter.

"Thank you for that; it helps."

Vesta pulls me against her shoulder, hugging me so tight with one arm I wonder if she's part bear. "Count yourself lucky."

"Lucky?"

"Mm-hm, lucky. To have had someone so special it's hard to say goodbye. It means you had someone in your life who was really worth knowing. That's lucky," she smiles as if there is no more to be said. She ruffles my hair like I'm a child and then stands up. "You just sit as long as you need. I'll make sure nobody bothers you. And if you want someone to talk to, I'll be right over here."

When I don't leave for a while, she brings me a plate of food and insists I eat it.

"I made that special. Fill you up nice and tomorrow, when you wake up, you'll notice you're starting to feel better."

I laugh at the notion but finish the plate. It's the first full meal I've eaten since Becka died. I thank her and decide to turn in early.

The next morning, the fog surrounding me feels lighter. Maybe Vesta's food was magical. When I open my eyes, Kane is standing over my bed.

"Come on, you need to see this." He guides me out of the cave and across the elevated plateau. Telmen and Olivia are standing in the distance, backs to us, trying to coax someone away from the edge of the cliff. As we get closer, I see him—pale, freckled skin, lean build, and light, messy hair. The swelling and cuts on his face have improved tremendously, but his skin is still discolored. He's still wearing his tattered, tan tunic and light brown pants.

"Weeee," he cheers, his voice sounding childlike and gleeful. Even from a distance I can see he is precariously close; no—he's right *on the edge*. His bare feet move back and forth like he's twirling on a balance beam. His arms are extended out. He moves and spins with the smooth grace of a dancer.

"Jensen?" I shout, confused as to what he is doing.

"He's been like this for hours," Olivia explains. "Just got up and came frolicking out here. We can't get him to come back inside. Jensen hums a little song in response,

> "Line up, sit straight
> Obedience makes life great
> Fit in, blend in
> That's how you get to heaven."

"And he's been singing nonsense this whole time," Olivia adds.

"What's that from? I feel like I've heard it before," I ask.

Kane and Olivia just shrug.

Telmen won't even look at me. I'm not sure if that's intentional or if he's just focused on helping Jensen.

"He's going to fall if he stays out here," Kane suggests.

I step closer to him, trying to keep my voice soft. "Jensen, come away from there."

"Away? No. Everyone goes away. Away is alone. Alone is pain. No away. Go away," he responds.

I step closer. His expressive hoping halts, and he swirls to face me, the balls of his feet resting on the edge of the cliff. If his weight shifts back, he'll fall.

"He won't let us get close; we've tried," Olivia shouts over my shoulder.

I take another step. "Jensen, can I come out there with you?"

"Get away from him! If you—" Telmen's voice is filled with anger.

"I'm not losing another friend. Not today," I snap at him before turning my focus back to Jensen.

He cocks his head to the side as if confused by my presence.

I hold out my hands and move slowly, trying to disarm his suspicion. "Jensen, it's me, Jett. Since when do you dance?"

Jensen smiles proudly and sings:

> "Dancing is defiance.
> Dancing is sin.
> Don't let the wickedness dance it's way in."

That's an odd jumbling of Patriarch propaganda.

"Do you know where you are?"

"Jett. Jett. Don't forget. Don't forget, Jett." He twirls in a circle before planting his feet half on and half off the ledge. He moves well—surprisingly well—considering I've never seen him so much as hop before. Just a few more steps, and I can reach him, but if he goes back, I won't be able to catch him in time. I need to keep him distracted.

"Jensen, please, come away from there. You're scaring me," I plead.

"Don't be scared. I'm a bird. I will fly around like weeee!" He spins again. I can see his foot shift back slightly.

I can't watch this happen—not again.

I drop to my knees, and my head falls into my chest. "Jensen, what did they do to you? You shouldn't be out here. You should be back at the Lazy Loafer driving some poor girl crazy with your obnoxious views on everything. If I'd just . . ." I exhale deeply, trying to breathe out my guilt. "Gibbs, Becka—we'd all still be together. I was so focused on all the things we didn't have, on all the injustice that surrounded us, I couldn't see how much I had. Forgive me."

I feel a hand on my shoulder. Jensen is standing over me smiling. He slides down to his knees and hugs me tight. Is Jensen being sympathetic? He's worse off than I thought.

"Don't cry; they only hurt you worse when you cry." He squeezes my neck tightly.

I hug him back, turning a little to move him further from the ledge. Hope flaps its feeble wings. Somewhere in this broken shell of a person is Jensen. After we get him back inside, Telmen volunteers to keep watch. The rest of us step back outside, joined by Kali and Rowan.

"What happened to him?" Kane asks.

Olivia sighs, "When they took us, they told us they were going to train us to be Marauders."

"I thought Marauders didn't train women to fight," Kane interrupts.

"They train them to fight; they just don't treat them with respect or believe they are worthy of honor," Olivia explains.

"Don't interrupt, Kane," I say.

"Training meant they had to break us down to nothing. They were going to push us to our limits and forge us into weapons. It was brutal. It wasn't just physical. After they had pushed us all day, they would tie us to chairs, tape our eyes open, and force us to watch projections of violence and murder all night. It was like they spent their whole lives dreaming up ways to get in your head and make you believe things you don't believe."

"That's how they trained you?" Kane asks.

"Yes, but every day was different. One day they'd train us with blunted weapons. Then, they'd have us run until we passed out. The next day they'd have us walk between two rows of Marauders who hit us with sticks until we collapsed and then they'd beat us more as a punishment for collapsing. The one thing that remained the same: every day was worse than the one before it. They wanted to push us so far that we'd let go of ourselves and become whatever they wanted. There's this part of you screaming to just give in, do whatever they want, just to make it stop. Each day that voice got louder. The more we resisted, the more they hurt us. I stopped resisting. Telmen too. But Jensen never did. He fought back every chance he got until they stopped trying. They took him into that back room, and I have no idea what they did after that. Just that he was screaming all night every night. We could hear him begging for them to stop. They never did."

Kane exhales, "Best prepare for the worst, then."

"The worst?" Olivia's voice shakes.

"As a bit of an expert on torture, I can tell you that if they pushed him too hard, there may not be much of your friend left."

"I don't accept that. I won't! Jensen is strong. He's in there somewhere. We just need to help him find his way back," Olivia snaps.

"Didn't Jensen drive you loopy?" I ask.

"Every day! But he is my friend—my family; I won't give up on him."

"Kali, do you think Doc could help him?" I ask.

"Maybe; he's probably the best bet, but he's in Red Clay," Kali responds.

"There's a doctor there who could help Jensen! What are we waiting for? Let's take him there." Olivia's eyes light up.

"We can't," Kali retorts.

"Why not?" Olivia presses.

"We burned that bridge when we left. The Elder who runs the town will have us killed on sight. Jett, I told you when we left there was no going back," Kali counters.

"Elder Schmitty is a problem. I would be more than happy to solve this problem," Kane adds.

"No," I interrupt.

"No? We got a problem. I can solve that problem. So what's the problem?" Kane glares at me.

"The guards will be on high alert. You wouldn't be able to get close enough," Kali explains.

Kane grins, "You let me worry about that."

"No," I say again. "Becka wouldn't approve. Since she's not here to object, I'll do it for her. If we take Red Clay by force, how are we any better than the Marauders? We can tell ourselves we are operating out of necessity, doing what we have to do for the greater good, but that doesn't change anything."

"You want to talk about Becka? Becka wouldn't have been at the camp in the first place if it wasn't for Schmitty. He sells people as slaves. He's a villain who deserves to die." Kane's voice is agitated, his face flushed.

"Tell me—if in our fight against a villain, we become villains, what have we changed?"

"Jett, you'd be doing Red Clay a favor. They'd thank you for it," Kali adds.

"Victor used to say, 'The problem with rolling downhill is once you start, you can't stop until you reach the bottom.' Once we start rolling that justification downhill, you really think we can stop it?"

"Some people need killing and you know it! Sometimes killing is the right thing to do," Kane adds.

"We aren't just talking about killing Schmitty. We are talking about taking a town by force."

"So?" Kane snaps.

"If we start deciding what is best for people without their consent, how are we different from the Patriarch? We can't make the world a better place by making the same mistakes and expecting different outcomes. I get it; I'm angry too. In Dios, I let that anger drive me. I see now why that didn't work. We need to be different." For the first time since Becka's death, I feel the weighted fog dissipate, replaced by a clarity of focus.

"How do *you* suggest we solve our little Schmitty problem?" Kane's annoyance rings through his tone.

"We do what Victor would have done. We let Schmitty solve our problem for us. We liberate Red Clay from his rule, and let them decide what to do next," I say.

"You set them free from Schmitty, and they will choose to follow you. What's the difference?" Kali asks.

"The difference is, it's their choice. I know what to do." My smile only seems to enhance the confused expression on Kane's face.

"You're going to have to give us more than that." Kali looks at my eyes as if trying to see my thoughts through them.

"We need to talk to Lilly." I walk off, leaving the others staring and confused. This is fun; I see why Victor always enjoyed being the man with the plan.

Lilly and Brock are arguing when we walk into the cave's command center.

"Look at how that worked out. We spent a week setting up that trap, and did anyone show up? No. The whole thing was a heaping waste of time," Brock shouts.

"The plan wasn't the problem. The Vanguard screwed it up, not Jett."

"Stop defending him, it was his—"

"It was you who brought Kyle in, remember? Maybe you should be careful before you go slinging blame around," Lilly snaps back.

"Are we interrupting?" I ask. I try not to grin, but hearing Brock get put in his place makes it hard not to.

Lilly turns toward us, yells, and charges at Kali. "You've got some spheres showing your face in here! I knew there was something off about you. I should have listened to my gut."

I step between them, catching Lilly's arm before she thrust it into Kali's face. "Lilly, have you crashed? What's gotten into you?"

"Remember before you left, we saw the soldiers scan and then kill that Marauder girl?"

"Yeah, what of it?"

"I told you, Jett; I told you she was hiding something. I was right. She's with the Patriarch, or at least she was." Lilly shoves her finger at Kali.

"I am not with the Patriarch! I never have been! I hate them!" Kali's agitation sounds genuine, which adds to my considerable confusion.

"I bet you do. So why do they want you so badly? Hmmm?"

Kali doesn't answer that.

"You knew, didn't you?" Lilly asks. I've never seen Lilly's thermals going like this.

"Wait, what are you saying?" I look at Lilly, who is glaring at Kali and then at Kali, who is staring at the floor.

"I'm saying she knew the Vanguard was after her, and she lied to us about it."

"I didn't lie." Kali's voice sounds shaky and weak.

I stare at her in raw disbelief. It couldn't be. She couldn't have known. A picture forms in my mind as the pieces of the puzzle click together. Despite my desire to deny it, they fit perfectly. Every time we saw them, she would act strangely or change the subject. It makes sense.

"Is that why you wanted to travel through the night after the Skylari swarm passed? Did you know?" I stare at her. Her face blurs behind the wall of tears forming in my eyes and distorting my vision.

"Jett, it's not that—"

"Did you know?" I almost shout, enunciating every word.

Her shoulders sink, her head turns even farther down. It takes her a minute to respond, "Yes."

All of my internal cooling systems fail at once. My skin is fire, my breathing heavy. "You knew a highly trained group of soldiers were looking for you, and you didn't think to tell us?"

Kali stares at the ground, tears pooling in her eyes. "They've been searching for years and never gotten that close. They were more annoying than anything. I never imagined they'd actually catch up to me. I knew if I told you, you would have sent me away. You wouldn't have let me help."

"You're right! Because it was a stupid risk! You knew how important this was. If the Vanguard hadn't showed up—if Kyle hadn't stopped us—we'd have been stocked. Becka would still be . . ." I can't bring myself to say it.

"I . . . I didn't know they had a spy. I was careful, stayed on the move. That's why when I came back to Red Clay, I agreed to scout for Schmitty. Their trackers never got them close enough to be a real threat. How was I supposed to know that they'd all of a sudden start being able to track me?" She's scrambling, frantically trying to find some foothold to stand on.

I'm not about to give in to her.

"You should have told us," I glare at her.

"I didn't think—"

"No, you didn't care! You knew they were after you, knew just traveling with you was a risk. You didn't care. So long as Kali gets her vengeance, who cares what happens to anyone else, right?"

Understanding crumbles like dust, leaving behind a sea of untamable rage.

"That's not fair. I was just trying to help! Rowan and I have been alone for so long. Traveling with you, it was different. It was like getting something back that we'd both lost years ago. I didn't mean for anyone to get hurt. I thought I had it under control." Kali's tone is pleading.

I can hear the pain in her voice, the sorrow, the shame, but I don't care. Every time I hear her voice, I see Becka's face. I see Morton's blade piercing through her again and again and again. It doesn't matter what Kali says. None of it will change what happened.

"Becka is dead. Dead because of you—because of who or what you are. She's dead because you weren't honest with us."

Rowan steps between us, using his body to shield Kali from my words. My anger, spilling past any barrier of reason that might have normally held it, turns to him. "What about you? Did you know, too?"

Rowan stares back, deliberately not indicating one way or the other.

I swing my focus back to Kali. It feels like my rage is radiating from my skin.

A tear runs down her cheek. "I . . . I'm so sorry, Jett. I never meant—" she starts.

"You should go," I cut her off. "There's no place for you here."

She stares in silence. No one else says a word. After a painfully long moment, Kali swallows and nods. "I guess this is goodbye."

"Rowan, you should go with her," I grunt.

The two slowly sulk their way out of the room. Kali looks back over her shoulder but says nothing. Silence persists after they leave.

Lilly rubs my arm softly. "The world's a darker place without Becka in it."

"It is."

"I'm sorry if I overstepped a bit."

"She was your friend too. You have every right to be angry." I force a smile to try and shake the feeling that comes every time I think about it.

"Do you need some time?" Lilly's voice drips with concern. We stand silent for a minute as I let my rage cool.

I shake my head. "The distraction is helpful. Plus, I have an idea."

"Because your last one turned out so well? Or was it the one before that?" Brock chirps. A second later he gasps and coughs, crouched over with Kane's fist in his stomach.

"Go ahead, friend." Kane smiles like he's posing for a picture.

"If we are going to survive here long term, we need a place of our own. We need access to resources. We need allies. Your cave here is an impressive outpost, but it's not a home."

"You want to make the Outlands our home?" Olivia's voice jumps. "What about Dios?"

"Even if we wanted to go back, we'd need an army amongst a long list of other things we don't have." This answer seems to satisfy Olivia's objection.

"Where do you have in mind?" Lilly asks.

"Red Clay is the most logical place. It's also the first place most exiles end up."

"That's your plan? Red Clay? They will kill you on *pfffhhh*—" Brock's words are cut short by the sudden expulsion of air as Kane hits him again.

The warm smile on Kane's face is almost comical as he taps Brock on the back like they are old friends.

"Red Clay has space, resources, infrastructure, medical and training facilities, defenses, weapons . . . We could make it a home," I suggest.

"My Raiders are tough, but I'm not sure we could take Red Clay on our own," Lilly notes.

"Well, we are back to where we started. Jett, you going to tell us your plan now?" Olivia asks, putting her hands on her hips.

"Let me worry about Red Clay."

"OK, so what do you want from me?" Lilly asks.

"I want you and your Raiders to join us."

"You want to join forces, make Red Clay our home?" she asks.

"Not just our home. A haven for all who need it."

"Alright, I'm interested. Let's hear this plan," Lilly says.

"We know Schmitty provides Morton with slaves. If we cut off that supply, that will make Morton upset."

"Have you crashed? Morton is a psychopath with an army. You want to antagonize him? Haven't you gotten enough people killed?" Brock covers his chest as he speaks.

This time Kane doesn't try to hit him.

"I'm not sure this is a great idea, Jett. We got lucky last time because Morton was more focused on dealing with the Vanguard than he was with us. I saw enough of him when I was his prisoner to get a sense for the kind of man he is. He's obsessed with control and completely possessive. When someone takes something of his, he becomes like a rabid bear. If you do this, he's going to come for you," Olivia says.

"I'm counting on it," I smile, trying to project as much confidence as I can. The future is locked behind the attic door, but for the first time in my life, I can see every step that leads up to it. It's not just an idea, but a vision of what the future could look like. The different parts flow together, connecting in my mind. This could work. I can see how to make it work. Now, I just have to do it.

"We can't beat the Marauders. Even with all the defenses and soldiers in Red Clay, they'd wipe us out with ease," Lilly objects.

"I don't want to fight the Marauders," I explain.

"People call *me* a looper," Kane chuckles.

"Do you remember what Raggy told us? The two ways we could deal with Morton without bringing down the wrath of Marauder kingdom?" I ask.

Kane sneers, "Oh, what fun! You never disappoint, friend."

"What are you talking about?" Lilly asks.

"He's going to pick a fight," Kane answers for me.

Lilly covers her face with her hand and sighs in frustration.

"Not with the Marauders. He's going to pick a fight with Morton," Kane chuckles.

"Jett, no!" Olivia objects.

"It's not like we can just go back to Dios and pretend this never happened. So long as we are out here, Morton is going to be a problem," I explain.

"But Jett, you don't have to—" Olivia starts.

"He killed Becka right in front of me. He doesn't just get to walk away."

"OK, walk me through this," Lilly starts. "Your plan gets us into Red Clay where we can set up our base of operations. We get rid of Schmitty. Morton doesn't like that. Brings his Marauders to come kill us. You get Morton to challenge you rather than just wipe us all out and be done with it. Let's just say that works . . ."

"No vote of confidence from you, then?" I try to sound playful to keep the doubt from my voice.

Lilly sighs, "You're scrappy, Jett. I doubt that. While you've been in fights, Morton lives to fight. He's a warrior and a killer. He's bigger than you, stronger, faster even. What chance do you have against him?"

"I guess I'll just have to be smarter. I'm not saying it's a great plan. It's our only shot at this. We can run and hide. We can survive, at least for a while. Little by little, one by one, our people will die. We have this chance to make a difference. It's a risk. Any time you fight, you might lose. We can run today and spend the rest of our lives trying not to die. Or we can stand up and say, 'enough.' I'm done running. I'm done hiding."

Silence surrounds us as everyone contemplates in unison.

"Win or lose, live or die, we'll do it together," Olivia smiles, always so quick to throw in her support. Her words make the whole room feel different. When she speaks, hope cuts through the veil of doubts.

"Just so we are clear—no matter what happens, I'm not calling you king." Lilly shakes her head. "You can just forget it."

Kane cackles an eerie and off-putting laugh. "This is what I like about you, friend; you pick the best fights. First the Patriarch, now a Marauder king."

"Who knows, if we actually live through this, we may even—" I start.

"Have a home," Lilly finishes. "OK, Jett, I trust you. You think you can pull this off, we're with you."

"Are you serious? How many times do his plans have to—" Brock moves to block his chest from another strike.

Kane doesn't move. Brock exhales in relief. As soon as he does, Kane turns and drives his fist into Brock's stomach. Brock barely catches himself on the table as he gasps and sputters desperately.

Kane whispers in his ear, "How many times do I have to hit you before you keep your mouth shut?"

"Kane, I need you to stop," Lilly glares at him.

Kane smiles. "Happy to, just as soon as he—"

"Now," Lilly persists.

Kane lifts his hand up, showing her his palms and steps away. "Yes, ma'am."

"I'm going to go check on Jensen, then we will head out. If all goes according to plan, Red Clay will be free of Elder Schmitty well before you arrive," I say.

"We will head to you as soon as we pack up camp. Might take a few days." Lilly turns to her brother and shoves his shoulder.

I hear her chastising him as we walk out of the room. "*I swear to Bealz, what is wrong with you?*"

Olivia and Kane follow me out. Kane gathers supplies before making a point to say goodbye to Vesta. He seems very amused and oddly intimidated by her. Olivia goes in to see Jensen first while I wait outside the room. After a few minutes, she returns with a pack on her back. She puts her hand on my shoulder.

"It'll be OK, Jett; we will get him back. I just know it." Her comfort is appreciated.

Jensen is sitting on one of the beds along the wall, far away from the others. He's rocking back and forth slowly as if in a trance. Telmen is kneeling in front of him, trying to talk to him. Jensen is unresponsive. I stand there for a minute, trying to think of what to say.

"He's been like this since we got him back inside," Telmen reports. "I don't know what to do for him." He sounds defeated, his words heavy and slow to exit his mouth.

"There's a doctor in Red Clay. He has medicine and equipment. I'm heading there to see if he can help."

Telmen keeps his focus on Jensen, forcing his gaze away from me. "Red Clay is not a good place. They—"

"I know."

"Why go there if you—"

"I've got a plan. I just want to speak to Jensen before I go."

Telmen nods and steps away from him, giving me enough room to talk but hovering near by like a protective mother bear.

This is a side of him I've never seen before. I kneel down and take Jensen's hands in mine. I don't know if he can hear me or if he can process what I'm going to say. I look into his eyes and smile.

"Hey scrap sink, we never really got along back in Dios. I used to think you were a real brain buffer. It's like you had this ability to get everyone's thermals going without even trying. Even when you drove me loopy, you were always there. Even when I didn't want you to be, you were always there. That means more than you know. You may not want to see me. You probably blame me for everything that has happened. I would understand if you did. I know I can't change the past or fix any of my many mistakes. I'm not going to leave you like this. I believe you're still in there. I'm not going to rest until I've found a way to bring you back. I've lost too many people I care about already. I'm not going to lose you, too, OK? Jensen, if you're in there, I need you to keep fighting. Come back to us, OK?" I squeeze his hands, feeling a little silly.

Telmen cuts me off before I can walk away. "Jett, about what I said before."

"I'm doing everything I can to fix it, just give me some time," I plead.

"No," Telmen shakes his head.

Sensing his rejection stabs into me like a knife. My family of misfits is falling apart. One betrayed us, two are dead, one is broken, one is missing, and one no longer wants anything to do with me. Out of the eight of us who lived together for years, Olivia is the only one I have left. I am Jett: destroyer of worlds.

"Jett."

And now he's going to twist the knife.

"I'm sorry. I never should have said any of those things to you. It's been rough out here. Seeing what they did to Jensen, then Becka. I couldn't take it. The Marauders messed with our heads. They wanted to make us angry all the time. They tried to channel our hatred to turn us into fighters. I let them. Those are just excuses. I know you didn't mean for any of this, truly I do. I know you'd have traded places with Becka or any of us if you could. Victor betrayed you too. Honestly, he betrayed you even more. I know you are doing the best you can. I should not have attacked you for trying to pick up the pieces. This isn't your fault. It's Victor's."

CHAPTER NINETEEN

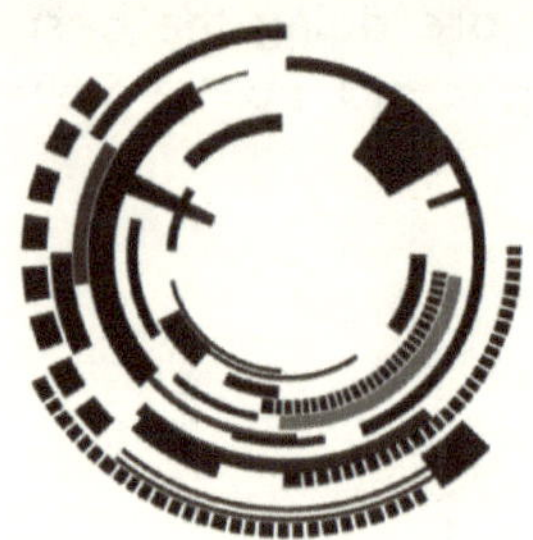

I try to think of something to say, but blinking is all I can do.

"Victor's fault. No! Victor no fault. Victor friend. Trust Victor," Jensen says.

Telmen and I exchange a look. Telmen swoops down and looks into Jensen's eyes.

"Jensen?"

He stops talking and turns his head from side to side.

"Jensen, what were you saying about Victor?" Telmen tries to coax more words from him.

Jensen's words weren't exactly coherent, but it was something.

"Oh, pillow is soft." Jensen picks up a pillow from the bed and nuzzles his face into it.

Telmen sighs and looks back at me. "I'll stay with him."

"Good, it'll be safer to travel with the Raiders. I'll see you in a few days." Before I can leave, Telmen hugs me. A little reconciliation lifts the spirit a lot.

As I make my way out, I bump into Benji. He steps back, and I hear a clang like metal bottles banging together inside his jacket.

He glares at me with a sniff. "Watch where you're going, will you?"

His pupils are so large I can't even tell what color his eyes are. In his eyes, there's not even a glimmer of recognition. Benji's pale skin looks almost slimy. I apologize and he grunts and walks off. That's rude.

Our journey toward Red Clay is surprisingly uneventful. We don't see another living thing for most of the day. As the sun starts to wane, I hear a nocstra howling. I picture my previous encounter with the creature and my whole body shivers. At least this one sounds far away. High above us, there are a few aestroths dancing in the sky. This trek is probably the most uneventful experience I've had since my exile. The light starts to fade as we see the wooden walls in the distance.

It's odd seeing Red Clay again. It hasn't been that long, but it feels like so much time has passed. Olivia and Kane stand beside me, looking at the town in the distance. The sun is setting, and it's almost time for the Dusk Descension. That will provide us with the perfect opportunity to sneak in. We'll wait for morning to put my plan into motion. I half expect to see Rowan and Kali walking ahead of us. They've been with me almost the entire time I've been out here. Now that they aren't, I miss them. I shouldn't have been so harsh. At this point, I wonder if I'll ever see them again.

"You sure about this, Jett?" Olivia turns to look at me. "If you want to bail out, I'm with you for that too."

I shrug. "Who knows how this will go?"

The siren rings out, eerie and off-putting as ever. We wait a few minutes and then approach the gate. We need to time it just right to make it inside the walls before the force shield goes up but after the guards have moved from their post. Kane takes the lead, claiming he memorized the guards' patterns when he was here last. Let's just hope they haven't changed.

"*Now!*" he whispers. We rush after him, crouching low, heads down. We clear the gate and move alongside the outer wall, finding a stack of barrels to hide behind. The *whoosh* of the force shield activating behind us makes me jump. We are in the clear.

"I'm telling you, I saw them—Kali and that dirty Tribling—when I was out scouting with Krista. It looked like they were headed toward Dragonvale." Two guards are walking in our direction.

They shouldn't be here. They should be making their way underground by now. Kane and I exchange a glance. Attacking the guards is going to make my plan much more difficult; not attacking them may make it impossible. Just once, I'd like to make a choice where at least one of the options could bring something good. Kane readies his knife.

I shake my head at him. "We can't kill them."

"Oh, come on—just a little?"

I shake my head again.

"You think they'd come back here after breaking that psycho out of prison? They'd have to be mad," the second guard responds. The pair moves past us. I look over the barrel I'm hiding behind to see them reach the gate. They work it closed and put a thick wooden beam in a latch halfway up the gate to lock it in place. That's new.

"Come on, we're going to miss the start of Grim Collapse."

"Fine by me; let them lose their money before we get started."

"You're just nuked you lost on that terrible bet last night."

"Shut up, I still think Gareth is cheating; no one is that lucky."

We listen until their voices fade along with the remnants of light. Relief washes over me. The threat has passed, for now.

"My job's done; what's next?" Kane grins.

"The doctor lives in the underground infirmary. We'll rest there for a bit and go over the plan for tomorrow."

"You trust him?" Olivia asks.

"I do."

"Alright, show us the way," she replies.

I lead them into the building near Schmitty's little palace.

"Well, this is a lovely log cabin, isn't it? How are we supposed to get down?" Kane wanders around the room before looking back at me.

I point to a spherical glass in the corner of the ceiling. I wave casually at it. A moment later there is a click. We step in, and our descension begins. The elevator door opens to a long hallway leading into the main office where Doc had treated me before.

"Jett Lasting, as I live and breathe. Didn't think I'd be seeing you again." Doc stands behind us, his smile practically larger than his stature.

"Doc! It's good to see you! These are my friends, Kane and Olivia."

Doc grabs my hand and pulls me into a one-armed embrace, forcing me to lean down into it. He slaps my shoulder and then pushes me away, still maintaining the handshake. It's a strange, but oddly bonding way to greet someone. After, Olivia shakes his hand. Kane just stares at him, keeping his arms folded across his chest.

"You're the doctor who can help Jensen?" Olivia can't hide the note of excited earnest in her voice.

Doc looks at me, raising an eyebrow. "What kind of trouble are you in now?"

We explain about Jensen's condition while Doc takes notes. When we finish, he scratches his head before circling something on his datapad.

"Do you think you will be able to help?" Olivia's urgency is endearing.

"Difficult to say without knowing more. Is it brain trauma or psychological or physiological or some combination? The human body is perhaps the most complex organism on the planet. The brain is the most complex structure of the human body. It doesn't just govern our thoughts but also the systems that make up who we are."

"Are we supposed to understand what he just said?" Kane scratches his head.

Doc smiles. "There's no broad-spectrum treatment. Things like this have to be handled case by case. Without seeing him in person, there's just no way to know."

"That's not very hopeful, Doc," I say.

"Listen, I have some ideas to try, and if those don't work, I know someone who might be able to help. You'd need to bring him here, which has its own complications thanks to our mutual friend, Schmitty. He's been enhancing security ever since you left. If he finds out you are here, it's not going to go well."

"I have a plan to get rid of him, but I may ne—"

"I'm in! What do you need from me?" Doc responds before I can finish.

"Firstly, can we rest here tonight?"

"I'm insulted you'd even ask. What else?"

"In the morning, can you get everyone to the Town Square?"

Doc rubs his chin. "I'll get Cooper and a few others to help me—should be doable. Why the Town Square?"

"Elder Schmitty is going to unburden himself. I want to make sure everyone hears it."

"How will you pull that off? He's smarter than he looks. He's not about to say anything in front of a crowd."

"I wouldn't expect him to. Kane, can you get Doc into the Great Hall?" I request.

Kane laughs, "Course I can."

"You want us above ground *at night*?" Doc's voice trembles slightly.

I nod. "We have a lot to do to make this work." I pull back my sleeve and type something into my datapad before sending it to Doc.

He opens it, reads it, raises an eyebrow, then smiles.

"Can you do it?" I press.

"My brother was a technician in Dios; I think I learned enough from him to pull it off."

"Good, that's the easy part. Kane, get Doc in, keep him safe, get him back here as soon as he's done."

Kane grins, "Come on, Doc; let's go have some fun."

Kane and Doc disappear inside the elevator, leaving Olivia and I in the underground infirmary.

"What do you want me to do?" Olivia questions.

"You have the most important job of all," I say.

She smirks, "Oh, is that so?"

"Schmitty is a revolting human being."

"I know, Jett. He did sell me into slavery." Olivia shakes her head at me.

"Right. But he's cunning—at least normally. His weak spot is women."

"I don't like where this is going," Olivia starts.

"No, I don't need you to charm him. I need you to challenge him."

"Challenge him?"

"He thinks of women as inferior creatures by design. Honestly believes Bealz made them lesser."

"Just when I thought a person couldn't get more terrible," Olivia replies.

"It's awful but incredibly useful. I will start and get him riled up as best I can. Then, you come in, challenge him, find his buttons, and push them. He'll lose control."

Olivia smiles. "You want me to give him the rope he'll use to hang himself?"

"Exactly."

"What makes you think I can do it?"

"Something you said when we were on the rooftop in Dios."

Olivia raises an eyebrow. "And that was?"

"You mentioned being frustrated because everything you did and all the skills you had were attributed to your looks. That got me thinking. I started replaying some of the grabs I saw you make when we were partnered together. That's when I realized it. Your gift at distraction isn't just about how you look. You are incredibly good at reading people. You could just look into their eyes and know how to play them. Your tone, demeanor, the way you'd move or laugh was different every time. I learned to size people's physically qualities to see who I could steal from. You were doing the same thing, only you sized up what was going on in their heads."

Olivia's natural, easy smile extends wider than I've ever seen it. Her eyes shine brighter than usual, "Jett Lasting . . ."

I put my hand on her shoulder and look into her eyes. "I know you can do this."

I walk her through the rest of my plan, so she knows what to expect. Then, she heads into Doc's quarters to get some rest.

About an hour passes before I hear the elevator door ding. Kane and Doc emerge.

"How did it go?" I ask.

Doc nods, "It's done. In the morning I'll gather everyone in the Town Square. The rest is up to you."

Doc walks to the door of his room. He reaches for the handle and then looks back at me, pointing to the door. "Is she . . ."

I nod, "Yeah, pretty sure she decided to take your room."

Doc chuckles and heads into one of the side rooms of the infirmary.

"Alright, then, see you in the morning," Kane says.

"Actually, I need to go over one more thing with you."

Kane stops, raising an eyebrow.

"You're not going to like it . . ."

I walk Kane through my plan as I had with Olivia but emphasizing his part. As I expected, he was displeased.

"Disable them. Don't kill them. They are not the problem." I give Kane a firm look.

"You can't be serious," he protests.

"I am."

He pouts, "You never let me kill anyone anymore."

What it must be like to live in Kane's head.

"Alright, let's get some rest. We're going to need it."

Something about having a clear direction makes sleep come easy. I drift off, despite laying on the world's lumpiest couch. In my dream, I see Victor, Spike, Olivia, Becka, Jensen as he was, Telmen, and Lilly. We are all sitting outside our rundown house, laughing and talking. Little Brelar is running around, chasing his birds and playing hide the Undesirable with Victor. Even Gibbs is there, sitting off by himself, watching. I can't make out any of the words being said, but I feel the warmth and bond of being together. Nostalgic happiness blends with woeful despair as even in my sleep I know this scene will never be again. It's amazing how much you can have without even realizing it.

I wake with a sense of longing—longing to go back and tell my younger self what I know now. If only contentment could be learned without loss. Idealism so often dies with youth. The price of it is higher than most are willing to pay. I shake the thoughts from my head. Victor always used to say: *Looking backwards is how you trip over what's in front of you.*

The alarm on my datapad tells me it's time. I slide off the couch and get myself ready. Olivia, Kane, and I take the elevator up. It's still dark, but the sun is peeking over the horizon. We make our way toward Schmitty's palace of corruption. Olivia stops at the front door and kneels, examining a small, light blue flower that managed to spring up through the clay.

"What are you doing here?" she says to the plant.

"Olivia?" I whisper to her softly.

"This is an emeraldus paradoxa; they used to grow near my family's farm."

"It's a beautiful flower," I comment, not sure what else to say, but it is clearly important to her.

"It's a tough little plant. One of the things that would grow close to the Rim. I haven't seen one of these since I was a girl. Never thought I'd find one out here." She stands up and rubs her palms against her pant legs. "I used to run around in fields of these when I was a girl." She lets out a happy sigh.

I wait to see if she has more to say.

"Sorry, just brings back memories." Her lips curl into a soft smile.

"No reason to be sorry. I don't know much about your family. Maybe you can tell me more when we are done here?"

Her smile is hesitant. "I'd like that."

The front door to the Great Hall is still unlocked from when Kane picked it last night. We step inside. The entrance of the Great Hall is in the center of the building. With an ornate red carpet running all the way to the stairs directly in front of Schmitty's throne. The Hall is open in the middle and has a room tucked back on either side of the entryway. Arching columns line the walls on either side of the hall. Between each of the columns, there is an inset that is used to hold serving tables, barrels, and other miscellaneous items. To keep these functional but unimpressive things out of view, each inset is covered by a decorative red curtain. Olivia hides behind one of the insets on the outer wall. I take one on the inner wall nearer to the entry door. Kane disappears. We wait in our positions as time oozes along painfully. Finally, we hear the back door open and multiple sets of boots thunk against the ground. I can't afford to risk a glance, but my guess is there are at least four guards.

"Sweep the room," I hear a voice say. They really have increased security. Olivia and I are hidden from view but not well enough to avoid detection during a sweep. My heart pounds loudly in my chest. I listen as boots stomp and clunk around the room. They are getting closer with every step. Two guards move in on our hiding spot like the pinchers of a claw. If I don't do something now, we are heaped.

I exhale slowly and act against every instinct I have. I slide my foot out from under the curtain I was hiding behind, intentionally making it visible. The loud thumping turns to a quieter creeping that stops directly in front of me. I feel two hands push the fabric out of the way, grab me, and tug me from my hiding spot.

"Get Elder Schmitty; he needs to see this," one of the guards says. He shoves me onto the ground in the middle of the floor. I keep my head down, glancing back to make sure Olivia remains hidden. The loud grind of chair legs sliding against a smooth wooden floor echoes around me and indicates the oversized elder has taken his throne.

"You dare show your face here after what you did?" I can hear the disdain in Schmitty's voice.

"After what I did?" I look up and stare into his eyes. "What I did?" I repeat.

"What are you doing here?"

"I came here to make you answer for your crimes."

Schmitty whispers something to one of his guards, then leans back on his chair, causing the wood to creak. "Check the room for others."

My eyes widen, and I feel a nervous desperation take hold of me. I need to keep his attention.

"You sold my friends into slavery!" I stand up and point my finger at him accusingly. The two guards who were posted at the front door stand behind me. One puts his hand on my shoulder and kicks the back of my leg, dropping me back to my knees. The two guards who were posted behind Schmitty move toward the wall where Olivia is hiding. Heap.

"You're trying to distract me, which tells me you have an accomplice. Find them!"

Kane drops down from above, landing on the middle of the walkway behind Schmitty. He must have climbed up and hidden himself on one of the rafters. Impressive. With the guards out of position he rushes to Schmitty. The guards whirl around and lift their rifles, but they are too late. Kane has his knife to Schmitty's throat, his own body shielded by Schmitty's chair.

"Now, tell your men to drop their guns before I give you a permanent smile," Kane grins.

Schmitty gestures for the guards to lower their weapons. As they do, I stand upright with a confident smile on my face.

"Elder Schmitty, you are a vile, detestable human being. I can't imagine someone more revolting. You pretend to be this great leader, but you're nothing more than a self-absorbed manipulator. You use the people who trust you, who rely on you. The days of your corrupt rule and abuses of power are over. I am here to liberate Red Clay from your fat, disgusting little fingers." I put as much edge on my words as I can.

Schmitty smiles, seemingly unaffected by my words. He reaches under his right armrest. I lunge toward him, but I am too far away for that to make a difference. He pushes a button under the armrest. Great, his chair has a camera switch on one side and some kind of alarm on the other.

Kane gives me a confused look before glancing around nervously. The guards raise their weapons again, forcing Kane to return his focus to them.

"Stand down, boys," Kane instructs.

This time they don't listen. Schmitty makes no effort to encourage them to do so either. Why? Just then, natural light pours into the room as the door at the end of the walkway behind Schmitty's throne flies open.

"Kane! Look out!" I shout, but it's too late.

Kane holds the blade tight against Schmitty's throat, but with guards moving in behind him, there isn't much he can do. If he moves to fight them off, he will expose himself to the guards behind me, and we will lose all of our leverage. The guard behind me has his rifle aimed at Kane. I activate my energy blade mid-swing and cut through his gun. His arm drops as his rifle gives way in the middle. I bring my free hand around, driving it into the surprised guard's face.

Before I can turn, the butt of a rifle crashes into my back, sending me to the ground, my energy blade sliding away. I spin around to see the business end of the rifle aimed at my face. My eyes squeeze closed, and I wince instinctively.

What an absurd reaction this is. You can't shoot me if I'm not looking, *Na na na na naa naa*. Yet here I am, staring at the back of my own eyelids, waiting for my end. The gunshot doesn't come. No energy cutting through my body. Just silence. I guess Schmitty wants to gloat before killing us.

I open my eyes to see Kane on his knees with his arms behind his head. One of the guards lifts him up and guides him next to me. They position us both on our knees facing the now giddy-looking Schmitty.

"Did you really think you and your friend could come into my town and try to ruin the peace I have created? Hmmm? I didn't get here by accident. It is my duty to protect this town from the likes of you," Schmitty boasts.

"If the people of this town knew what you were doing, they'd hang you up themselves," I counter.

Schmitty's eyes glance up at the cameras in the corner of the room. I see his hand move to the panel underneath his chair, the same way it did before when he turned off the cameras while arguing with Kali. His smile turns sinister.

"Did you really think the two of you could bring me down? I've been preparing for your return since you left. Though I was certain you'd have Kali and her little pet with you as well. You made it too easy."

I turn to the guards behind us. "You can't be OK with this. You are supposed to be protectors. The man you are protecting is a slaver. Is that really what you signed up for?"

Schmitty laughs, "You think they didn't know? All of the guards on my personal detail are fully aware; they even help me with it. You can appeal to them all you want; it won't save you."

"This was your great plan?" Kane sneers, "Should have let me do it my way."

Schmitty laughs, "Any last words?"

"I have some." Olivia steps out from behind the curtain.

The guards spin around, aiming their weapons at her. Seeing her, they pause. Olivia walks casually, hands empty as she makes her way over toward us.

"Olivia, what are you doing? This was not . . . ," I start.

She shrugs. "Your plan didn't work, Jett. Time to give it up. They'd have found me eventually."

"Guards!" Schmitty commands.

"I think you're going to want to hear what I have to say." Olivia bats her eyes at Schmitty.

He pauses for a moment, thinking it over. "Doesn't really matter; you'll be dead soon anyway," Schmitty starts. He stares at her more closely. "Wait, I recognize you. You're that girl . . ."

"You remember me—I'm flattered." Olivia smiles sweetly. "After all, you sold a lot of people to Morton Ghood. I met hundreds of them when I was in his camp. It was almost impressive how many people you betrayed. How many people came to your town looking for a safe place only to find shackles instead? How do you sleep at night?"

Schmitty's demeanor shifts. His confident, giddy expression sours into annoyed frustration. "Everything I do is for the good of this town."

"The town?" Olivia chuckles, her voice sweet and soothing. "Just how has selling people benefited this town?"

"What would you know of such things? Do you carry the weight of responsibility on your pretty little shoulders? No. The Marauders demand an offering. I pay it. I pay it to keep my town— my people— safe."

"What about Tomisina, Gladriel, Yen, and Killian?"

Schmitty clears his throat. "Where did you hear those names?"

"Hear them? I met them. They told me all about how you had asked them to come speak with you before you kidnapped them, kept them in the prison and then sold them. I wonder, do their families know?"

"I don't have to listen to this. Guards, kill them."

"Before you do, I should warn you," Olivia says, her voice still impressively calm.

Schmitty grins. "Warn me; what could you possible warn me about?"

"How did I get here?" she asks.

Schmitty just stares stupidly at her.

"You sold me to Morton. Yet here I am; how do you think that happened?"

Schmitty's eyes grow larger as realization strikes him. "How?"

"A group of Patriarch soldiers attacked the Marauders, weakening them. That allowed Moon's Raiders to rescue us. All of us. Every person you sold is now free and they are headed this way. Very soon all of Red Clay will know exactly what kind of man you are." Olivia smiles and bats her eyes innocently at Schmitty.

"You're lying!" he glowers, his face red. The vein in his forehead throbs so hard it looks like it could burst.

"I just wanted to make sure everyone knew what a horrible, incompetent, useless excuse for a man you actually are. See, it doesn't matter if you kill us. Everyone is going to see firsthand what you are."

Schmitty pushes his large self onto his feet. "You stupid woman! What gives you the right to lecture me? I am the reason this town exists. I am the reason the Marauders didn't wipe us out years ago. I am this town. You dare to question me? To think you, a stupid girl, could possible ruin all that I have built. So what if the price is a bunch of outsiders who happen to stumble upon our door? I exchange their freedom for our safety. Yeah, sometimes Dios doesn't exile enough people to make our offering. So I take what I need to for the greater good. That's the kind of sacrifice you have to make in leadership. I wouldn't expect you to understand that."

"We will see," she shrugs dismissively, which only seems to agitate him more.

Olivia, you brilliant, clever, wonderful woman.

"You will not. You'll be dead. Anyone who comes here—they'll be dead, too. There won't be any proof. The people will believe whatever I tell them to believe because they are stupid and they need me."

"You sure about that?" I look at up at Schmitty with a smile before nodding to his cameras.

He turns to look at them and the color leaves his face.

"Now you get it. Kane and I weren't here to stop you. We were just the distraction."

"Distraction? What are you talking about?"

"Nobody gets to where you are without being cautious. If I'd have confronted you, you'd have just denied it. You're right, it's your word versus mine; no one would believe me. But if you thought we'd tried and failed, then you'd let your guard down. It's amazing what people will say when they think they've won. I mean, did you really think your guards got the best of Kane?" I laugh.

Kane spins around and in a single swift motion, disarms the guard behind him and bashes him in the face with the butt end of his own gun. Before the others can react, he aims the gun at Schmitty's head.

"Hope you enjoyed it; that's the last time I'm throwing a fight," Kane sneers.

I stand. "The last time we met, I noticed when you were arguing with Kali that you had a switch under your chair. You flipped it and the cameras turned off. Last night, Kane and Doc came in. You already had the signal being sent to the projection screen in the Town Square; all Doc had to do was spin the switch around. That way when you thought you were turning the cameras off, you were actually turning them on. This morning, Doc and Cooper got everyone to gather in the Town Square. They saw everything."

As if waiting for the perfect cue, the front doors push open and an angry crowd pours into the room. The guards stand down, surrendering immediately. The mob storms the platform where Schmitty is standing. The large man comes crashing down the stairs, being tugged and shoved out toward the door.

We follow the mass of angry townsfolk out to see Schmitty rolling awkwardly down the hill. The mob carries him to the Town Square. It's almost impossible to hear what anyone is actually saying as they all scream and throw things at Schmitty.

"Get away from me, you foul creatures!" he blurts. "You can't touch me! I don't answer to you!"

Olivia snaps and pushes her way through the congregants. She pulls a knife from her pocket and holds it under Schmitty's chin. The whole square goes quiet.

"You heapin' scrap sink! We came here looking for a place to rest. You promised us we'd be safe. Then, you sold us. You sold human beings to stock your own accounts! My friend is dead because of you. I will never hear her laugh again, see her smile, because of you!"

Schmitty swallows forcefully and drops to his knees, groveling for his life.

"It's not my fault; I had to do it. They would have killed me if I didn't."
He clasps his hands together as if in prayer.

"You don't deserve to live," Olivia scowls.

I move my way into the clearing that surrounds Schmitty. I put my hand
on Olivia's shoulder.

"Hey, not like this," I say softly.

"Jett, he deserves—"

"He does. But this is not what Becka would want," I say.

Olivia lets her hand fall back to her side.

Schmitty's fine robes are caked in red powder. He tries to crawl
backwards, away from Olivia, but one of the shop walls cuts off his
escape. The crowd grows louder again. I turn to face them, holding my
hands in the air.

"Citizens of Red Clay, this man whom you trusted has betrayed you.
He has robbed you, lied to you, used you, and worst of all, he has
shamed the most basic code of humanity. You deserve better. You
deserve a leader who will protect you, look out for you, and strive to
improve the quality of your life. I will deal with him. You should find
a—"

Doc steps next to me. "My friends," he interrupts me. "This man standing
before you—his name is Jett Lasting."

"Doc, what are you doing?" I ask, grabbing at his arm. He pulls it free
and ignores me.

"You don't know him, but you know me. I've been with you in the good
times and the bad ones. I've tended to your wounds, treated your
pains. I do all I can to make life here as good as it can possibly be. I
believe we deserve a leader who will do the same. We deserve a
leader who will fight for us, defend us, look out for us. This is our home.
We have a chance to make it a better one than it has ever been. We
need a leader. I tell you this man, stranger though he may be, is a
good man. This isn't his home. We are not his people. Yet he risked his

life to free us from Elder Schmitty's deception. I ask you—who better to lead us than someone who has already risked their life for us?"

"I'm not trying to be your leader. I just needed to get rid of—" I start to protest. The people begin to chant, drowning out my words.

Doc smiles at me and lifts my hand in the air. "To our new leader!"

I pull my hand down. "Doc, no. I am not a leader."

"You are." Cooper steps into view from his place in the front of the crowd. "The fact that you're not trying to take it means you may actually be a good one."

"I don't know the first thing about running a town," I protest.

"You can learn how to lead. Being a person worth following—well, that can't be taught," Doc counters.

In an instant, the mob is surrounded by the town guard, all armed and at the ready as they rush into the Town Square. One of them is wearing a long, brown coat and a light blue beret on his head. He pushes into the circle.

"What is the meaning of this?" The man in the blue beret scans the scene.

"Oh, thank Bealz!" Schmitty rises to his feet and points at us. "Dakkin! Dakkin! Kill these rabble rousers for me."

"You have—" he starts.

Cooper leans over and whispers something in his ear.

Dakkin hesitates for a moment before turning from Schmitty to me.

"What is your name?"

"Jett Lasting," I answer.

He crosses his arms in front of his chest, holding his hands on his shoulders and bows his head. "What are your orders, Mr. Lasting, sir?"

The panic in Schmitty's eyes is one of the most gratifying sensations I have ever known. He drops to his knees, grabbing my coat and tugging on it. "Please, please don't kill me. Have mercy on me!"

I pull my coat away from his groveling hands. "Stand up."

Schmitty stands nervously. Before he can dust himself off, I drive my fist into his stomach so hard I feel his folds rubbing against my wrist. He coughs and gasps before dropping back to the ground.

"Everything in me wants to kill you. I would like nothing more than to make you suffer for what you have done. That's not who I am. That's not what Becka would want me to be. Schmitty, you will leave Red Clay, never to return. I sentence you to wander the wilds alone. If you enter another settlement, I will find you, and I will kill you. If you settle down someplace, I will find you, and I will kill you. If I ever see you again, I'm going to kill you. Now go!"

Schmitty nods and reaches for Dakkin. "Yes, yes, I'll go; just help me up."

Dakkin extends his hand and struggles to lift Schmitty to his feet. Schmitty stumbles forward into him. With a sudden jerk, Schmitty pulls the sidearm free from Dakkin's hip and holds it to Dakkin's head. He wraps his other arm around the guard's neck and uses him as a human shield.

"You think you can just come in here and take what is mine? Who do you think you are?" Schmitty points the gun at me. The crowd moves back. Screams fill the air and chaos ensues as men and women scatter in every direction.

I see Kane gripping a knife in his hand, waiting for the right moment.

I sigh. "You can't even lose gracefully, can you?"

"We both know I won't make it in the wilds. I leave here, I'm as good as dead. At least like this, I can take you with m—"

Phwaahhh!

He gasps and leans forward as Dakkin drives his elbow into Schmitty's chest. The guard slides out of Schmitty's grip, grabbing for his own weapon. He's too slow. Before he can pull it free, Schmitty straightens up and lifts his gun. Schmitty moves surprisingly fast; Olivia moves faster. Two quick steps, and she ducks under his extended arm. Her knife plunges into his stomach all the way to the hilt.

Schmitty sputters, and his gun drops to the ground. His hands move to the blade in his stomach. Olivia doesn't let go. She stares into his eyes as he looks at her in surprise.

"You are a pathetic excuse of a man. The world will be better without you in it." Olivia grits her teeth, and her wrist turns hard, twisting the blade in his chest. She lets go of the blade, and Schmitty stumbles back, slamming against the shop wall behind him. His body slides down until he's sitting on the ground. He blinks but can't form any words.

Kane pats Olivia on the back. "Nicely done."

Schmitty coughs for another minute before he finally closes his eyes and goes still. Couldn't have happened to a nicer guy.

"I'll get some people to take care of this. Why don't you go get settled in," Cooper says as Doc joins him, looking down over Schmitty's dead body.

I happily take him up on his offer.

Now we have a safe place to call home. Just like that, I am no longer an exile. I am the head of a community. Just like that, I go from exile to the head of a community. Now, I just have to figure out how to govern it.

CHAPTER TWENTY

Kane, Olivia, and I head back up the hill into the large ornate building. I look around the main hall, which is like a tribute to wasted space. Tables and chairs are scattered everywhere with no form or reason. There's so much potential, but Schmitty clearly didn't know what to do with it. He used the building to prop himself up, his throne chair elevated and placed at the focal point of the room.

"Well, Jett, we did it. We managed to get to Red Clay and get rid of Schmitty." Olivia pats my arm. "What now?"

"First, I'm going to smash that abomination of a chair," I answer.

Smashing the throne that symbolized Schmitty's rule and abuse of power feels wonderful and, it turns out, a great way to work off some stress. As I finish breaking it down, Cooper walks in.

"What's going on here?"

"Making a statement. Schmitty used this as a palace to remind everyone they were beneath him. I want to make it into a proper Great Hall."

"What exactly does a proper Great Hall do?"

"It's a place for sharing meals, administering justice, and bringing people together."

"Well, that's a bit different than we are used to, but I like the idea. How can I help?"

"This space to my left—can we run long tables in a few rows with benches on either side? We can use it to eat with guests, maybe even for entertainment someday. And the space to the right—can we wall that off, make it a private meeting room?"

"For what?"

"The community leaders will need a place to gather and have discussions without everyone being able to listen in."

Cooper shrugs, "Should be easy enough."

"Inside the room, I'd like a perfectly square table large enough to seat three chairs on each side."

"Why?"

"When I was an Undesirable, I spent a lot of time dreaming of change. Victor used to ask me what I would do differently if I could. I tried to say everything, but he made me answer specifically. When every day was a struggle to survive, I found that there were four things I really wanted. A safe place, a purpose, support, and opportunities to grow. What if we built this community around those ideas? We appoint community leaders to focus on growing the town, leaders to keep everyone safe, leaders to care for the people and offer support, and leaders to dream of the future and unite us behind common goals?"

Cooper stares at me before blinking. "I like the idea. But what does that have to do with a square table with three chairs on each side?"

"The table symbolizes all four values are of equal importance."

"And the chairs?"

"I was thinking, we appoint three leaders for each value. When one person wields power, it's too easy for them to use it for themselves. Power needs accountability," I explain.

Doc and Dakkin walk in as I finish. They stand next to Olivia and Cooper but don't interrupt.

"Anything else?" Cooper asks.

"One more thing. I'd like to divert the main path and entry to the door Schmitty used."

"Really? Why?"

"Schmitty acted like the people existed to serve him. I believe leaders exist to serve their people. I want to flip the room. Rather than the lowest level being where people come to grovel before their glorious leader, I want them to stand proud from the tallest steps, looking down at the people who are here to serve and protect them. We will place a long table where several members of the leadership council can sit and listen to the needs of their people. This will be how we make Red Clay different," I explain.

Cooper exhales. "Can I make a suggestion?"

I nod.

"You want to show people Red Clay is different—we should give her new name," Cooper suggests.

"A new name?" I ask.

"That's a great idea," Doc inserts. "Names are powerful things. Changing the name of the town is a big statement."

"What would we call it?" I ask.

Olivia tugs on my arm. "Our name should be a declaration of what we want to be. With all the darkness and all the pain in the world, we should make it something hopeful."

The room goes silent as we all think.

"What about Dawn Haven?" I suggest.

"Dawn Haven?" Doc repeats.

"Dawn—symbolizing newness. Haven—being a declaration of our purpose: to be a safe place for all people. We want to do more than just survive in this hostile land. We'll become a beacon of hope."

"Dawn Haven—I like it," Doc nods approvingly.

The others agree, except Kane, who is sprawled out on the floor snoring.

"Good. Let's talk about the future. Dakkin, you are captain of the guard?"

He snaps to attention. "I am, sir."

"Am I to believe that you were unaware of the Elder's actions?"

"Completely, sir. I wouldn't stand for that."

"How is it the leader of the guard would be ignorant to such behavior?"

"Beg your pardon, sir, I am not the leader of the guard. I am the captain. I answer to the commander of the guard."

"And where he is?"

"The elder sent him to escort some criminals to Dragonvale. I've had suspicions for some time. After Tomisina and Gladriel went missing and then Yen and Killian also disappeared without a trace, I started noticing new arrivals almost always vanished within a few days. I knew in my gut something was off. When my commanding officer told me it was nothing, I took him at his word." Dakkin reaches into his coat and pulls out a silver decorative badge with a couple of stars under it. "Please accept my resignation, sir. I am charged with the protection and safety of this town. I have failed in my duty. I am prepared to accept full responsibility and submit myself to whatever punishment you deem necessary."

"Failure indeed, Captain. You allowed yourself to be deceived by a corrupt leader and your commanding officer."

"Yes, sir."

"A true man of justice must serve truth above all else. He must never blindly accept the word of others. I expect that you will not repeat that mistake again."

"No, sir."

"Very good, Commander Dakkin."

He looks befuddled. "Sir?"

"I accept your resignation as guard captain and name you commander of the guard. Your first duty will be to arrest your former commander and any guards with him who knowingly participated in Schmitty's trafficking of human beings."

Dakkin nods enthusiastically. "It will be my pleasure, sir!"

Doc gives me an approving grin.

"Now that we've resolved that, you all know this town far better than I do, so I will need to lean on you for a while. I have some ideas as to how to change things. How much housing is available within the walls?"

"We have approximately one hundred homes unspoken for," Cooper answers.

"Good, that's more than I expected. How many people could stay in the underground structure of each home?"

"Comfortably, six. If you're desperate, twelve—maybe a few more. What are you thinking?"

"Expansion."

"Not much room for that. We're wall-to-wall as it is."

I nod, "That's why we need new walls. The hills that surround us will be our walls. We line the hills with stone to make tall rock walls around us. We build elevated walkways for guards to patrol and towers for supplies and sleeping quarters."

"On which side?" Cooper asks.

"All of them," I answer.

"Sir, that would make Red . . . Dawn Haven almost twice the size of Dragonvale. That's a lot of land. We don't have that many people," Dakkin objects.

"Not yet. We are surrounded by natural defenses. We should use them. Larger borders mean more space for homes, for shops, for farming. We are the closest settlement to Dios. Why should people need to travel farther?"

"Sir, walls aren't the only problem. Our force shields are barely strong enough to surround the town as it is," Dakkin continues.

"I know a man in Dragonvale who can get us the supplies we need to not only expand our shields but to improve them in the process."

"That won't be cheap, sir."

"No, but my guess is when we raid Schmitty's house, we will find more than we need to pay for it."

"But sir, with Schmitty now gone, all his possessions are rightfully yours."

"I don't care for his ill-gotten gains. We will use every last credit's worth to make Dawn Haven a safe place for all who live and reside here."

Doc, Dakkin, and Cooper exchange glances.

"How do we help you?" Doc asks.

"Dakkin, I need you to clean house within the guard. Anyone who may share Schmitty's vices or greed needs to be removed. Once that's done, I'll need you and your men to work as security for the builders while they expand our walls. Cooper, I want you to take charge of the construction. Take as many able-bodied men and women as are willing to work and get started on the walls."

"I don't know much about construction," Cooper confesses. "But Pryon was an engineer in Dios before his exile. He might be good to—"

"Recruit whoever you need. I'm not asking you to design it. I'm asking you to help me get it done."

Cooper nods in agreement.

"Doc, I want you to handle the tech. Send a team of our best tech experts to Dragonvale to get the supplies we need to expand and protect our borders."

"I know just who to send," Doc answers.

"One last thing I need from you: I want the names of a few people from town who are wise and well-respected in the community. We are going to create a team of leaders to help manage projects and developments. Time to recruit, train, get everyone up to speed."

Doc, Dakkin, and Cooper each cross their arms with their hands on their shoulders in a formal bow, then exit.

I stand over Kane's sleeping body. One of his eyes peeks open and he grins, "You got plans for me too, then?"

I reach down and help him to his feet. "Kane, I want you to test security. Find our weak points and fix them. Train the guards until not even you could get in undetected."

"No guards are that good, my friend." Kane strikes a proud visage.

"Teach them to be," I answer.

"What about me? I'm pretty good with plants; maybe I can help the farmers set up crops? I want to help," Olivia says.

"If you want to help the farmers, that would be great. While you're doing that, there is one other thing you can do to help me."

"Anything."

"Spike. Think you can find out if he's been here?"

Olivia nods enthusiastically. "You think he's here?"

"I honestly don't know."

"If he's here, I'll find him."

I hope with every fiber of my being that Spike is here. "Oh, talk to Dakkin first."

"Did you just call me 'O'?" Olivia seems shocked.

"What? No, I was saying oh, like in OK . . ."

Olivia closes her eyes and nods. "Yeah, that makes sense. Sorry."

"You going to explain that?"

"'O' is what my dad used to call me. Whenever he wanted to get my attention, he'd just step outside and shout 'O!' When I was a kid, I hated it. Now, I'd give anything to hear him call me 'O' again."

"I had no idea. How has that never come up before? People say 'oh' all the time."

Olivia chuckles. "No, they do. I think after seeing those flowers that reminded me of home, I've just been thinking about my family a lot more."

"Well, if you ever want to talk about them . . ."

"Thanks, now let me go find Spike." Olivia winks at me with a little half grin on her face and she exits.

I spend the rest of the day reorganizing the Great Hall. At the end of the day, the guards try to escort me to Schmitty's home. I try to refuse, but they insist. Olivia and Kane join me as we descend on the elevator to the dwelling below.

The doors open to an embarrassment of riches. Pristine furs line the ground. Large, colorful gems in glass cases decorate shelves along the walls. Everything down here looks ornate and lavish. We walk around, opening the doors to the many rooms only to find more treasures. I push one door open and discover it's filled with square and triangle coins made of a shiny, dark metal. The coins sit in a giant mound on the floor. The coins represent a different number of credits based on their thickness and shape.

It's so odd. Do people carry around actual coin purses to hold their credits? Purses. Coins—that you carry! If they had done this in Dios, we'd have lived like kings. Digital credits—easier to manage, harder to steal. Schmitty had an entire room filled with coins. Why? Did he swim in them or something? What's the point of storing all this?

I'm as impressed as I am disgusted, knowing how he earned them. But he'd left behind the fortune we'd need to make Dawn Haven into the pearl of the Outlands. We'll make a better life here than we ever had there. That'll show Victor.

In addition to the treasure and credits he has stashed everywhere, there are a stack of datapads, a refrigerator stocked with all kinds of delicacies, and the most troubling portraits I've ever seen. Schmitty had six different paintings of himself hanging on his walls in ornate, gold frames. In all of them, he is shirtless and looks like an athlete in peak physical condition. That must have taken some imagination on the artists' part. In one, he is riding a unicorn. In another, he's wrestling a bear. A third has his face and fake abs on the body of a horse. Of all the things I've seen in the Outlands, these paintings may be the most disturbing. I remove them from the walls and shove them into the closet to get them out of sight.

The next day we focus on maximizing occupancy in each home to free up as many units as possible before the Raiders arrive. Preparations consist of planning, introductions, building teams, and listening to ideas from various townspeople. Some of them are more bizarre than others.

Cooper walks over to me with a middle-aged woman wearing a light purple outfit and carrying a digiboard.

"Jett, this is Sala. Sala is a bit of an organizer by trade," Cooper explains.

"Organizer? No, I am a highly trained, highly proficient experience guide. In Dios, I put together the finest custom events for Primes. I'm a holistic planner. I take everything into account and put the right people in the right places to create the perfect experience."

"Wow. Um, what does that mean, exactly?" I ask.

Sala ponders for a minute. "Well," she sighs. "It means I organize things really well."

I look at Cooper, and we both start laughing.

Sala's face turns red. "That's not funny."

"No, I suppose to you it isn't," Cooper says between laughs. "Anyway, Sala here can help get all our new friends settled in when they arrive."

"Perfect, what's your plan?"

"Well, the first thing we have to do is create a registry. Obviously, I don't know these people. So it will be important for us to figure out what skills or talents they may have to see how they can be of use." Her tone is so superior that I wonder if it hurts her neck to look down at such a steep angle.

"That's a great idea. Let's include the current residents as well. That way we know what we are working with," I add.

Sala rolls her eyes. "Naturally. Once we know what everyone is good at, we can organize them into categories; farmers, builders, medical workers, merchants, teachers—you know, then we will group everyone according to their category and—"

"No," I say loudly and firmly.

"No?" Sala cocks her head and puts a hand on her hip. "What do you mean—no? This is the best way to create an ordered system. We will—"

"No," I repeat. "We can have people in similar fields work together—that's fine, but we are not making a little Dios here. People can live where they want. Spaces can be assigned or chosen. I want people with different skills interacting and engaging with one another."

Sala sighs, "Fine, what do I know? I was only top of my class. But sure, we can do whatever you say. We are in the Outlands after all; what's a little more chaos? You're the king or whatever. May I continue, your majesty?"

Oh, she's going to be a lot of fun.

"Please do."

"We will build teams based on skill and ability. Each team will be given a project to work on to help with the development of Red Cl . . . Dawn Haven."

"You have projects ready for these teams?" I am surprised and impressed by her organization.

"Naturally."

"Can I see these projects?"

She sighs loudly and hands me her digipad. "The file is pulled up. Just swipe to move between projects." Her voice sounds so annoyed.

I look through her plans. She has designs for everything: tapping into the river to create natural irrigation for the farmland; large underground housing facilities that operate like inverted cloud breakers; using one elevator leading down to multiple different units, allowing us to fit five or six times the number of people in the same amount of space; a proper market center in the middle of town with organized spaces around it. She's thought of everything.

"This is brilliant. There's no way you just created all of this, is there?" I hand her back the digipad.

"No, I've been working on it for three years. That pig, Elder Schmitty, said it would be too expensive and wasn't worth the effort."

"Well, this is truly incredible. Sala, I would like you to make this happen. Will you be the official highly trained, highly proficient experience guide for Dawn Haven?"

Instantly her demeanor changes. She smiles, her eyes light up, and she starts hopping in place. "Oh, yes, yes, yes! Thank you!"

"OK, I'm counting on you, Sala," I say.

"You won't regret it, Mr. King man."

"Jett."

"Mr. King Jett."

"No, just Jett is fine."

"Oh, OK. Jett." When she smiles her eyes squint closed. She turns and frolics off.

"What a strange woman," I mutter.

"Oh, you don't know the half of it," Cooper chuckles.

The next few days are a blur of planning and trying to organize the chaos that Schmitty left behind. I'm starting to get concerned. It must have taken Lilly a little longer than expected to pack things up—at least I hope that's all it is.

In the afternoon of the third day, Olivia rushes to me, practically floating in with excited energy.

"Hey, Olivia, what's up?"

"Spike—one of the guards told me he might have seen him."

"Who? When? Where?"

"According to the guard, he arrived about two weeks ago, stayed for the day and then left toward Dragonvale. I haven't found anyone else who recalls seeing him, but it could be him. Jett, Spike could be here."

"If he is, he's all alone."

All I want to do is run to Dragonvale—leave all this behind and find Spike. If it weren't for the impending doom that is Morton Ghood, I'd do it. If Spike is out here somewhere, I'm going to find him. I need to find him. I have to talk myself out of leaving anyway, despite how dangerous and foolish it might be. The resounding of the alert siren from the town walls expels the thought from my mind. Someone is coming. From the walls, we see a large group of people approaching. Finally, they are here. Things are about to get exciting.

Lilly and Brock lead the Raiders into town. The large group of fighters and former Marauder slaves file in and are directed to the registry tables Sala set up. The line runs from the Town Square all along the main road with plenty of Raiders who haven't even made it through the gate.

"Welcome to Dawn Haven. This is Sala. She will be getting some information from you as we help get you settled into your new homes. Please be patient; we will go as fast as we can," I say.

Sala waves her hand in the air. "This way, this way. Please form an even line in front of one of the four tables here. Once you give us your information, you will head to the Town Square. There you will get into groups with five other people. Each group will be given access to a home and shown around by one of our local volunteers. If you do not have a group, we will assign you one."

The line moves faster than I expected. Having a few people recording data at each of the four tables speeds things along.

Toward the end of the herd, I see Telmen and Jensen. Telmen is holding a rope in his hand, the other side of which is wrapped around Jensen's waist. I chuckle; it's crude but effective. I hate to think what caused this to be necessary. Just seeing them both fills me with a sense of peace. The band's almost back together. We're just missing Spike. I escort them in and away from the line of Raiders.

"Doc!" I wave my hand in the air, and he makes his way over to me.

"Your friend?" he asks, inspecting Jensen.

"Oh, stick! A stick!" Jensen reaches out and tries to run.

Telmen wraps the rope tighter around his arm and pulls back to keep Jensen in place.

"It's been a walk to remember. He keeps trying to run off and grab whatever he sees. I haven't slept since we left the outpost."

"Doc, this is Telmen and Jensen. Jensen's the one we were telling you about."

Doc steps closer, tapping his chin. I have no idea what he's looking for, but I can't stop myself from trying to see what he sees. All I'm really doing is getting in the way. When his appraisal ends, he turns to Telmen.

"Bring him to my facility. I'll run some tests and see what I can do."

"Telmen, get some rest; you've got to be zeroed. I'll take Jensen from here—" I start.

"No, I'm fine. I'm staying with him." There's a firm determination to his voice. I decide not to press the matter. Telmen follows Doc to the infirmary, towing Jensen behind them.

Lilly walks over to me as she looks around. "Wow, you've been busy."

Brock stands silently with his arms folded across his chest like a perpetually annoyed lawn gnome.

"This was the easy part."

"Deposing a corrupt leader, liberating a town, and somehow becoming its new leader—is easy?" Lilly chuckles.

"Compared to what comes next, yes."

Lilly shakes her head. "It's never easy with you, is it?"

I shrug. "Just trying to keep things interesting."

"Well, you got us here. What's next?"

"Can you spare some scouts? I'd like to get as much notice as possible if Morton starts heading this way."

"You think he'll come?"

"Eventually, but we are not ready. Can you scare up a couple of Raiders to help guard the gates, stop anyone who doesn't have permission to leave?"

"You turning the town into a prison?"

"I can't rule out the possibility that Morton has a spy. My plan doesn't work if Morton comes to us before everything is set."

"Plan?"

I grin, channeling my best Victor impersonation. "Yeah, I have a plan to bring an end to Morton Ghood."

"How?"

"I'm going to make him so mad he challenges me to a fight."

"You want to . . . ," Lilly stops herself and buries her chin into her chest before looking back at me. "You know challenging him is loopy, right? It's reckless, impulsive, maybe even downright salvage."

"Just keep filling me with confidence."

"Morton is not a fool. We have what, five hundred fighters, maybe six? He has ten thousand. They are warriors whose greatest desire is to die in battle. If he comes, he's just going to wipe us out. He has no reason to challenge you. No one in their right mind would."

"You're right. For this to work, we need to make sure he's not in his right mind."

"I'm not going to like this, am I?"

"You still have the explosives?"

Lilly sighs, "I really didn't want to be right about that."

"Same plan as before? Didn't work then, so why not try the exact same thing again?" Brock snaps.

"Not exactly the same. Last time, we were aiming for maximum impact: kill as many Marauders as we could. The goal this time is different. We use the explosives to harass him."

"Great. So now you want to take the best weapons we have and deliberately use them ineffectively? Brilliant plan. He definitely won't see it coming."

Brock's contempt is thick enough to cut with a dull stick.

"Exactly." I could answer in a way that doesn't antagonize him more, but at this point, I'm just owning it. The look on his face is priceless. If it were possible for steam to spout out of a person's ears, Brock would be doing it. I give it a minute before Lilly smacks me in the arm.

"Jett, behave."

"A few years back, Vic and I were on a job in the mining sector. It was a simple job, easy money. Couldn't figure out why nobody wanted it until that night. Job required us to get across a quarry that was being blasted to break up the ore. Victor had mapped out a safe path. As we went, they kept exploding these blasters. Rocks and debris were flying everywhere. Even though we knew we were a safe distance away from the explosions, every time one went off my whole body tensed up. My nerves were like exposed wire. After the third one, I thought I was going to rip my hair out. I was on edge for three days after that. I about pummeled Telmen for saying good morning. If Becka hadn't stopped me, I would have."

"You want to use the explosives to create so much tension and anxiety that Morton goes into a blind rage, so he challenges you without thinking?" Lilly summarizes.

"Exactly."

Lilly rests her face in one hand. "You're insane, but it might work. I'll send a few scouts to keep an eye on Morton's camp. At least it will give us some notice."

I reach into my pack and pull out a pair of datapads. "Give two of them these; they can message us directly. I have datapads for you and a few other key personnel to help with communication and coordination."

Lilly looks genuinely impressed. "You really have been busy. Now it's just a matter of setting the explosives."

"I'll get them placed," I offer.

"We have a demolitions specialist; Brock and a few others will go with him to get those set. You are in charge here, Jett; you can't just go running around doing whatever you want. You've responsibilities to think about."

Somehow Lilly acknowledges my role as leader and bosses me around in the same breath.

Three days later, the scout team leaves with Brock and Isilda, the demolitions specialist. Cooper is proving to be a very capable building supervisor. The Raiders are settling in well and finding ways to get involved, thanks to Sala's organization. Vesta takes it upon herself to provide a community dinner every night. She enlists a few townsfolk to help her. Even without a lot of ingredients to work with, she somehow manages to make some incredible dishes, which brings up the morale of the entire town. Something about everyone eating together each night really helps integrate the Raiders and former slaves with the residents. Perhaps that was what Vesta had in mind. Who would have thought food could be such a powerful tool to bond people together?

I sit down for dinner. Olivia slides across from me. She doesn't say anything, just occasionally looks up at me and smiles.

"Everything OK?" I ask after her fifth look.

She nods. "I wanted to ask about your friend, Kali—the girl that helped you rescue us."

I sigh. "What about her?"

"Are you still angry with her?"

"Yes, it's because of her that Becka—"

"Do you think she wanted Becka to die?"

"No . . ."

"She made a mistake, and someone else got hurt because of it?"

"Yeah . . ."

"I think that's something we can all relate to." Olivia puts her hand on top of mine. "Jett, people make mistakes, but we can't give up on them."

She has a point. Olivia gives my hand a squeeze and then gets up from the table. "I'm going to take some food down to Telmen; he still hasn't left Jensen's side. I'll see you later."

A moment later, Dakkin replaces her.

"Sir."

"Yes?" I set down my food, giving up the notion of eating in peace—or at all. "The former commander, Ted Oaklan, and his guards have been spotted. I thought you might want to be there for the arrest."

"You thought right." I slide away from the table. "Make sure everything looks normal. We will wait until they are inside the gate, then surround them. I don't want them trying to escape if we approach too soon."

"Yes, sir." Dakkin slings his energy rifle from his shoulder. "You should know, sir—Ted is a proud man with a short temper. He will likely lash out."

"Cornered beasts usually do. Do everything in your power not to kill them. But if they become a risk to your men or to anyone else, do not hesitate."

Dakkin nods at my instructions. "I'll post some extra men on the walls just to be safe."

I stand alone at the point where the path forks inside the gate, far enough back for Ted and his guards to get inside before we spring our trap. Ted is a tall, lanky man with short, brown hair, a thin round chin, and an almost dopey expression cemented on his face. His eyes are bulbous and unusually far apart. He looks like the human version of a groundhog.

When he sees me, he cocks his head to the side, and an easy but lifeless smile forms on his lips. "And just who might you be?"

Even his tone sounds off, like he's just a walking shell of a person.

"I'm Jett."

"What are you doing standing in my way, Jett?"

"Oh, sorry, that's my fault. I just wanted to stop you here long enough for us to surround you so that I could have the joy of telling you you're under arrest."

Ted's bulbous, lifeless eyes narrow, and his face scrunches. "Excuse me?"

"No, there is no excuse for you. Scum like you shouldn't be allowed to live."

"I don't know who you are, but you've got some nooma talking to me like that," he says through gritted teeth. "Do you know who I am?"

"Of course, your Ted Oaklan, former commander of the guards of Red Clay—slaver and soon to be inmate at Dawn Haven prison." I smile for added effect.

"Boys, take this crag and teach him some manners for me," Ted sneers and starts to walk past me.

"That will not be happening." Dakkin steps around the building behind me with several guards. The humming of the rifles' energy cores charging up fills the air.

"Dakkin, I should have known a parasite like you would be involved in this. We will see what Elder Schmitty has to say."

"Didn't you hear? Elder Schmitty is dead. I gave him a chance to live. He rejected it. Now, I'm going to give you one chance. Surrender peacefully, and you and your men will not be harmed. Do not, and I'll make sure you get everything you deserve." The handle of my energy blade rests in my hand as I stare Ted down.

"Who do you think you are, hmm? Some domie from Dios? I bet you haven't even survived your first year out here. You presume to lecture me? I am the guardian on the wall. I am the shield that keeps this town safe."

"No, you're the disease this town needs to be cured of." When I cut him off his eyes go wide. He grunts loudly and swings at me. His long, thin arms move clumsily and slow. Is this a joke? I've seen children throw better punches. It's so easy to dodge, I almost let it hit me, thinking it has to be some kind of distraction. I move under his arm and then drive my weight into the back of his shoulder, sending him to the ground.

"You dare touch me?" He's on his feet and pulls the rifle from his shoulder, aiming it at me. My energy blade sings to life, cutting through the air. I arc my blade, so it cuts the rifle in half. Before he can react,

I rest the edge of the blade against his neck. Ted's whole body begins to shake. He drops both halves of his rifle and holds his hands up.

"I'm sorry. Please, don't hurt me. I didn't mean it. I surrender." He sniffles and tears well up in his eyes. Is this guy for real?

"Let's go." Dakkin grabs him and pulls his arms behind his back. He snaps energy shackles around his wrists and pushes Ted forward.

Ted looks over his shoulder at me and glares. His men, seeing their cowardly leader surrender, do the same. One, a bald man with a crooked nose, drops his rifle and bolts toward the gate. He shoulders past the guard who tries to intercept him. The guard tumbles while the man with the crooked nose rushes to the gate and his freedom. Kane steps out of nowhere, slamming his fist into the man's face and knocking him on his back. Kane's knife is in his hands. Before the guards can reach him, Kane slices the man across the face.

"A mark to remember," Kane chuckles and gets off the man just before the guards grab him and pull him up. He puts his blade away.

Part of me wants to scold him. Part of me wants to pat him on the back.

Dakkin and his men escort the former guards down the street toward the prison. Now, finally, all those who were involved with the slave trade of Red Clay have been dealt with. The ugly chapter in my new town's history is over. We are free to move on. At least that's something.

I make my way to the infirmary to check on Jensen when a woman in a hooded, red cloak cuts me off. She bows her head low.

"Now that you are the leader of this town, I'd like to request an audience." Her smile feels warm, but her gaze is frigid.

"What is it, Janelle?"

Her smile shifts to a sneer. "The Children of the Dome have a sacred mission. We are Bealz's instruments to find his chosen one! To do that, we need a temple."

"You want to build a temple?"

"Yes! To train new recruits, to teach the word of Bealz, to seek the will of Bealz."

"I'm sorry, I don't see that being a high priority right now."

. . . or ever. The last thing loopers need is that kind of validation.

"Do not be a fool; there is nothing more important than the will of Bealz. Those who oppose him shall burn in the acid river for all eternity. But if you support his mission, then you shall be invited into paradise and allowed to return to the Holy Dome!"

"I appreciate the offer, but we have other things to worry about. Your temple will have to wait."

She makes several more attempts to change my mind before finally giving up and storming off.

Four days later, Brock and the demolition team return.

Ah, just when I was getting used to the joy of his absence. Upon his return, he informs me the job is done, and everything is in place. Then, he shoves past me to "get some well-earned rest."

The alarm from the front gate sounds, indicating someone is approaching. It can't be Morton, can it? We haven't heard anything from the scouts. Who could it be? Perhaps a new exile from Dios? My mind races with possibilities as I make my way to the guard tower, curious to see our visitors. Three travelers approach, the hoods of their cloaks pulled up to protect them from the sun but also serving to hide their faces.

"Halt, who goes there?" a guard shouts.

"We are here to see Jett Lasting," a woman's voice answers. I recognize it immediately.

"I didn't ask why you were here, did I? Identify yourself," the guard calls back.

"Open the gate," I instruct, hopping down from the wall. The wood creaks as the gate splits down the middle, opening wide. I step outside to face them.

"Kali."

CHAPTER TWENTY-ONE

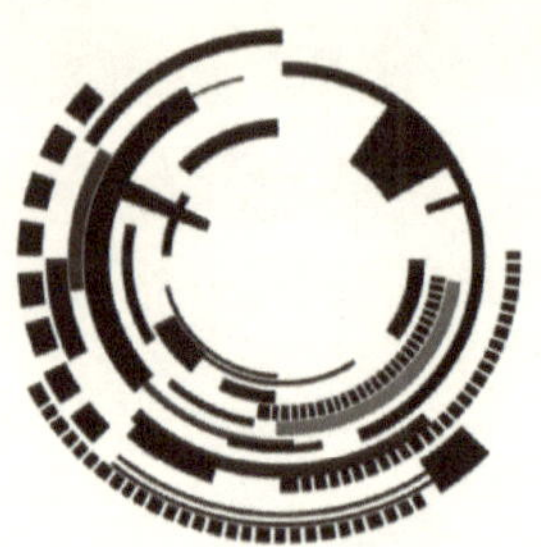

Kali keeps her head lowered, avoiding my gaze.

"I know you don't want to see me. I'm not trying start anything. I just want you to know how truly sorry I am. I've been on the run my whole life. I've been hunted my whole life because of who my father is. Outside of Rowan, everyone I've ever trusted with my true identity has betrayed me or rejected me. Knowing how much you hate the Patriarch—how much they hurt you—I was afraid if you knew, you would too. I know I should have told the truth; I got so used to keeping my secret, it never occurred to me someone else might get hurt because I didn't share it."

I fold my arms across my chest as I listen. I feel the pangs of guilt nibbling at my gut mixed with the anger I can't seem to escape. As angered as I am by what happened, it still feels good to see her.

I sigh, "I just don't get it. After everything we went through, why didn't you tru—"

"Oy, after everything the lass just said, that's what yer going with? Try again, brother, but this time, do betta."

My eyes swell. My jaw drops. My body freezes in place as excitement, hope, disbelief, confusion, and pretty much every other emotion imaginable swell up inside me all at once.

"Spike?!?!" I manage.

The middle traveler straightens and pulls his hood back, revealing his salt-and-pepper hair. The scruffy facial hair that typically lines his jaw has blossomed into a full and wild beard. Standing tall, broad shouldered, and grinning like a kid in an ice cream shop is my favorite living person. Before I can blink, Spike has crossed the drawbridge and scooped me up in his arms, squeezing me so tight I feel like my shoulders may actually touch.

"I've been looking for ye, brotha. Seeing yer face again fills me with joy. I've been worried all kinds of sick. Where are the others? Are they here?" Spike releases me and starts looking around.

It feels like a heavy blanket is suddenly dropped on my shoulders. My knees wobble, and I look away from him. I don't want to see his face when I tell him.

"Spike, I need to . . ." My heart is an anchor untethered by a chain, plunging into the ocean with nothing to stop its descent into darkness.

His hand clasps my shoulder, and he pulls me back into another hug. "I know, brotha; Kali told me. She found me in Dragonvale. Apparently, someone told her a wee bit about me. She filled me in on the journey back."

My anger surges back up, and I push myself back away from Spike. "Did she tell you what she did?"

Spike nods. "Aye, she did. Can you blame her, brotha? We're in the Outlands. Everyone here hates the Patriarch. Being the daughter of a Patriarch official puts a target on her back. Plenty of people would kill her on that alone. Hard to blame her fer keeping something like that a secret."

"But if she'd said something—Becka . . . "

I glance up to see Rowan standing behind her with a hand on her shoulder, her gaze fixed on the ground by her feet.

"Aye, there are no words for the loss of someone like Becka. The world is a lesser place without her in it. I hate that she's gone. I hate that I wasn't here. If I had been, maybe things would be different. I understand your anger, brotha, but we both know that wasn't Kali's fault. She'd no way of knowing that the secret she kept for her safety would end up hurtin' Becka."

Leave it to Spike to ruin a perfectly good grudge with his reasoning. He's right. When I found out about her lie, I was so angry. I convinced myself it played a part in Becka's death. I lost control of my rage. Even then, in the recesses of my mind, I knew it was not really her fault. I was just desperate to unleash my pain, my anger, my sadness onto someone; punishing her was a substitute for punishing myself. I know I should tell her that I understand why she did it and that what happened wasn't her fault; I just can't seem to form the words.

"I've missed you."

"Well, I'm here now. Stop trying to change the subject."

"You're right, I need to talk to her. The others are probably in the infirmary. Give me a minute, and I'll take you to them."

Spike squeezes my shoulder and hugs me again. "I'll be waiting inside, brotha."

I go to Kali, who still refuses to look at me.

"Why?" I ask.

Kali's shoulders slump even more. "After you sent us . . . after we left, we weren't sure where to go. We met this very unusual man who claimed to be a merchant. While we were talking, he told us he'd just passed a man with a strange accent headed toward Dragonvale. I remembered you'd told me about Spike and his accent. I knew it was a long shot, but it was something. We went to Dragonvale in search of the man with the strange accent. I thought if I could at least find him, if I could reunite you, maybe that would help. We found the man in a pub. I approached him and sure enough, it was Spike. I know I can't fix what happened. I know it's my fault. I just thought maybe if I could—"

"No."

I hear her sniff. "I understand. We're leaving." She turns to walk away.

"Kali, no." I reach out and grab her arm, pulling her into me as I hug her tight.

"I was asking why you would go through so much trouble for me after how I treated you. Both of you." I step back and look between her and Rowan. "I'm not going to insult you by making excuses. I took Becka's death hard, and I projected my anger onto you. It wasn't fair or right. I reacted badly, and I'm sorry."

"I should be the one apologizing," Kali objects.

"Well, how about this. From now on, we are honest with each other—as friends should be."

"Friends?" Kali repeats.

Rowan slaps my arm and smiles brightly before walking into Dawn Haven, leaving Kali and I alone . . . or as alone as two people can be when they are standing outside the town gate being watched by a half dozen guards.

"Too presumptuous?"

Kali shakes her head, a subtle smile forming on her lips. "No, I like it."

"There's a lot I need to tell you. Can we chat later? Right now, I need to get to Spike."

"Of course, I'll be here."

Spike is waiting just inside the gate, looking around at all the activity. He follows me through town to the infirmary. We ride the elevator down and head into the room where Doc is treating Jensen. Sitting next to him is Telmen, who, apart from sleeping, hasn't left his side.

As soon as Spike steps into the room, Telmen rushes us. Tears well up in the corner of his eyes as he laughs awkwardly.

"Spike! You're alive! When did you get here? Are you ok? Where have you been? Did they just exile you now? Why did they wait so long? Did they talk to you before they exiled you? How did you find us?"

I can't help but laugh as Telmen returns to form. Spike hugs him tight and squeezes him hard enough to choke off his endless stream of questions.

"Hey, Doc, I think I found the stuff you asked for. Is this—" Olivia walks into the room and nearly drops the vial in her hand. Her body freezes like a statue. She blinks and then blinks again. Her mouth drops open as she stares in stunned silence.

"Don't just stand there catching flies in yer trap, get over here." Spike reaches out and practically lifts Olivia off the ground, tugging her into a hug. "It fills me heart with joy seeing you both!"

"What? When? How? When did you? Where . . . ," Olivia stumbles over her words as she steps back.

"Yer starting to sound like Telmen," Spike chuckles.

"Oh, come on. I don't sound like that," Telmen objects.

Spike laughs, "Brotha, you talk so fast it's like yer words are running for their lives."

"That's not true! I don't talk fast; you just listen slow. I just have a lot going on in my brain all at once. So excuse me for sharing some of it with you!" Telmen protests.

Spike just grabs him around his shoulder and squeezes him, forcing Telmen to lower his head and stop speaking. Watching them warms my heart. My little family went from eight to two. Now it's back to five.

"How's Jensen?" I ask Doc.

"Tough. His jaw was dislocated. He had four broken ribs. Internal bruising over most of his body. The good news is, I don't see any brain trauma that should keep him from recovering. I've given him some meds, treated his wounds, which should help. Bad news is the mental trauma of what he endured may be very difficult to mend. He's going to need a different kind of healer for that."

"Know someone?"

"I do; she lives outside of town on a little, solitary farm where she grows herbs and crops."

"Isn't that dangerous, living by herself in the wilds?"

"It is. She's figured out a way to keep the corrupted away. Somehow she makes it work."

"Can we bring her here?"

"Possible, but you'd have to be pretty convincing. She hasn't left her little homestead in years."

"Show me." I pull up a map on my datapad. Doc draws a path from where we are to where this healer lives.

"Her name is Willow Lane. Be careful. She's not someone you want to trifle with. She's a survivalist and quite a good shot. When you approach her, make sure you're clear that you mean no harm. If she's not interested in talking, don't press the issue."

I nod. "Spike, you up for a field trip?"

"You have to ask, brotha? Just let me say hello and then we will go."

Spike kneels in front of Jensen, who is still rocking back and forth.

He speaks softly. "Alright brotha, don't ye worry about a thing. Spike will get ya back to normal in no time."

I watch Jensen's face, but he doesn't show any reaction.

"You really think he'll be ok?" Telmen shuffles his feet nervously.

Spike stands up, turning to face Telmen. He wraps his hand around the back of Telmen's head and looks deep into his eyes. "I know he will, brotha. Jensen is tough as houses. Give him some time to recover, and he'll be right as rain."

"When are we leaving?" Olivia stands at the doorway, making it clear the only way out is through her.

"Olivia, ye should stay here. Jett and I can handle this."

"Spike Joseph Raynar, if you think for one second that I'm just going to stay here, you've got another thing coming. Our friend needs help. I'm going with you. If you don't like it, you can stay here, and I'll go handle it myself." Olivia places her fists on her hips and glares.

"Hold on just a minute," Spike starts.

His words are cut off by a sudden expulsion of air. Suddenly a pair of long arms are wrapped around his waist squeezing him tight. I blink as I realize it's Jensen. Jensen is hugging Spike and holding the side of his head on Spike's back. To everyone's shock, he practically lifts Spike off the ground in his strong embrace.

"No fight. Family no fight," he says before letting Spike go.

He sounds coherent. I look at Doc, who shakes his head, seeming as surprised as we are.

Hope floats like a duck on water.

"Jensen?" Telmen's voice sounds nervous.

Jensen turns to face him. "Telmen family, too." His words sound almost childish, but they make sense. "Oh, lights." Jensen wanders over to inspect a monitor.

Doc takes some notes while Telmen tries to coax Jensen into talking more. After a few minutes, it becomes clear whatever happened with Jensen was momentary.

Olivia turns back to Spike. "I'm coming with you."

Spike holds up his hands in surrender. "Sorry, luv, heat must have gotten to me. Course we want you with us. Somebody's got to keep Jett out of trouble."

"Now you've got it. Let's go find this Willow lady." Olivia's tone softens.

While they pour out of the room and down the hallway toward the elevator, Doc grabs my arm.

"Jett, I wanted to say I'm sorry for what happened to Becka."

I nod; saying anything will just make me think more about it.

"Also, thank you for looking out for Kali."

"I appreciate that." We stand in silence for a moment. "I do have a question. You never told me why you care so much about her. Who is she to you?"

Doc looks off in the distance as if watching a memory on some invisible screen behind me. "She reminds me of my daughter."

"I didn't know you had a daughter."

"When I was exiled by the Patriarch, my wife and my daughter were not. Instead, they were stripped of their class and sent to live in the Rim. Part of my punishment was the Patriarch ensuring I'd never see them again. My daughter is about Kali's age. I see a lot of her in Kali: her strength, her stubbornness, her wild spirit. I can't be there to protect my daughter. But looking out for Kali makes me feel a little more connected to her. I know it's silly."

"It's not. Not at all. What's your daughter's name?"

"Evetta." He says her name like it's a bad word he doesn't want to get caught using.

I nod. "Well, Doc, maybe one day we can reunite you with Evetta."

Doc smiles. "Nothing in all the world would fill me with more joy."

We shake hands and part ways. I join the others in the elevator. When we step outside the infirmary, Kali is waiting for us while Rowan is leaning against a post on the other side of the street.

"How is he?" Her expression is sincere.

"He's getting there," I reply. "We are heading out to find a healer who lives nearby."

"Willow?"

"You know her?"

"Only by reputation. She's a bit feisty. Can we tag along?"

Spike shrugs, "I dunna mind some extra company."

"That would be wonderful, thank you," I agree.

"Alright, let's get going brotha." Spike adjusts the pack draped over one of his shoulders.

"We need to let Lilly know first," I note.

We find Lilly in the Great Hall looking over some designs on the newly built but unfinished square table. She smiles at me as I walk in. Kali steps in behind me, and Lilly's smile fades. There's a strange tension in the air.

"Lilly!" Spike bellows, pushing past me.

Lilly's smile returns as she rushes over to Spike and hugs him.

"Spike, I am so glad you're ok. You look well!"

"Course I do; I always look good, it's part of me charm." His wink is almost ruined by his laugh.

Lilly steps back and looks at us. "Alright, so what's going on?"

We fill her in on the plan. She shakes her head in disapproval.

"Jett, you can't just take off. You're the leader here. These people are counting on you," she protests.

"If there is a chance Willow can help Jensen, all the Marauder armies couldn't stop me."

Lilly sighs, looking annoyed. "I admire your desire to help Jensen, but what happens to the people here if something happens to you? Leadership transitions are hard on a community. Even if the last one was a complete scrap sink. Jett, this is not the time for you to put yourself at risk."

"At risk? This is the Outlands, Lilly; everything we do is a risk. These people don't just need a leader. They need an example, an ideal to unite them together. I can't stand here and tell them a community should look out for each other and take care of each other while I sit safely behind the walls while other people take all the risks. That's not the kind of leader I want to be."

Lilly closes her eyes and takes a deep breath. "I can see there is no talking you out of this. At least, promise me you won't take any salvage risks."

I nod in agreement, and we say our farewells.

We make our way out of Dawn Haven toward the home of Willow, the healer. Rowan takes the lead as is his custom. Kali slows down to walk next to me.

"Can we talk?" she asks. Spike and Olivia hang back a little in response.

"Everything ok?" I ask.

"When I first met you, I thought you were going to be another insufferable domie. But the more we spent time together, the more I . . . I didn't expect that I'd miss you." She avoids looking at me as she says it.

"I kind of missed you too. It was weird not having you around."

She smiles and looks over at me. "It means a lot that you accepted me. Thank you."

We look at each other, neither of us saying anything for a moment. The longer the moment goes, the weirder it starts to feel.

"What was Kyle talking about? He called you something . . ."

"Filia Lucem," she interrupts.

"Yeah, what is that?"

"It's like a title that I have because of my dad."

"You ever going to tell me who your mysterious father is?"

She hits me on the arm. "We're having a moment. Don't ruin it."

"Oh, a moment? I'm so glad you told me. I might have missed it."

She rolls her eyes and rushes to catch up with Rowan. No sooner than she catches up to him, I feel a strong arm wrap around my neck.

"Well, this is new." Spike grabs me and pulls my head into his chest, rubbing my hair.

"Don't you start too." I glare at him, pushing him away.

"Too? Ye mean I'm not the first one to notice the obvious?"

"No, I just don't know what to do about it." I straighten up and readjust my clothing.

"Well, what's happening with you and Lilly, brotha? Seems like yer out of sync."

I sigh. "Ever since we reunited, things have been different. At first, I thought it was just the situation, but I'm not so sure."

"Have ye told her that?"

I shake my head. "Not yet. I didn't know what I was thinking. When Kali showed up at the gate with you and Rowan, I think that's when I realized it."

"Well, there's nothing wrong with not knowing. But now that ye know, brotha, ye need to talk with Lilly."

"Becka said the same thing."

The mood shifts at the mention of her name. Spike's whimsical demeanor sobers.

"Then ye know it's the right thing to do; Becka always had a sense of that." Spike sighs, and the moment lingers in silence.

"How long ago did they send you out?" I try changing the subject.

Spike shakes his head. "'Bout two, maybe three weeks after ye. Had a wee bit of trouble dealing with those heaping dog things. By the time I reached Red Clay, ye were gone."

"How did you avoid Schmitty's guards?"

"I got the sense something was off about that one. I noticed after we spoke he had two guards tailing me. Amateurs. I stayed near crowds, figuring he wouldn't move on me openly. Gave me a chance to ask around. I met the Doc, who brought me to his lab. He's a good lad. Thanks to him, I had a chance to rest and recover while he snuck supplies and got me stocked. Twas probably a week later when I left just after dusk and started searching for ya. I'm not much of a tracker, though. Took me a wee bit to find my way to Dragonvale. When I got there, I learned ye'd already left."

"How did Kali find you?"

"Haven't the foggiest. I was trying to get a lead in one of the pubs when she and Rowan came up to me. Seemed they knew who I was and were looking for me."

"Well, we're together now. That's all that matters."

"Aye, couldn't agree more. How are ye holding up, brotha?"

I shrug. "You mean with Becka?"

"I mean with Becka, Jensen, Gibbs, Victor. Everything really—ye've been through a lot lately."

"I've been trying to understand why, trying to look at it from Victor's perspective. I don't even know when he turned on us. It couldn't have been before the battle in the Market, could it?" I wave my hand absently. "I don't know, Spike. I don't know if I'm angry or hurt. I don't know if I hate him or feel sorry for him. I just feel lost. You and Victor are two of the only people I've trusted completely in my life. I just don't understand how he could betray that?"

Spike grunts, "I loved Victor like a brotha. I'd have died for him a thousand times over if he'd asked me to. After all he did for us over the years, I thought there was nothing on this earth that could make me angry at him. What he did—it's unforgivable. The longer I've been out here, the angrier I feel. Friendship is a sacred bond. It's not just about trust. Friendship is openness and intimacy. Friendship is vulnerability. It's having someone you can let yer guard down with, and know whatever happens, they will always be on yer side, even if yer on the wrong side. The greatest sin—the most wicked, heinous act in this world—is the betrayal of friendship. Victor's betrayal was conscious, willful, and calculated. That makes it so much worse."

"Why do you think he did it?"

"I honestly don't care. There is no reason, no justification, no excuse that could ever pardon his actions. If I ever see him again, I'll send him to the special circle of Sheol reserved for murderers, racists, people who chew with their mouths open, and people who betray their friends."

Something about Spike's anger helps me find peace with my own. Just having my feelings validated allows me to put some of that anger to rest. My anger doesn't do me any good right now. The only person who is suffering because of it is me.

Rowan comes to a sudden halt and holds his hand out flat. He uses two fingers from his other hand to simulate legs and then holds a finger to his lips.

"Try to step quietly," Kali explains.

We've reached the crossroads where we first encountered the Vanguard. Rowan leads us down the path to the left. We follow it until it opens up to the canyon swarming with trematerras. They look so much bigger down here than they did from the top of the cliff. Great, we're walking through them. I've always wanted to dance with the possibility of becoming human jelly under some giant monster's foot. It's a dream come true.

"We have to go through?" I whisper.

Kali points. "Only access to her land is through here unless you can fly. They react to sudden movement. Just don't move quickly, and you should be fine."

"Should?"

Rowan holds his finger to his lips again as if to emphasize his point. He moves silently, stepping into the clearing and starting to weave through the Trematerra herd toward the opening that leads to Willow's home. Now I understand how she manages to survive on her own. She's behind a terrifying wall of monstrous creatures not even the depraved would challenge. Spike goes next, following the path Rowan sets. Olivia follows him. Kali insists I go before her. I close my eyes and exhale long and slow before entering the canyon. The one thought that echoes in my mind is the first warning Kali gave me about these creatures: don't go into their territory. Here we are, middle of the day, wandering right through it.

Every step feels painfully slow, and yet terror presses down on me that it may be too quick. I feel hot and cold at the same time. The farther in we get, the more my legs shake. My body starts to feel weak, my hands sweat, my breathing becomes labored and irregular. I feel a soft hand grab mine and squeeze. Kali exaggerates taking a deep breath. I do as she instructs. It helps. My thoughts shift from impending death at the edge of a Trematerra horn, which up close look like giant barbed spears, to the feel of her hand in mine. I expected it to feel rougher, more callous. We move together with our hands locked as we weave and dodge, each step bringing us a little closer to the goal. I remind myself that this is how we get Jensen back, provided Willow is able and willing to help us.

Rowan reaches the open path out of the canyon. We are almost there. There is a loud grunting sound just in front of me. Steam bursts from one of the Trematerra's nostrils and cuts off my path. I freeze and feel Kali do the same. Right next to us, a large Trematerra that had been laying peacefully on its stomach having a leisurely mid-afternoon nap rises to its feet. I close my eyes and flashes of bugs hitting windshields pop into my mind. Only, in these flashes, I'm the bug. I don't move; I don't even breathe. The creature shakes its head, and the force of the wind it generates nearly topples me. It opens its mouth in a yawn, revealing its pointed, jagged, sharp teeth. The Trematerra starts slowly sauntering right in front of us. The bottom of its belly is at my eye level. A quick run, and I could clear it. Kali's tightening grip on my hands advises against it. Spike makes his way out. I see Olivia do the same. The Trematerra's step makes the ground beneath us shake.

This is it; this is how I become a human pancake.

When the creature finally clears the path, Kali and I exhale. After letting our heartbeats slow, we resume our trek, slightly more hurried than before but still careful not to move too quickly. The path leading out of the open canyon narrows, making it much too small for a Trematerra to get through but easy enough for us. It's a long path, but even from here, I can see it open again to a waterfall, small lake, and actual green grass. I'd completely forgotten what the color green looked like. Hidden off the path, out of sight unless you were looking for it, is this little paradise oasis surrounded by nightmares.

The ground underneath us goes from feeling dry and hard to soft and squishy. We reach the edge and enter the clearing. Along the back wall of the oasis is a solitary house made of wood and surrounded by crops, flowers, and herbs. I start down the path toward the house. This was like something out of a dream. *Zttchh-pfffd.* A ring of black char appears on the ground just in front of my foot. I freeze in place.

"That wasn't an accident. Kindly turn yourselves around and be off, or the one I put in your brain won't be an accident either." The female voice blares around us, but I can't tell where it is coming from.

I pull out my energy blade and hold it away from my body, dropping it to the ground. "We're here to see Willow Lane."

"Good for you, honey, but she's not interested in being seen—not by you."

This is going wonderfully.

"Please, we need her help. Our friend—"

Zttchh-pffd. Another hole—this one an inch closer to my foot.

"Just in case you're hard of hearing. Go away!"

"Shoot me, then!" I shout. Spike and Kali express their displeasure with this remark. There's no answer.

"I apologize for our intrusion. You may be the only hope I have to get my friend back. I've lost too many people to give up on him, not when there's hope. If you have to shoot me, do it. But I'm not leaving until I know my friend is going to be ok."

"Why should I care?"

"You shouldn't, I suppose. None of us should be here risking our lives to help someone else. No one should do anything that isn't in their own best interest. But we do—we do because that's what being human is all about. We build bonds, forge connections, even make sacrifices. Every relationship is a risk. We take that risk because we know it's better than the alternative."

"What, pray tell, is this alternative?" The voice sounds softer and less hostile than before.

"Being alone," I answer.

"Good speech. You can go back and tell your friend that you gave it your all. I'm not interested in getting roped into whatever you have going on."

"Excuse me, is that Zainweed I see?" Olivia cuts me off before I can object.

There's a moment of silence before the disembodied voice responds, "It is. How do you know about Zainweed?"

"My family are farmers back in Dios. My dad told me about it—said it was one of the most potent cure-alls he's ever seen."

"He knows his plants. Doesn't change anything."

"I think it does. If you're growing Zainweed, you're not just an herbalist. You're a healer. Our friend needs a healer. We've risked our lives to find you. Are you really going to send us away without even hearing us out?" Olivia's voice sounds oddly confident.

The responses stop. We look around at each other, not sure what to do. A minute passes before the door to the house swings open, and a woman steps out. She's in her late forties by the look of her, with mostly black hair with some silver trimmings. Her clothes are handmade looking, both practical and decorative. Her eyes scan us like a hawk as she sets the butt of her rifle on her deck and leans the weapon against her house.

"Well, come on, then; I've put the tea on." She waves us toward the house. I gather my blade, and we tentatively make our way inside.

Willow's home smells strongly of lavender and mint. Green leafy vines hang from floor to ceiling along the walls. Shelves and cabinets are littered with jars of colorful plants and powders, none of them labeled. A cauldron sits in the back of the room, a small kitchen in the corner. Between brewing bottles, flasks, and other containers, she must be part herbalist, part alchemist.

"Sorry for the extreme test. I've had a lot of unwelcome guests as of late." Willow welcomes us into her home and closes the door, pointing to a sitting area near her large stone cauldron.

"Unwanted guests? Out here?" I ask.

"Well, when you get a reputation like mine, a lot of people want access to your skills. I have no interest in patching up Marauders or bandits so they can carry on victimizing innocent people. That's why I moved out here. They can't bring enough people through the canyon to force me to go with them."

"This place is amazing! I can't even remember the last time I saw real grass. How did you find it?" Kali asks.

"Find it? Honey, I grew it. The only thing that was here when I arrived was the waterfall. The rest are alterations I made."

"How did you get supplies through to the canyon with all those creatures there?" I ask.

"She didn't," Olivia grins. "You used aromatic plants to lure them in, didn't you?"

Willow laughs. "Just how did you figure that out?"

Olivia shrugs. "Aromas are powerful. I caught a strange scent when we were making our way through the pass. Back in Dios, I remember reading about how there were certain plants that were used to attract certain creatures. Luring those things in knowing they wouldn't be able to navigate the narrow pass is a brilliant way to protect yourself all the way out here."

Spike and I stare at each other in shock. I knew Olivia liked gardening but had no clue she was such an expert. I glance over at Willow. She stares at Olivia for a moment, shaking her head slowly.

"Well, aren't you something? You didn't come here to discuss my living situation; what do you need?" Willow asks.

I explain to her what happened to Jensen, trying to provide as many details as I can. Willow listens, frowning the whole time. "Oh, honey, I'm very familiar with Morton Ghood. I knew his parents, actually. Poor boy never had a chance."

"Poor boy?" Kali tenses up, gritting her teeth as she tries to control herself.

"You don't know the half of it, honey. There's no excuse for what he's become, mind you, but his parents were just about the nastiest couple I've ever met. When I was first exiled, I set up a shop in Red Clay, applying my trade to help people with their afflictions. Morton was in my shop once a week at least with a new injury and a story to go with it. His dad was a raging drunk and a doltine addict. He used his son as a punching bag. Morton's mother was no prize either. My guess is her parents were Primes, and she never had to work for anything a day in her life. She used her affection to manipulate her son. She'd only hug him or tell him she loved him if he stole things for her. She had that little boy wrapped around her finger. He'd steal, get caught, get beaten, go home, and get beaten. That was his childhood. Least, until his mother tried to trade up. She told his father she was leaving him. He didn't take it well. He dragged Morton and his mother into the wilds of the Outlands and left them near a Nocstra den. Morton survived— his mother didn't. I think that's when he started down the dark path. Sad, really. When I knew him, he was a sweet, silly boy with a wicked sense of humor. Now, the wicked is all that remains."

We sit in silence, not knowing how to respond to this insight into the madman.

Spike breaks the silence, "Ma'am, I know it's a lot to ask, but our friend, he's suffered a lot. The Doc has been treating him as best he can, but he needs more. Can ye help us?"

Willow doesn't even acknowledge the question. She just suddenly starts pacing back and forth, muttering under her breath to herself. Her hands dance in the air like she's conducting an orchestra. It's like she's having an intense debate with herself inside her head.

"I'm sorry, honey, I want to help, but I can't leave. It's too dangerous. Too many people want access to my skills. If someone like Morton finds me, I'll be a prisoner for the rest of my life. I can't be used like that. I won't be. I'm done helping people who do not deserve it."

Before I can speak, Rowan places his hand on the pacing woman's shoulder. He looks into her eyes deeply before stepping back and gesturing. His hands move fast from one thing to the next; I can't get any sense of what he is trying to express. Willow nods, the tension in her shoulders lessening. She sighs and sits down across from me.

"Tell me about your friend; what was he like before all this?"

"Jensen is . . . well he's complicated. We didn't really see eye to eye on much. He has a way of pushing people's buttons and driving them absolutely loopy. He always seems to say the wrong thing. Honestly, I spent much of my time trying to stop myself from punching him in his face."

"Goodness me, why would you go through all this for someone like that?" Willow asks.

"Because he's family. You don't ever give up on family." Olivia's voice is passionate and determined.

Willow gets up and walks over to her, looking in her eyes as if trying to read them. "I see. You intrigue me. You said your parents are farmers in Dios?"

Olivia nods. "Yes."

"I can feel your conviction. Yet you are in the Outlands without them. Tell me, honey, why isn't your family here with you?"

Olivia averts her eyes. "They weren't with me when I was exiled. I haven't seen them in many years actually."

"Why not?"

"That's not a story I like to dwell on."

"Tell me, girl," Willow says.

Olivia seems reluctant. "Technically, we were plebs, but we lived on the edge of the Rim. Our land was barren; our harvests barely enough to live off. Growing up, we were always hungry, always scraping to get by. One summer, after a particularly bad harvest, we were starving. I guess my parents realized if they didn't do something, we'd all starve to death. One day my dad took me into the Rim, told me he needed my help finding a very special seed—a seed that would revitalize our soil, so we could grow better crops. He said it would be hard to find, so we needed to split up. We'd meet back by the flower cart before heading home. I looked and looked and looked but never found the seed. So I waited at the flower cart for my father to finish his search. I waited and I waited until late into the night. That's when I realized he'd left me there. I was too young to find my way home. I didn't even know what direction it was in."

"He just left you there?" I blurt out in surprise and disgust.

Olivia nods. "Too many mouths to feed. Guess they decided they'd be better off with one less. For a long time, I wondered—why me? I have two brothers and a sister. Why didn't they want me? Why was I the one they got rid of? Maybe if I'd been better, if I'd known more about farming, been more useful, they would have kept me. That's how I got into gardening. Whenever I'm working in a garden or growing something, I imagine my family is out there somewhere doing the same thing. In a weird way, it's like we're still together."

Spike walks over and rubs his hand slowly over Olivia's back along her shoulder blades without saying anything.

"Hold on," I interrupt again. "If your family abandoned you in the Rim, why would you want to feel connected to them?"

Olivia shrugs, "They are still my family. Just because they gave up on me doesn't mean I'm going to give up on them. I can't imagine it was easy for them. They could barely feed themselves, not to mention four kids. I guess for me, gardening is my way of staying a part of their lives since I can't be with them."

"I just thought you liked getting away from all the guys commenting on how good ye looked all the time." Spike gives her a wink.

A smile grows on Olivia's face, and she starts to laugh. "I suppose that was an added bonus."

"Why didn't you ever say anything?" I ask. "I would have helped you try to find them."

"Victor knew. He'd been trying to find them for years."

"At least he told you he was trying to find them," I snap.

"He was trying. I think he still is," she answers.

"You're defending him; after he sold us out to save himself?"

"Do you hear yourself? That's not Victor. How many times did he put himself on the line for us? How much did he sacrifice for us? I think he's earned the benefit of the doubt."

"The doubt?"

"I don't know why Victor did what he did. He was always seeing more than we did. Maybe he had no choice. Maybe this was somehow for our good."

"For our good?"

Olivia's voice gets firmer, making her sound almost stern. "Victor asked us to trust him. I do. I think he's working out some grand plan, and we just don't see what it is yet."

"No wonder you put up with Jensen so well; you never give up on anyone."

Willow walks back to Rowan, taking his hands.

"You were right; thank you." She holds him in her gaze for a moment.

"Right? What did he say?" I ask.

"He told Willow that if she gave you a chance, you would restore her faith in humanity," Kali answers.

"Maybe not humanity as a whole, but you, honey," she points to Olivia. "You are someone worth helping."

Willow lets go of Rowan's hands before walking over to her cabinets and pulling out a large bag. She tosses it to me, then retrieves another and another, tossing one to each of us before pulling out one for herself. "Fill those with as much as you can carry. Let's go help your friend."

CHAPTER TWENTY-TWO

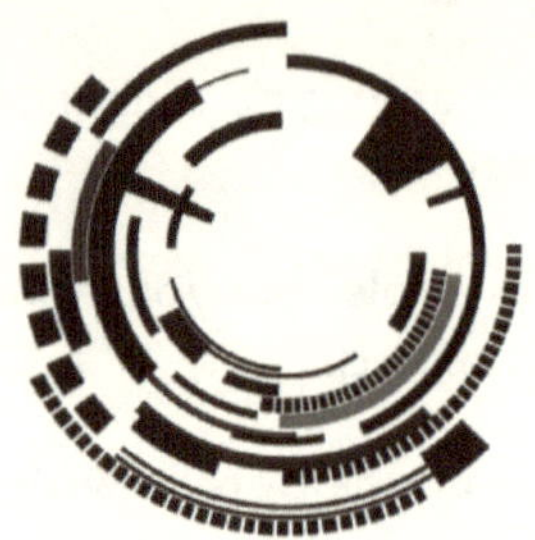

My body shakes with excitement as I stuff vials, plants, and containers into my bag until it's hard to zip up. Willow's house looks bare by the time we are done. She leads us to the pass, where she pauses for a moment. She turns and looks back at her home and then waves us on.

Not even the trematerras can bring down our soaring anticipation as we slowly creep our way through the canyon on our journey back to Dawn Haven. We practically race to the gates once the town is in view. There, standing just outside the gate waiting for us, is Kane with someone on their knees in front of him.

"Spike, glad to see you again." Something about Kane's full smile makes him look so much creepier.

"Kane . . . ," Spike responds dryly.

"I got you something." Kane kicks the man on his knees, sending him tumbling down the hill.

"Not a great time, Kane." I shake my head.

"He's a spy for Morton," Kane replies. Willow freezes and looks at me. Her body tenses as her eyes stretch wide open.

"Willow, let's get you to the infirmary to see Jensen." Olivia takes the herbalist's arm and guides her past Kane into town.

"Kane, that's not a spy; that's Kevin. He has a small shop in the Town Square," Kali says.

"That's what I've been trying to—" the man called Kevin slams forward, face smashed into the ground as Kane puts his foot on the man's shoulder.

"You think spies just sit around spying all the time? Course he has a job. Best way to get information is to look like you're not trying to. Living like a member of the community lets him gather information without raising suspicion," Kane says.

"What makes you think he's the spy?" I ask, looking at the man sprawled out in front of me.

"*The* spy? How did ye even know there was one?" Spike asks.

"Morton always seems well-informed. He's also been doing shady deals with the former Elder for some time. It makes sense that he'd have someone in town keeping him updated. It's also the first thing Victor would have looked for," I say.

Spike seems impressed. That makes me feel good, like somehow I'm on the right track. "Why him, then?" Spike presses his inquiry as Kane lets Kevin sit back up.

"Caught him making his way toward the pass," Kane says.

"That means he's a spy?" Spike asks.

"You know a lot of people who go wandering into the wilds on their own?"

"I keep telling him; I was headed out to gather some supplies for my shop. He won't list—" Kevin's objection is cut short by Kane shoving his face back into the dirt.

"That's hardly proof," Spike responds.

Kane pulls a disc out of his pocket and tosses it to me. "How about that, then?"

"What is it?" I examine the disc. When I click it, I see a drawing of Dawn Haven's layout, guard numbers, weapons, defensive locations, and pretty much every possible bit of data an attacker might want or need.

"Had that in his pocket along with some notes about you, the Raiders, and your current plans for expansion." Kane pulls out a knife and grabs the man's head, pulling it back.

"Wait, don't kill him," I instruct.

"You stopping me from killing people is becoming a bad habit," Kane objects.

"Take him to Dakkin; let's see what he knows and what he's told Morton. Then, we will talk about what to do with him."

"You want him interrogated?" Kane breaks into a smile. "And I didn't get you anything."

"Interrogated by Dakkin, not you," I insist.

Kane puts his knife away dramatically and starts hauling the man off toward the prison, dragging him with one hand by his hair. The man kicks his feet, trying to get up but can't find his footing.

Under normal circumstances, I might feel bad for him.

We make our way into town. Rowan wanders off without a word. Spike decides to check on Jensen and make sure Willow has everything she needs.

I start toward Schmitty's former palace. Kali grabs my arm to stop me.

"Jett, we need to talk."

"Is something wrong?"

"No, everything's fine. I just . . . I heard about your plan to get Morton to fight you."

"Wow, word travels fast. Is there a problem with it?"

"It's not bad. It's just not going to work."

Oh, how Kali so casually stomps on my dreams.

"What do you mean?"

"Your plan—to use explosives to get Morton so nuked he challenges you to a dual—relies on using chaos and tension to stress Morton out. Morton isn't like normal people. He thrives on chaos. You want him nuked, you need to get in his head and push his buttons."

"How do you suggest I do that?"

"I'm not sure exactly. I've been trying to come up with something, but I can't figure out what's missing."

"I was afraid you'd say that." I run my hand through my hair, trying to think about what else we could do to increase our chances.

"Afraid . . ." Kali lets the word hang in the air without context or explanation. The grin forming on her face betrays the idea developing in her mind. "What do we know about him? He's ruthless. He hates being challenged. He's possessive. Fear is his greatest weapon."

"And that helps us because . . ."

Silence. If only there were some crickets chirping nearby it could really set the mood. She rests her chin on her fist. I guess the idea is still in its infancy.

Kali breaks the silence. "My mother used to say: people who hurt others typically do so because they themselves are hurting. When we can't deal with our own issues, we project them onto others. What if he doesn't just want people to be afraid of him?"

I feel my eyes light up. "That's it! You're suggesting he needs them to fear him because that's where his power comes from? He's not the rightful king of the Marauders, and he knows it. Everything he has he stole. Everything he has is built on fear."

Kali's grin turns into a bright smile. "Yes! Exactly!" Her smile fades into a look of disappointment. "But how does this help us?"

"If Morton uses fear as a weapon against others in order to hide his own, that's something we can use against him," I note.

"How? We'd have to know what he's afraid of," Kali points out.

I nod. She has a point.

"Well, if we build off what your mother said; maybe what he does to invoke fear in others is to hide what he fears," I say.

"Based on his behavior, his fear would be being powerless. Losing. He takes because he's scared to lose."

Clarity strikes like a bolt of lightning in my mind. "According to Raggy, when Morton took over, the Marauder presence in this area was much smaller."

"That's right!" Kali's excitement grows. "Most of his fighters aren't true Marauders. They are slaves he bought, then conditioned to fear him."

"They aren't following him because they believe in him, but because they are too scared not to?" Our thoughts are so perfectly in sync we build off one another seamlessly.

"Yes! His grip of fear may be strong, but he knows that's the only thing keeping them. There's an old saying: 'it's a house of cars.'"

I put my finger over my mouth to stop myself from chuckling. "That's definitely not the saying."

Kali scoffs, "Yes, it is! Think about it—a house of cars wouldn't work. They'd just roll off each other, and the whole thing would come crashing down."

My hand covers my eyes. "The saying is: 'a house of cards'. It means being built on a shaky foundation that can be toppled by the faintest breeze."

Kali gives me an incredulous look. "Who builds a house out of cards? That doesn't even make sense."

I wave my hand dismissively. "If what Raggy told us is true, I can't imagine the true Marauders are that thrilled with his leadership."

"Right, so all we need to do is break his hold and then—"

"Kali, we don't even need to break it. We just need to threaten it. If Morton is as afraid as you suggest, simply trying to lure his people away should play into that fear and be enough to nuke him."

"What are you thinking?"

"We offer them a way out. We openly, brazenly, invite them to join us. They won't do it, of course, not at first. When they don't, we provoke them. Then, we run, and if all goes well, they follow us right into the valley of boom."

"You think it will be enough?" Kali asks.

"I hope so."

"You're risking a lot on a hope."

"Not just hope. If we're going to survive here, we're going to have to deal with Morton. This is our best chance of success."

"I'm with you either way; once you—"

"No, no, not me. We. If this is going to work, I'll need you and Rowan with me. I promised you revenge. I aim to keep that promise."

"You don't have to do that. I can't do it anyway, not without putting the lives of everyone here at risk. I don't want more people dying because of me."

"You let me worry about that. Pack your bags; we need to move first thing."

"If you think imma let ye run off on some fool's errand without me, ye got another thing coming, brotha." Spike appears as if out of nowhere.

"Spike? When did you—"

"Forgive me for eavesdropping, miss." Spike bows politely to Kali. "Me friend here has a wee bit of a history with rash decisions. If it's all the same to you, I'll be joining ye. If it's not, I'll be joining ye anyway, so I guess that's that." Even when he's being obstinate, Spike can't help but make me feel at ease. His very presence is reassuring.

"Don't you want to—" Kali starts.

"Don't bother; once Spike has made up his mind, there's no reasoning with him," I warn.

"'Bout time ye learned that, boyo. So when we leavin'?"

"As soon as you're ready. You'll need to see Cooper to get you an energy rifle."

"A rifle—why?"

I smile, "You'll see. Get two. One for you and one for Rowan."

"Anything else, brotha?"

"Only other thing you need is some rest. We'll meet at the gate at sunrise," I instruct. Spike nods and walks off.

Kali stares. "You sure about this?"

"I'm sure it's the best chance we have."

"Morton is a really good fighter. I hope you're ready."

"Me too."

"Tomorrow, then," she smiles sheepishly.

"Tomorrow." I start to walk off. Kali catches my wrist to stop me. I look at her. Her face soft, eyes bright—she looks almost nervous.

"Thank you. For everything." She releases my wrist and rushes away toward her residence.

In the Great Hall, Lilly, Brock, Sala, and Cooper are discussing how to organize the town as it expands. Sala wants to maximize the design of the town. Cooper's focus is on defensibility. Brock—it's hard to tell what Brock is actually arguing about; he's just arguing. When I reach the table, they stop and look to me.

"How'd it go with Willow?" Lilly asks.

"Good; she's here looking at Jensen now."

"You got Willow to come here?" Cooper sounds shocked.

"It was all Olivia."

Cooper claps his hands together. "Do you think you could convince her to stay? Having her around would be a real boon for the town. It might even draw people from some other towns."

"Really?" *People would move to a new place for an herbalist?*

"Without question. She is a highly prized commodity. She doesn't just heal. She knows how to cultivate the land better than anyone."

"She also seemed to know how to attract certain creatures," I add.

"Not just attract. She found ways to repel them as well. Even if she'd just share her knowledge with us—this is huge," Cooper says.

"Alright, slow down. We might be able to. First, we need to make sure she's safe here. To do that, we have to deal with Morton."

"We're working on it. If your plan doesn't work, we're heaped." Lilly smiles. "So don't screw it up."

"About that, we've made a few changes."

"What now?" Brock rolls his eyes.

"I'll try to keep it simple for you, Brock," I say sarcastically. "The only way we can defeat the Marauders is to get Morton to challenge me to a dual. Since there's no good reason for him to do that, we need to get him so angry he does it without thinking. Here's what I've got so far. Step one: Spike, Rowan, Kali, and I make our way toward Morton's camp here." I point to the Marauder base marked on the map, stretching across the table. "Step two: I offer a safe place to live for any Marauder who wants to join us."

"Are you completely salvage? No Marauder is going to abandon their ranks just because you invited them," Brock interrupts.

"Course they won't, but it will show Morton what we are trying to do, and that will start getting him worked up. Step three: We provoke them. Shouldn't take much. We run, and they chase us right through the valley here." I trace the path on the map.

"Jett, you can't use yourself as bait; it's too dangerous." I can see the concern in Lilly's eyes as she protests.

"I'm not bait. I'm the fuel we're pouring on the fire."

"That may actually work," Brock says. Everyone looks at him. "What? Working someone into a blind rage? Getting them so nuked they can't think straight? Talk about playing to your strengths."

A compliment wrapped in an insult. We're making progress.

"Step four is the plan we previously discussed: Lead them through the valley, and use the explosives to harass them and reduce their numbers. I may have something else to help with that, but I'm not certain yet."

"Not certain? Jett, this isn't the time to——" Lilly starts.

"It's more of a backup anyway. Step five: We head back here. The Marauders should be rattled enough that when I try to invite them to join us again, some will consider it. Morton will lose control and challenge me."

"You want to lead them back here?" There's intensity in Lilly's voice.

"It's the only way this works."

"You can't do that. The risks——" Lilly protests.

"I know the risks."

"Not for you. For everyone else. Jett, you're talking about waking a sleeping dragon and then luring him right to our front door. What happens if it doesn't work? What happens if Morton doesn't challenge you? Everyone here will be trapped inside. We don't have the numbers to fight off his army, even if you weaken it in the process. You're not just betting your life; you're betting the life of every person here. I can't let you do that. I can't believe you'd even suggest something so reckless."

I close my eyes and take a breath, trying to keep my voice calm as her reaction stirs a fire in my guts. "I thought of that, thank you. I have a plan."

"Oh, he has another plan. What are you going to do now to keep from getting us all killed?" Brock snaps.

I turn to Brock. "You kill me."

For the first time, he shuts up. The room stares in silence. "The only way Morton is going to believe that you weren't all involved is if you claim I acted on my own and execute me. That's why it needs to be here. We do this someplace else, he kills me and comes here anyway. If we do it here, you can turn on me. That should prove to Morton you weren't involved. I'll die, but the town will be spared."

"We're not going to kill you, Jett." Lilly folds her arms in defiance.

"Hold on, sis. I never thought I'd say this, but he has a point," Brock sighs.

"It's not going to happen; how can you even—" Lilly turns to face Brock as she speaks.

"It's one life to save thousands; that's a fair trade. If he's willing to pay that price, we have to let him," Brock interrupts.

The tension in the air becomes as thick as gelatin. The longer the quiet lasts, the greater the tension becomes.

"Lilly, I'm betting my life on this either way. I just don't see any other option. This way—worst case scenario, I die."

"That's not a great option, Jett," she glares at me.

"It's not my first choice either. But if I have to die so you all can live, that's a fair trade."

"Jett . . . ," Lilly starts.

"Lilly, will you run things here until I get back?"

Lilly sighs and nods. "You are a very frustrating man."

I smile. "I've been told that. One more thing." I turn to face Sala. "Sala, I need you to get Spike one of the datapads from our stock."

Sala seems too stunned to speak. She nods in confirmation and then walks out of the room. With the plan in place, the others gather around me, each expressing a variation of 'good luck'. With all the best wishes expressed, I depart.

Two guards follow me as I make my way home. They post outside my door as I take the elevator down to get some much-needed rest. I soak in the last calm before the coming storm. Rather than sleep, my mind plays every possible scenario and outcome imaginable for my confrontation with Morton.

I get up early after a mostly sleepless night, so I can see Jensen before I go. Spike is already there, kneeling down and talking with Jensen while Olivia and Telmen look on. I am not sure how much Jensen comprehends, but after seeing his earlier reaction to Olivia and Spike arguing, I'm certain something is getting through. When Spike finishes, he steps aside. I kneel down in front of Jensen and put my hands on his knees. If he knows I'm here, he doesn't show it.

"Hey Jensen, Spike and I are going to be gone for a bit. We shouldn't be long, but in case something goes wrong and I don't make it back, I wanted to tell you that despite growing up with nothing, I was the wealthiest person in Dios. I had all of you in my life. I know we didn't always, or even often, get along, but you were family. Willow is going to help you get better. When I get back, we're going to sit around a fire like we used to and laugh at all the times Telmen made a fool of himself."

"Hey!" Telmen objects.

"That's what you get for eavesdropping." My hand wraps around the back of Jensen's neck as I press my forehead to his. I notice the wound on Jensen's face is healing nicely, but it's definitely going to leave a scar.

"Jett. Safe. Back," Jensen says.

It feels like my heart does a pair of summersaults. I smile and nod to him. "Don't worry. We all just found each other again. I'm not about to ruin that."

"Ready, brotha?" Spike walks to the door. I nod and follow him out, looking back to say goodbye.

We pass Willow, who is organizing supplies in the next room.

"Goodness me, where did they put that corlael powder? This will not do, Willow; no, it will not." At least her conversations with herself are spirited. Knowing she's here makes it easier to leave.

We meet Rowan and Kali at the gate just as the sun clears the hills to the east. I fidget with the remote to the explosives in my pocket as we embark without exchanging a word. This is it—our final showdown with Morton Ghood. Our lives, our future, our hope all rests on my ability to beat a vicious, cold-blooded murderer in a fight to the death. No pressure.

We reach the crossroads we used when fleeing Red Clay after rescuing Kane. The path to the right leads to Dragonvale and Morton's camp. The path to the left—to the trematerras herd and Willow's hut.

"Spike, Rowan, this is where we leave you."

"Notta chance, brotha; I'm staying by your side," Spike objects. Rowan nods in agreement.

"You can't help me if you're with me. For this to work, I need you here."

"You need to give me more than that, brotha."

"You are step five in my plan. I'll signal you on your datapad; when you get it, start shooting."

"Shooting?! What are we supposed to be shooting?"

"You'll know. Follow Rowan's lead; he knows exactly what to do."

I wink at Rowan and watch the corner of his mouth turn up into a grin.

Rowan confirms with a bow and starts climbing up the cliff. A protesting Spike follows.

Kali and I make our way back down the pass to the right—toward Morton.

Kali looks at me. "Morton is not going to be easy to bring down, even if he is in a blind rage. He's got size, reach, experience, and probably a good bit more skill than you."

"Is that all? I think I can actually feel my confidence rising."

"Your advantage will be speed and agility. Don't let him fool you; even though he has an actual sword with an energy edge to it, he can wield it very quickly. You'll need to be careful. Also, it may help to know he's left-handed."

"That is helpful, thank you."

"Jett, I need you to do me a favor."

"What's that?"

"Don't die. I really, really don't want to watch someone else I . . . someone I care about die."

"Believe me, I'm going to do everything in my power not to . . ." I look into her eyes and try to project as much confidence as possible. We both know what this moment could be. "If something happens, I need you to do something for me."

"Name it."

"Get my friends someplace safe. Someplace they can be happy and at peace."

"You have my word."

We journey the rest of the way in silence. There's a lot I'd like to say to her. So many things I'd like to ask. For now, I just want to clear my head and not think at all. If I spend too much time thinking about what I'm about to do, I may lose my nerve entirely. We walk slowly, conserving our energy. We'll need it all for the journey back. We stop for food and to rest for a bit as we get closer to the Marauder base. My nerves feel like a string being pulled taut and then stretched to the point of breaking.

The camp comes into view as does the large stone that rests in the middle of the path almost like an elevated platform just before reaching the gates. I hand Kali the remote to the explosives. I grit my teeth and exhale through them, climbing onto the rock with Kali remaining on the ground to my side. There's a time to think and a time to act. Sometimes, one negates the other. I can't think, can't question, can't wonder. I need to just know that this is going to work.

"Marauders! My name is Jett Lasting; I've come here to offer you an opportunity!" I yell as loud as I can, hoping to gather as much attention as possible. I wait as Marauders pile into view, many pushing their way past the gates to see me. I can't imagine they've ever seen something like this before. People usually run and hide from them. Here I am, like salvage scrap sink calling them out. The sea of faces parts and through it walks Morton. He gets to the front and stops, folding his arms across his chest and glaring at me.

"Well, well, well . . . if it isn't my little friend. Did you come to bring me back what you stole?"

"No. But I did want to let you know in person—Elder Schmitty is dead. Red Clay, the place from which you were betrayed and sold into this life, is no more. We have taken the town and remade it. Dawn Haven, a place of hope, is a home for all who would desire it—including you."

"That's cute; now what? We sit around and braid each other's hair?"

"You'll have to bolster your ranks some other way, Morton. You have taken your last slave from us."

Morton's calm visage starts to crack. "You're going to want to rethink that, boy—"

"Not only that, but I'd like to invite your men to join me."

"Join you?" Morton's body shakes as he starts to laugh. "You think my men are going to join you?"

"You stole their lives, their freedom, their honor; I'm going to give it back."

"Sir, let me kill him," the man standing next to Morton pleas. He's a short, bald man with a thick goatee. He looks tough but not so tough as Morton.

"Hold on, Fallan, he's just started to amuse me." Morton turns his focus back to me. "Well, let's hear your sales pitch, boy."

"My people are working to expand our town, build up our defenses, to make Dawn Haven a safe place to live, to grow, to start families. I'm offering you a chance to do more than just survive, but to come with us. To help us build a place we can thrive together. All you have to do is join me."

I might as well be talking to the canyon walls. There's not so much as a visible stir in their ranks.

"You still don't get it, do you, boy? All that time living safe inside your city walls with your fancy little dome made you soft. I'll bet when you went to sleep, you never once wondered if something was going to be trying to eat you when you woke up. That's the difference between you domies and the rest of us. You're soft and weak; that's nothing to be ashamed of, it's not your fault. Here's your mistake: you think there's some humanity left out here. There ain't. This is a world where you get killed or you do the killin'. We're the ones who do the killin'. You, on the other hand, well, maybe we should ask your friend, what was her name again? Becky? Beth? They all kind of bleed together after a while."

"Becka." I am supposed to be getting him riled up. Not the other way around.

"Becka, that's it! Doesn't really matter now, though, does it because, well, she's dead. I'm standing here asking myself: Morton, when is this boy gonna learn? How many of his friends am I going to have to kill before he realizes how this works? I mean, look at you, standing on that rock, acting all superior. You come here talking about a better life, offering my men a place in your town. This will not do."

"Worried they will join me?"

Morton grins. "What you don't understand, but you will by the time we're done here, is the only reason you have anything is because I let you have it. You think that town is yours? It's not. It's mine. I let you play boss man, so you can feel all big and important. So long as you remember who the real boss man is around here. That's me. I don't appreciate you coming here and trying to steal my men from me. It's rude, and it's downright disrespectful. I'm sorry to say, I'm going to have to punish you for it."

"I had this friend who used to say, 'You can't win a war if you fight the wrong battles.' That's why you're going to lose. You picked the wrong battle. I'm not afraid of you, Morton. You should be afraid of me."

Morton laughs, his one eye squeezing closed as he holds his hand over his chest. "Why would I ever fear you?"

"Because you and I both know that the power you wield is an illusion. You're nothing more than a bully with an overinflated ego. Your men— they don't respect you. They don't believe in you. Fear is the only hold you have. That's a hold that can easily be broken."

"Is that so?" Morton grins as if fighting back a laugh. "And just how are you going to do that?"

"Your men follow you because they want to live. I'm going to show them that following you is the thing that's going to get them killed. But before I punish them for your sins, I thought I should offer them a way out."

Morton claps his hands together while shaking his head. "You really are unbelievable. We were born for this life. You don't know our ways. Let me educate you, boy. We don't fear. We don't farm. We fight. We don't ask. We don't offer. We take and we take. We don't settle. We don't build. We don't break. We take and we take and we take. We are Marauders."

"Are you, though?"

There it is; I see it—that little glimmer of doubt in his eyes. That's the spark I was looking for.

"Marauders are born. Marauders are a breed. The men with you are slaves you trained to look and act like Marauders. Any real Marauders who have the misfortune of suffering the shame of your leadership can't be happy with this violation. You've turned a proud people into nothing more than thugs for hire. You have tainted what it means to be a Marauder."

The spark ignites into a flame. His face reddens. The vein on his forehead grows more prominent. He's angry. Not angry enough. I need more.

I extend my hands and raise my voice. "To all of you who stand with Morton, I understand your fear. He seems too big, too strong, too powerful to resist. All he is, he is because of you. His power, his influence—it rests on your shoulders. The only reason he has power is because you give him yours. All you have to do is stop. I'm offering you a chance. Come with me. Following this maniac is only going to get you killed. When it does, he won't bat an eye. You are nothing to him but a tool to be used. You're nothing but kindling for him to toss on the fire of his own ego."

I wait. No one moves. Morton looks around and laughs. "You see? You got nothing but empty words."

"Last chance—come with me and live. Stay with him, and I can't promise you'll make it through the day."

"You think you're going to scare my men?" Morton laughs. "You? You are nothing!"

"I was the leader of the Market Rebellion. My friends and I took the Market Sector from the Patriarch. A small group of disorganized beggar gangs with inferior weapons and almost no time to prepare. Still, we defeated the Patriarch in battle. We had a chance to bring down the Patriarch and change Dios forever."

Morton's voice waivers, "And yet here you are, just like the rest of us. You're nothing more than a failed rebel."

"True, we did fail . . . because we were betrayed. I haven't been here long, but I've already taken control of one town. Imagine what I'll do next." I grin confidently for good measure.

Morton's eyes narrow as he glares at me. I can see his chest rising and falling heavily. I think this is working.

"You are getting on my nerves, boy," he warns.

"Don't worry, you and any who remain with you are about to die."

My threat triggers them. Weapons rise, eyes move to the cliffs above, scanning for dangers. It's just enough distraction for us to make our move. I jump down from the rock.

Kali has already activated her energy bow. She pulls back an arrow and fires it just over Morton's shoulder. Her aim is perfect, missing him but near enough to startle him. The arrow drops a Marauder standing behind Morton to the ground.

"That's your plan? Let your little girlfriend shoot at us with arrows?" Morton laughs.

Kali fires again; this arrow passes so close to Morton's neck it breaks the skin. The nice thing about having an army packed together so tightly is it's almost impossible to miss. Another Marauder falls. Morton looks back, and his eyes narrow.

"I've had just about eno—" his words are cut short as he's forced to duck, the arrow sailing right past where his head had previously been. She had aimed that shot right at his forehead. I look over at Kali. She smirks, offering a quick shrug before pulling back another arrow.

"I'm going to kill you," Morton seethes.

Another arrow flies, and I sense the levy breaking. Kali fires two arrows in rapid succession, and two more Marauders fall.

"Enough! Bring me their heads!" Morton shouts, and the Marauder horde charges toward us.

"We need to get clear and fast," I shout.

Kali nods, and we run back in the direction we came through the explosive-lined path.

"Whoever brings me his head can name their price," Morton shouts. A loud roar comes from behind us as the Marauders give chase.

It's weird that the plan is actually working. Thankfully, our head start gives us a healthy lead. We sprint as fast as we can with the Marauders in our wake. All we have to do is reach the explosives before they catch us. I struggle to keep pace with Kali, despite the throbbing, knotting pain in my side. Breathing starts to burn as we run for longer than I've ever run in my life. We must have been running for more than an hour. I can feel my body aching and screaming for a break. There's no time. The Marauders are too close. We rush ahead, and the path narrows; that's the cue. Kali's hand grips the remote, her finger on the first button. Looking over my shoulder, I see the mob of Marauders bottlenecking as they reach the narrowing path.

"Do it!" I shout. She's faster than I am, a full two strides ahead of me as we run.

"Just a few more seconds." Kali waits until our pursuers are further in.

Three more steps, then she clicks it. The explosion booms and echoes around us. The ground shakes. Rocky debris flies from either side of the pass. Screams of shock and pain pour from the dust and smoke. Some of the Marauders made it past the blast zone. The shock either knocks them over, or they stop to look back. Our lead extends. The first explosion will have the most shock value and should slow their advance. After that, it'll be all about the timing.

"Do not lose them! Get moving!" Morton's voice bellows from behind us. Shadows emerge as a wave of Marauders charge through the smoke. That didn't slow them down nearly as much as I'd expected.

My datapad is programed to vibrate when we pass points where explosives have been set. All we have to do is be far enough ahead to get out of the blast zone before detonation. The Marauders have already poured past the first explosion and are gaining on us again when I feel the *vvvt vvvt* on my wrist. I nod to Kali, and she clicks the remote, causing another explosion and more screams. The devices were placed to maximize chaos, not causalities, by sending rubble and debris flying everywhere. Even still, plenty of Marauders will certainly die. Our pattern goes smoothly. *Vvvt vvvt*, click, boom. Repeat. Each explosion is like a wave crashing on the shore; the wave pulls back for a moment only to be replaced by another. The Marauders keep coming, driven forward through the waves of destruction by Morton's relentless will. It's almost impressive how they press on despite so many explosions cutting them down.

Each explosion gives us a little time to stop and catch our breath while the Marauders regroup. Then, it's back to sprinting. We should be close to the path leading to Dawn Haven. As we run, I tap on my datapad to send a signal to Spike. We are reaching the last of the explosives. One more boom and then the crossroads to get back to Dawn Haven. The ground starts to rumble and shake. If she sends the signal even a moment too soon, this was all going to be for nothing. No time to think about it now. The Marauders are nearly upon us when I feel the final *vvvt vvvt*. Their boots land in our footsteps; we are barely past them when Kali detonates the final explosive. The blast is far enough behind us that we avoid any debris but close enough to send us flying onto our stomachs. My ears ring. My eyes water. My body stings from sliding across the stone ground. I push up. Kali is already on her feet. She grabs my hand and pulls me. No time to catch my breath. No time to breathe. The crossroad is ahead, but the shaking under our feet has grown from a soft vibration to a disruptive shake. The ground itself feels unstable. I then see the cause. Crashing around the turn, roaring in agitation as they charge toward us: trematerras.

Something that big should not be able to move that fast.

Just a few more paces, and we're clear. We may not make it in time. My body surges forward as I push with every ounce of strength I have. Nothing like charging head-on into a raging stampede of giant monster bulls to make you reevaluate your life choices. The path back to Dawn Haven opens to the left. Kali is running on my right. She cuts in and shoulder-checks me, knocking me out of the way as a razor sharp horn slides right where I had been. Ducking back in an impressive feat of agility, she slides out of the creature's path and into the clearing of the crossroad. The trematerras charge, roaring and lowering their heads. Screams fill the air, occasional gunfire, and a lot of crunching as the Marauders are caught in the path of the angry stampede.

Rowan and Spike drop to the ground from the rock wall near us. Spike helps me up; Rowan tends to Kali.

I see a cut on her arm from where the trematerra's horn grazed her. It's a cut she got from slowing down to knock me out of the way.

"Yer a heaping madman." Spike hugs me before pushing me away. "Ye played that too close, brother; if the lass here hadn't—"

"It . . . worked out . . . didn't it?" I counter between gasps for air. I'm still in disbelief myself. It actually worked.

"Let's get to Lilly and her Raiders; whatever's left of the Marauders won't be able to put up much of a fight after that," Spike says.

I grab his arm. "This isn't over, Spike; we need to be ready."

"Aye, they come knockin, we'll make 'em pay, brotha," Spike nods as we start walking to Dawn Haven.

"No. Spike, I'm going to need you to do something for me."

"Name it, brotha."

"You're not going to like it."

"I'm starting to get that sense. Best just get on with it, then." Spike folds his arms in front of his chest.

"I need you and Rowan to get the others ready and wait by the prison. If something goes wrong—if I can't beat Morton, or he doesn't take the bait—things are going to get heaped really fast. Get some guards and as many people as possible, and take them down to the prison below. The hallway will serve as a choke point. Their numbers won't matter. Barricade yourselves in, and you'll have a good chance. After it's over, take as many people as you can to Dragonvale. You should be safe there."

"Ye know I love ya, brotha, and I'd do anything for ya. But if ye think for one second I'm gonna sit back and do nothing while ye risk yer life fighting that beast, ye have another thing coming."

Rowan folds his arms across his chest and stands defiantly next to Spike.

"Spike," I protest.

"Ice cream would have a better chance in Sheol, brotha."

"I can't fight him if I'm worried about our friends."

"Aye, if ye thought I was gonna let ye fight him, yer truly daft. He's the one that killed Becka." Spike looks into the distance as if preparing to march off and find Morton right then and there.

"This is my fight, Spike."

"No, brotha; you and I—we're family. Yer fight is my fight. I'm not sitting this one out."

"Spike," I start.

"For once in yer life, Jett, don't argue. You've never fought someone like Morton."

"You don't even know him."

"Don't have to, brotha; I know the type."

"What do you mean?"

"Fighting is like learning a language. The earlier you learn it, the easier ye pick it up. Learn it young enough, and it becomes a part of who ye are. Ye grew up thievin'. He grew up killin'. Not even Victor's training can prepare ye for that."

"You sound pretty confident in that; how would you know?"

"I lived it, brotha. Talia and I both did."

It occurs to me that I know remarkably little about Spike's life before I met him. I didn't even know he had a sister until recently.

"When?"

"We were born in the Rim. Never really knew our parents. I knew we wouldn't survive that glorified concentration camp. When I was six, I got us out of there, into the Market Sector. Right away, I joined a beggar gang."

"At six?"

"Aye, that's when they recruit you. Train 'em young enough, and the possibilities are endless."

"They made you fight as a child?"

"Aye, not just fight. They taught us to kill. Made us believe it was natural and normal—that all the other gangs were these horrible people who stole children away from their families, and we were supposed to stop them. I took to it like a fish to water. Thought I was doing good. I trusted the gang because they looked out for us. Wasn't till Talia and I joined up with one of Grent's rebellions that my eyes were opened. That's when I saw the pettiness of the beggar rivalries. I thought Grent was a visionary. He gave us a higher purpose: free Dios from the oppressors. Turns out that was just another lie."

"How did I not know this?"

Spike's normal lighthearted nature is replaced by this heavy, somber expression.

"Not exactly something I'm proud of, brotha."

"How did you get out of that?"

"After Talia died, Victor found me—pulled me out of that life. He gave me a true purpose."

"Spike, I—"

"My job is to protect ye. I wasn't here fer Becka; I'm not gonna make that same mistake with ye. I'll handle Morton."

"No. Spike, you're not just our protector. You are the heart of our family. I need that heart to keep beating. Spike, I have to do this."

"The sheol ye do, brotha. I'm a better fighter than you. It's not particularly close either. I've a much better chance."

He's right; Spike is a far better fighter than I am. Still, I'd rather die than risk losing someone else.

"You're also stronger than me." I put my hand on Spike's shoulder and look into his eyes.

"Aye, that I am," Spike grins proudly.

"You're strong enough to go on even if I lose."

Spike's eyes glisten as water builds up in them. "No, dunna even say that."

"Spike, Victor betrayed us. Becka died in my arms. I can't lose you too. If you died, I wouldn't be able to go on."

"Brotha, you—"

"I need you to trust me; I have a plan."

"Jett, you're not a fighter, I'm not even sure I can take him."

That's comforting.

"I know. In a proper fight, you've got a better chance at winning. This isn't going to be a proper fight."

Spike stares at me, testing my resolve. "I don't like ye facing him alone."

"He won't be alone." Kali moves next to me. She puts her hand on the back of Rowan's neck and leans her head forward, holding her forehead against his.

Rowan's folded arms drop to his side.

"Go with him," she beckons. "If things go meltdown, they will need you to help fend off the Marauders."

Rowan signs something, and Kali shakes her head.

Spike looks over at Kali and then back at me; he grits his teeth, concern replacing his normal calm demeanor. "Fine, I'll take care of it. But don't ye dare die, brotha. I'm warning ye."

We hug before Spike and Rowan run ahead. Kali hangs back with me. At this point, I'm surprised the Marauders haven't emerged from the pass. Either they are taking their time to regroup, or the tremateras did more damage than I expected. We waste no more time making our way back to Dawn Haven.

"What if he got killed by a trematerra?" Kali asks.

"We'd have to hope the Marauders are reasonable enough consider that. Not sure what their code says about a king being crushed into jelly."

When we get to the bridge leading into Dawn Haven, I sit down on it, dangling my feet over the edge and leaning back on my elbows. Kali sits next to me.

"You really are an impressive man, Jett Lasting." She tucks a strand of hair behind her ear while swaying her body to bump her shoulder into mine.

"Me? You just saved me from being gored."

"That's three you owe me."

"Three? How do you figure?"

"Nocstra—the day we met, Skylaris—at the Raider cave, and now trematerra: three."

I laugh, "Well, at the rate we're going, you'll have saved me from every monster out here by month's end."

"Nah, three's my limit. Next one, I let get you."

"Good to know. Thanks again."

"Can't have you getting killed now, can I? Who will kill Morton for me?"

"I knew it! You're just using me for my assassination skills."

"Why did you think I was keeping you around? Your delightful personality?"

"That's seem like a stretch——"

"Jett Lasting!" Morton roars, his voice lacking its usual charm.

I close my eyes and take a breath before forcing myself to my feet. Even a trematerra herd couldn't stop the inevitability that is Morton Ghood. He's breathing heavily, covered in dust and patches of blood. He stands on the other side of the bridge, his long sword is in his hand. Behind him are his remaining Marauders. Even after all that, their numbers look overwhelming. While numerous, their ranks appear exhausted, many of them panting for air.

I shout to the weary army behind Morton, "You see the kind of man he is? How he throws you at his problems? He can't do anything without you. Why else wouldn't he just fight me himself? He's afraid. He's no Marauder; he's hardly even a man."

I need him nuked.

"I tried to be civil." His breath pushes through grinding teeth, making him sound like a growling bear. "I send my people to kill you, and you kill them instead. I take that personally. I was going to let my men kill you quickly. *Bam Bam*, get it over with. Not now; this is going to suck for you. I'm going to take my time. When the stories of what I do to you spread, people will be lining up to give me all their treasures," he growls.

"Be ready," I whisper over my shoulder before walking down the slope toward Morton.

CHAPTER TWENTY-THREE

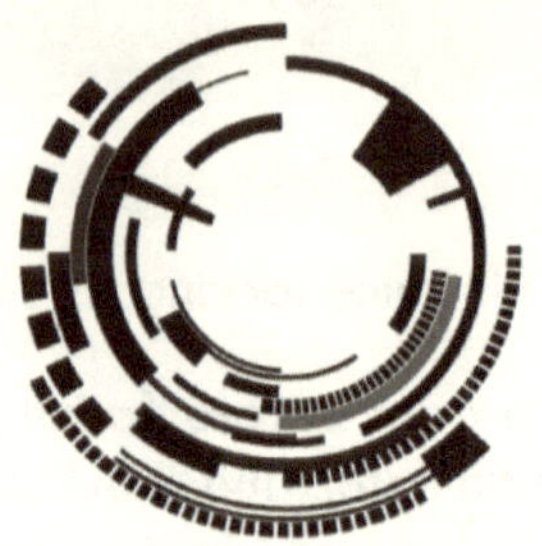

I take a breath, trying to calm my nerves. None of this will matter if he senses my fear.

"No one is going to give you anything, Morton. You violated everything the Marauders stand for. The Marauders are a proud people. You made them nothing more than slave traders. You hide behind them like a child. The only reason anyone fears you is because of them. You are a fraud king."

Morton glares at me; my words, though seeming to agitate him further, are not enough. His eyes are locked on mine as he paces back and forth, restraining his rage. He is holding on to control. I have to push harder. The lives of everyone in Red Clay may depend on it. I see how to do it, but it feels wrong. Then, I remind myself what he did to Becka.

"You think you're so tough, but I know different. I know you're afraid. No use hiding it here. This was your hometown, wasn't it? Everyone remembers, even if no one wants to talk about it. You're afraid because you know mommy didn't love you."

"Watch it, boy." Morton's head twitches. His grip is slipping.

"Everyone seems to think that your mother was trying to get away from your father. I think she was trying to get away from you. I think she realized what a pathetic excuse for a man you were, and she was ashamed. Hard to blame her really. I mean, look at what you turned into."

Morton screams into the air, extending his sword in my direction. "Enough! You vile little scrap sink; you want to do this the Marauder way, fine. I, Morton Ghood, King of Marauders challenge you to a duel. Once I defeat you, I'm going to make you watch as I cut every one of your friends into pieces. Then, when you've had your fill of their screaming and begging for mercy, then I'll—"

"Will you ever shut up?" My energy blade hums to life, and I lift it toward him.

Morton activates the energy beam that runs around his steel blade. He charges at me, swinging his blade in a wide arc. I duck down and thrust forward, using the opening created by his exaggerated motion. He blocks it, whirling his sword back with alarming speed. His fist catches my jaw, knocking me back. I shake it off, trying to focus through the lights dancing in my vision. Another swipe, then a thrust—his blade whirls faster and faster, the momentum of each swing allows his attacks to pick up speed. It's all I can do to deflect them.

Speed was supposed to be my advantage. I'm not sure it is. I switch the setting on my blade, activating the shield. Maybe I can tire him out.

"All that talk, and this is the best you can do? I'm disappointed in you, boy," Morton growls and continues his onslaught. Each time his blade hits my shield, it knocks me off balance. My reflexes barely keep his energy-edged blade from slicing me in half.

Morton grunts and growls with each attack. If his goal is to add a psychological element of intimidation, it's working. I dive out of the way of his shoulder as he tries to knock me over with it. I tuck into a roll, spring back to my feet, then spin. No good, he's already turned and closed the window I was hoping to gain. I'm not sure how long I can keep this up. At this point, I'm just biding time. I need to strike back, but there's not enough time or space between his strikes. Kali was right; he's leagues beyond me in both skill and experience. He seems to anticipate and block every move I make to give myself an edge.

I need something drastic, something unexpected, or one of his attacks is going to get past my guard and end me. Then, at the end of the day, I can take comfort in the fact that I both chose and started the fight that killed me. It's the little things really. Then, I see it: he's smiling from ear to ear. The scrap sink is having fun toying with me. He brings his blade down in a wild strike. I pull my arm up, and his blade locks against my shield. He chuckles, pushing down and dropping me to one knee as I push up against his sword, trying to get out from under it. He has strength and better position. I feel the heat from the energy edge of his blade as it pushes closer to my skin. Having the steel sword gives extra weight and force to his weapon.

I grit my teeth and push up with all my strength, shoving my arm out and barely getting the blade away from my body as it falls. The edge catches my shoulder and burns my skin. I jump back and switch the setting back to my blade. This is not going well.

He dashes forward, and his sword is flying toward my neck. I swing my hand up, catching the edge of his sword with my blade and deflecting it just a little. My move manages to move his blade away from my neck, but the blunt end of his sword smashes against the side of my head. I stumble to the side and fall to one knee as my head rings with pain.

"Bet you're wishing you'd kept your mouth shut now, aren't you, boy? Don't worry, I'll make sure all your friends suffer for your mistake. Least I can do for an old pal," Morton grins as he points his sword at me, mocking me. He could finish me off easily but now he's just playing with me.

What are you doing, Jett? Victor's voice echoes in my mind. Suddenly I find myself back in Dios, five years ago, in the backyard of our rundown house in Sector C. Weird time for a memory flash, but here I am. Victor always told us, "You should never fight. Fighting is for fools. If we do get into a fight, make sure to win."

"It's not fair, he's bigger and stronger than me!" I hear my younger self-objecting. Vic had partnered me with Spike that day. I was still growing then, and Spike was twice my size. Even though he always took it easy on me, I rarely won.

"Fights aren't won with strength alone. You can't win a fight here." Victor holds up a fist. "Unless you win the fight here." Victor taps a finger on his temple.

"You want me to headbutt him?" my brilliant younger self asks.

"I want you to think—be smart. Don't let your opponent pick the battlefield."

"We're in the backyard, Vic; this is where you told us to fight."

"Don't fight a fast opponent with speed, a strong opponent with power, or an experienced opponent with technique. Don't play to their advantage. Make them play to yours."

The second-worst part of having my brilliant best friend betraying me is that I apparently can't stop thinking of his advice in times of need, and it's always annoyingly insightful. How am I supposed to maintain a healthy hatred for someone when even my memories of them are helpful? The burning of my skin as Morton's blade nears my shoulder brings my mind back to the painful reality of the moment.

Don't play to their strength. Victor's words repeat in my head. Fighting Morton like a warrior isn't going to work. It's time to fight him like a thief. I charge him as if I'm about to take a swing at his neck. Morton brings his blade up to block my attack. Instead of attacking, I slide down, my body gliding smoothly under his arm. I click my energy knife on and drag it across his thigh as I slide by. Morton grunts and whirls around, lashing out with his sword, but I'm too far out of reach.

"That one was for Lenard." I charge at him again, making the same motion as the last time. He lifts his blade to deflect mine, but this time steps as he does to keep me from sliding past him.

Just before my blade makes contact with his, I lighten my grip on my handle enough to turn off the energy beam. Once my grip is past his blade, I reactivate the beam. Having an actual blade gives his strikes more weight and power. He can't deactivate the metal to make his weapon easier to maneuver. He's already committed to the block and can't adjust in time. I pull my arm back, stabbing my blade into his shoulder. He roars in pain and clutches his shoulder with his free hand.

"For Jensen."

He glares, returning his hand to his hilt. "Cute trick, but it's not going to save you, boy!"

Morton charges and swings. He's not as fast with an injured shoulder. I use the sword setting and deflect his strike with just enough energy to move his weight to the side. Clicking back to my knife setting, I slash back and forth as fast as I can, catching his arm twice, his shoulder, and his back. Blood stains his skin but doesn't spill as the heat from the energy blade cuts and cauterizes at the same time.

"For Valami."

With each attack he makes, I switch the setting of my weapon, forcing him to commit to a move without any idea how I plan to adjust. The misdirection slows him down, confuses him just enough. Before long, he has a couple dozen cuts on his body. He's panting and struggling to hold his blade up. He roars and charges at me, shoulders wide. He's trying to tackle me. It's a desperate move. I dodge his blade and start to move into position to strike back, when his leg catches my gut. The wind flows out of me. That was a good misdirect too. He spins, looking to take advantage of his move.

I stand up, trying to steady myself, but he sweeps my feet from under me, dropping me onto my back. He has me, and he knows it.

"You did better than I thought, boy, but you never had a chance."

He lifts his sword up and prepares to drive it down into my chest. I swing my arm up, clicking the hilt to turn the blade on as I release it. The beam sings to life and catches Morton in the stomach, burning through him until the hilt hits his skin. He coughs and stumbles back, the sword dropping from his hands.

"For Becka." I put one hand on his shoulder and grab the hilt of my blade with the other. Morton clutches his wound and drops to his knees. Is this it? Did I actually win?

"Do it; send me Roth Shalar. My name will be remembered throughout the ages." Morton sneers.

"I'm not sending you anywhere."

Morton balks, "Not man enough? If you don't kill me, boy, I'm going to—"

"No, you're going to die. But Roth Shalar is not your destination," I shrug.

Morton looks confused.

"Kali." I toss the energy blade to her. "Time to fulfill my promise."

Kali catches the handle and looks at it and then at me in both shock and confusion.

"What are you doing?" Morton's voice sounds suddenly nervous.

I smile. "Can you imagine what happens to your name, to that terrifying reputation you worked so hard to build, when the word spreads that Morton Ghood was killed by a girl half his size?"

Morton's eyes widen. "Wait a minute, wait a minute. She can't kill me. If she kills me the Marauder army will descend on this place, and everyone in it will die. That's the code. You can't deny me my honorable death."

Kali tosses me back my weapon and shakes her head. "He's right, Jett, it's not worth it."

I smile; this was going to feel better than killing him would anyway.

"If you were a true Marauder, you'd know the Law of Retribution is invalid if either of the following occur: the king is killed in battle, or if the king challenges someone to a dual and is defeated. It doesn't say killed. When the king is defeated, he ceases to be king. All rights afforded to the Marauder king no longer apply. Upon defeating the old king, the winner becomes the new king. You challenged. I defeated. That makes me the Marauder king. Which means the Law of Retribution no longer applies to you, and anyone can kill you in any way without reprisal."

"No, that's not right. I become king emeritus, and I still—"

Fallan walks over, standing just behind Morton. "King emeritus only applies if the king willfully steps down. You didn't step down. You were defeated and therefore are stripped of your kingly title and all the protections that come with it." He actually sounds happy.

"That's wrong. You're twisting the rules," Morton complains, sounding like a disgruntled child.

Fallan looks up at me and nods before turning his attention back to Morton. "You twisted our customs to steal power and serve your agenda. It's only fair that a twist would bring about your end. Mr. Lasting, beg your pardon." Fallan kneels, forming an "x" with his arms across his chest. "My King, I and all the Marauders are yours to command."

Just like that—from reject, to rebel, to ruler. The mass of Marauders litters the horizon behind Morton while behind me the people of Dawn Haven have gathered along the walls and at the open gates. Spike, Rowan, Telmen, Olivia, Lilly, and Brock have pushed their way through the crowd and are crossing the bridge. There is a nervous energy in the air, but no one dares break the silent stillness.

"Fallan, you spineless worm; I will—"

Kali drives her fist into Morton's face, cutting him off and knocking him to the ground.

I turn to Kali. "For your mother, for Becka."

She mouths, "Thank you," to me before turning to face Morton. "I've been waiting so long for this moment."

Out of the corner of my eye, I see movement from among the Marauders.

"Nooo!" Olivia rushes toward me. She dives, knocks me to the ground, her body landing on top of mine. A beam of light flies past my head, just missing me thanks to her tackle. A metal can clanks against the ground, bouncing into the middle of where we're standing. Thick smoke hisses from it, causing us to cough and choke. I cover my mouth and my eyes begin to water.

What is this?

I see something in the smoke and try to reach out for it, but I can't pull my arm from my mouth without choking on the gas. I step toward where Morton was kneeling.

Shinshew! He's gone.

"Hey!" Kane shouts before the sound of bone cracking against bone cuts him off. I stumble back, trying to get out of the cloud of smoke. As I inhale clean air, my lungs cough violently to expel the gunk in them. I wipe my eyes and blink repeatedly to restore my vision. It feels like my eyes are on fire as tears well up trying to put it out.

By the time my vision clears up, the smoke is dissipating. Rowan is chasing after our assailant.

"What was that?" Lilly asks, still coughing.

"Morton is gone," I answer.

"No!" Kali tilts her head back and screams into the air, her arms rising up as if offering a hug to the sky. She growls, her chest heaving and falling dramatically. She looks around back and forth. "He can't be gone! He's here somewhere. Where are you, scrap sink? Come out and face me!" The words seethe from her lips.

"Kali . . ." I keep my voice calm and step toward her.

"No, Jett!" she snarls, pointing her blade at me. "He's here somewhere, hiding. We just have to find him!"

She rushes over to the ditch that surrounds town, frantically looking over the edge.

"Kali . . . ," I repeat.

"You hear me, coward? I'm going to find you! I'm going to make you pay!"

I move next to her and put my hand on her shoulder. She turns around and pushes past me, walking back to where Morton had been.

"He was right here, Jett! He was right in front of me. All I had to do was . . ." Kali drops to her knees staring at the place where Morton had been. Her face rests between her hands as her head shakes from side to side. Kali rocks back and forth.

I put my hand on her shoulder. "We'll find him, Kali; he can't get far."

"Who was that? A Marauder?" Spike asks.

"Could be, but I wouldn't bet on it. He was wearing this." Kane tosses a mask onto the ground in front of me. The mask covers the whole head with a large, clear front to allow the wearer to see and a filtered air vent on either side of the bottom.

"A gas mask?"

Kane nods. "Whoever it was came prepared."

Rowan comes running back to us, gesturing something to Kali. She wipes the tears from the corner of her eyes and stands back up.

"You saw them?" she says, her eyes lighting up.

Rowan gestures something else. Kali's eyes close. She takes a deep breath before nodding and walking over to us.

"Morton was rescued by a man with a motorbike. He's gone," she says, sounding defeated.

"We can—"

"I can't right now." Her tone is sharp. We observe a moment of silence to allow her to process what just happened.

"What kind of motorbike was it? Old world or hover tech?" Spike asks.

Rowan gestures a response.

"Hover," Kali translates reluctantly.

"No wonder we didn't hear it. Hover tech bikes are quieter than walking. I didn't know they had those out here," I reply.

Kali sighs and shakes her head. "We don't. I've never seen a working vehicle out here."

"Brotha, far as I know, hover bikes are highly controlled and only permitted for official Patriarch personnel."

The heaping Patriarch.

"Why would the Patriarch want to rescue Morton?" I ask.

"I doubt they would," Kali replies. "Rowan saw the man's face. It was Kyle."

"Kyle? That doesn't make any sense. Morton killed Kyle's entire team. Why would he help Morton now?"

Kali shakes her head. "I don't know. Maybe he wanted vengeance for his team. Maybe he knows something about Morton we don't. Maybe the Patriarch banished him for letting me get away, and now he's trying to buddy up with someone who could help him survive. Does it really matter?"

"That's the least of our problems. Jett, Morton's not going to let this go. So long as he's alive, he's a threat," Lilly notes.

"I know, but he's alone now. Without an army behind him, he's just one man. We will find him and deal with him."

I can see the disappointment and frustration return to Kali's face. "If I'd just—"

"It's not your fault, Kali. No one could have seen that coming."

Spike puts his hand on her back. "Dunna worry; I swear to ye, one way or another, we will find him and put an end to him. After what he did to Becka, he dunna get to live."

I sigh. I can't believe he escaped. First Stone, now Morton. My list of enemies who are out of my reach grows longer.

"What now, brotha?" Spike interrupts my thoughts.

Leave it to Spike to ask the question that matters most. Our friends are rescued. We have a place to call home. We can just settle here and be done. Or I can hold onto my desire for vengeance and try to find a way back to Dios. Part of me wants both. I take a minute to mull the question over in my mind.

"Today, we start building a better tomorrow," I finally answer.

"Aye, that sounds good. So long as by today, you mean later. You need rest, brotha; let's get you home. We can meet in the Great Hall after dinner and start making plans."

I'm too tired, and Spike is too stubborn to fight with.

Fallan stands straight in front of me. "My King, I could send some scouts to search for him."

I shake my head. "We'd just be putting them in danger. If he's on a motorbike, they'd never catch him anyway. Why don't you take the men inside Dawn Haven? We've got some work to do, and we can use your help to do it."

"My King." Fallan shouts some instructions, and the surviving Marauders make their way into town ahead of us. I half expect them to be met with aggression or hostility from the townsfolk, but the gathered crowd parts to allow them entrance. We make our way inside. I half expect to see the Marauders brawling with the guard, but so far everything appears to be going well.

Fallan lingers behind. "My King, what are your plans when we are done here? Are we returning to our base?"

"Leave him be; he needs to rest." Spike steps between us. I put my hand on his shoulder and motion for him to step aside.

"Yes, Fallan. Right now, I want them to rest and tend to their wounds. Then, when they are ready, I want you to take the Marauders back and gather everything of use. Wood, containers, supplies, weapons, anything and everything you can carry, and bring it back here. Dawn Haven will be our home."

"My King, Marauders are not civilians. As distasteful as Morton was, on that point he was right."

"Many of those with you are not true Marauders. They will be given the opportunity to return to a normal life and join this community."

Fallan smiles approvingly, "Yes, my King. For the rest of us?"

"Warriors can have homes, can they not? Does the Marauder code prohibit having a reason to fight or a place to defend?"

"No, my King."

I put my hand on his shoulder. "Fighters don't have to be pillagers to be warriors. Dawn Haven will need an army. We will need men and women who can fight to keep the civilians safe from the many dangers here. In return, the people will provide support and a comfortable place to rest for the warriors who protect them. Acceptable?"

"Yes, my King." Fallan snaps to attention.

"Fallan, are we going to have any issues?"

"My King?"

"I am not a Marauder. Is that going to be a problem?"

"For years I have seen the glory of the Marauder name run through the mud at the hands of a dishonorable man. On my honor, I had to serve this man, bringing constant shame to myself. You have liberated us from him. There are no issues."

"Good. Can I trust you to communicate issues to me if they arise?"

"My King?"

"I am not an expert on your customs. I imagine there will be many growing pains as we start this journey. I need you to ensure that tensions and conflicts do not arise."

"Yes, my King. It shall be done. I will take them and return with the supplies. We can rest when the work is done."

Before I can object, Vesta appears, holding a wooden spoon. She pokes Fallan in the chest with it. "Well, if you're planning on taking all these people out without a proper meal, you've got another thing coming."

Fallan steps back and stammers, looking at me with an expression of shocked confusion.

"Don't look at me; I'm not crossing her."

Fallan attempts to protest, but Vesta grabs him by the arm and practically drags him into town. The other Marauders follow much more willingly.

Spike puts his hand on my shoulder. "Ye've come a long way. I'm proud of ya, brotha. Now go rest before I drag ye down there meself."

When I reach my new home, I detour from Spike's instructions and walk to the small yard next to the house. I take a shovel from the worksite, and I dig two small holes. I tear the title page from Gibb's book and place it in one of the holes before pushing dirt over it. I mark the mound by shoving a tall, thin stone shaped like an oval into it. In The World That Was, they called it a gravestone. I always thought the idea was interesting—having a place to go remember those who were no longer around. I stick the shovel down into the other mound so deep only the wooden handle remains visible. I take one of Becka's colorful shoelaces and tie it around my wrist like a bracelet, sliding it just under my datapad. It makes me feel like she's still with me somehow. I take the other shoestring and tie it around the top of the shovel. The only visible reminder of one of the most amazing people I've ever known is a solitary shovel stuck in the ground. She deserves more. She deserves better. For now, this will have to do.

Rest comes easy. I fade into a dreamless sleep. The alarm on my datapad wakes me in time to meet with the others. For their sake, I take a quick shower before making my way to the Great Hall. Everyone is standing around a table. Brock intercepts me before I can make it through the door.

"Listen." He starts talking as if I have nothing more important to do than stop and hear him out. "I don't like you. I'm probably never going to like you."

Wow, so glad I stopped for this.

"But I get it now. I never expected you'd be able to pull it off, but you did. For the first time since we were exiled, I have hope that we may actually survive this. I'm not making any promises, but I'm going to try to take it easier on you."

The end was much better than the start.

Brock offers me his hand. I shake it and give him a nod before walking the rest of the way into the room.

Kali and Lilly are in the back corner away from everyone else, having a private conversation. Something about it makes me feel nervous. Kali nods, and they exchange an oddly friendly embrace. Questions race through my mind, but I silence them. When their hug ends, they both make their way over to the table. Lilly clears her throat and looks directly into my eyes.

"Well, Jett, you did it. You got rid of Schmitty. You got rid of Morton. We're still here. Ever since I've known you, you've had this vision of what the world could be. I always thought life had to be in Dios. Now, seeing what's happened, I think we should start working on that dream right here in Dawn Haven. I spoke with Cooper, Doc, and Sala. I'd like to catch you up to speed if you're ready." Lilly says.

"You mean, think about something besides how to not die? I'd be delighted."

"Between the Raiders, the Marauders, and the prisoners you rescued, Dawn Haven will become a very large town. Maybe even a small city. In addition to the social challenges of managing a diverse community, we need to manage infrastructure, defense, development, resources, not to mention any laws that need to be put into effect. It's a lot. We've started recruiting people for the leadership and advisory board based on your vision of how to run the town. We've filled most of the positions," Lilly explains.

"That's great!" I smile.

"After working with Sala, here's what we came up with. Dakkin will be the commander of the guard in charge of training officers, enforcing rules, and maintaining order within the town limits. Sala will be our town administrator. She will organize our groups and keep development running. Doc and Willow will be in charge of health care. Doc will also work with technology until we find someone more versed in that. Willow will head up our agricultural development. She's going to teach us how to reclaim the land and get crops and other plants growing as well."

I look to Willow. "So you're going to stay?"

"With Schmitty dead and Morton gone, this place should be as safe as any, honey. I'm looking forward to being around people again. All I ask is that I can set up a place on a remote part of town. I've gotten used to some privacy."

"I'm sure we can arrange that."

"Thanks, honey; that's all for me. I'm going to go." She walks out while everyone else watches. I guess she didn't want to be part of the whole meeting.

"Cooper will be in charge of trade and whatever market gets set up. He has a knack for that sort of thing. Kane has requested to be in charge of intelligence gathering, whatever that means. We need a construction manager to head up the development and building projects. Cooper's doing it for now, but it's outside his expertise. We're still looking into a couple of other areas, but we haven't been able to inventory everyone's abilities yet," Lilly continues.

"Fallan will be in charge of our military when the Marauders get back. We'll try to keep the Marauders out in the wild, dealing with threats before they reach our walls," I add.

Lilly nods. "Anything else?"

"Yes. I want you to be charge of education."

"Education?"

"You were a teacher; I want this to be a place where people can have families, raise children, and as such, someone will need to help teach them."

"That's fine," Sala replies. This is just the starting point. I'll have other ideas and other candidates to suggest once I'm done surveying all our residents."

"What do you think, Jett?" Lilly asks.

"It looks like a great start to me. Thank you for putting it together. In the morning I'd like to address the town, get us all on the same page."

Lilly nods. "I look forward to hearing what you have to say."

As everyone makes their way out of the Great Hall, Lilly catches my arm and gestures for me to hang back. I wait until we are the last two in the room.

"What's going on?" I ask.

"Jett, I know a lot has happened. After everything, I feel like I found my place in the world. I've felt more alive, more like myself out here than I ever did in Dios. I know we've sort of drifted in different directions, and I hope you won't hate me for this, but I want to do more. Teaching is important; I'm happy to help, but I want more. I want to be a part of shaping what this place becomes."

"Lilly, I don't hate you. I don't think I ever could. You've always been looking for adventure, ever since we were kids. You finally found it; I don't want to take that from you. We may not always agree on how to handle things, but you are a great leader. If you're looking for something different, we can figure that out. I just don't know what that would be yet."

"Thanks, Jett." Lilly kisses me on the cheek and walks away. Something about it feels like a conclusion. A kiss on the cheek to end the relationship that never really was.

I spend the rest of the day walking around town, trying to visualize what it could become. I used to daydream like this in Dios. It's weird to think my daydream might become a reality—and in the Outlands of all places. As the daylight wanes, I walk back toward the center of town. I grab dinner and then head straight to bed. I feel like I haven't slept in weeks.

I wake to my body bouncing on the bed. Opening my eyes, I see Jensen jumping on my mattress and giggling like a child. Olivia, Telmen, and Spike are standing at the entrance to my room, chuckling in amusement.

"Wakey, wakey, Jett." Jensen bounces high and then drops on his butt, nearly springing me off the bed.

"I'm up, I'm up. What's going on?"

"Time to get up!"

I almost jump when he speaks. "Jensen?"

He smiles, "That's my name."

"How are you . . .?"

"Willow helping me. Doc treats outsides. Willow treats insides." He wiggles as he speaks, giving himself the appearance of a very large toddler.

I blink, trying to process it all. "That's great. Does that mean they think you'll get better?"

Telmen rattles out a full-on report. "We're not sure yet. He seems to be improving, which I think is promising. But he's been through a lot. You never know with these things. Willow told us he was walling himself off in his mind. It's how he protected himself from what was happening to him."

Jensen strikes a heroic pose. "I strong."

I chuckle, "I can see that. It's good to have you back!"

Jensen smiles and nods.

"Willow seems to think he will have moments of clarity and some lucidness, but it'll be a while before he's fully functional again," Telmen explains.

"I get there. Don't worry 'bout Jensen," Jensen says. Before I can hug him, he's wrapped his arms around me. He squeezes me harder before finally letting go.

I just stare at him in joyous disbelief. "It's a start. We'll be here to help you. Do you feel different?"

"Different?" Jensen cocks his head sideways, looking confused. He shrugs, "I don't know different."

Just seeing him functioning somewhat normally gives me a warm feeling of hope. A shirt crashes into my face.

"Come on, brotha, you've got a speech to give. Your people await ye," Spike interrupts.

"Yeah, let's go. Jett, don't worry; you'll do great. I'm sure you've got this. Nothing to worry about. Have you thought about what you're going to say? Are you nervous? I'd be nervous. You've given speeches before, though, so you should be fine." Telmen blasts his usual burst of excited and unfiltered thoughts.

Before I can answer, Spike turns. "Alright, let the man get ready in peace; see ye out there, brotha."

Jensen and Telmen follow Spike out.

Olivia kisses my cheek. "You'll do great, Jett. We'll be cheering for you."

After getting ready, I head back to the Great Hall. I stand outside as all the people of Dawn Haven crowd around to listen. Doc wired a microphone so everyone would be able to hear me.

"People of Dawn Haven, friends, many of you don't really know me. I hope in the months to come to change that. When I was exiled from Dios, I thought my life was over. Like many of you, I grew up hearing about the horrors of the Outlands. Yet here I stand in a place that already feels more like home than Dios ever did. We live in a world of pain, suffering, and injustice. Where those in power use it for their own benefit at the expense of others. No more.

"Dawn Haven shall be a beacon of hope and a place for healing. We will show the world what the future can be. I know things changed in a short period of time. More changes are coming. I won't promise it will be easy. There will be bumps along the way. I promise we can overcome them if we stand together. Like most of you, I grew up being told our differences divide us. That they were dangerous and needed to be stamped out. That is a lie. Our differences are our greatest strength when we learn to work together. When we work together despite our differences, seeking to understand each other and appreciating our unique qualities, we become an impenetrable shield wall.

"Now, I will not stand here and pretend to be a perfect man. I am far from it. I've made many mistakes, and I expect I'll make many more. I am not a savior. I am not a hero. I am a man just like any of you. I believe that together, if we can learn to accept the differences and flaws in each other, we can become a place where everyone has a place. Where every person, no matter their background or their creed, can be treated with respect and kindness. For this to happen, we must learn to work together. Everyone here has a purpose and a role to play. I see a bright future ahead of us. But I need your help to make it a reality. Will you join me?"

The crowd erupts in cheers and applause.

I feel Spike's hand on my shoulder. "This, brotha—this is what Victor always saw in you."

"What do you mean?"

Spike gestures to the roaring crowd. "Anyone can lead by force. Anyone can lead by fear. Having the ability to inspire people to work together—that's what a real leader does. Ye've just given everyone here a reason, a purpose, a shared goal worth fighting for. I couldn't be prouder, brotha."

Spike's words fill me with warmth. This should feel like an unbridled celebration. Something feels like it's missing. Maybe it's just knowing that Morton and Kyle are still out there somewhere. Maybe it's knowing that settling here means I'll never have the chance to confront Victor. Maybe it's that Becka isn't here to see it.

I notice a man in a cloaked hood pacing back and forth just behind the back end of the crowd. I squint my eyes, trying to get a better look. He stops and stares at me, nodding his head to the side as if instructing me to follow. Something about him looks familiar and suspicious. I can see just enough of his face to see him grin and then turn and walk away.

"Hey, you! Wait!" I call out, rushing toward him. The crowd of people swarm around me, shaking me, grabbing my hands, shouting too loudly for me to hear. I smile and nod, trying to push through. When I finally break out on the other side, the man is gone. I rush off in the direction he was walking. I see no sign of him. Wandering around in aimless pursuit, I end up in the Town Square.

"Nice speech." The voice comes from an alley next to one of the shops. The cloaked man is leaning with his back against the wall, keeping his head down to hide his face.

I step closer to him. "Who are you, and what are you doing here?"

"A storm is coming, Jett Lasting. Your actions have drawn the Patriarch's gaze. While I applaud your passion, setting up shop so close to their backdoor wasn't the smartest play."

"Excuse me?"

"Now that you've dealt with the Marauders, you've gone from being an annoyance to a threat. We both know how the Patriarch deals with threats."

"Who are you, and what do you want?" I repeat.

"I want you to be smart. Much rides on you and your little friend, the Filia Lucem."

"Isn't playing cryptic games while the sun's still up a little weird?"

"Joke all you want; the Patriarch is not going to stop until they have her."

All my playfulness vanishes. "What do they want with Kali?"

He laughs, "I'm surprised you don't know. You should really talk to her about that."

"I'm done with all this cryptic shinshew; you want to talk, talk. Otherwise, I've got things to do." I turn to walk away.

"Jett!" The man steps out of the shadows and pulls his hood off. I'm suddenly staring at the face of the most memorable stranger I've ever known.

"Kegan. Why do you insist on doing everything so mysteriously?"

"It's part of my charm."

"It really isn't."

"I'm here to warn you. The Patriarch knows who Kali is now. They know she's here; they will stop at nothing to get her back. They will bring an army here and destroy everything you're trying to build just to get to her."

"Come on, she's that important?"

"You don't know the half of it. The Vanguard is just a part of it. They've been hunting her for most your life. You've seen it and not even known."

"What do you mean?"

"The Middling Days. They weren't promoting people to Primes. They were recruiting people they could send out on a holy mission to scour the Outlands until they found her. So long as she remains here, everyone is in danger."

"Oh, so I should just cast her out?" I can feel my frustration rising.

"No. You should fight them. But you're going to need allies to do it."

"Let me guess, that's where you come in?"

"You still don't trust me?" Kegan raises an eyebrow. He looks almost hurt.

"I'm not just going to follow you because you say I should. I don't know you."

"I know you—like I knew your parents."

"What do you know about my parents?"

"I can tell you, but for that, you'll need to come with me."

"You want me to leave here? Abandon these people after promising to look out for them?"

"I am asking you to keep your promise. Leaving is how you keep them safe, at least until you have an army to match the Patriarch's. We may be able to help with that."

"We?"

"Surely you don't think I am doing this all on my own. I am part of a group that has been working against the Patriarch for some time. We have most of what we need to bring the fight to the Patriarch. Before they commit forces, they want to meet you. For that, you'll have to come with me to Solis."

"Solis? The largest domed city?"

"Yes."

"That's on the other side of the Outlands?"

"Yes."

"Even if I wanted to, how would we get there?" I ask.

"Through Dios."

"The cryptic thing is just automatic with you, isn't it? Do you know how to get back into Dios?"

"The 'how' is on your datapad."

"What are you talking about?"

"The copy of the codes you made for Dios. I have the access points. You have the codes. Together we can sneak into Dios. Inside the city, I have contacts who will help us."

"Help us how?"

"We sneak aboard the underground train, which will take us to the arena where the City Wars are held. From there, it's just a matter of sneaking aboard the train that leads to Solis. Before you know it, we are there."

"Wow, that's amazing. You just made something borderline impossible sound quick and easy. Congratulations, I'm out."

I turn to leave.

"Jett, look." Kegan types on his datapad, and his screen projects. On it I see a feed of PDF forces standing in neatly packed rows and columns as far as the screen can show. Announcements play over the speakers: *"Incursion to the Outlands authorized. Mandatory preparations in process. All units check in to your assigned stations for gear and supplies. Officers gather for mandatory mission briefings. Mission launch in five days. Failure to report will result in disciplinary action."* The voice sounds like a female robot.

"What am I seeing?"

"This is live footage from one of our sources inside Dios. They are preparing to bring their army here."

"Heaping scrap sinks, why can't they just leave us alone?"

"I told you they will not stop until they have Kali. If she stays here, they will kill everyone."

"How does leaving help?"

"As you may have gathered, Kali has a small tracking chip inside her body. While it's defective, it will be scanned when we enter Dios. That will alert the Patriarch, telling them she's in the city."

"So then they will start searching the city?"

"Yes, they will deploy their search parties in Dios and abort their mission here. No reason to send their armies if what they are looking for is already in Dios."

"Won't that make it hard for us to get around?"

"It will. Not to worry, we have plenty of agents to help us and a high-value contact within the Control itself to ensure our passage."

"How is it you're so well connected?"

Kegan smirks. "I assumed you'd figured it out. I am a Sanduran."

"The ancient order who built the domes?"

"The same. The Patriarch wants everyone to believe we died off after they exiled us. Maybe they even believe it themselves. We did not. We moved our home to Solis where we wield a great deal of influence. But we have never forgotten about the city that was taken from us."

"I see; and tell me, why should I trust you? How do I know you aren't just trying to lure us into Dios, so you can turn Kali in yourself?"

He laughs.

"Something funny?"

"You want to know how you can trust me?"

"Yes, you're asking a great deal for a virtual stranger."

"I'm not a stranger, Jett." He pauses as if that should explain everything. All it really does is make my heart race. *What does he mean he's not a stranger?*

"My full name is Kegan Lasting. Matteo was my older brother."

Pretty sure my jaw just turned into a cartoon and dropped to the floor.

"You're . . . you are my . . . you—"

Come on, brain—process the information.

"Jett, I'm your uncle."

CHAPTER TWENTY-FOUR

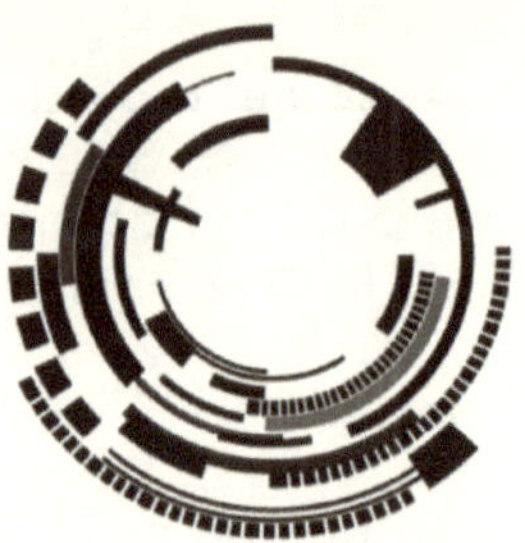

"**H**ow are you . . . where have you been? Why didn't you ever . . ."

"I'm sure you have many questions. I promise you, I will answer them in time. For now, I need you to get Kali and come with me."

"You want me to just take you at your word? You say, 'Jett, I'm your uncle,' and that's supposed to convince me to just go somewhere with you?"

Kegan grins. "Good, you're learning." He taps on his datapad, and I feel mine vibrate. It's a video with my father and mother talking. The audio doesn't seem to work, but I recognize them. Seeing them looking just the way I remember them makes me feel happy and sad at the same time. In the video, Kegan walks behind them and leans against the same counter they are talking at. The three of them laugh for a minute, and the video fades to black. I blink, trying to keep my brain from overheating from too much emotional stimulation.

"I haven't seen them since . . . ," I start, barely able to keep myself from sniffling.

"I know. Also, there's this." Kegan reaches into his pocket and pulls out an old photograph, something that looks like it came out of The World That Was. "Since we both know video can be edited." The front of the picture is the three of them—my dad in the middle with arms stretched out, one over my mother's shoulder, the other over Kegan's. I flip it over and read:

"My dearest brother,
A reminder of simpler times.
-Matteo"
"You realize if they can fake a video, they can fake a—" I object.

Kegan hums a tune, cutting off my response. There's something oddly familiar about it. I've heard it before. Suddenly Kegan breaks into song:

"Like a great silver streak,
You shine in the sky,
I catch you in the corner of my eye,
Where are you going,
Where have you been,
My little shooting star,
I'll sing it again."

"That . . ." My jaw drops.

"You remember it—good. I was afraid you wouldn't."

"How do you know that song?" I ask.

"How do I know the lullaby your mother used to sing to get you to sleep every night? How do I know the song she made up just for you? Or that she used to call you her little shooting star? Come on, Jett, I can lead you to water, but I can't make you drink."

I stare dumbstruck at him.

"I trust that is sufficient evidence?" Kegan asks.

I manage a nod. "That's why you keep showing up? Because we are family?"

Kegan smiles. "In part, yes. I've tried to keep an eye on you as best I could since Matteo's death. Approaching you would have only put you in danger. But I did what I could from a distance."

"Like warning me about Victor. Wish I would have listened."

Kegan shrugs. "The past is set in stone. It cannot be changed. No sense in wondering what could have been. What we do now has the power to shape the future."

I sigh. "Where are you suggesting we go?"

"I'll explain. We need to leave soon if we are going to make it into Dios before the PDF deploys."

"Well, I do hope yer plan allows for a few others, or yer gonna have a tough time getting out the gates." Spike folds his arms across his chest.

Kegan glances over his shoulder, looking surprised. I get the sense he doesn't get surprised often. Next to Spike is Rowan, who is leaning casually against the side of the building.

Kegan grins. "You're welcome to join us; we just need to get—"

"Rowan, why dunna ye go fetch the others. I'm gonna have some words with this lad," Spike says as he steps toward Kegan with a wicked grin plastered on his face. Rowan nods and walks between the buildings back toward the Great Hall.

Kegan backs away from Spike, holding his hands up.

"Spike, it's ok; he's my uncle," I speak in Kegan's defense.

Spike extends his hand. "Aye, so he claims. I'm gunna need a wee bit more convincing."

"How do you suggest I convince you?" Kegan asks.

Spike shrugs. "Ye let me borrow yer datapad."

"My datapad?" Kegan repeats.

"Aye, the little thing wrapped round yer wrist. Hand it to me. If yer telling the truth, it'll help me verify it. If yer telling a Tod Tale to try and get something from me brotha here, I'm gonna make ye wish ye didn't have any bones."

Kegan chuckles and unsnaps his datapad, offering it to Spike. Spike takes it and runs his fingers over the surface. A projection screen appears as he starts tapping furiously, glancing back and forth between the screen and the datapad itself. He swipes between a few more screens, muttering something undiscernible under his breath. After about a minute, he looks up and offers the datapad back.

"Well, brotha, it checks out. He's got a birth certificate, identification number, and a series of other documents suggesting he is, in fact, Kegan Lasting. If these files aren't authentic, they are the best fakes I've ever seen." Spike rubs the back of his head before turning to Kegan. "His uncle, ye say?"

Kegan nods. Before he can say anything else, Rowan returns with Olivia, Telmen, Jensen, Kali, and Lilly in his wake.

"Jett, what's going on?" Lilly asks.

I take a breath, trying to figure out how to explain it. "Well, this is Kegan. You may not know him, but Victor and I met him in Dios when he saved us from some Levites. Met him later when he tried to warn me about Victor's treachery. I didn't listen. Now, he's here with another warning."

"A warning about what? How could he be here if he was in Dios? Was he exiled too? If he was exiled, why haven't we seen him until now? What warning could he have?" Telmen starts. Olivia nudges his shoulder, and his questions come to a halt.

"For a long time, the Patriarch has been looking for Kali. Now, thanks to Kyle, they know she's here. They are currently preparing to invade the Outlands in order to capture her and take her back to Dios," I explain.

"What? No, I'm not going back there!" Kali's voice raises suddenly, and she steps back away from the group as if distancing herself from the words could somehow help her escape the reality that comes with them.

Lilly's eyes grow large. "Jett, if they come here looking for her, they will kill everyone."

I nod. "I'm not going to let that happen."

Kali starts pacing back and forth, her face red as she mutters under her breath, "I've got to go! Now." Kali turns to leave. Rowan steps in front of her, blocking her exit.

"We don't have time to discuss this, Rowan," she snaps. "We need a big head start if we're going to disappear."

Rowan folds his arms across his chest and shakes his head.

"Let's not get ahead of ourselves. There has to be something we can do," Lilly offers.

"Aren't you listening?" Kali barks. "There is. I run," Kali says, her voice still overly loud.

"Where would you go?" Lilly asks.

"I'll head to Dragonvale and then just go north from there. This is my problem, not yours."

"It won't matter," Kegan responds. "They know you were here. They will wipe this place out just to ensure you have one less hole to hide in."

"I'm not going back there! I won't let them take me. I'd rather die!" Kali's grits her teeth.

"So what do we do?" Lilly asks.

"Kegan has a plan to get us into Solis, but we have to go through Dios to do it."

The statement results in a cacophony of questions. I lift up my hands to silence them.

"I know it sounds crazy, but it's the only way." I explain.

"In Solis, we will gather some allies who will help us fight and take down the Patriarch," Kegan adds.

"Sorry, who are you again?" Lilly asks.

"He's my uncle," I answer for him. Everyone looks at each other in confused silence.

"We don't have time for this." Kegan turns on the projection of the assembling armies in Dios. "If we don't get Kali inside of Dios before the PDF deploys, everyone here will die. Time to decide."

"I never thought I'd go back to that place," Kali shakes her head.

"I'm going, too," I announce.

"Jett," Lilly objects. "You can't just—"

"We may have a chance to stop the Patriarch, to help all the people who are suffering under their tyranny. Lilly, if there is even a chance this could work, we have to take it."

"If he's going, we're going," Olivia states.

"Wait a second. Wait. Did you all forget about what got us out here in the first place? We wanted to fight against the Patriarch. Victor had a plan. We trusted Victor. Then, we got exiled. Now you want to do the same thing but replace Victor with Jett's random uncle no one knew existed? This is crazy. We can't do this again," Telmen protests.

"You don't have to come, Telmen. You're more than welcome to stay here."

"That's what you said last time. It didn't stop me then. It's not going to stop me now. But if this goes bad, I'm going to tell you that I told you so for the rest of our lives."

I chuckle, "That's completely fair."

"Very well. Say your goodbyes; do what you need to do. We leave at daybreak." Kegan pulls up his hood and walks away, disappearing into the shadows.

I look around at my gathered friends. "Thank you. I don't know what I'd do without you all."

"Ye'll never have to find out, brotha." Spike walks over and puts his hand on my shoulder as he often does. His little method of transmitting comfort always works. "We're in this together."

"I can't believe we are going back to Dios; that's going to be so weird. Do you think we will recognize it? Maybe we can go see the old house or, at least, where it was? Stop at the Lazy Loafer?"

I sigh and shake my head.

Telmen clasps his hand on my shoulder. "Don't worry, Jett. Nothing bad will happen so long as I'm with you. All of us together, back in Dios like it should be!"

Jensen steps beside me. "I go too! I help!"

I smile and shake my head. "No, Jensen, I'm sorry. I wish you could come, but in your condition . . ."

"I can help!" Jensen puts his hands on his hips in defiant protest.

"You will." Olivia puts her hand on his shoulder. "You will help us by staying here and looking out for everyone. We need you to get better."

"I get better?" Jensen repeats.

Olivia nods. "Yes, that would help us more than anything. Work with Willow and the Doc and keep getting better. That way when we come back, you'll be ready for us. Can you help us with that?"

Jensen smiles and nods, striking a childish heroic pose.

Everyone lines up to hug Jensen and express their farewells. Once he's thoroughly hugged, Spike gathers the others.

"We'll go get ready; see ye in the morning, brotha."

Rowan gives me a nod and walks off, leaving Kali and Lilly. The two exchange a glance. *Why does this feel so awkward?*

"Can I have a minute?" I hear Lilly whisper to Kali, who nods in response.

Lilly walks over and grabs my arm, pulling me away a bit and speaking in a hushed tone. "Jett, I want you to know if you need me, I'm with you. But I hope you don't. I believe in this place. I believe in your vision for it. Someone has to make it happen. I'd like to stay and do that."

"There's no one I'd trust more to lead Dawn Haven than you. I'll leave instructions for Fallan to make sure the Marauders stay in line. I'm sure everyone will happily follow your lead, Mayor Lilly." I bow my head to her. She laughs.

"Thanks, Jett." She nudges me and looks back over her shoulder at Kali. "One more thing . . ."

I brace myself.

"I know I wasn't her biggest fan, but I can see what you like in her." Lilly looks at me and smiles.

"Are we having this conversation?" I ask, feeling suddenly uneasy in my own skin.

"Relax, we are still friends, right?"

I nod.

"Just be careful, ok?"

I nod again.

"And try not to do anything stupid. I am counting on you to come back." She grins before walking away, leaving me alone with Kali.

"Hi." Kali's voice is quiet, almost timid. "I guess it's time to tell you who I really am."

I look at her; even the bright midday light seems pale in comparison to the way she shines. I feel a strange bond like I'm being pulled to her.

"I told you my father was an important man in Dios. He exiled my mother and I to avoid a scandal. At the time, he was younger and had two other children, both boys. A few years after I was exiled, I heard that one died in an accident and the other of an illness. He was getting older and didn't have any other children. Not long after that, the Vanguard started searching for me."

"Right," I nod along as she speaks.

"You heard Kyle call me the Filia Lucem. Here's what you don't know: the Filia Lucem and the chosen one are the same person."

"Wait, the chosen one is a girl?"

Kali scrunches up her face. "That's real nice, Jett. Everyone knows the chosen one has a to be a man." She slugs me in the arm.

I laugh but rub it. She hits hard.

"Wait, so the Children of the Dome and the Vanguard are actually searching for the same person?"

"Yes."

"Who are you?"

Kali sighs. "My father is Gregory Ignatius, the High Father of Dios."

Enter cartoon jaw drop to the floor take two; this time add tongue rolling out for added effect. Just like that, discovering that a strange man who has been showing up randomly in my life is actually my uncle, who I didn't even know existed, is not the most shocking thing I've heard in the last ten minutes. I know myself well enough at this point to know that if I try to say anything, it's going to come out as stuttering nonsense. I close my mouth and let the information sink in while Kali just stares nervously at me.

When enough time has passed for my brain and tongue to reestablish a link, I take a breath. "You're the daughter of the High Father and his only heir?"

Kali nods. "That's why they want me so badly. They've been telling people for generations that his line is the link between Bealz and Dios. I'm the last chain in that link."

"Riiiighhhtt . . . so when he dies, you become the High Father? Or High Mother? Or how does that work?"

"I have no idea. I can't imagine they are thrilled by the thought of a woman leading them."

"Probably not. How crazy would it be if you were the ruler of Dios?"

Kali shakes her head.

"You don't want that?"

"I'd rather be free and fighting to stay alive than a prisoner in a palace to be used as someone else's puppet."

"Agreed. I'd rather bring down the Patriarch anyway," I smirk.

"Now that the Patriarch knows who I am, there's no reason to hide my identity. If it's something we can use against them, let's do it."

"We will cross that bridge when we come to it. You sure you want to walk into the lion's den?"

"If that's where you're going, that's where I want to be."

I smile. "Is that so?"

"As long as I can remember, I've been wandering. Never staying too long, always on the move. Even here, we stay, but we don't stay. I've never had a place to call home. But ever since you showed up, being around you feels like home."

She steps closer, looking up into my eyes with a subtle smirk gracing the edge of her smooth lips. Her cheeks flush with a soft pink hue. There it is, that magnetic drawing feeling pulling my head toward hers.

"Shinshew, if you don't kiss her after that, I will."

Her eyes widen, and she steps back, chuckling nervously.

Kane walks into view. "Oh, I killed the mood, didn't I? Sorry."

"What do you want, Kane?"

"I just heard from Spike; we're leaving?"

I nod. "That's right. Back to Dios, then on to Solis."

"I'll get my stuff."

"Wait."

Kane raises an eyebrow and looks at me.

"You're not coming with us."

"You're leaving me behind?" Kane sounds genuinely hurt.

"No. I'm setting you free."

"I don't follow."

"Do you remember what you told me back in the prison?"

"I do." Kane looks confused.

"You said you were a warrior and that this place felt like home."

Kane nods.

"The dangers we are going to face next are of a different kind. You'd hate it."

"I've been in this fight too long not to see it through." Kane's tone is almost pleading.

"You will. This isn't goodbye; it's divide and conquer. I need people here to get our forces ready while we build new alliances. If we are going to bring the Patriarch down, we will need to throw everything we got at them. If you come with us, you'll have to behave—sit, listen, talk. No violence. If you stay here, there are plenty of things that will need killing."

Kane's expression warms. "Well, then, guess I'll stay here and have all the fun for myself."

"I do need you to do something for me. Lilly and Jensen are here. I need you to watch their backs the way you've watched mine. And if anyone gets out of line . . ."

"Oh, I'll kill 'em right back into place."

A bright smile forms on his face, and a spark of gratitude glimmers in his eye. He grabs my forearm, locking it tightly against his.

"I'm counting on you," I say.

"When you get back, you'll be amazed at what this place looks like. I promise you that." He pulls me in for a hug and smacks my back with his other hand.

"I'll hold you to that."

Kane nods. "Please, carry on," he winks at me.

I turn to Kali, whose face is bright red. "I better get ready. Don't want to forget anything." She scampers off.

Kane—killer of people, killer of moods.

I spend the rest of the day saying goodbye to Doc, Willow, Sala, Cooper, Dakkin, Vesta, and several other people I don't actually know. They all express the same sentiment: hurry back, be safe, we got this while you're gone. Vesta insists on cooking us all one special meal before we go. It's like she's trying to convince us not to leave with food.

I wake up the next morning and wander into the yard of the house. I sit just past the mound of dirt and shovel I placed in the ground. My fingers slide idly over the shoestrings around my wrist. I know she's not there, but it comforts me to think that somewhere, she could hear me.

"Hey, Becka, so I met my uncle; that's pretty crazy, right? Turns out after everything we did to make a home, I have to head back to Dios if you can believe it. I didn't want to go without saying goodbye. I miss you, Becka. I think about you all the time. I want you to know I'm going to make this place a place you'd love to be. I'm going to make you proud." I stand up and dust myself off. For a few minutes, I just stand there and look at her grave.

Once I'm finished, I head to the town gate where the others are already waiting. I take one last look at Dawn Haven. It's weird how much I've bonded to this little town. I haven't been here long, but a part of me is sad to leave. Another part is surging with questions that my newly discovered uncle has promised to answer.

"You ready?" Kegan asks.

I nod and we walk. We take a pleasant pace until we reach the dark pass where I first encountered the night stalkers. Between Rowan and Kegan, navigating the pass seems easy; nothing more than a light stroll through a creepy dark tunnel filled with cave monsters.

"I don't like this place. It always feels like something is watching, you know? Did you feel that way when you came through here? I did. I was so sure something was going to crawl down from above and snatch me, I stayed in the middle and just ran," Telmen rattles on.

"Good thing you did," Olivia chuckles. "If you'd walked along the walls those monsters would have eaten you."

"Monsters? What monsters? There are monsters here?" Telmen's voice shakes.

"Aye, brotha." Spike pulls him into a headlock. "How did ye avoid them, Olivia?"

Olivia smirks, "Oh, I know a lure trap when I see one."

Maybe just being with other people makes the trek feel less terrifying. Or maybe I've just grown more accustomed to terror.

On the other side, the bright sun stings my eyes. I almost don't notice the eight-passenger jeep parked just in front of us.

"How did you get this?" I ask.

"I told you, the Sandurans have many resources."

"We really need to work on your question-answering skills," I glare at him.

Kegan smirks, "Old habits. Ever since the Patriarch banished us, we have been gathering strength, pooling resources, and waiting for the right time to strike. With Solis backing us, our strength and resources rival those of the Patriarch. A jeep is not a very hard thing for us to get."

We pile in, excited to avoid having to trek across the Sand Sea. As an added bonus, the jeep has air coolers, which we haven't felt since our exile. A journey that took me almost a week on foot takes only about an hour in the jeep.

Kali is sitting next to me. I look over at her as we drive.

"Are you nervous?"

She scowls, "No, I'm not nervous."

I smirk, "This is your first time going back to Dios since you were a kid, right? Everyone there is looking for you. You're not nervous at all?"

Her scowl turns into a glare, and she punches my arm. Even without much effort and while sitting, she hits hard. She shakes her head, but the grin on her face betrays her attempt to appear frustrated.

She sighs. "Yes, I'm nervous. Even if we are sneaking through, it's going to be weird going back there. Knowing that my father is there somewhere. He has his men looking for me but not because he cares about me; he just wants to secure his legacy. I don't even know what I'm supposed to feel about that. My father is the most powerful man in an entire city, but to him, I'm nothing but a tool to be used."

I listen, trying to keep myself from reacting too much and distracting her from sharing. "Wow, yeah, I can't even imagine what that must be like."

She smiles softly. "It's odd. Then I don't even know if I have other family. My mother never mentioned anyone, but do I have grandparents in Dios? Are they still alive? Do they know about me? Know who I am? It's . . ."

"A lot," I finish her thought for her. She nods. I leave it up to her if she wants to say more on the issue. She doesn't say anything, so we just listen to the purr of the engine as we rumble across the waves of endless sand.

Across the Sand Sea, the great walls of Dios tower over us, casting a looming shadow. I am once again reminded just how massive the city is. Seeing it from the outside somehow makes it look even more impressive. Rowan, who is in the seat behind me, grips the back of my seat so firmly with his hands I feel my head shift on the seat. His eyes are wide. He looks the way I felt when I saw a nocstra for the first time.

"Won't the Patriarch see us coming?" Spike asks.

"They don't monitor the walls as much as you might expect. They have two techs in a room full of screens, watching every camera along the exterior walls. The techs don't pay much attention to the screens; they just look for the red, flashing light that blinks when the camera detects motion," Kegan explains.

"Aye, motion like a large jeep driving up?"

"Normally, yes, but we disabled the motion sensor lights for this sector. Unless they happen to look at the exact right screen at the exact right moment, we might as well be invisible."

"Disabled?"

"We have contacts inside the Patriarch who are working to ensure we pass through without incident."

Kegan drives along the edge of the wall for about twenty minutes before pulling the jeep to a stop and turning off the engine. "Alright boys and girls, time to go." His voice is annoyingly chipper in contrast to the sudden onset of ominousness surrounding what we are about to do. We pile out of the jeep and wait. Kegan runs his datapad along the wall. A soft blue scanning light moves up and down. A faint clicking sound is followed by a single brick in the wall giving way to reveal a screen.

"Jett, you're up," Kegan calls out.

I walk over and open the file with the codes on my datapad. Under the screen is a small keypad. I start punching in the code from the file: 43952BC234LP87640VERRIDE342315SE154.

I can't imagine a lot of people guess that on their first try.

Nothing happens. I look at Kegan and then start comparing the code to what I typed in.

"Did I do something—"

The ground underneath us shakes. Sand gives way as I feel myself starting to slide down. The rumbling gets louder as a path appears, the slope leading down into a tunnel below the city wall.

Kegan cracks a lumeflare and starts down the slope into the dark tunnel below. "The Sandurans built these access tunnels to allow key personnel to get in or out of the city as needed. They were also used by maintenance workers who needed to do repairs to outside walls. Once the Patriarch took over, they had no way to access the original codes, so they just ignored them," he explains as we follow him into the abyss below.

"We're following a stranger into a dark tunnel to hopefully sneak into a city where everyone wants us dead so that we can sneak into another city. Seems we've gone quite mad, brotha."

"What would Victor think?" I jest.

"I can tell you what I'm thinking, brotha." Spike's tone is hushed and lacking its normal playfulness.

"What's that?" I whisper back.

"Even if we are sure he is yer uncle, we dunna know him, his agenda, his character, or what he's willing to do. Something dunna set right with me. Ye said he was in Dios. Then, he left Dios to find ye in the Outlands. Why does he need yer code to get back in? Yer telling me he left without being sure he could get back?"

Spike's suspicion makes a little too much sense for my comfort. I glance over at Kegan and then turn back to Spike.

"You're right. Gregor told us the codes we got were from an old Sanduran datapad. If he's Sanduran, he would have those codes, wouldn't he?"

"Aye, something is off here. We need to be careful, brotha. We can't trust him."

"You might be right, but here's one thing I keep coming back to."

"What's that, brotha?"

"He's not making any effort to get us to trust him. If he was against us, wouldn't he be trying harder to win our trust?"

Spike bobs his head, contemplating. "Well, that's a thought, isn't it? I'll give him the benefit of the doubt fer now, but Imma keep me eyes on him."

Kegan looks over his shoulder. "Jett, a word."

There's no way he heard us. Right?

I walk ahead of the others to catch up to him. "What is it?"

"You and your friends will need to be careful around any guards. You do not have the same anonymity you once did. You were the face of the rebellion. He," Kegan gestures to Spike, "killed their puppet, Grent. The Patriarch doesn't take kindly to people messing with their toys."

Just the mention of his name makes me grit my teeth. Grent, the rebel leader who rallied enemies of the Patriarch and led them like lambs to slaughter to help quell unrest in the city. What a despicable human being he was. Thinking of Grent reminds me of Commander Stone. I wonder what happened to him; last I saw he was being arrested for killing Gibbs.

"I should tell you," I start.

Kegan raises an eyebrow.

"Commander Stone is the one who killed your brother."

Kegan stares expressionless into the void ahead. "No, I highly doubt that."

"What do you mean, no? I remember him. I saw his face. It took me awhile to put it together, but it was Stone."

Kegan shakes his head again, "That is called transference."

"What?"

"Memory is a fluid thing. Unreliable at best. You saw Stone as a nemesis. A nemesis like the person who killed your parents. Your brain fused the memory with the man."

"You don't know that; I remember—"

"How old was the man you remember?"

"I don't know, maybe twenty-five or thirty."

"The same age Stone was when you met him."

"What?"

"Strange coincidence, don't you think? The man you remember and Stone were the same age. Maybe he just didn't age for an entire decade."

My eyes widen as I stare ahead into the darkness. "You're saying he's not the one . . ."

"I'm saying the world is a big place. It's possible, I suppose, but I wouldn't be so certain. You should consider the possibility that your parent's killer is still out there."

After dropping that little mind-bomb, Kegan picks up the pace and starts walking several paces ahead of everyone else. The silence is pierced only by the sound of our boots stomping onto the wet stone path beneath us. The tunnel has no other light source, at least that I can tell. Rowan remains at the back, holding a lumeflare, leaving us to walk quietly in the low light between the two flames. It's strange not seeing him in the front. I wonder if he's hanging back to give himself more time to process all this. I imagine it's a lot to take—sneaking through an underground tunnel into a domed city.

I feel a hand, small and soft, bump and grab hold of mine. I look over to see Kali attempting to not look at me as she walks beside me. We walk for what seems like an entire day, though it's impossible to tell when you're underground. The lumeflare in front of us stops. I see the silhouette of a small train car. Kegan walks us over to it and opens the door.

"How does he know how to navigate these tunnels so well?" Kali whispers.

I shake my head and realize she probably can't see the motion in the low light. "I'm not sure."

"First the jeep, now this thing—for someone who showed up yesterday, he seems very prepared."

"I agree," Olivia interjects, suddenly dropping back next to us. "There's no way this was put together last minute. Orchestrating all this takes time and planning."

"Right. He left Dios; it's not strange he'd have a plan to get back in," I counter.

"Jett, he didn't just have a plan. The motion sensor lights were disabled—the jeep, this train car, all here right when we need them to be. He couldn't have set all this up last minute," Olivia adds.

"What are you saying?" I ask.

"He had this plan in motion long before he knew about the assembling army. He's hiding something; I can sense it." Olivia has always had a good sense about people. She's like a human lie detector. If Kegan is setting her off, there's a good reason. Perhaps this was not a good idea.

Kegan stands at the door. The others reluctantly start sliding into the tight space of the train car. Rowan remains at a distance, looking at the vehicle suspiciously. I walk back to him, whispering to keep Kegan from overhearing.

"You ok?"

Rowan's eyes narrow.

"Concerned about the car or the person leading us into it?" I ask.

Rowan smirks and turns his gaze to me.

"I can tell you the train car is totally safe. It's just like the jeep. It's a metal container with seats, propelled by an engine."

Rowan sighs and nods slowly.

"I've ridden in it thousands of times. If I can do it . . ."

Rowan smiles and taps me on the shoulder before walking over to the car and ducking inside. Once we are all in, Kegan walks to the front of the car where a dashboard of buttons and screens light up. He slides his fingers between screens, pushes a few random buttons, and lights inside the train car turn on. I hear the familiar hum of a hover track, and the car lifts up into the air slowly.

"Next stop, the Temple Sector," Kegan announces, and the train car rushes forward with a *woosh*.

The air feels cooler as the sound of rushing wind grows louder. We are gaining speed. Rowan clutches the armrest of his seat, leaning back to look around as if trying to make sense of what is happening. His head turns rapidly from side to side. I realize he's never seen a hover train car before. I try not to laugh, but his expression is priceless.

I lean back and get as comfortable as I can in my seat, my mind wandering wildly. I can hear the others whispering their concerns. Kali scoots over suddenly as Spike sits down next to me.

"Brotha, we gotta decide right now if we are gonna follow him or bail. Our window is closing."

I remain still, keeping my eyes closed. "If it's a trap, he'll almost certainly spring it on us when we get to into the city."

"If I was going to trap you, I'd have had guards waiting to surround you when we got into the tunnel," Kegan says.

I open my eyes, heart racing as I see him standing in the doorway to the command module of the train car. We all just stare at him with our mouths open. He lifts his hands.

"I don't blame you for distrusting me. You don't really know me. I can't prove that I'm on your side, but maybe knowing this will help." Kegan reaches into his jacket and pulls out a small pistol. He offers it to Spike.

"What's this?" Spike asks.

"Call it a token of trust. You trust me not to betray you—I'll trust you not to shoot me." Kegan grins. Spike seems receptive to the idea but inspects the pistol anyway.

Spike steps froward and leans close to Kegan. "Trust that if ye even think about betraying us, I'll make ye wish I used this." Spike slaps Kegan on the shoulder hard enough to knock him forward a half step.

Kegan seems a little shaken for a moment. "If you have doubts, I'll reverse course and take you back out. Everything I told you is the truth, but I am not going to force you to accept it. We will need some trust to move forward."

"You want us to trust you? It might help if we knew why we should. You seem to know all about us. We don't really know you or why you're fighting the Patriarch. It's hard to trust someone you don't really know," I point out.

"Very well. You want to know why I fight. I'll tell you. When we were children, Matteo and I used to play. One day, in the Market, we crashed into a Levite by accident. We apologized, but he insisted we be punished. He chained us to a wall and started using his thrasher on us. Our father came looking for us and saw what was happening. In a blind rage, he tackled the Levite to the ground. He hit the man several times and then got up to unchain us. Before we could get away, a group of Red Caps rushed over and arrested him."

"For defending his children?" The disgust oozes from Olivia's voice.

Kegan nods. "Apparently, the Levite was a vindictive man. He came to our home and threatened to kill Matteo and I, unless my father did what he said. He made my father give my mother a shot of something that looked like medicine. Then, he left. The next day he came back and made him do it again and again and again—every day for two months."

"What was in the syringe?" Kali asks.

"A medicine that my mother was allergic to. He started with a small dose. Not enough to really hurt her, just enough to make her sick. Every day he came back, the dose was a little bigger. Every day our mother got a little sicker. Until one day, she just didn't wake up."

There is an audible gasp from pretty much everyone in the train car, including Spike.

Kegan takes a breath. "He made my father kill my mother. Not immediately. He made sure to make it last, to make her suffer for as long as possible. Then, just for good measure, when she died, he had my father arrested for poisoning his wife. Our mother died. They took our father away, and we never got to see him again."

The car falls completely silent. There's an odd tension. I feel like I should say something but can't think of anything that seems an appropriate response.

"Matteo was my brother," Kegan continues. "I loved him. He was the kind of person who would do anything for you. Falli was one of my closest friends. They didn't want to fight. They just wanted to live in peace as a family. The Patriarch murdered them. I hate the Patriarch. I swore an oath that I would not rest until I saw their reign in ruins. You don't have to trust me. Know this: I would never help the Patriarch."

I look to the others. Spike shrugs. Olivia ponders for a minute before nodding. Rowan just smirks.

"I can't believe we are in this situation again. How does this keep happening to us? Isn't there anyone else who could risk their lives to save the world?" Telmen asks.

"You want to back out?" I ask.

Telmen sighs and shakes his head. "No, I guess not."

"We've come this far," Kali adds. "We know what could happen if we turn around. This may be the only way to keep everyone else safe. It's a risk, but it's better than the other options."

I nod. "Well, there you have it. Let's continue."

Kegan returns his attention to the command panel.

I close my eyes again, trying to process everything until I feel a jolt, and the train car slides to a stop. We pile back out as Kegan shuts the car down. I can't tell if I'm more nervous or excited. A thought nags at the back of my mind. Even though Kegan is my uncle, I don't really know anything about him. How can I be sure he's not using me—or worse, Kali—for his own benefit?

"This way." Kegan leads us by the light of his lumeflare up a winding set of stairs to a door. He punches in a code, and the door swings open, leading into a small hallway and another door. He pushes in another code, and it swings open as well. We step into a second hallway—this one without a door. We face a solid black, brick wall.

"Well, that doesn't seem good. Where's the door? Who builds a hallway with no exit door? Did they wall it up? Is it supposed to be like this? How do we get out? Why did we come up here if there is no other exit?" Telmen comments incessantly.

Kegan laughs and counts bricks from the ceiling, sliding his hand to the side until he stops. "Ah, there you are." He pushes, and the brick clicks deeper into the wall. A rumbling sound echoes around us as the brick wall is pulled back like a sliding door. We step through into a green area near a small stream and many large, well-groomed trees. I've seen images of it since I was a kid; it's far more spectacular in person— we are in the Temple Sector. Just like that, I'm back in Dios.

"Let's go, we don't want to linger here too long," Kegan whispers, putting out his lumeflare. I look around in disbelief as the others follow Kegan. We make our way into an elegant garden with stone paths, fountains, and beautifully colorful plants. Everything is perfect. Not a blade of grass out of place or weed in sight. It looks like a little paradise utopia. Quite the opposite of what the rest of the city is like. We follow a path down a set of stairs and into a large courtyard.

"Up here, the building on the right provides access to an underground tunnel; we will use the tunnels to stay out of sight for as long as possible. From there, we can . . ." Kegan freezes in place. Standing in front of us is a line of PDF soldiers blocking our path. This is not good. My hand moves to my weapon. It won't do any good. There are far too many of them.

The soldiers don't react to our presence. We didn't stumble upon them; they are waiting for us. How did they know we were coming? Was this all a trap after all? Did Kegan play me? I spin around, looking back to the tunnel we just came from. Maybe we can still make a run for it.

"Good to see you again, Jett." The voice comes from behind me.

I'd know that voice in my sleep. Hearing it makes my skin crawl and every muscle in my body tense up. Victor.

END OF BOOK 2

GLOSSARY

AESTROTH (Mutated Creature) *Tribling for light of the stars.* Large butterflies with colorful almost glowing wings, their wings emit a powder that causes hypnotic trances. They swarm to blood like sharks. Their tongues have a sharp tip like a little spear which they stab into their victim and drink them dry leaving a mummified corpse behind.

ALUMA (Tech/Object) Technology from the Outlands, Aluma generates light with running water inside a tube.

ARTISANS (Group) Responsible for the design and logistics of Dios, the Artisans are the middle-class. Relatively small in number they are educated but not scholarly. Artisans are gifted with a lot of the practical arts, like design, technology, architecture. They are meant to take the vision of the Prime's and turn it into a realistic design

CHILDREN OF THE DOME (Group) Believing their exile was the will of Bealz, this cultic group views themselves as the Patriarch's missionaries to the Outlands. They seek to please the High Father and will do anything possible to serve his will. Their sacred mission is to find 'the chosen one' who will save the bloodline of the High Father and supposedly bring salvation to the world. They use their own version of the 'Sacred Texts' and demand strict allegiance to their teachings.

CITY WARS (Event) are a once-a-year sporting competition. Each of the five cities sends their best athletes to compete for the Great Golden Trophy. The other cities provide a bounty of special resources, like sugar and various sorts of fruits, to the winner as a reward. This is the only time the cities interact in any public way.

CONTROL (Group) The Control is one of the primary groups governing Dios. They are in charge of civil matters. The Control is run by the Ruling Counsel. The Counsel appears to be elected, so the people of Dios believe their voice is being heard. In reality, the Ruling Counsel consists of the most manipulative, egotistical, and ruthless men in the city. It's a pit of vipers. They operate in the name of protecting the peace and unity of Dios. This is all smoke and mirrors. They exist to carry out the High Father's wishes. They are in charge of law making, law enforcement, and maintaining order in Dios. Groups under their charge consist of: Red Caps, the Patriarch Defense Force, and cam drones.

CORLAEL POWDER (plant) A powder used for a variety of medicinal purposes to reduce fever, pain, and helps with focus.

CORRUPTED (Group/Mutated Creatures) The general term used for all creatures and people who were altered or mutated in the Outlands.

CRAG (Term/phrase) An Idiot

CRASH (Term/phrase) Lost it (typically in reference to self-control)

CRASHES MY SYSTEM (Term/phrase) To frustrate, agitate, or bother someone equivalent to 'put a bee in my bonnet'

CREATURES TO CREDITS (Term/phrase) It's a good bet

DEPRAVED (Group) Considered by some to be nothing more than a Tod Tale, The Depraved are people how have turned away from their humanity. The worst monsters are people. It is not known how they came to be. They are a death cult that worships death. They are drawn to dead bodies and use them like incense. They hate life and wish to destroy all of it they find. They love only one thing, consuming and destroying life. They insert metal and bone into their skin and face, cut themselves, graft skin from their victims onto their own bodies. Paint themselves with blood. File their teeth into fangs. Cut out their own tongues. They torture, kill, skin, and eat, people but not always in that order.

DIOS (Place) One of the five domed cities that remain after the Great Collapse. Ruled by the Patriarch Dios is a caste-based society of forced conformity. It is the setting for the story of book one and the home of Jett and his Undesirable family.

DOLTINE (Tech/Object) A type of drug similar to meth, but consumed in liquid form from a metal bottle, like a beverage. It creates a euphoric sensation that provides the user with a mental escape from the harsh realities of the Outlands. In the Outlands, it also runs the risk of rotting the brain and turning the person who takes it, into a Foamer.

DOMES UP (Term/phrase) to give someone a heads up or a warning

DOMIES (Term/phrase) An insult used by Outlanders to refer to new exile. Similar to the term "fresh fish" in prison. It generally refers to ignorance or inexperience.

DRAGONVALE (Place) The largest community in the territory near Dios. Dragonvale is a melting pot of different groups that maintains peace by a strike code of non-tolerance. Home to the dark market, Dragonvale is a well-protected town with access to many tressures from the World that Was.

DRAGONVALE CITY GUARD (Group) They wear a smooth grey jacket tucked into matching grey pants with a green stripe running from the collar, across the shoulders and down the sleeve. Over the heart, like a badge is an embroidered green patch with black trip in the shape of an arrow. Inside the patch, the black stitching of a dragon with outstretched wings.

DRUKANI (Mutated Creature) *Tribling for Toxic Dragon.* like a Komodo dragon, size of a horse, fast with sharp bones at the ends of their lizard tails. They spit a corrosive acid and hard to pierce hides.

DRY ROT (Term/phrase) A waste of space / deadbeat / useless person or thing.

DUSK DESCENSION The practice of some Outlander communities where they go underground to sleep where they can be safe.

FEELING LIKE A HAMMER (Term/phrase) feeling like a tool. An expression used when one makes a fool of themselves.

FILIA LUCEM (Term/phrase) *Literally Daughter of Light.* The Filia Lucem is a very important person to the people of Dios and the Patriarch hierarchy. The Vanguard's mission in the Outlands is to find, retrieve, and bring the Filia Lucem back to the Temple Sector.

FOAMERS (Group/Mutated Creatures) Exiles from Dios who coped with the Outlands by consuming a liquid drug called Doltine. The drug degraded their mind of all humanity but enhanced their speed and reflexes. Foamers are rabid and completely devoid of reason or higher thought. They are unnaturally fast, and merciless. Called Foamers because of the foam that forms on their mouths foam. They are primal creatures who act only on instinct.

FORCESHIELD (Tech/Object) A protective energy barrier used around builds and town both in Dios and the Outlands. Force shields are lesser versions of the technology used to create the protective domes around the five remaining cities.

GREAT COLLAPSE (Event) As increasingly corrupt leaders began losing the trust of their people their power began to wane. Factions rose up each promising a better way. Disillusioned and divided the people began fighting with each other, each in pursuit of their own agenda. Families turned on each other. Neighbors became enemies. The world fell into chaos. As the conflict intensified so did the weapons used in it. Until finally, the earth itself became victim to the chaos within it. The ground was made barren, water undrinkable, the air itself became a toxic fume. Most living things died. The things that did not, mutated into monstrous creatures. This hostile and deadly new world became known as The Outlands.

HACK IN (Term/phrase) To eavesdrop

HAVE THE SPHERES (Term/phrase) A crude way to say courage or guts. Similar to "you've got some nerve"

HEAPED (Term/phrase) Commonly used term meaning to be filled with or surrounded by trouble. It's to be screwed or could be used as a vulgar way of saying "screw you"

KATHAR AERA (Tech/Object) Is a solution given to people from Dios to help them breath the toxic air of the Outlands. Without it, the toxins in the air slowly close the person's lungs until they suffocate. The solution must be taken every eight months until the body adapts to the toxins in the air.

LEVITIES (Group) Religious zealots in charge or ensuring the people of Dios remain under control. While paraded as spiritual leaders and ministers the Levites are incredibly cruel and sadistic in their punishment of those who do not conform to the Paragon virtues of their class.

LOOPER/LOOPY (Term/phrase) A term used in the Outlands to describe a crazy person or to note that something is crazy.

LUMEFLARE (Tech/Object) A Torch

LUMEGRIN (Term/phrase) Used in both Dios and the Outlands. Can refer to a know it all, an annoyingly argumentative person, or a sarcastic / sassy person.

MARAUDERS (Group) Marauders operate in tribes. Each tribe controls a territory of the Outlands and operates autonomously from the others with a few exceptions. Each tribe answers to the High King of all Marauders. Marauders are warrior who long for glorious death on the battlefield. They pride themselves in being fearless. Marauders are governed by a code of honor and are typically very savage and barbaric in their behaviors.

MIDDLING DAYS (Event) The Middling Days are designed to weed out any outliers in the city of Dios. Those who are deemed considerably below average—either too slow, too weak, or too dumb—are gathered up and turned into Outlands Officers. This is done to help alleviate the burden they place on society. They also offer an opportunity for exceptional people to advance to a higher-class, or at least they claim to. No one who has been taken from a Middling Day assessment has ever been seen again. Their actual purpose is still unknown.

NIGHTLINGS (Group) The Nightlings are a beggar gang turned freedom fighters. They seek to overthrow the Patriarch and rule Dios for themselves. They are well-connected and organized but what they envision for the future, should they succeed, remains to be seen.

NOCSTRA (Mutated Creature) *Tribling for stalkers of the night.* Nocstra have black fur on its legs and back with a dark tan-red underbelly and mouth. It has a long thick tail with an almost spear like point at the end. It looks in many ways like a wolf coated in grease, except it's the size of a bear. Its maw is filled with little dagger teeth. The back of its throat glows with flame. Sharp bones grow up from its ankles like spikes. It appears to have a second set of ribs growing on its back like a jagged bone saddle complete with a bone collar that wraps its neck. Like its throat the creature's eyes glow with a red orange blaze. Two bone horns grow out of the side of its head where its ears should be.

NOOMA (Term/phrase) Used by Outlanders to refer to a person's spirit, consciousness, or awareness.

NUKED (Term/phrase) To be extremely angry

ORDER (Group) The Order is the Spiritual Branch of Dios government. Led by the Warden of Law. He deals with any discipline or unpleasantries on the Spiritual side in the name protecting the faith. The High Father rules everything. The Order and the Control. The Order is in charge of Levites, Assessors, and Potters.

OUTCASTS (Group) Radicals who hate the Patriarch. They are well-organized and largely supported by exiles. Consisting primarily of Outlands Officers not only do they want to bring down the Patriarch. They want to kill all who support them and all who aid them with complicit silence in order to give Dios to its "true citizens".

PATRIARCH (Group) Ruled by the great prophet and High Father The Patriarch seeks to control every aspect of life in Dios, ruling as both civil and spiritual authority. They believe by making everyone the same they will remove conflict and division from the world. To create a society that lives in harmony they will stoop to unspeakable cruelty.

PATRIARCH DEFENSE FORCE (Group) Is Dios's military. They are highly trained, well-armed, and well-organized. The PDF is typically called in for suppressing riots in the event things escalate behind the Red Caps ability to manage. They wear black body armor and helmets that make it difficult to distinguish between them.

PHARISITES (Term/phrase) a hypocritical person or a derogatory term for someone who was born out of wedlock

PINGING THE FIREWALL (Term/phrase) Shooting the breeze, making small talk, pointless conversation.

PLEBS (Group) Plebs live in Sector C and are the largest class in Dios. They work to build and maintain the city. They are trained to be hard-working and submissive as they work to bring the plans and ideas of the other two classes to life. Plebs have barely enough to survive and live in the worst conditions of any of the classes.

PRIME (Group) The Prime's are the social and intellectual elite of Dios. They provided the idea and the resources to build the city. Primes represent less than one percent of the population but control over eighty percent of the resources in Dios. They hold almost all of the power and are the most devoted to the Patriarch.

PROGRESS BAR STALLING (Term/phrase) literally refers to being slow. Is often used to describe someone who is engaging in crazy or irrational behavior.

RED CAPS (Group) Called Red Caps for the hats they wear, the city guard is in charge of crime prevention and maintaining order in Dios. They can be harsh in their execution of the law, especially for lower-class or classless citizens.

RED CLAY (Place) The closest city to Dios. Red Clay is a mid-sized town that barely manages to get by. While on the surface it appears to be a primitive settlement, it does boast impressive unground farming, houses, and a medical facility.

ROTH SHALAR (Term/phrase) The warriors paradise and where every Marauder longs to go. Only warriors who die in battle, with their weapon in their hands can enter Roth Shalar.

ROTH THRUNE (Term/phrase) Marauders who maintain their honor in life but fail to die in glorious battle go to Roth Thrune, it is a peaceful and pleasant place but not one Marauders long for or honor.

ROTH DESPOR (Term/phrase) This is the place of shame. It is for cowards, traitors, and Marauders who have lost their honor. The greatest desire of the Marauder life is to avoid a death that would lead to Roth Despor.

SALVAGE (Term/phrase) Stupid

SAND FOR BRAINS (Term/phrase) Stupid or dense person

SANDURANS (Group) The original builders of the domed cities, the Sandurans were in charge of Dios before the Patriarch launched a successful coup and banished them and all their supporters to the Outlands. It is generally believed, within Dios, that the Sandurans died off.

SCARED THE SUN (Term/phrase) To be startled or surprised in an unpleasant way.

SCRAP SINK (Term/phrase) a jerk / rude person or a general way of expressing dislike.

SHEOL (Term/phrase) Hell

SHINSHEW (Term/phrase) typically considered a rude term for feces.

SKYLARI (Mutated Creature) *Tribling for death from above.* They appear like humanoid / praying mantis hybrid. Their exoskeleton is a greenish plate-like armor that spikes in the back. They walk on two legs, run on four, and are the size of a large human. They have four transparent wings on their back which provide them with short-term limited flight. Their heads look like an eagle with a long beak and pinkish red orbs for eyes. At the ends of their arms are hooked, spike bones for impaling on the outside, with a clear-ish crescent shape blade on the inside, like a scythe. They are fast for short windows of time and are ambush hunters, typically perching someplace out of view, descending, attacking, and disappearing. Some travel by themselves while other times they swarm. Swarms live in hives and have a queen. Skylari hate water.

SPLITTING PIXELS (Term/phrase) Being petty, splitting hairs

STREET MILES (Term/phrase) to look or appear much older than the person actually is, as if prematurely weathered.

STOCKED (Term/phrase) to be ok or all good

STOCK YOUR ACCOUNTS (Term/phrase) Line your pockets or steal

TECHAPOSTS (Tech/Object) like cards or emails used to send messages without a datapad.

TERASTRUM (Mutated Creature) *Tribling for the bane of travelers*. They appear much like an Angler Fish sticking their antennae out of cave entrances. With a lantern at the tip the light draws travelers and prey in. When someone gets too close, they lunge forward out of the cavern entrance and consume whatever is in front of them with large mouths wide enough to swallow a jeep and three rows of sharp jagged teeth.

THERMALS GOING (Term/phrase) to be fired up, angry, or frustrated.

THRASHERS (Tech/Object) energy whips with nine strands that Levites use to punish people for crimes or just to amuse themselves.

TOD TALE (Term/phrase) a fairy tale or fantasy story told to children, something that is not true.

TREMATERRA (Mutated Creature) *Tribling for Shakers of the earth*. Bull like creature with sharp teeth, larger than an elephant. They have Two sharp horns that point forward just off the side of their head, and two longer, hooked horns that grow off a plate on their neck. They are passive unless you wander into their territory. They react to sudden movement and move in herds. Energy weapons don't wound them but agitate them greatly.

TRIBLINGS (Group) Native to the Outland, not outcasts. Triblings ae people who survived the Great Collapse. While the chemicals and toxins wiped out most of humanity that remained outside the Domed cities, the Triblings were not only survived, but developed enhanced mutations making them faster and stronger than normal humans. Not much is known about their. They are polytheistic and often nomadic. Many Outlands consider them savages and treat them poorly as if they are less than human.

UNDESIRABLES (Group) Anyone living in Dios that doesn't fit into the caste system for one reason or another is classified as an Undesirable. They are not given jobs and forced to live in the Rim, a grounded slum that surrounded the inner walls of Dios.

VANGUARD (Group) A specialized unit of the Patriarch military that is sent into the Outlands with a sacred mission to find and retrieve the Filia Lucem.

VOMITOUS MASS (Term/phrase) to consider someone worthless trash or a waste of space.

ZEROED (Term/phrase) to be beat, worn out, or tired.

ZOOMERS (Tech/Object) Binoculars.

ACKNOWLEDGEMENTS

Were I to endeavor to thank everyone who influenced, supported, or encouraged me over the years and specifically with my writing I fear it would require its own tome. For any and all who might be included in this area: thank you. Thank you to my mother for not only sharing her love for reading and writing but for helping fine-tune this story. To "Momma" Mountain one of the fiercest and greatest supporters anyone could hope for. To Amanda and Johnny, whose insights and feedback went above and beyond expectation and challenged me to grow as a writer and storyteller, I offer an extra special thank you.

MORE FROM AUTHOR

The Outlands (The first book of the Outlands Saga)

Next in the Series: The Rise of the Fallen

Dear Reader,

I hope you enjoyed book two of the Outlands Saga. If you did and would be willing to do me a favor, I would be grateful. Ratings and reviews on sites like Amazon and Goodreads make a huge difference for Indie Authors. As well as talking about the book with your friends or sharing a post about it on social media. If you would like to support this series, that's a great way to do. Thanks for reading!